A
F.R.E.A.K.S. SQUAD
INVESTIGATION
FIVE

JENNIFER HARLOW

DEVIL ON THE LEFT BOOKS

COPYRIGHT

ALSO BY JENNIFER HARLOW

THE GALILEE FALLS TRILOGY
Justice
Galilee Rising
Fall of Heroes
Nemesis: A Sydney Rye Kindle World Novella

THE F.R.E.A.K.S. SQUAD SERIES
Mind Over Monsters
To Catch a Vampire
Death Takes A Holiday
High Moon
The Sin Eater

THE MIDNIGHT MAGIC MYSTERY SERIES
What's A Witch To Do?
Werewolf Sings The Blues
Witch Upon A Star

THE DR. IRIS BALLARD SERIES
Beautiful Maids All in a Row
Darkness At the Edge of Town (out November 2017)

A HART/MCQUEEN STEAMPUNK ADVENTURE
Verity Hart Vs The Vampyres

This book is dedicated to you.
Yes, you.
The ones reading this right now.
The ones who take a chance on my stories.
Who leave reviews. Who tell your friends.
You rock.
I truly adore you.

From the bottom of my heart…thank you.
Thank you.

"We can easily forgive a child who is afraid of the dark: the tragedy of life is when men are afraid of the light."
–Plato

"Yeah, but I'll bet the dark side's better. I hear they even have cookies."
–Beatrice Alexander

CHAPTER ONE

I DREAMED A DREAM

"Welcome to the world, William Price, Jr. You are...*so* loved."

He's perfect. Our son is simply perfect. The most beautiful child ever to grace this earth. He has his father's eyes, an intense emerald green practically piecing my soul as he stares up at me, his mother, in wonder. The same way I gaze down at him. Our boy also has Will's strong jaw, which he'll be thankful for as he grows into his teens. He's going to be a looker, just like his father. Ruggedly handsome with broad shoulders perfect for resting your head on. But judging from our son's smile and cheer, his curiosity at the wonders of the world, he's inherited nothing of his father's hard personality and constant grumpiness. His father's good looks and my personality. Our son inherited the best of us both. Our little blessing. Everything I've ever wanted in this or any world.

"Thank you."

It takes mental fortitude, but I manage to unglue my eyes from the Ninth Wonder of the World to the source of the voice. Oh, if our son grows half as handsome as his father the boy will have a charmed life. He'll have a charmed life regardless with us as his parents. Two people who love one another, what more could a child need?

"Thank me for what?" I ask as the man I love sits beside me on the bed.

Will wraps his arm around my shoulders, pulling us against his warm body. I rest my head on his broad shoulder. My favorite spot in the world.

"This. You. Him." Will kisses my temple. "For my life. I love you, Bea. I love you *so* much. Don't ever doubt that."

"Trixie..."

"I love you too," I say, never taking my eyes off my son.

"Trixie..."

No. *No.* Don't...

I can't help it. I peer up. Oliver, once the most breathtaking man I've ever encountered, looms beside my bed with his once angelic face torn to pieces. Claw marks run all the way down to the bone and still bleed. "It's time to wake up, Trixie."

"No," I whimper as I return my gaze to my baby. But he's gone. My arms are as empty as my soul.

"You deserve nothing less," Will says.

I turn to Will, but instead of my lover, I find the wolf. The snarling, rabid wolf who stole my life with blood and saliva dripping from his snout. There isn't time to scream before those teeth descend toward my jugular. When I snap awake I can still feel those fangs in my neck. The agony. It hurts even to gasp.

"Jesus. Jesus," I pant. "Goddamn it."

Goddamn it.

I hate that dream. *Hate it.* I thought last time would be the last time. It's been two weeks since I've had it. The damn day's ruined before it's even begun. All damn day I'm going to sense the empty space in my arms my baby should be. Smell that newborn scent. Crave the sensation of Will's arms enveloping me. His kisses. It's damn near impossible to keep the thoughts and misery at bay after I dream of him. Of them. What could have been. It's hard enough on the best of days, forget with them haunting me at night. Yeah, I'm done with today already. I wouldn't even get out of my childhood bed except I have to pee. I linger as long as I can because it takes too much energy just to get mobile, and that's when I have to drive to do so. Today isn't one of those few and far between days.

Somehow I borrow from my empty reserves and force myself upright before making the long trek all the way to the bathroom. And…my drive's gone. Nana's left for the day already so I can avoid her concerned eyes at least until she returns from her shift at the library. She's doubled her volunteer hours since I moved back to San Diego three months ago. I don't blame her. Each morning, okay *afternoon*, since it's past noon, when I catch sight of myself in the mirror, I want to cringe myself. I wasn't a beauty queen before, but with my limp mousy brown hair I barely bother to brush, pasty skin, and dark circles under my amber eyes, I resemble a corpse now. And I've fought corpses better looking than I am right now. I have the scars to prove it too. If I removed my clothes I could double for Frankenstein's monster. Two zombie bites, one vampire bite, a scar running the length of my elbow on the left, and another from the wrist to elbow on the right. At least my new bangs cover the scar on my forehead.

But without question my heart and soul are the worst. They're torn to shreds anew every damn day when I think about him. About what I lost. "Fuck you, dreams."

I go through the morning ritual on autopilot, brushing my teeth and hair before popping a Lexapro. I don't know why I still do that last one. The drugs haven't helped one iota. Pretty sure there's not a pill that combats the level of guilt and desolation that stems from shooting your werewolf fiancée with a shotgun and watching him die a foot in front of you. I've been watching a lot of *Intervention,* maybe crack and meth would do the job. Of course I don't even have a pot connect. I do however have a great liquor store, Benadryl is over the counter, and my second week home I bought every video game system on the market. The combination of those three wonderful inventions makes every long, grueling, shitty day of my existence almost bearable.

Almost.

The house phone rings when I step into the living room. Thank God I was so immersed in *Mass Effect 2* yesterday I only had one drink so no hangover because my passive aggressive grandmother left all the blinds up. As if the peach walls with turquoise accents weren't bright enough. Twenty-seven and back living with my grandmother. *That's* enough to drive a girl to the bottle. It's not as if I can't afford a place of my own—being a member of a secret monster hunting organization proved quite lucrative—but at first I was too physically weak let alone emotionally to care for myself. Then after I just didn't know where to go.

God Nana welcomed me back with open arms. Of course I all but shoved those arms away my first week and haven't apologized since. She cooks but I barely eat. She cleans up my messes and only gets a curt thanks. She tries to get me to open up, and I literally just walk away. I know she's at her breaking point. Not only can I sense her emotions with my minor empath skills but the dreaded "What are your plans?" question now leaves her lips every other day. Apparently the answer "romance a space dinosaur" isn't enough for her anymore. Her worry comes from the best of places, I know that, but I truly don't have an answer. I'm not ready to leave purgatory yet. I can't. I'm not strong enough. Hell, I don't think I ever will be again.

The machine picks up as I start the coffee. "Beatrice, this is George again." My heart seizes in my chest when I hear his voice. Oh, not today. Please, I can't handle this today. "This is the third time I've phoned. It is imperative I speak to you. Your suspension is up and we need to discuss what happens next. If I don't hear from you soon…please call, Beatrice. I do hope you're well. Bye."

I've already begun adding the Kahlua to my mug. My suspension's up. I knew that was on the horizon, but…I sigh. Why couldn't it have been six months? They should have just fired my ass. Or sent me to The Facility in Montana. I tortured then released a confessed murderer. Worse, my actions set in motion a horrific chain of events that left one of my best friends centimeters from death. It made me…I chug the Kahlua outright.

I should have been shipped off to preternatural prison. Because it was me. It was *all* me. It was all my fault. If I'd trusted my fellow agents. If I'd listened to reason. But I was stupid. My fiancée was held hostage by a rapist werewolf. Nothing mattered but getting him back. *Nothing.* But I lost him anyway. And Oliver...the memory of Will's powerful jaws biting Oliver's neck. The claw marks ravaging his perfect face. I can all but feel the warm blood pouring out of his jugular onto my hands. All because he wanted to help me. I've become Lady Macbeth, staring at my blood stained hands, driven to madness by them.

I haven't seen or heard from Oliver since that night. I didn't even say good-bye. I couldn't look at him at first. Part of me hated him for his weakness. He's a five-hundred-year-old vampire, he can't subdue one werewolf? They hated each other. Maybe a small sliver of him wanted to force my hand. Force me to blow my fiancée's brains out. But those thoughts came in the darkest days when I hated everything and everyone. Another sin added to my tab. Thinking the worst of a man who almost died helping clean up my mess.

He must hate me. I hate me. We weren't on the best of terms before that night. I chose Will. I pushed my friend away even though I swore I never would. And he still...I don't blame him for not wanting to see or talk to me. But I miss him so damn much. Laughing with him. Our hours long conversations and verbal sparring. Going to the movies and making witty comments about how terrible they are. He's alive, but he's as far away from me as Will right now. Maybe forever. I lost them both that night. And I deserve nothing less.

Hurry the fuck up, coffee. I just stare at that blinking red light on the answering machine. It's as if every blink whispers, "Call me. Call me." If I'm fired I wish he'd just say it. But I don't think that's the way the wind's blowing. The only F.R.E.A.K. I've had contact with is Nancy when we're gaming together online. Most of the time she doesn't say anything non-game related after I told her I'd block her if she did, but once or twice she's mentioned they've kept my room exactly as I left it, and George stopped recruiting when a married werewolf couple from the Eastern Pack joined. If that's true, and if by some miracle they do want me back, I don't know what to do. Quit is winning by a mile. Hell, it shouldn't even be a damn race. Then why the hell is it so hard to tell George that? Probably the same reason it's almost impossible to leave the house most days. Depression and guilt devour all my energy and drive. I barely have enough of either today to pad back to my bedroom and switch on the PlayStation.

Saving the universe with a team of misfits is a hell of a lot easier in video games than in real life. Of course that second shot of booze I had gets one of my team mates killed, but I do beat the game a few hours later. Now onto killing cops and prostitutes in *Grand Theft Auto*.

I'm so immersed in my bank robbery I must not hear Nana return home until she knocks on my door. As always, she enters before I can invite her in.

My grandmother's aged well. A few wrinkles on her tan face, silver hair freshly cut into a bob, like me medium height and weight, though I've gained ten pounds in limbo, and the same slightly upturned nose. Her face remains neutral, but as always her brown eyes deceive her. I should be used to her constant air of worry and helplessness, but it hasn't happened yet. "There's a message on the machine for you. Dr. Black called again."

"I know," I say, shooting a cop.

"Did you call him back?"

"Not yet. Damn it!" Bank heist failed. I'm dead.

"You have to call him, Bea," she chides.

"I will."

"When?"

"Soon! God, get off my back!"

My grandmother simply stares at me, mouth slightly gaping open as if she doesn't recognize me at this moment. I sense her melancholy and hint of anger too. I never used to talk back, even when I was a teenager. I always was a late bloomer.

She shakes her head and leaving without another word. Crap. That's the second time this week I've snapped at her. I shake my head too. She means well, but I just cannot deal with her questions and oppressive worry. I guess I should feel guilty but can't muster another drop. Okay, maybe there's a drop or two in there.

Without the distraction I complete the bank heist and storming the drug kingpin's home. There's an idea. Maybe I should become a criminal. Rob a bank. I do have a unique skill that would make it easy as pie. I probably wouldn't even need a gun. My telekinesis could finally improve my life, not hinder it for once. Maybe I've been going about life all wrong. I wanted to save people. I *did* save people. Dozens are alive because of me. They're eating dinner, laughing with family, falling in love. And here I am. Scarred, depressed, twenty-seven, and living with my grandmother. Life is so fucking unfair. Fuck being good. Fuck love. Fuck selflessness. Fuck it all.

I beat another four levels unmolested. Maybe Nana's gone next door to Mrs. Ramirez's to vent. She's been spending more time there than here. Though I barely leave my room I've taken over the house. I've sucked it into a black hole.

"Abandon hope all ye who enter here" should be carved above the front door. Only one brave soul dares enter. My best friend just strolls into my bedroom without knocking. Damn it, I was so immersed in my game I didn't hear the front door. Again. Yeah, law enforcement agent of the year here. April Diego is a knockout: tall, curvy, full lips, hell she's often mistaken for Eva Mendes. Right now I want to knockout the knockout for barging in here and ruining my game.

"What the hell—"

"You haven't been answering my calls," she says, hands on her hips.

"I've—"

"Save it. You haven't been answering my calls *and* now I hear you've been mean to Nana Alexander?"

I pause the game and set down the controller. "You two have been talking about me behind my back?"

"Damn straight we have been! You look like crap! You never leave the house. You aren't talking to us. What would you do in our shoes?"

"Have a little compassion? Respect my life choices?"

"Maybe we would if you were choosing life!" She walks over and shuts off the TV.

"Hey!"

"Well, tonight you are. You are going to take a shower, let me do your hair and make-up, then put on your nicest dress, and come out with me, Yo, Marina, and Kenny for his bachelor party. His commitment ceremony to Scott is next week. We're going to Cougar's to watch the male strippers and eat the best chicken wings in San Diego. And *you* are coming."

"No. I'm not." I switch back on the TV.

April immediately shuts it off again. "Oh, yes you are!"

On. "Nope."

Off. "Yep."

On. "I'm not going."

Off. "I have three young children, Bea, I can do this all night!"

"I don't want to go!"

"Yeah, but you *need* to," she states with absolute certainty. "You missed Carlos' birthday. You have barely left this room in three months. Your grandmother's reached the end of her rope, Bea. She will kick you out, you know. Maybe she should. Is that what you want? She's about given up on you. Is that what you want? To break your grandmother's heart like you're breaking mine?" My jaw sets at this emotional blackmail tactic. My obvious displeasure doesn't stop her from walking over to the bed, sitting on the edge. "One night. That's all I ask. Come out with me tonight and tomorrow you can spend all day in here hiding away from the world. But you gotta give us tonight."

Maybe this will buy me some time. I just have to *pretend* I'm trying, right? That I care. I can sit there drinking and watching male strippers for a few hours then feign a headache. Two hours for two weeks of no questions or looks or oppressive emotions. God, I just *so* don't want to, yet I find myself saying, "You're buying."

April grins from ear to ear and holds out her hand for me to take. "Come on. Let's get Cinderella ready for her night of debauchery."

I can fake it. I can fake being a living human being for one night. I can. I will. But sadly, wherever I go, I take hell with me.

CHAPTER TWO

LOTUS

Not even two rum and cokes can make watching male strippers interesting. I'm a butt girl but after watching the fifth butt twerking in a G-string inches from my face, I don't ever want to see another ass for a while. And they are nice. Round. Muscular. But nowhere near as gorgeous as Will's. Our one night together I finally got to do what I'd been fantasizing of since I'd met him: nibble and kiss down that fleshy mound as he chuckled and moaned. I wonder if that bitch Patsy did the same to him. If he trailed kisses from behind her ear to her toes as he did me. When I begin going down this train of thought I order a third drink to derail it. I promised April I'd at least *attempt* to have a decent time. This is Kenny's bachelor party. He's committing to the love of this life. He doesn't deserve Debbie Downer ruining the fiesta. So I drink and somehow maintain a smile on my face as the others from April's salon whoop it up and stick singles in G-strings. Yeah, I would so rather be fighting Nazi/zombie/aliens at home.

At least I resemble a fully functional adult person tonight. April really knows her stuff. The natural wave in my hair shows, the gold specks in my eyes glow, and despite the extra ten pounds I've packed on, in my black satin pants and long-sleeved maroon lace top, I have an hourglass vavoom happening. Too bad ninety-nine percent of the men at Cougar's are gay. Not that I'd go home with any of the even if I could. Okay, maybe the one dressed as Tarzan.

I've only been with three men, and it wasn't until Will I figured out what the fuss was about. Now I miss sex. *God* I miss sex. My vibrator's just about worn out, not to mention all the furniture I've busted and had to replace when I lose control and orgasm. I think Nana's bought my "I'm clumsy when I drink" excuse. Another wonderful side effect of my psychokinesis. If I'm not careful I can literally kill my partner when I come. That puts a big ass crimp in dating and sex. Hell, I can't even spend the night with a guy on the off chance I levitate something in my sleep. But Will didn't care. He truly knew *me*, all my faults and quirks, and he loved me anyway, as I did him. Who will want me now? Scarred, freakish, depressed, overweight. Godddamn it, there I go again. As if fucking some random guy will exorcise Will from my very atoms. It might be nice to try though. Why the hell not? I—

"Bea?" Yo, one of April's co-workers, shouts from across the table.

I snap out of my head. I realize everyone's rising from our table. "What?"

"We're going!" Yo shouts over the music.

Thank God. I collect my purse and follow the four others past the other happy bachelorettes whooping it up on their last nights of freedom. I wonder if I would have had a bachelorette party. I wonder if I'd be Mrs. Will Price right now. Probably. I might have even been pregnant already. We both wanted children so badly. I broke down in tears for an hour when I got my period a week after Will's death. God couldn't even give me that.

More than once tonight, when Kenny began talking about his honeymoon to Cancun or the ceremony, I had the strongest urge to throw my drink in his face or flip the table. I contained myself though. I just smiling and nodding while chugging my rum. I am happy for him, I truly am, I'm just sadder for me at the moment.

We step out of the club into the perfect June night. Not too hot, not too cold with a breeze from the Pacific wafting down the streets of the historic Gaslamp District. Small boutiques and restaurants line the sidewalks as gas lamps flicker above instead of boring electric street lamps. Young couples and groups like ours stroll hand-in-hand laughing as they pass us. April latches her arm in mine too.

"So, where to next?" Marina asks.

"Home?" I suggest.

"Hell no! It's only ten-thirty!" Kenny says. "Let's hit a club! I wanna dance! Silhouette's just around the corner." We turn the corner, running smack dab into the line to get inside. "Fuck!"

"It's Saturday night. They're all gonna be like this," April points out.

"But I wanna dance!" Kenny says, pouting. "Bea wants to dance too. Don't ya, Bea? You love dancing."

I do love dancing. And with all the rum and cokes I'm too wired and drunk to fall asleep for hours yet. I need to work off the chemically induced energy. A truly terrible, *terrible* idea only alcohol could produce creeps into my mind. No, that is a very, *very* bad—

"I can get us into Gaslamp," I find myself saying. The others look at me, eyebrows raised in surprise. "What? I know the owner."

April's grip on my arm slackens. "I don't think that's a—"

"Awesome!" Kenny says. "Gaslamp ho! I love that place! So sophisticated."

Our bachelor takes off like a marching band conductor minus the baton. Someone's excited. When I try to follow, April yanks me back. "Are you nuts? What if *he's* there?"

"He probably won't be. He's a busy guy."

"But what if he is?" she hisses. "The asshole threatened to kill you."

"He didn't mean it," I say, literally waving it off. "We're so past it."

"Bea—"

"You're the one who wanted me to get out and do something. And I wanna dance!" I start walking. "Besides, he so won't even be there!"

Though part of me, the drunk part most likely, really hopes he is. About a day after I returned to San Diego, a giant bouquet of lilies arrived on Nana's doorstep with a card that simply read, *"If there is anything I can do, anything at all, do not hesitate to ask. –C."* I'm not hesitating tonight.

Gaslamp is four blocks away and one of those blocks has a line stretching to the very end. We garner more than a few questioning or envious stares as we walk past the have nots, but at least they weren't the downright glare the hulking doorman gives us the moment he sets eyes on little old me. You threaten to shoot a vampire once, and he never lets it go. *I've* moved on.

I plaster on my sweetest smile as I approach. "Howdy."

"May I help you?"

"We'd like to come in."

"Is he expecting you?"

"Isn't he always? And do you really want to keep me waiting out here? I doubt *he'll* like that."

The sides of his mouth twitch, but he does unclip the velvet rope. "Go right in, Agent Alexander and enjoy your night."

"Thank you very much. We will. Wonderful seeing you again." With a wink, I step into the club.

Gaslamp is one of the classier clubs I've been to, and in my tenure as a F.R.E.A.K. agent I found myself in a fair share. Gaslamp is designed to resemble a hunting lodge or English gentleman's social club with brown leather booths with brass buttons, wooden tables and padded matching chairs, and a beautiful chandelier with flickering gas lamp flames dancing in time to the patrons below. The bouncer must have radioed in the moment I turned my back because we barely make it out of the foyer to the main dance hall when a familiar African American man with an earwig and clipboard blocks our path.

"Agent Alexander, how lovely to see you again," he says with a British accent. "Right this way to our VIP area."

"Why thank you!" At least *he's* forgiven me.

The vamp leads us toward the staircase. "Why do they keep calling you Agent Alexander?" Yo asks me.

"Inside joke. Take too long to explain," I reply without missing a beat. I have gotten so good at lying I impress even myself.

The VIP section is a large booth just off the staircase in the corner of the second story overlooking the dance floor. The British minion parts the velvet rope. "All your drinks tonight are, of course, on the house, and Malia will be your private server. If you desire anything else, please let Malia or another member of staff know, and we will accommodate you immediately."

"Thank you." The vampire nods before leaving. I reapply my lipstick after I sit. Have to look my best.

"I could get used to this," Kenny says. "What'd you do? Save the manager's basket of kittens from drowning or something?"

"Or something," I say. "He's a friend."

"Must be a damn good friend," Yo says.

"You consider *him* a friend?" April asks, eyebrow raised.

"We've got free drinks all night. Tonight he's my *best* friend."

April rolls her eyes with that one.

Our waitress promptly comes for our orders. I quickly gulp down half my fourth rum and coke of the night before it's dancing time. Kenny, Yo, and I slink down to the dance floor and begin bumping and grinding with the rest of the wild throng. I can actually allow myself to get lost in the beat, in the energy of the crowd tonight. The majority of clubs I found myself in, I was there stalking prey. Places like these where alcohol and drugs flow like water, lowering everyone's inhibitions and common sense are the best hunting grounds for almost every monster out there. I spot a few such creatures of the night nearby, working on their nightly victim. I'd estimate about twenty percent here are vampires. As long as their prey is over eighteen, isn't forced to have sex, and lives to see the sun, the F.R.E.A.K.S. have a live and let undead policy. Yet I've lost count of how many vamps I've had to put down for breaking the rules. Two dozen? More? And I still don't feel a kernel of remorse, at least not for that.

I—

During the second song, a techno mix of Missy Elliott's "Get Your Freak On," an arm suddenly glides around my torso before pulling me back against his body, all but pinning me against him. Even with all the bodies writhing against me from all corners this act shocks me. I spin around, ready to shove the creep away, but the mischievous grin on his familiar, fine face quells the rage. Damn, I forgot how hot he is. Not gorgeous like Oliver, maybe two men on the planet are, but with the smiling, crinkling violet eyes, wiry yet muscular body currently looking damn fine in black jeans and gray V-neck sweater with the sleeves pushed up, way auburn hair, and air of mischief the Irish just have, he is one sexy ass vampire.

"About time you showed up!" I shout over the music.

"I was about to say the same thing," he shouts back. Frak me, that accent. Melt. I'm shocked I'm not sliding off my panties right this instant.

I don't put up a shred of resistance as Connor wraps his arm around my waist again or as I collide with his body. I drape my arms over his shoulders as he slips his leg between mine so I'm all but sitting on it. Never taking our eyes from each other's, our grins growing with each passing second, we swing our hips in time to the chaotic music. The rest of the club fades away, all that remains are those smiling eyes and the heat growing between my legs. Okay, *this* is why I wanted to come here tonight.

I wanted *him*.

Lord Connor McInnis, ruler of every vampire from Tijuana to Santa Ana, and my next giant mistake. We met over five months ago when he tried to blackmail me into becoming his concubine. An asshole move to be sure, but it was mostly my telekinesis he was after. *Mostly*. He made up for his bad behavior by helping me take down a troll cult led by my ex Steven. The man I'm currently dry humping offered me money, power, privilege, wild hot sex, and companionship until the end of my days, and I said no. For true love. Yeah, look where that got me. I don't think I should ever make that mistake again.

The song ends and Connor sadly releases me, all but my hand. He guides me toward a hidden mirror enclosed booth in the corner. The VVIP section. We can see everyone, but they can't see us. How voyeuristic. There's already a drink, I assume rum and coke, waiting for me on the table. The moment the door shuts, the music becomes nothing but muffled beats. For whatever reason, I guess without the noise overwhelming my already addled senses, when he shuts the door, I tense. Okay, maybe *all* sense hasn't been washed away by alcohol. Hopefully this will do the job. I grab the drink and take a gulping sip as I slide into the booth. He does the same, sitting *right* beside me so our thighs touch and even drapes his arm over the back of my seat. Liquid courage don't fail me now. "So," he says with that mischievous smile affixed. I swear I grow wet between my thighs every time he crinkles those eyes.

"So," I reply before taking another swig. Think, Bea. Think. "Uh, I meant to call you and thank you for the flowers. They were beautiful."

"I never saw much point in sending something that would soon wither and die to console another who is dealing with a loved one withering and dying."

"Then why did you send them?"

"It is what one does. Though I want it noted I did take my life into my own hands with the gesture. Your Oliver phoned me the day you returned to our fair city. I believe his exact words were, 'If you go near her, if you bother her in any way, I will burn all your properties to the ground before I flay you alive.'"

"He-he did that?"

"You seem surprised."

"We didn't exactly part on the best of terms."

Connor's violet eyes narrow. "From what I understand you saved his life at great personal cost. *I* am surprised he is not by your side moving heaven and earth simply to bring a smile to your gorgeous face."

"Actually, he hasn't called once," I say, falling back against the seat.

"Perhaps he was doing as I was. Giving you time and space to grieve until you emerged from your mourning period. I will say I am honored you came to *me* first." His arm moves onto my shoulders. "You look well."

"Only well?" I ask with a pout. "I was going for beautiful. Enchanting. Ravishing."

"Your beauty is unparalleled. You are Helen of Troy for the modern age, Agent Alexander."

I sip my drink. "It's just plain old Beatrice now, Danny Boy. I think."

He stares at me, head slightly tilted to the side. "You are no longer with the F.R.E.A.K.S? I assumed you were on medical leave."

"Suspended without pay until...I guess today." I chug the rest of my booze. I am going to regret that one tomorrow morning. Hopefully it won't be the *only* thing I regret come morning. "How much do you know about what happened?"

"Only rumors. Oliver did not delve into the details between his threats. I know you sustained grievous injuries, and that Agent Price perished in the line of duty. The obituary claimed he died in a car accident."

I scoff. "Yeah. I guess...he kind of did." At least the Will Price I knew and loved did. God, I need another drink.

"We do not have to talk about—"

Before I lose my nerve, or regain my sense, I grab the back of his neck and draw his lips to mine into a fierce kiss. The alcohol's making everything a little numb and unreal, but I forgot how much I enjoy kissing. The raw pleasure from tasting another. From the mere touch of lips conjoining. Connor doesn't hesitate a millisecond. His lips match mine caress for caress. I pull away a few seconds later to breathe. "I don't wanna talk. I wanna dance."

Those ridiculously pretty eyes of his crinkle as he smiles. Definitely wet now. "Your command is my wish."

His arm never leaves my waist, his hungry eyes never leave the rest of me as we return to the dance floor and allow the music work its magic. There's no guilt, no future, nothing but the beat, my body against his, and those fangs and lips grazing over my flesh every chance he gets. Please don't let the music ever stop. I want to become a lotus eater and stay on this island forever. Let me stay here. I want to *die* on this dance floor with his hands roving my body.

Not to be.

Around our sixth dance, I notice someone fighting through the crowd toward me. It isn't until she's right in front of me I realize it's April, sporting a scowl for my dance partner before turning her glare to me. Even without that hostile expression I can sense her nerves and undercurrent of anger. "It's time to go!" she shouts over the music.

"I don't want to go!" I lean back against Connor. "I'm having fun!"

"It's time to go now, Bea," she says sternly. "We're all leaving!"

"I can see she gets home safely," Connor says, I'm sure with a smile.

She flashes him another sneer before taking my hand. "Come on."

I rip my hand from hers. "I'm not leaving yet."

"Bea, you're—"

"Having fun! Like you wanted me to!"

"Drunk," she finishes. "You're drunk."

"I'm not that drunk," I say. "I know exactly what I'm doing, okay? Really. And I can take care of myself."

"Bea, this is—"

"Ma'am," Connor says. April peers up at him and her eyes suddenly go vacant. "Go home to your family and do not worry about your friend tonight. No harm will come to her. Go. Now."

April nods and without another word turns her back on us, walking away. I should chastise Connor for putting the whammy on my best friend, but I'm just glad she's gone. She'll be fine. I'll be fine. There goes the guilt again but I shut it down. I'll be guilty tomorrow. I can give myself that at least.

I wrap my arm around Connor, picking up where we left off, hips gyrating to the music, but the interruption has drained the fun. I'm also now aware I'm dripping with sweat and my legs are aching since I haven't exercised in months. Fucking April. "I think I need a drink!" I shout.

Connor nods, slips his hand around my waist again, and leads me toward the private room again. I can walk straight. See? Not drunk. But instead of entering the mirrored enclave, we move past it to another dim hall and another door with a keypad at the very end. "Close your eyes," Connor requests. I do. He presses in the code, and I'm yanked forward. I open my eyes to find myself in yet another hallway moving toward another door. It better have a bed inside. Or…fuck I can't wait.

Just as we reach the first door on the left, I shove Connor against the wall and give him a steamy, panty dropping kiss. He spins me around, this time pinning me to the wall as we devour one another. Someone likes to be in charge. I pull away to breathe, and he trails kisses down my throat as his hands reach under the back of my shirt to dig his nails into my flesh. But the moment I sense fangs against my jugular, I push him away with a laugh. "Nice try. I'm not that drunk, Danny Boy. For that privilege, you have to buy me dinner first."

He smirks. "I do believe eating out can be arranged."

He punches in the code for the door, takes my hand again, and leads me through and into a two-story apartment, I assume his. I have just literally entered in the lair of one of the most feared and powerful vampires in North America. He's gone for modern simplicity with lots of space, a few pieces of black leather furniture, rich wood tables, a pool table, and tiny kitchenette with bar stools at the counter. For whatever reason—*booze*—I can't take my eyes off the billiard table. Oliver taught me to play. He was so patient, always cracking jokes when—

Oh, we're moving again. Connor must shove me down onto the couch because one second I'm upright and the next I'm on my back with a vamp looming over me about to pounce. Some voice deep, deep down, the only part of me not drunk as a skunk right now, screams in terror. That this is nuts. That—

Connor presses his body against mine, kissing me again, and lowering the voice's screams to a whisper. God, this man can kiss. Centuries of practice. We break apart so I can remove his shirt. Nice. Thin but toned. Mama like. He—shit. Connor grabs my shirt to take it off, and self-consciousness adds its voice to common sense's protests. Besides not being model thin my ugly, huge red scars are on full display. At least I wore a lacy bra. Connor's too busy burying his face in my breasts, kissing and licking across my cleavage, to notice the scars. I forget them too when he pushes up my bra, freeing my left breast and taking my erect nipple into his warm mouth, tongue flicking it in time to the thrusts of his bulge against my equally titillated center. Damn, that's nice.

His mouth moves up to kiss my lips again as his hand takes over torture duty, rolling and pinching my nipple in his expert ways. After a long, lingering kiss that mouth moves southward, kissing my chin, my neck, between the swell of my breasts. I'm so awash in pleasure I fail to realize he's removing my pants and underwear until they're rolling down my thighs. This act cranks up the two voices of reason to rock concert loud and even adds a third, guilt, to the cacophony. What the hell am I doing? I barely know this man and what I do know I don't particularly like. He's undead. He threatened me. I'm not this kind of—

Connor buries his face between my legs, tongue playing my clitoris as if we're in the sexual World Series, and all higher thought proves impossible. Dear God, that's amazing. He kisses it with tenderness before his tongue takes control again, rolling and pressing, only to exchange kisses for playing every few seconds. I'm not used to oral. It's so animalistic, even more so than penetration itself. Steven barely did it, but Will loved to. It was his first destination almost every time. He…oh, God. God. *Will*. No, I—

I burst into tears, jarring both Connor and myself. What the hell am I doing? Connor stops his feast of me, and I barely notice. The waves and waves, fucking tsunamis of guilt and shame pour out in time to my sobs. They won't stop. I can't stop them.

"Beatrice?" Connor asks, sitting up. I pull my legs to my chest and hug them to hide my nakedness, even resting my head on my knees so I don't have to look at him. "Did I hurt you?" I can't answer. "Beatrice..." Tentatively, he touches my bare knee.

"I'm sorry," I cry. I gaze up and wipe my tears so I can see. "I'm sorry. I thought I wanted this." I shake my head. "I'm sorry."

"You have nothing to apologize for," he assures me.

"I thought...this would help. That I could forget him and what I did, for just one fucking night. For one fucking night I could forget to hate myself," I sob.

"Why do you hate yourself?"

"Because I couldn't save him. Because I killed him. Because he left me alone. We were getting married. We were starting a life together, and I killed him," I sob. Connor moves closer and drapes his arm over my shoulders, pulling me against him. He hugs me as I literally cry on his shoulder. "I don't know what I'm doing..." Connor pets my hair and kisses my forehead. "I don't know what I'm going to do." I cry for another full minute until I finally begin to calm down. When I realize I'm naked in every way conceivable with a veritable stranger, I pull up my bra with a sniffle as I sit up. "Oh, gosh, I'm so embarrassed."

"There is no reason to be," he whispers with a sincere smile. "Absolutely none. I understand."

"Well, that makes one of us," I say with another sniffle. I stand up and put on my underwear and pants. My head's swimming. Standing was a mistake. Okay, this whole night was a mistake. I'm never leaving my bedroom again.

"I will have someone drive you home," Connor says as he stands as well.

I put on my shirt. "Thank you," I whisper. "And I'm sorry—"

Connor presses a finger to my lips and shakes his head. "I meant what I said. There is nothing to apologize for, fairest. I had a wonderful time tonight. One of the best I have had in ages." He smiles and places a gentle kiss on my lips. "I look forward to our next." Another sweet kiss. "Now, let me get you home."

Ever the gentleman, Connor escorts me back to the club and even waits outside until his driver pulls up to the curb. I let him kiss me once more, but a giant weight lifts the moment the car door shuts, and I'm away from him. I want this night over with. I want to be home. I rest my head against the window as the car drives away. What the hell was I thinking? I'm mortified, scared, remorseful, but now I get to add sexually frustrated as well. I can still feel him licking me. I'm still wet and on edge and...excited with no relief in sight. I deserve to be. It was stupid, reckless, and dangerous. So not like me. Of course being me has only gotten me heartache and pain. At least tonight, for a few short hours, there was no Will. No F.R.E.A.K.S. Just me and a gorgeous man dancing and flirting. I felt almost human for the first time in months. And I ruined it. I've faced vampires, werewolves, witches, and none have done as much damage as I've done to myself. I am without a doubt my own worst enemy.

Perhaps it's time to vanquish the bitch like I have all the others.

CHAPTER THREE

SCAR TISSUE

At least I have a legit reason to stay home the next day. Hangovers are the worst. I throw up twice before the sun even rises, and the headache and body aches keep me in my dark bedroom all day. I don't even have enough brain cells to play video games. Another day avoiding decisions and delaying the inevitable. Almost worth the pain.

Unfortunately I wasn't drunk enough to black out. I remember everything. Every kiss. Every caress. Every word I said. The fact he saw me naked. The fact I let the vamp literally brainwash my best friend. He could have told her to jump off a roof and she would have. I'm such a shit. I'm more of a shit for caring more about the other stuff than what he did to April. And I'm supposed to go over to her house tonight for Javi's birthday supper. God I wish I could get out of it but Nana's made him a cake and she'd never let me miss it. It'll be my penance for the violation and just being a general bitch last night. Nana loves being around the kids. I've barely seen them in all the months I've been back. I'm a sucky Godmother. Despite the summer heat, to hide the scars I put on a long-sleeved green and black striped shirt. Don't want to scare the babies.

As I step out of my bedroom, Nana hurries down the hall. "You have a delivery."

"What?"

I follow her to the kitchen where an edible fruit arrangement, giant box of Godiva chocolates, and envelope with my name scrawled on it. Inside I find a card, a gift certificate to a spa, and two tickets to the ballet *Swan Lake* at the Dorothy Chandler Pavilion for tomorrow night. "Who is it from?" Nana asks.

I don't even need to read the card. "My friend Connor."

Written on the card is just a local phone number with "-C" written on it. How cryptic. At least he's not angry about my being such a tease. I am intrigued. And I do sort of feel like I owe him after my shameful display last night.

Don't be stupid, Bea. Don't—

"I have to make a call. Be right back."

I take the portable phone to my bedroom and shut the door. This is truly a hellacious idea. Yet here I am. Listening to it ring. "Connor McInnis," he says with that Irish brogue. Yum.

"Hello Connor McInnis, this is Beatrice Alexander."

"Well hello," he practically purrs. "How are you feeling?"

"Hung over. Mortified. Now I can add perplexed."

"Why perplexed?"

"I was just wondering if you send all the women who burst into tears and run away after almost sleeping together ballet tickets and fruit arrangements."

"Only about half," he quips. "The others receive opera tickets and gift baskets."

I chuckle. "So. I assume you intend for me to go to the spa to ready myself for the ballet? My only question is, why give me two tickets?"

"Why do you think?" he asks.

"Well, one ticket would make sense."

"Why? Do you often attend events alone?"

"No. It's just…a person would assume *you* would need the other ticket currently in my possession."

"I merely thought perhaps you had others in your social circle who you would prefer attend with you. Your surly friend from last night as example. Or your grandmother. Though I will say *Swan Lake* is my favorite ballet, not that that fact should color your decision on whom deserves that second ticket and the chance to spend the evening with you. The fate of that second ticket is left entirely in your exquisite and surprisingly deft, skilled hands."

I chuckle again. Well played, Danny Boy. "Your fate is in my hands, you say?"

"At least tomorrow evening's fate."

"Okay. Fine. Connor, would you like to go to the ballet with me?"

"I thought you would never ask, fairest. I would enjoy nothing more."

"You should know there's only a slight, *miniscule* chance you'll actually get laid tomorrow."

"But there is a chance," he points out before going radio silence for a few seconds. "I can still taste you, you know. I am literally *aching,* pulsating to taste you again."

Thank God he can't see me because I blush from tip to toes. "I…enjoyed last night as well. I'm just sorry my nervous breakdown spoiled the end."

"I am nothing if not patient, fairest. I shall have my driver pick you up at six-thirty tomorrow night. Enjoy your day at the spa. Good-bye."

"See you tomorrow. Bye." I hang up.

Okay, how long have I been playing with my hair? I let the strand go and bask in the warmth that call brought. A sexy, rich man asked me out. It's certainly an ego booster. Sure he scares the crap out of me, and I don't really trust him, but it's just a date. One date. I've never been to the ballet, *and* he kisses like a demon tempting my soul. Good thing I buried that annoying thing right beside Will.

I know Nana's dying to know about my mystery benefactor but doesn't ask on the drive to April's house. Maybe she's afraid to. Whatever the reason, I'm glad. She's worried enough about me without adding the fact I'm dating a Machiavellian vampire with a body count no doubt in the triple digits to the pot. We park in April's driveway behind her husband Javi's Stanza. As always the front yard's littered with balls and other toys. They live in a modern ranch with attached garage like millions of other families, mine included. Wholesome as a nun. I carry Nana's homemade fudge chocolate cake that she spent hours on inside the house.

"Hello?" I call, stepping inside.

"*Tia* Bea!" Flora squeals before running into the messy yet homey living room from the kitchen.

My Goddaughter is her mother's mini-me with the same pillowy lips and huge chocolate brown eyes. It appears she'd moved on from her pink phase to purple as she's dressed head to toe in lilac. Flora latches onto my waist with a big hug. I pet her black hair. "Hi, sweetie."

Javi steps out of the kitchen next, all smiles. I wouldn't call him good looking, more striking with a square, Mayan face and squat, strong body, but he's a good one. He treats April like a queen and is the best damn father I've ever encountered. Not that I have much to compare that to. The closest thing I had to a father tried to molest me right before I literally broke his heart. May he burn in hell for all eternity.

"Is that my cake?" Javi asks. "I smelled it from the kitchen."

"Nana spent all day on it," I say.

"Is it chocolate?" Flora asks.

"Chocolate fudge," Nana replies.

"I love you Nana Liz," Flora says, releasing me to hug my grandmother.

"Love you too, honey."

Javi kisses my cheek and whispers, "April's on the warpath about you."

"Thanks for the warning," I whisper back.

"*Tia* Bea, I wanna show you my ponies!" Flora says. "I've gotten five since you were here!"

"Five? Wow. Lead the way, sweetie." Flora takes my hand and drags me down the hall to the bedrooms. One door is open, and I peek in to find Carlos and Manny playing video games in their room. "Hi, guys."

"*Tia* Bea!" Manny says with a smile.

"What are you guys playing?"

"*Star Wars*," Carlos answers, never taking his eyes off the screen. He's in the zone. I love the zone.

"See you two later," I say as Flora pulls on my arm. "Have fun defeating the dark side!"

It's definitely purpler in Flora's room than before but not much else has changed. It's like a Disney Princesses, *Dora the Explorer*, and *My Little Pony* showroom in here. "Here's their castle!" Flora says. She plops down on the carpet in front of a sparkly purple castle where pastel ponies lie in a heap in front of it. I sit beside her. "This is Sparkle Face! She's my favorite!" Flora hands me a pink pony and tiny brush. "Brush her hair!"

I know better than to disobey. I start brushing her mane. "These are pretty ponies. You're taking very good care of them."

"I love them so much. More than I love Cinderella *and* Dora."

"My goodness! That's an awful lot."

As I continue brushing, Flora begins arranging the ponies in their castle. "Are you still sad?" she asks nonchalantly.

"I'm sorry?"

She keeps setting up the toys. "Mommy said you were really, really sad because your friend died. That's why you haven't come to see me. Are you still sad?"

"Yeah, sweetie, I'm still sad. I loved my...friend very, very much."

"I'm sorry, *Tia* Bea. You can keep Sparkle Face until you're not sad anymore. She'll make you feel better."

My heart feels as if it literally swells. I kiss the top of her head. "Thank you, sweetie. I'd like that."

Flora nods and begins feeding the green one from the trough. "You can't keep her forever though. You can't leave with her when you go back to Kansas. I'll miss her too much."

"Don't worry. I don't know if I'm ever going back to Kansas, sweetie."

"Because of your friend?"

"In part. Yeah."

"Will the nice man still visit? He's handsome like Prince Charming."

"The nice man?"

"He said it was okay to call him Oliver. Mommy says its not umpolite if he says it's okay."

Oh. "*Impolite*," I correct. "Not umpolite. That's not a word."

"Oh. Sorry." She feeds the blue pony. "I want to show him all the paper snowflakes I made. He showed us how to make them at Christmas. They're fun!"

"I don't think he's coming back here, sweetie. But you can make him your snowflakes if you want and I'll send them to him. I know he'd love them."

"Or you could call him," April says behind me. I spin around and find her standing in the doorway, arms folded across her chest and scowl affixed. "Like you should have done months ago. Maybe he could knock some sense into you."

Great. Lecture time.

"Be right back, sweetie. I think your mommy wants to talk to me." I stand up and sigh. Let's get this over with.

I follow April to her bedroom. At least she waits until I've shut the door to begin her tirade. "Wasn't sure you'd show up tonight."

"The hangover wasn't too bad."

"That's not why I thought you'd chicken out."

"What? *You're* the one who wanted me to get out."

"Get out. Not get shitfaced, abandon us, and screw a monster who threatened your, mine, and your grandmother's life not even a year ago."

"I told you. We're past that."

"Why? Because you didn't have to physically fight him back then? Because Will got him to back down? What if Will couldn't? Do you think your new boyfriend would have let his psychotic scheme go?"

I don't know. "Yes," I lie.

"Liar," she spews back. "What if this is another play of his? Bea, you cannot trust this guy."

"April, I can handle myself. And it's not like I plan to marry the guy. I just want to have fun."

"Then find someone who isn't a literal blood thirsty, homicidal, supervillain without a damn pulse! He's a fucking vampire for God's sake! I thought the undead thing skeeved you out. It's the only conceivable reason I could come up with for why you didn't gain some goddamn sense and—" For whatever reason, she stops her train of thought and shakes her head. "You know, yesterday I was concerned about you but right now I'm shit scared *for* you. I'm more scared now than when I thought about you out there fighting trolls and ogres. You're so vulnerable right now a newborn could take you in a fight. Maybe you should go back to the F.R.E.A.K.S. At least with them you had an anchor. You're adrift here. You're drowning and instead of paddling to shore or grabbing the life preservers people keep throwing you, you're swimming toward the sharks.

"I know you. I know you're lost. I know the guilt is eating you alive. I know you think you deserve every pain the world can dish out because of what you had to do to him. But you don't. You were put in an impossible situation, and Bea, you made the right choice. The *only* choice. Look, I didn't Will that well and what little I did I didn't much like, but I think even *he* would agree with me on this. And I sure as shit know he wouldn't want you jeopardizing your life, your self-respect, your soul by jumping into something even you know is wrong for you." She takes a step toward me. "I love you. You're *mi hermana*, Bea, and you're lost right now. I just want to help you from making another massive, *massive* mistake."

"Okay, melodramatic much? I *almost* screw one hot, sexy guy and you're ready to call an exorcist. Ten years ago you would have jumped his bones in a New York minute."

"You're not me, Bea, and I'm not that girl anymore," she says with a sneer. For a reason. "And thank God I'm not. You don't do casual sex. You need a connection."

"I slept with Steven for two years, and I never loved him," I point out.

"Yeah, and look how *that* turned out," she spews back.

I scoff. "Oh, so it's my fault he went postal and become a serial killer?"

"No. Not…he had that ugliness inside him before he met you. He had to have. But maybe, just maybe, you sensed that and it…drew you to him. Like now with Connor. Hell, like with Will. He—"

"Don't," I warn, voice titanium. "Don't you *dare* say a word against—"

"The guy who treated you like shit for months because you wouldn't ghost your friend? Who left Oliver to be tortured and murdered? Who shut down every one of your ideas to help save people's lives out of spite? Who *you* even admitted had a temper and controlling streak? Hell, he wasn't a fucking saint, Bea. He didn't even seem that nice most of the time."

Why the hell did I have to tell her *everything*? I want to punch her. Scratch her pretty face until she bleeds. Rip out that horrible, offending tongue. But I just clench my hands to stop the impulses. "You don't know *anything* about him, so shut your damn mouth about him. Now. You don't know…*fuck you*. Fuck you." I storm out of the bedroom before I really lose it.

"Bea!" April calls.

I continue down the hall into the living room then kitchen where Javi and Nana chat and cook as Flora looks on. "I want to go," I tell Nana. "I want to leave. We're leaving."

"What?" Nana asks.

"We're going. Sorry, Javi."

"What happened? Wh—"

"You are not going anywhere," April says behind me.

"What's going on?" Javi asks.

"I want to go!"

"We just got here!" Nana says.

"Don't be like this, Bea," April says.

Flora jumps off the counter and circles around toward me. "*Tia* Bea! *Tia* Bea!"

"You want to stay, stay. Just give me the keys!" Flora keeps pulling on my hand to get my attention. "*Tia* Bea! *Tia* Bea! Don't go! Don't—"

"Will you stop that!" I snap at my goddaughter. The little girl's eyes bug out and her mouth falls at the same time all the adults gasp. I'm as shocked as the rest of them. I've never lost my temper around children before. I was a teacher for God's sake. Flora releases my hand, staring up with those huge brown eyes as if I were a stranger. She takes a step back toward her mother. Good thing too because the little girl's confusion and sadness overwhelm me.

"My keys are in my purse by the door. Take the car," Nana says.

"How—"

"We'll bring her home," Javi says.

"Just go," April says, putting her arms around her whimpering daughter.

Crap. I spin around and move toward the nearest exit before I have to look at them. It isn't until I'm outside that I can breathe again. What the hell just happened? April and I never fight, well not until recently. The last time was when I wanted to get pregnant right after Will and I started dating. I hung up on her when she attacked him that time too. It was annoying then but despicable now. I'm not sure if we can ever come back from this. Right now I don't want to. Right now I don't want to see or talk to her ever again.

I climb into the car and drive away but not home. I wind up at The Hotel Del Coronado. Well, the beach behind it. I love the beach. I remember the first time I ever saw the ocean in person, just one week after Nana collected us from that police station in Arizona. To my eight-year-old eyes this natural wonder was grander than I'd ever imagined. Blue water, soft sand, the gentle splash of the waves. Tranquil, beautiful, majestic. Even at night it's glorious. You can actually see the stars and the moon above illuminating the water, making it sparkle in places. I flop down on the sand and just stare at the twinkling horizon. I can always think here with those lapping waves and no other sounds. This place never fails to calm me enough to think. I came to this exact location when I was deciding whether or not to break up with Steven. I came here at Christmas when I considered leaving the F.R.E.A.K.S. Will and Oliver were at war with me caught in the middle, and the entire team were at odds. The last time I was here was the day before I returned to the squad. I had decided to continue the good fight against the monsters threatening innocent lives. Okay, really I was going back for *him*. The man I loved who I knew loved me in return, even if he wouldn't admit it to himself. And I was right. Will Price loved me with all he had. How dare April question that? Question him when he's not here to defend himself?

She *didn't* know him. They only met a handful of times with most of those interactions occurring when they were losing their minds after I was kidnapped and tensions were high. So high Will beat Connor and Oliver bloody. He had a lot of anger inside, a lot of hatred, though most of it directed at himself. It's why he pushed me away for so long. He was mad at life, at fate for the night a werewolf attacked him and killed his wife. He thought I couldn't handle his wolf, his darkness. But in truth he was the one who couldn't. I wanted to prove to him he was worthy of love. That he deserved the home, the children he always wanted despite his affliction. I was going to save him and instead I literally destroyed him.

He would have made a good father. We would have had a good life. When he died, he took that life from me. I want children, I want them more than words can express. I want the white picket fence. I want PTA meetings and barbeques and Saturday date night. I want pure, accepting, respectful, true love. And I almost had it. It was *right there*. I latched on with both hands, holding on for dear life, and it still wasn't enough. I still lost him. I lost *us*. I can't go through that ever again. I don't have the strength. I barely have the strength to lift my head in the morning. And April thinks I should go back to the F.R.E.A.K.S? She is right about one thing, I am weak and vulnerable. A pixie could kill me at this point.

I wish I'd never joined them. Okay, that's not entirely true. If I hadn't I never would have met Will. Nancy. Irie. Carl. George. Andrew. Wolfe. Oliver. My stomach clenches as it usually does when I allow myself to think about *him*. Especially tonight. Five hundred plus years on the planet made him knowledgeable about people and their needs. He'd know the exact right thing to say or do to make me feel better as he had countless times before. Sometimes I wouldn't even need to utter a word. He'd just look at me, frown, take my hand and off we'd go for a drive while I vented. To the roller rink or Dave & Buster's to belt out terrible karaoke. Even without his years to expertise I could somehow do the same with him. One look, I'd know he was down in the dumps, and off we'd go shopping or just sitting in the living room watching TV as we talked it out. Shit, how long have I been playing with the compass on my necklace? "To always find your way back to me."

As I have a trillion times in the past three months, I stare at my purse with my phone inside. No. *No*. I can't. Not even just to hear his melodic voice. I'd lose what little grip on myself I'm grasping onto right now. And God knows he's better off without *me*. In the whole year we've known one another he's almost died twice trying to save my worthless life. I've assaulted him, rejected him, insulted him, worse I didn't trust him when he gave me precious little reason not to. I've inflicted too much damage. Our relationship's probably more scar tissue than anything else and like everything with us it runs so deep, to depths I didn't know I possessed. I look away from the phone back to the stars, but he's even there. Somewhere on this world he's looking up at those same stars with me on his mind. I don't know how I know it, but I do. I wonder if he senses me too. "Help me," I whisper as the tears begin. "Help me."

My only response is silence.

CHAPTER FOUR

SWIMMING WITH SHARKS

A day at the spa. Just what the doctor, or I suppose vampire in this instance, ordered. I can see why it's a billion dollar industry. Connor treats me to the works. Facial, massage, mud bath, sauna, mani/pedi, make-up, even a brand new hair color, a caramel brown that, with the highlights, shines blonde in a certain light. I skipped the colonic and waxing though. Even without them I no longer feel like or resemble a drunk on a bender. On the Uber ride home—I really need a new car ASAP—I actually find myself smiling. If today's any indication, tonight might not be the big mistake everyone seems to think it will be. Hell, it might be precisely what I need. I hope so just so I can rub it in all their faces.

My smile wanes as we turn down my street and I notice Nana's car in the driveway. I only have thirty minutes before Connor's driver arrives, and I really don't want to harsh my expensive buzz by having it out with Nana. Last night I just drove around until I was sure she'd be asleep and left early this morning to the spa. I know I crossed a line last night, but so did my supposed best friend. I did send her a text asking that she apologize to Flora for me before I shut off my phone. *She's* not getting an apology until she extends it first. Not that Nana will agree, hence my nerves.

When I step inside the house, my grandmother's on the couch watching the news. She glances at me then back to the screen. "Hello," she says, voice as blank as her face.

"Hi," I say, quickly passing through.

When I shut my bedroom door, I sigh. So far so good. Maybe I've worn her out. She's finally done with me. Don't know how to feel about that. Relieved? Sad? Both I suppose. Whatever. Keep the high going, Bea. Don't think about it. I already decided on my Monique Lhillier long-sleeved black baroque satin and lace knee-length dress with bright red tights and black strappy high heeled sandals. The dress still fits but barely. I so need to get back to the gym or take an exercise class. I actually enjoyed learning boxing, karate, and any other martial arts disciplines the other F.R.E.A.K.S. were willing to teach me. I learned some during my training but then Will, Oliver, and Wolfe continued my ass kicking regime. I can disarm a person pointing a gun at my face, flip a two hundred pound man onto his back, and even perform a roundhouse kick. Now I'd probably just sit on the perp to incapacitate him. But tonight thank God for Spanx. We're definitely not having sex tonight. Spanx is so the new chastity belt.

I'm putting on the final touches when the doorbell chimes. Perfect timing. I fasten the strap on my shoe when Nana knocks and steps in. "There's a car here for you."

"Thanks."

"You look pretty."

"Thank you."

Her lips purse in disapproval a second later. I don't even need to look at her to know what she thinks about this date. Fuck you, empathy. "So you're going out with that...*man* tonight?"

"Yeah. To the ballet."

She pauses, then, "Are you sure that's a good—"

"Yes. I do. I'll be fine. I promise."

"Bea, I don't think—"

"No," I state. "I don't want to hear it." I walk to her and quickly peck her cheek. "Don't wait up. I love you."

Connor's driver waits outside on the porch and escorts me to the limo, even opening the door for me. Oh, nice. I've never been in a limo before. It's so long. Spacious. And there's even a bottle of champagne and a plate of chocolate covered strawberries on the tiny bar. Nice touch, Danny Boy. Since I only ate a salad at the spa, I devour the strawberries but leave the champagne corked. I need all my faculties tonight for obvious reasons.

We drive downtown, which is gridlocked this time of day. How we're getting to LA in under two hours for curtain is beyond me. Maybe Connor has a teleporter. We're not in traffic here too long, the usual ten minute drive takes twenty. The limo pulls into a tall skyscraper's parking lot. O-kay. The driver climbs out and opens my door. "This way, ma'am."

Curiousier and curiouser. The driver escorts me into the building then the elevator. "What's going on?" I ask.

"Mr. McInnis asked I not spoil the surprise, ma'am."

"Okay. But you should know if this is a trap, I can kill you with my brain."

"Uh…okay," the driver says. He takes a step to the side away from me.

The elevator doors open to the top floor and once again I follow the driver, this time up a stairwell to the roof. When he opens the door, I find my surprise. A helicopter waits on its pad with the pilot standing by it. Holy shit. No way.

"Hello, Miss Alexander, I'm Jeff," says the pilot as he shakes my hand. "Mr. McInnis is running a few minutes late but will be here soon. I should still have you both in Los Angeles in time though."

"Uh, okay."

Jeff slides the helicopter door open. "Please make yourself comfortable. There's fruit, chocolate, cheeses, and champagne inside."

"Wow. Okay. Thanks."

The pilot helps me into the helicopter where a plate of goodies and more Cristal wait just for me. I scoot over on the bench to the left and begin chowing down again as I survey the whirlybird. Small, only seats four, but the windows are enormous, perfect to take in the scenery. I especially drink in the sight of Connor, dressed in a tailored gray suit with white shirt and aviator sunglasses striding toward me a few minutes later. I run my tongue over my teeth to wipe away the stray cheese and smooth my hair. "I apologize for the tardiness," he says as he climbs in. As if it were the most natural act in the world, he leans across and quickly kisses my lips like Javi always does to April. "I rose early but apparently not early enough."

"It's okay."

Connor fastens his seatbelt and slips on the headset from a hook so I follow suit. "You look ravishing by the way."

"Thank you."

Even with the headsets, when Jeff starts the helicopter, the chop of the blades are loud. Really loud. I hope it doesn't ruin the experience. "We should be in LA in under an hour, Mr. McInnis," Jeff says over the comms.

"Thank you, Jeffery," Connor replies before turning my way. "Have you ever ridden in a helicopter before?"

"Nope."

"A virgin then. Excellent." Connor takes my hand and smiles slyly. "Simply sit back and enjoy the ride."

"Guess that's better than 'Brace yourself, Bridget,'" I quip.

The helicopter gently lifts up, leaving my stomach behind for a moment but it catches up by the time we've cleared the skyscrapers. I still squeeze Connor's hand in an attempt to stave off the few nerves emerging with this new experience. Thankfully those nerves quickly vanish once I get a gander at the vista. Damn. The sun has just set under the ocean so the sky is all dark blues tinged with orange and pink with a few twinkling stars sharing the sky. The Coronado Bridge rises above the blue water with stripes of red and white lights from the cars running along it. In the front of the helicopter sit the green and brown hills with more lights from the houses and cars scattered around. To my right, the city of San Diego. Glass behemoths rising to the sky with homes, schools, and shopping centers laid out around it. "This is…"

"The only way to travel," Connor finishes for me.

I glance at my date, and my smile fills my whole face. The vamp gives good first date, I'll give him that. A girl could get used to this. "I don't know. I was kind of hoping for another ride in your Ferrari."

"I shall give you any type of ride you desire, my fair Beatrice," he says with that crinkly eyed grin of his. Too bad I can't see his eyes behind his aviator sunglasses. "Simply say the word." My own grin grows. I have missed smiling. "Now, are you not glad I am the one you chose to accompany you tonight?"

"I don't know. Nana's helicopter is a bit roomier."

He smiles again. "Well, thank you for the invitation regardless. Have you ever attended the ballet?"

"No. Oliver and I had tickets to The *Nutcracker* at Christmas, but I came here instead."

"Did you and Oliver often attend live events alone together? I cannot imagine Agent Price approved considering the wolf almost ripped my tongue out for merely *speaking* to you."

Crap. I forgot we told him Will and I were together for months when we met him. "We didn't *always* go alone together. Will usually came too, and Oliver would sometimes bring a date. Will would skip the musicals though," I lie. I can't see Connor's eyes behind his sunglasses but I'm fairly sure they're narrowed at me. Yeah, not sure I sold that lie too well. Change of subject. "So, is this your standard first date M.O.? Champagne, limos, and helicopter rides to LA?"

"No. Normally I escort my paramour to Wings 'N Things followed by laser tag. But I did not want to reenact a date Agent Price and Officer Weir no doubt took you on already."

"Hey. Don't knock Wings 'N Things. Their honey bar-b-que sauce is unparalleled."

He smiles again. "Next date perhaps."

I pop another strawberry in my mouth. "You're being quite cocky there, Danny Boy. This date's just begun and you're already sure you're getting another? This may surprise you but I prefer substance to flash."

"But look at *this* flash," he says, gesturing to the helicopter. "Not to mention I am taking great risk to my physical person this evening simply by setting foot in Los Angeles so you can experience a ballet masterpiece. Surely that warrants a second evening of your company."

"Why are you taking your life into your own hands by going to LA?"

"I am not on the best of terms with its current ruler."

"Oh, yeah. I vaguely remember Oliver mentioning something about that. What happened? You sleep with his wife? Steal his herd of cattle a century ago?"

"Nothing so simplistic I am afraid. Lady Antonia and I have had our dust ups for over a century, but our little rivalry especially flared over sixty years ago as most wars do, over land. My territory used to span to the edge of Orange County, but Antonia secretly purchased large parcels of property and built homes and the like on them. By the time I discovered the subterfuge, she and her fellow vampires were firmly entrenched. Back then Orange County was nowhere near the population center it is now. Her vassals far outnumbered mine in a very short time. She agreed to parlay, but of course would not remove her business interests and naught was solved. So, with no other option, I dispatched people to surgically demolish the properties and those closest to her in an attempt to destabilize her operation. Unfortunately she launched a counter-attack, slaying my second in command and burning down many of my interests in Orange County. Eventually our war began making headlines so the King sent emissaries and gave us a choice: cease hostilities or he would strip us of our posts and exile us from North America. She was granted all territory north of Santa Ana. Since then we have engaged in a Cold War of sorts. Dispatching spies, undermining business deals, and of course waiting for the first sign of instability to strike."

"Why? Why live like that?"

"To become the most powerful vampire on the continent, if not the world," he says with the briefest of smiles. "I would control a hundred thousand vampires and become a billionaire a hundred times over."

I shake my head. "Or you could be content with what you have," I offer. "Lord of San Diego ain't too shabby."

"A shark must always keep swimming forward, Beatrice, or it perishes."

"You know, you're the second person in as many days to compare you to a shark. It's a tad disconcerting." Connor chuckles. "Well, if world domination is your end game, Lex Luthor, then why not just challenge her to a duel? Isn't that how you vamps become Lords and Ladies?"

"It is. However, Antonia is the greatest swordsperson inhabiting the earth. I have kept up with the sport, however I do not possess enough skill to face her in single combat. She has challenged me, but I am no fool."

"So she did kind of steal a metaphorical herd of your cattle," I quip.

"And made me appear weak in the process."

"So what will she do if she finds out about tonight's field trip into enemy territory? Should I have brought my machete?"

"*You* shall be perfectly safe. Antonia would never harm a hair on the head of someone so close to your Oliver."

"She's another ex of his?"

"Of course."

I frown. "Yeah. Not the most exclusive of clubs, is it? I think I'm the only woman, or man for that matter, to enter his orbit and not to join."

Connor stares at me behind his sunglasses, I think studying me. "You have truly never shared his bed, have you?"

"No, I haven't."

"But you desired to. Would you have succumbed to his temptation if not for the wolf?"

"I-I…can't answer that. I mean, of course the thought crossed my mind,"—nine million times—"but that doesn't mean anything. It crosses my mind about Chris Evans every hour too. Actions are what matter."

"Thoughts hold great power," he points out. "It must have been a great source of discomfort to your wolf knowing you harbored desire for another man, one known for his sexual prowess, and one in such close proximity to you. I simply cannot reconcile the brute who on two occasions attempted to tear out my larynx and an enlightened, secure male who would not protest as his paramour traipsed off alone with a man he obviously loathed."

Hence why we had our own little Cold War. "Will trusted me, and I never gave him a reason not to. But yeah, it got complicated sometimes and was a lot of hard work." All for nothing in the end.

"The important things in life often are," Connor says.

"Well, it left me exhausted."

Connor takes my hand again. "Then allow me to take care of you, at least for tonight."

"This is a good start," I say, glancing around the helicopter.

I suppose even sharks have their uses.

*

It's easy to see why *Swan Lake* is a classic. I always thought I'd find ballet dull and hard to follow, but I'm amazed how swept up I become in the combination of music and movement. What the dancers are able to do with their bodies is nothing short of astounding, and this is coming from a woman who can move matter with her mind. I'll have to attend more often.

It's almost midnight when the show ends, and I'm starving. My rumbling stomach began all but stealing the show around Act 4. I smiled apologetically to Connor and the others glaring at me in our box. Can't take me anywhere nice. When the curtain falls, Connor helps me into the limo that picked us up at the helipad in LA before climbing in himself. "Can we stop at Mc—"

"Driver," Connor says, cutting me off, "will you please take us to Taylor's Bistro at Mullholland and Cypress? Thank you." He rolls up the partition. "I am a tad peckish myself."

"You plan on eating the waitress?"

He smiles again. "It caters to both our kinds," he instructs me. "An old friends owns it."

"The last few times I've been to vampire/human establishments everyone was naked and holding whips."

"It is merely a restaurant, I assure you." His grin grows along with the crinkles in his eyes. "Though if you prefer whips to steak…"

"Not in this lifetime, Danny Boy."

"Then steak it is."

Taylor's Bistro appears to be precisely that, a small dimly lit restaurant. The only thing out of the ordinary is the fact there's not sign on the front above the empty store window, and we have to walk down an alley to reach the entrance, entering in the back. To the outside world it's an empty boutique. Guess they don't want some tourist to wander in and find people sucking down blood as three fourths of the current patrons are. As I do whenever I enter a potentially hostile territory, I instantly take in the patrons, the space, and locate the exits. Twelve vampires and three humans at the ten tables, all relaxed and not even glancing our way. Exit in the back left corner along with the door we came in. Still wish I'd brought a gun. Or Bette my machete.

Connor escorts me to the back by the exit, pulling out my chair before sitting with his back to the wall. Guess I'm not the only paranoid one. He continues to survey the restaurant as he's also done since we entered. It does nothing to lower my own nervousness. "Are you okay?" I ask.

He stops recon to look my way. "Yes. Of course."

"You know, I'd be fine if we just popped through an In & Out Burger or something."

"Nonsense."

A waiter in all black walks over. "Hello, welcome to Taylor's. Tonight we're serving chicken alfredo with antipasto, steak filets with sautéed onions and pomme frites, or nicosise salad."

"Steak, medium rare, and coffee with milk and sugar," I say.

"And I shall have the AB positive if you have it," Connor says.

"We don't, I'm afraid. We do have B though."

"That will do. Thank you."

"I will be right back with your drinks." He walks away.

We stare across the small table at one another, just smiling for a few moments. "This has been a wonderful night. Thank you."

"You are welcome, Beatrice," he says sincerely.

I shake my head and raise an eyebrow at him. "Who knew when I first met you, you'd turn out to be a pretty decent guy?"

"Yes, we did not have the best of introductions. Entirely my fault, of course. It is long overdue, but…I apologize. And I thank you for looking past my bad behavior."

I stare down. "You have, have you not?"

I give it a good think before sighing. "I…don't know," I answer truthfully. "Not completely. Would you have gone through with it? All your threats?"

"I would hardly call offering you privilege, power, and devotion a threat," he says.

"Accept or die is a threat, Connor," I point out. "Cake or death still has the death component."

"I suppose it does," he concedes with a slight frown.

"You had to know I wouldn't accept."

"Actually, fairest, I did not. You were the first to refuse my consortship in almost two hundred years."

"And what happened to her?" I ask.

"She died of consumption a year after our time together concluded. I miss her to this day."

The waiter returns with my coffee and Connor's blood before departing again.

"Well, you didn't even *know* me. So what was your endgame, Danny Boy?"

"What does it matter now?" he asks, sipping his blood.

"It matters if you want that second date," I say. "I like you. I do. I just…there has to be a speck of trust between us. So just tell me and we can put the past to bed. We can get that speck. Please."

Connor studies my face, no doubt the wheels in his mind churning at break neck speed, trying to figure out the best angle, his shoulders relaxing a little before saying, "The truth? I saw you as a weapon. You know the world I inhabit is little more than a jungle with predators behind every tree. To survive one takes every advantage they have at their disposal. I believed I had leverage over one of the most powerful psychics in the world, I would be a fool not to at least attempt to acquire said weapon."

I figured as much. "Okay. Fair enough. But now? Am I still just a gun to you?"

"No. I overplayed my hand. My ploy failed. I have no leverage. I still do not. And yet…" he reaches across the table for my hand. I let him take it, entwining our fingers together. "Here we are. Equals. Here because we both wish to be. No ulterior motives but that. I like you, Beatrice Alexander. Truly. I wish to spend more time with you because you are funny. Sexy. Interesting. A fantastic kisser. That is all. At least for me." He sits back. "So, now am I granted that second date?"

"Don't know how you're going to top this one," I say with a smile.

"I believe you have just thrown down the gauntlet, my fair Beatrice. I *will* come out victorious." He sips his blood. "As always."

"Not always," I point out, sipping my coffee too. "But a loss every now and then is humbling. And you *certainly* could use a humbling or two."

"I certainly have no problem with falling to my knees before *you*, fairest. I shall take any position you desire."

My face grows hot, and I know I'm blushing. "Jeez, you're almost as bad as Oliver."

"Except I shall succeed where he failed," Connor says with utter certainty.

"It's not a competition," I say, drinking my coffee.

"Everything in life is a competition, fairest," he schools me.

"Okay, this whole supervillain vibe you're giving off right now is a little off-putting, just so you know."

"Then how may I steer you back into the mood? I could tell you all the things I wish to do to you when I get you alone again?"

And we've gone too far in the opposite direction. "Tell me about Oliver."

"I beg your pardon?" he chuckles.

"I've never had a chance to sit down with someone who knew him in the old days. There wasn't much time between meeting them and them trying to kill us, which always seemed to happen. So. What was the legendary Oliver Smythe Montrose like?"

"The life of the party. Up for almost anything. We were not close by any standard, but I was close with his Grand-Sire Asher." I crinkle my nose at that name. "It was deplorable Peter traded Oliver's life for Asher's. It certainly did not endear your Oliver to me further, forget his continued relationship with Antonia."

"Asher slaughtered an entire family and kidnapped his ex-girlfriend while Oliver saved the life of a little girl. Your *friend* deserved everything he got. And Oliver more than paid for his part in that night. I have personally seen him save a dozen lives, mine included."

"If I am not mistaken he was forced into his position with the Federal Government. Forgive me but I do find it difficult to reconcile Oliver Smythe or whatever he calls himself now, risking life and limb for perfect strangers as if he were Superman when the man I knew could not think past his next bedmate or gala."

"Then I guess he's changed."

"Perhaps he finally had a reason to," Connor says, raising his eyebrow and sipping his blood.

"I had fairly little to do with it if that's what you're insinuating."

"Do not underestimate your power over the opposite sex, my fair Beatrice. I speak as one now trapped in its clutches. From all I have observed and learned, you two share a bond I have never known him to have formed before. Perhaps not even with Antonia."

"We're friends. Friends *should* have a bond. And ours runs deep because we've gone through the worst of the worst together and when it mattered, we've never let each other down. We understand each other. We recognize what each other is capable of, what the other can endure even if we ourselves don't recognize it. I don't think anyone wanted to put in the work with him. You all expected him to be nothing more than the life of the party, and after a while if enough people tell you what you are, even the strongest of us start to believe the propaganda. But he is so much more than that. He's smart, and funny, and has a good heart. One of the best I've ever come across."

Connor studies me again but his own face gives nothing away. "Then why is he not here? By your side in your time of need? You told me you have not spoken in months."

"Because…it hurts me too much, and I've met my pain quota for several lifetimes."

"But you miss him," Connor states as fact.

More than I care to admit. "Of course."

"More than you miss your fiancée?"

The question rattles me enough I can't hide my shock and uneasiness. My mouth flops open a few times. I don't know how to answer that. I've questioned my decision that night countless times. Would I make it again? The answer is always, *always* yes. If the roles were reversed and it was Oliver about to kill Will, I would have pulled the trigger too. But it wasn't. I miss Will like I'm missing a limb, but it isn't him I instantly turn to share a funny thought or have a conversation with only to realize he isn't there to hear it. "I guess I miss them in different ways," I answer, staring down at the white tablecloth.

"I did not mean to offend or upset you with the question," Connor assures me.

"I know. It's my fault for driving us down this road. Seems every one we go down is filled with crater sized potholes." I look up at Connor again. "I haven't been on a real date since Steven almost four years ago. I'm out of practice, and I was never good at this first date thing to begin with." I sip my coffee. "Shouldn't we be talking about our favorite movies or hobbies or something safer?"

"Very well then. My favorite movie is *The Lion in Winter*, what is yours?"

My steak arrives as we're discussing the time he met my favorite writer Charlotte Bronte—very timid and shy—and I begin relaxing again. Will and Oliver have no place at this table. I focus on the sexy Irishman sitting across from me and the equally yummy steak. "...and Byron even contemplated following her to Haworth, but the man has the attention span of a fly. He found a new virgin to seduce closer to home. I have never liked the man, especially after he and Richard had their falling out."

"So Lord Byron's still kicking around, huh?"

"Unfortunately. He has taken to writing erotica under multiple pen names. I hear they are quite good."

"What's one of the pen names?" I ask, eating a fry.

A half smile forms on Connor's face. "Do you read erotica, Beatrice? I am shocked."

"Why? I read a lot."

"But erotica?" he asks, fake scandalized.

"I am a red blooded, liberated woman, Connor McInnis. I have even watched porn." Once. Ick. "Is that so hard to believe?"

"You merely give off a certain air of innocence and purity, fair one. That is all."

"Excuse me, did we not spend all of Saturday night dirty dancing and...rounding home?"

"The mere fact you feel the need to use the euphemism 'rounding home' proves my point."

"My grandmother taught me not to be vulgar," I say, "especially when in public."

"Then she would be positively scandalized when I tell you it is taking almost every ounce of my willpower not to rip off your panties, bend you over this table, spread your legs, part you to glide my cock inside your currently wet cunny, and rut you mercilessly as you cry out in pure pleasure until you come six times whilst all these people watch."

I stare across the table, my cheeks as hot as my yes wet womanhood. I cross my legs under the table to help quell the not unwelcome sensations. "I..."

"Or perhaps you would prefer I finish what I began Saturday. My tongue still craves your succulent pussy. I could feast on you for hours. Flicking. Kissing. Suckling until dawn as you writhe above me, begging me to stop. To continue. As I give you no quarter. I could fall to my knees now if that is your desire. I know it is mine."

I have absolutely no idea what to say or do in this moment. I want to look away again but he's so freaking magnetic I can't unglue my eyes from his seductive face. In this moment, if we weren't separated by a table and in public,

I'd be unzipping his pants and ripping off my own panties before I rode him into orgasmic oblivion. He must have read my mind because the side of his mouth rises slightly, almost like a dare. It's just sex. He—

All the mischief drains from his face when he catches sight of something behind me. His mouth sets into a straight line, forming a slight scowl. My own eyes narrow at him as he sits up straight and folds his arms on the table. My spidey sense tingles. Trouble.

"What the hell are you doing here?" a man asks behind me.

I spin around and find two men, one Chinese and the other Latino, striding over to our table. If the fact they both aren't male model gorgeous each with cheekbones that could cut glass isn't a dead giveaway they're vampires then the exposed fangs on the Chinese man would be. Connor's expression remains neutral as the men step past me without so much as a glance so all I can see are their profiles and backs. I'd be offended by the snub, but I'm too nervous to care. I've developed a sixth sense in identifying when trouble's in the air. It's all but wafting like cartoon stink lines from these men.

"Waiting for my companion to finish her steak," Connor says. "Service here is abysmal."

"What…are you doing here?" the Chinese vamp asks again, each word harder than the last.

"I believe I responded to your query already. The answer has not changed."

Crap. The Chinese man's hand clenches into a fist. "You know you are not allowed in our territory, McInnis."

"It-it was my fault," I chime in. Both men finally look at me, the anger not dissipating one iota. "I-I insisted we see *Swan Lake* and was hungry afterwards."

"Fairest, it is alright," Connor says with a smile. "This need not concern you." Connor rises from our table, still maintaining a smile directed at the vamps. "We should continue this conversation outside, no? No need to disturb the other patrons."

"Fine," the Latino says with a thick Hispanic accent.

"Connor?" I ask.

He steps toward me and leans down to kiss me on the lips. "All is well, fairest. I shall return shortly."

He kisses me again, a long, lingering, probing kiss that stirs the lust again and for a millisecond I forget the surly jerks ruining my date until he breaks away. After a quick smile, Connor leads the men toward the door.

Crap.

Okay, what do I do? Connor obviously doesn't want me involved. He probably knows best. I...yeah, that's not going to happen. I turn around to keep an eye on the trio through the sole window. Our new friends grimace and glare at my calm date. Whatever Connor's saying they're having none of it. Connor continues speaking, now with a slight smile, hands gesturing as he tries to make his point, but the vamps both put their body weight on their left sides and lean in closer to him. Crap. Fighter's stance. Connor doesn't seem to notice or care, he simply continues talking and smiling as if they were having a conversation at a Farmer's Market about jam or something. He is a lawyer. Maybe—

The Latino cold cocks Connor, sending my date tumbling to the pavement. Oh, hell no. I snatch my purse off the floor and sprint toward the door without a second thought, my blood already racing as if Richard Petty were behind the wheel. By the time I set foot outside into the narrow alley, the Chinese vamp lifts a bleeding Connor by the collar. "You motherfu—"

"Get your hands off him," I order.

The man doesn't obey, he just stares at me, fangs exposed. "Get out of here, lady."

"I am fine, Beatrice. Please return inside," Connor says before spitting blood on the side of his attacker's face. The shocked vamp's gaze whips back to Connor, and at the same time he punches my date in the stomach. Connor doubles over with a groan.

"Stop!" I say, taking a step toward them.

"Go back inside," the Chinese vamp orders.

"Not without him," I say.

"Lady, we're not fucking around. Get insi—"

Taking a page from his attacker's book, Connor punches the distracted vamp in the gut. The man's stunned for a moment, folding in on himself too, but his friend isn't. The Latino vamp bashes Connor's face again, dazing him for enough time so the Chinese vamp to regains his own senses. He punches Connor in the stomach again as the Latino vamp cocks his fist back for another round. That bastard doesn't get the chance.

I haven't used my psychokinesis for anything but switching on the lights and the television in three months, but picking up the Latino vampire and flinging him a hundred meters down the alley proves as easy as the light trick. The other vamp momentarily stops his assault on Connor when his friend flies backwards for no apparent reason. Connor uses the confusion to get upright. By the time the Chinese vamp's returning his attention back to Connor, my date's own fist is on its way toward his assailant's face. It connects and it's the other man's turn to splat on the pavement. I'm about to send him flying too, but suddenly there's a vice tight grip around my arms and torso. Arms. Attached to...

Training is a brilliant concept. My instructors at The Building and sparing with the other F.R.E.A.K.S. drilled me on this very scenario. My body reacts on its own. I whip my head backwards toward the man's nose, and my high heeled foot stomps down on his foot. Both head and foot connect with their targets. The head butt hurts my own but not enough I can't perform the third attack. The vamp releases his grip on me and the millisecond I can, I smash my elbow into his solar plexus as hard as I can. I spin around to find the Latino stumbling back, bleeding from his lip and clutching his stomach. I lift him off the ground and just hold him there mid-air. I can sense him struggling against my invisible grip, but I've trained myself against that too. He's not going anywhere.

My gaze pivots back toward Connor and the Chinese vamp. Connor's pinned against the wall by the vamp's forearm, crushing his larynx. Bad boy. I grab him with my mind too. He levitates up up and away from Connor.

"Enough!" I roar. I glance back and forth at both men. "This is over!"

"Fuck yo—"

I squeeze the Latino's chest tighter to stop his words. "This is over," I say, drawing out every word. "I can hold you both all night and let you burn in the sun if I have to." I peer at the snarling Chinese vamp. "Or I can release you, you let us go on our merry way, and we all forget this misunderstanding ever happened. I vote for option two, no?"

The vamps glance at one another and both begrudgingly nod yes. Good enough. I drop both men. Hard. They both collapse in heaps, giving me a chance to hustle over to the smiling Connor. Not even a split lip and bruised cheek can stop his damn smirk. Without a beat, he grabs my hand

and begins hustling me down the ally, hunched over and holding his stomach with his other arm. I keep glancing back at the vamps. They don't follow. They just watch our retreat. Thank God.

My blood, my brain, my breath, my emotions still race as we climb back into our waiting limo. "Please drive. Now. Drive," Connor orders the driver the moment I shut the door. As the engine springs to life, Connor rolls up the partition. I need a second to regain some composure. My limbs, hell my every cell is tense. I fucking love it. I'd forgotten the thrill, the high that comes from intense situations. It's horrible and brilliant at the same time. I—

"Are you alright?" Connor asks, bringing me a step closer to reality.

"What?" I stare at his battered face. Split lip and a little blood on his chin. Slightly swollen and bruised cheek. He's already healing but still. "Am *I* okay?" I reach across and run my finger over his lip. "Are you?"

He cups my face in his hand with a smile. "I am fine." He gazes into my eyes, sending another shiver of pure lust to my already overtaxed cells. "I am...I..." His thumb traces my already plump, tender lips. My breath catches and that's all we need.

Fuck it.

As if reading my mind, Connor grabs the back of my head and pulls my lips to his, devouring me. Matching my madness, my passion for him with each stroke of our lips. He tastes of blood but somehow that just heightens the experience. Our tongues fight for supremacy in my mouth as his fingers dig into my back and neck as hard as his lips assail mine.

That's the only fight left in me. I don't put up an iota of resistance as he lowers me onto the bench seat. As his hands slide up my skirt to literally rip off my tights and undergarments, exposing me to the cool air and further tantalizing my hot sex with this new extreme. As he quickly undoes his own pants. At this moment there is only one thing I want in this whole universe. When he thrusts inside me with the force of a hurricane, as his thick manhood parts me, stretches me, fills me with pure pleasure and a tinge of pain, I finally get something I want. First time for everything.

With that first assault, I close my eyes and cry out in pleasure and clutch onto him. He's not as big as Will and is colder, but it's still wonderful. It doesn't matter who he is. All that matters is what he's making me feel. Full. Sexy. Wild. Brilliant. I wrap my legs around this thrusting hips to draw him in deeper. I don't want gentleness. No lovemaking. I want him to fuck me. Fuck the tension, the agony, the fear away. "Harder," I pant. "Harder." I dig my nails into his naked buttock to drive the point home. Connor complies, gliding inside me faster and harder if possible. "Fuck me. Just fuck me. Fuck me…" My own hips meet him stroke for stroke. Good. So good. The delicious tension, the pleasure inside rises a notch with each collision. "Fuck me. *Fuck me.*" Oh, God, I'm coming…I'm coming…

When the climax hits not even a minute after we began, I hold onto him as I spasm around his still erect penis. He continues thrusting, even as I hear glass shatter near us. Both shatterings clear my head and as he thrusts again and again I realize what I'm doing and who I'm doing it with.

Oh, fuck me.

"Wh-what was that?" I ask, eyes still closed, shoving his shoulder to get his attention. "Connor?"

I open my eyes, and his violet orbs search my face. I can't look at him. I gaze over at the mess on the other side of the car. The bottle of champagne and glasses have all broke into shards all over the car and floor. Thank God. I begin to sit up, and Connor takes the hint. He climbs off me, out of me, back onto his own seat. Away from me. "Sorry. That was me." I quickly pull back on my undergarments. "My power. When I…" Thank God, they're back on. It's over. "It happens. Sorry. I-I didn't mean to ruin the…"

"It is perfectly fine," he says, reluctantly dressing himself as well. "Just fine."

Yeah. Fine. Fucked up, insecure, neurotic, and emotional. That's what this is. What I am.

Just fine. I think. I hope.

CHAPTER FIVE

PANDORA'S BOX

A person can justify any of their actions. Hitler and Stalin exterminated millions to make their countries stronger. Serial killers murder and rape because they've had such crappy lives it's only fair others make them feel better. I slept with a vampire because he's magnetic, charming, and because we'd just lived through a violent, intense situation. If I had a dollar for every time I'd had the urge to jump Will or Oliver's bones after a fight, I'd be Elon Musk wealthy. What's the most life affirming act after facing death? Sex. I shouldn't feel guilty or ashamed. It's not as if I didn't *want* to. Or still want to if I'm being honest. I wanted to even before the fight. We're both single adults. The sex was good. Then why the hell do I feel guilty? Maybe guilt is just my default emotion now. All other circuits are broken.

  The ride home was an awkward nightmare. We barely exchanged five words. In the helicopter I pretended to sleep, which thanks to the adrenaline withdrawal soon became a reality. When we landed, he woke me, escorted me to the awaiting car, and faded into the night as I drove away. That was two nights ago without a word since. Not a bouquet of flowers, not a phone call or email. A huge part of me is relieved. He finally got what he wanted from me and is moving onto his next conquest. I've had a one night stand like a normal twenty-something. Better, there's no worry about pregnancy or STDs. Lucky me.

But another part can't help but be a little pissed. All that work, all that money he spent wooing me, we sleep together once, and that's it? Was it so bad he's decided I'm not worth the trouble anymore? I should have offered to finish him with my mouth or hand at the very least. He got me off, and I should have returned the favor. I was just so shocked at myself, at the situation, that I'd just had an almost stranger literally inside me, sexual decorum didn't enter my mind. This crap just hurts my head, so I've gone back to old habits spending a whole day at the movies and another playing video games. April doesn't call either, and Nana gives me wide berth. I seem to repel everyone now. Except George. No, he's left two more messages I've ignored.

I *almost* found the strength to call him yesterday. Had the phone in my hand even. I just couldn't punch in the numbers. Two words, that's all I need to utter. "I quit." End of chapter. I can return to teaching. If I can't find a job in San Diego, I'll apply all over the country. Some school in America must need a teacher. Let the fates decide where I should rebuild. Make new friends. Maybe try to find a man with a pulse or who doesn't turn into a wolf. Forget the past year as best as possible. *Then what the hell is stopping me?*

I pause my game to stare at my cell phone. Go. Do it. What the hell am I waiting for? *Do it.* Just—

My phone begins vibrating, damn near making me shriek in surprise. Jesus. I chuckle to myself. Two nights ago I took on a vampire duo in high heels and tonight the phone makes me jump. I don't really want to talk to anyone but check the display anyway.

Big fucking mistake. One more to add to the ten million.

My stomach physically clenches. *Oh God. Oh, my God. Nope. No.* I literally flee the bedroom as if he can physically yank me through the phone to him. I retreat into the bathroom, sitting on the toilet, even shutting the door for extra protection against that phone. Why is he calling me? Why now? It's been months. He—Connor. Oh God, he knows about Connor. How? Did April blab? Does he know I…no he can't know about *that*. What does he want? What do I do?

It takes me a two full minutes to pull myself together enough to leave my hiding spot and walk the ten feet back to my room. He left a voice mail. I don't want to know. I do but I don't. I don't want to hear his voice again, but I have been craving that sound since I left Kansas. My phone's become Pandora's Box. I don't think a damn good thing can come from listening to his message, but I punch in my code anyway. Here come the horrors.

"Hello. Beatrice," Oliver says haltingly as if nervous.

I was right. Two words and the first horror's been released. He called me Beatrice. He only does that when he's angry or we're in mortal peril. The name sounds wrong coming from him. Unnatural. Obscene. As if I'm a stranger to him now. So much a stranger there are several seconds of uncomfortable silence. We've never experienced that much either. Will and I made it into an art form but never Oliver and me. Another stab to the heart.

"I, uh, um, merely…my friend Antonia contacted me tonight. She…she had questions as to why you aided in the assault of one of her closest advisors and his husband the other evening with Connor McInnis."

Crap. Crap, crap, crap…

"I…had no answer for her, but I believe I did manage to convince her if you did resort to violence, it was because you were provoked. That you harbor no animosity toward her, and have only a…casual acquatiance with the Lord of San Diego. I think she believed me." He pauses again. "This is serious, Trixie. These are two of the most ruthless, powerful vampires on the planet and they loathe one another to almost unreasonable levels. Do not insert yourself in any way, shape, or form with either of them, and especially not between them. *Please.*" There's another voice over the phone, I think Chandler's. "I, uh, I must go now. We are on a case. I, Trixie, please…*please* take care of yourself. Please."

The call ends.

Yep. Freaking Pandora's Box.

Okay, this is bad. Last time I inadvertently got involved in vamp politics I was a hair's breadth from a massacre and becoming Connor's concubine. Freaking Connor. This is all his fault. *Again.* Now I have a total stranger gunning for me just because I defended my date and myself. This is my punishment for attempting casual sex. Most women have a one night stand and the only consequences are the walk of shame. Not me. Never me. Now I have to call him and find out if I need to stock up on silver bullets and stakes.

He picks up on the forth ring. "Connor McInnis," he says, all business.

"Uh, hi, it's, uh…Bea Alexander."

"Hello," he says, voice neutral. Not happy to hear from me nor nervous.

"Hi," I say before drawing a blank. I don't know what to say next.

"I have been meaning to phone you. Thank you for saving me a call. I apologize. It has been a madhouse here the past few nights."

I can't tell if he's lying or not. Guess it only matters to my ego. "I can imagine."

"You truly cannot, fairest," he chuckles. "Are you...well?"

"I don't know. You tell me. Apparently Lady Antonia called Oliver after what happened in the restaurant. He sounded concerned for me."

Connor's silent for a few seconds. "Shite. I was hoping to keep you out of this." He's quiet again. "Uh...can you come to the club? Now? Tonight?"

"I don't have a car. Nana's at dinner with her friend."

"You do not have a car? Then I shall send my driver post haste."

"How worried should I be, Connor?"

"The truth? I have no idea, and *that* worries me. I shall see you soon. Good-bye."

He hangs up. Crap. Crap, shit, fuck, crap, fuck. How is this happening again? How am I in danger just because I went to dinner with a guy? Maybe April's right. Maybe it's me. I attract this bullshit and am not strong enough to ignore or push it away. It's so freaking unfair. *I just wanted to go on a date!*

I change out of my pajamas into jeans, my Wonder Woman t-shirt, leather motorcycle jacket, and slap on some make-up before retrieving a box from my closet. I'd hoped I'd never have to open this one again. Before I left Kansas I took some parting gifts. Silver handcuffs, silver nitrate MACE, two boxes of silver bullets, a Glock 9mm, and my baby Bette. I take all but her. Hard to conceal a machete in my purse unlike the rest. Just a precaution.

Gaslamp hasn't opened yet as the driver pulls up to the curb. I don't even have to knock, the bouncer just opens the door without a glare this time too. The bartender smiles as I approach. Five months ago we almost killed one another and now she smiles at me. "Hello," the bartender, whose name I can't recall, says. "Let me call and let him know you're here."

She does just that, and a minute later Neil, Connor's second in command, walks down from the office. "Hello," he says curtly. "Come with me. The meeting is about to begin."

"Meeting?" Great. Not only is a vamp gunning for me but now I have to sit in a meeting about it. Ugh.

I follow Neil toward the back of the club then through the hidden hallways to Connor's apartment. The vamp himself is already holding court at his dining room table. Four men and one woman sit at the table with Connor at its head. Not one vamp sports a smile, not even Connor when he lays eyes on me. I just get a nod. Not going to lie, it stings a tad.

"Thank you for coming," Connor says to me.

Neil pulls out one of the empty chairs for me and I sit. "Yeah."

"My friends, this is Special Agent Beatrice Alexander of the F.R.E.A.K.S.," Connor says. I don't bother correcting him. "Beatrice, may I present Thomas," the blonde man nods, "Edgar," the Latino man nods, "Avril," the curvy brunette woman smiles, "Sean," the redhead nods, "Jack," the man with the eyepatch smiles, "and of course you remember Neil."

"Hello. All."

"So where were we?" Connor says, sitting as well.

"They made it look like arson, so not only are the Newport police involved, but I doubt we will receive a dime in insurance," Jack says.

"And the building today?" Connor asks.

"They finally put the blaze out," Edgar reports, "but I am sure it will be the same story."

"And the police?"

"You will most likely have to speak to them at some point," Neil says.

"We are cooperating with them," Avril says. "Day staff sent them all the files and paperwork they requested. We will do the same when the Oceanside department no doubt contacts us tonight. I—"

"I-I'm sorry," I cut in, all eyes jutting my way. "Can someone please tell me what you're all talking about?"

"Among other...troubling events, two of our CM Holdings recent real estate acquisitions burnt down," Connor explains. "One yesterday, one today."

"And the other troubling events?" I ask.

"Several of the restaurants and other establishments I own have received visits from every conceivable inspector following multiple anonymous complaints. Six have been shut down pending investigation. Not to mention the owner of the bistro, my friend Taylor, is missing," he says as the sides of his mouth twitch.

"Don't forget the IRS," Sean says.

"How could I forget the IRS?" Connor says with a sneer.

"It will take months," Neil says, "before they begin investigating in earnest."

"Are the books clean?" Thomas, the blonde, asks.

"As clean as they can be," Avril says, "considering we all use falsified IDs and social security numbers. It is so hard for them to hold up to scrutiny in this day and age."

"We can hire, what do you call them...hackers to shore them up further," Jack offers.

"We should do that regardless," Edgar says.

"And you all think this is the work of Lady Antonia," I say.

"Of course. Especially in light of the fact she is asking questions about you," Connor says.

"This is ridiculous," I say. *They* attacked *us*. We just defended ourselves."

"We engaged in violence in her territory. She could use the mere fact we were in Los Angeles without her consort to begin this nightmare."

"She could do it just because she is bored," Avril adds.

"Why does not matter anymore, Connor." Avril takes his hand, squeezing it. Great. And ex-girlfriend. Just wonderful. "All that does matter is what we do now. Where is she vulnerable? Where can we—"

"Uh, have you tried *talking* to her?" I cut in.

"I beg your pardon?" Jack asks.

Are they serious? "I just think that before you start World War III maybe you should pick up the phone and tell her our side of the story? Work something out before the bodies start piling up and you both get in trouble?"

Connor contemplates this foreign concept for a few seconds. The others exchange glances. "Sir, word could have spread about her actions," Neil says. "If we do not retaliate or face this head on, it could make us appear weak and not only to her."

"Or while you're fighting this idiotic war that the King himself threatened you with death about beginning, and all your attentions are focused on said war, who knows what can crawl through the cracks you're not watching?" I point out. "Heck, maybe she wants exactly this. *You* started the war. By taking me to LA, right? Allegedly. I mean do you have concrete proof she's behind this? You start raping and pillaging then she can turn around and say it was all your fault. You're a lawyer. Do you have proof that would hold up before this King?"

"Do we?" Connor asks everyone.

They all look at one another again. "We are still investigating, sir," Neil pipes up.

"That's a no," I say. "This is stupid, Connor. You're playing right into her hands. Just call her. Remind her if this escalates you could both end up dead or exiled. And if she doesn't listen then at least you've covered your butt. *You* tried to resolve this peacefully. That will count for something."

Connor surveys his advisors, most of whom remain neutral or contemplative. "Thoughts?" Connor asks them.

"Perhaps she...has a point," Jack says. "We should not rush to retaliation. Yet."

"We should build a case," Edgar adds. "Exercise prudence."

"Give her enough rope to hang herself and hope the King finally takes her out for us," Thomas says.

"Not what I was going for," I say to Thomas.

"Neil?" Connor asks. "Avril?"

"I think it is a risk," Avril says. "If you ignore her, not only do we appear weak but also ineffective. In our world violence is met with violence. What happens when she begins targeting our *people*? They will be asking why, if we knew about the threat, we did not act before."

"I agree with Avril," Neil says. "Antonia bloodied our lip. If we do not strike back, she will continue kicking us until we can never get up."

"Of course that's how this whole mess began," I point out, "and look where it's got us. 'An eye for an eye makes the whole world blind.'"

Avril rolls her dark eyes. "Thank you, Gandhi. He was assassinated, was he not?"

Bitch.

Connor sits back in his chair, staring contemplatively into space as he soaks in all our advice. "No, Beatrice is correct. The most prudent course of action is descelation or at least its attempt. Neil, do we have Antonia's number? Please retrieve it, a phone, and a recording device. I want this call on record with you all as witnesses in case it is needed down the road."

"Yes sir," Neil says, rising.

Avril's plump lips purse in disapproval. "And if she refuses our demands?"

"Then..." he glances at me then her, "we shall discuss that later." His eyes finally settle on me. "Beatrice, what precisely did Oliver say to you? I need all available information before I phone Antonia."

"I'll play you the message." I put it on speakerphone for the table to listen to. Hearing his voice again the second time only twists my stomach one time and not into an unbearable knot like before. A crisis is a good way to keep emotions in check I guess.

"That is all?" Connor asks.

"Yeah. But it's the only time he's called me since...you know, so he must think this is serious."

"Of course it is serious," Avril says. "We have lost millions in revenue and are under police and government scrutiny."

"Then it is in everyone's best interest to end this now," Edgar says.

God I feel like I'm back at the F.R.E.A.K.S. when everyone hated each other with me as the unwitting catalyst. That started with romance too. I really, truly should become a nun.

Neil returns a few seconds later with a slip of paper and small recorder which he sets up in front of Connor. "Thank you." Connor removes his iPhone from his pants before turning on the recorder. "Speaking is Connor McInnis, Lord of San Diego. With me are Neil Kilkelly, four other staff members Jack McCrory, Avril Norton, Edgar Gallego, and Thomas Neville, along with Special Agent Beatrice Alexander of the F.R.E.A.K.S. Squad. The time is 9:34 PM on June 11th. This is a live, unedited recording of my call to Antonia Sabatini, Lady of Los Angeles. I am making the call now." He punches in the number on the paper. Over the speaker we all hear it ring three times.

"The Crimson Longue, Alejandro speaking," a man says with a familiar Hispanic accent. "How may I help you?"

"This is Lord Connor McInnis. I am attempting to reach Lady Antonia Sabatini on urgent business. Please connect me immediately."

The other end is silent for a few seconds. "You have a lot of nerve calling—"

"Connect me immediately please," Connor demands hard as granite. "Thank you."

More silence, then, "*Pendejo.*" But the hold message begins a second later.

"How rude," Avril says.

"I think that was one of the men from the bistro," I say.

"I believe you are correct," Connor says. "The one who put his hands on you."

"Didn't have them on me for long," I say with a hint of pride.

The hold music cuts a second later. Showtime.

"Connor McInnis, this is an unexpected..." a woman, I presume Antonia says with only a hint of an Italian accent.

"Is it? I believe we have much to discuss."

"True, but that never made you pick up the telephone before. I believe this is an unprecedented circumstance."

"Well, we are in the technological age where connection is far easier. I am finally embracing that fact."

"Yet not enough to use this new skill set to call or email me to ask permission when you enter my territory," Antonia says.

"I did not see the need to bother you with such a triviality. And I need not remind you we reside in the land of the free. As a taxpaying citizen I am afforded the right to go where I please without permission."

"And beating my second bloody in an alley? I must have missed the news they passed a law in California that allowed assault."

"I am unsure what your man told you, Antonia, but there was a restaurant full of people who can attest your Mr. Wu physically engaged me first."

"After you called him the vilest—"

"What was said is irrelevant. My freedom extends to speech as well. Your man assaulted me and his partner assaulted my date, a Federal Agent, I might add."

"Suspended Federal Agent so technically not an agent," Antonia points out. "And what are you doing with her in the first place? I heard all about your little plan to force her into becoming your consort. Low, even for you, McInnis."

"My relationship with Ms Alexander is private and irrelevant to this discussion."

"Is it? Because it seems as if you are up to something again."

All eyes at the table move to me to gage my reaction, but I remain neutral.

"You are a fine one to speak about subterfuge, Antonia. Two of my buildings destroyed by arson? Inspectors and the IRS plaguing me the past two days?"

"I have no idea what you are talking about," she says.

"Of course you do not because that would be violating our treaty, which means I can contact the King who will strip you of your lands and titles."

"But you have no proof of my direct involvement or you would have phoned him already. Although the King might be interested in the few things I have dug up. However who needs that scrutiny again?"

"I could not agree more," Connor says. "With all this wondrous technology and connectedness it becomes harder and harder to hide anything, let alone our misdeeds. The King will learn of our war and strip us both of our lands before we inflict any true damage to one another. Which is why I am calling to propose a truce."

"A truce?"

"No further escalation on either of our parts. We chalk it up to a simple misunderstanding and move on."

"We simply turn the other cheek?" she chuckles. "Who are you and what have you done with Connor McInnis?"

"To be quite frank, Antonia, I have better things to do." He glances at me. "Far more pleasurable endeavors I wish to focus my attention on than a pointless war with you. I am sure you do as well. We have traveled down this road before and it almost led us both to ruin. Nothing has changed since. If

I, the truly injured party here, can forgive and forget, you can as well. You are a smart woman. Please see logic and agree here and now. Truce?"

She's quiet for a few seconds. "You are up to something. I can sense it. It has to do with that—"

"All I am up to is attempting to save the lives of my subjects who will be caught in the crossfire of our insipid war. And you should know I am recording this conversation. I am coming to you in peace. That is all I desire in return. Antonia, I will put my proposal in writing. I will have it notarized. I will sign it in blood. Just...agree and we can go back to attempting to forget the other exists. Peace?"

More silence. Oh, come on, lady. Just say it. "Peace," Antonia says.

Everyone's shoulders slump with relief. Connor even smiles. "This is for the best. Without question."

"Just stay out of my territory from now on."

"I will try my utmost. Have a wonderful evening, Antonia." He hangs up.

"I cannot believe that actually worked," Neil says.

"Only time will tell if it truly did," Avril points out.

"I believe her," Connor says, turning off the recorder. "It truly is for the best for all parties involved." He smiles at his war council. "Excellent work, all. Please continue monitoring the situation, and keep me apprized, but the worst is over. You know what to do."

"Yes, sir," Neil says, the first to rise.

Unsure what else to do, I stand with the rest of them, Connor included.

"Beatrice, will you please remain behind?" Connor asks.

"Uh, sure."

Avril smiles at me as she passes, but it's about sincere as the one I give her. The others just ignore me as they leave the apartment. When the front door finally shuts, I avert my eyes to the ground. We're alone, and I have no idea what to expect. What to say. Connor has no such qualms.

"I am truly, truly sorry for dragging you into my mess," he says as he slowly moves toward me, stopping less than a foot away.

I gaze up at his contrite face. I think he actually means it. "It's okay. I'm a mess magnet. I'm just glad it's all settled. Thank you for listening to me."

"I am glad you were here to be the voice of reason. I believe a few of the others were thinking the same thing but were hesitant to voice their objections." He smiles down at me, a weary smile. He's had a long couple of days. "I am you are here for multiple reasons, your calm head the least among them." Tentatively, he raises his hand, hovering it an inch from my cheek before finally touching me. Even though his hand's cold, it's still nice. Sweet. "I wanted to phone you. I did. But with the maelstrom…I thought it best to shelter you from it as best as I could. It was not because of…"

"What happened in the limo?"

"Yes. I was also not sure if you desired for me to contact you."

"Yeah, I…" I chuckle, "wasn't sure either." I roll my eyes. "I guess, to be totally honest, asking me what I want about *anything* right now is like asking a deaf person to appreciate a symphony. The tools just aren't there. And this…whatever we have going on is so outside my wheelhouse, if I didn't already feel like I've been living on Jupiter, what happened in the limo would boost me into orbit.

I've never had a one night stand before. When you didn't call I just assumed that's what it was. Part of me was relieved, part of me was pissed at us both. All the crappy girl questions plagued me. Did you think I was ugly? Did you think I sucked in bed because you didn't orgasm? Did you not orgasm because you think I'm ugly? Did I scare you away with breaking the champagne bottle and glasses?"

"I am honored you thought about me so much when we were not together," he says with the crinkle-eyed grin. In this moment I'm glad I get to see it again.

"Not like I had anything better to do," I say. "The point is...I guess I don't have a point. Or a brain. Or courage. Or a heart." I chuckle. "You don't by any chance know the Wizard of Oz do you?"

"I am afraid not. But I can clear up any residual confusion, at least on my end." Connor leans down, softly kissing me on the lips. I don't stop him. The moment his lips touch mine, I don't want him to. With one kiss any doubts I never wished to experience this again evaporates. "I enjoy your company. I enjoy...your body," he says, drawing his free hand under my shirt against my bare back, his fingers caressing me with a feathery touch, leaving a trail of goosebumps in their wake. "And since I am shockingly the first of my kind you have deigned to take as a lover..." He unhooks my bra, my nipples already erect from his voice and the anticipation, "you should know a vampire can last *hours*," those expert fingers move forward to my now free breast, gently cupping it. My breaths stops again. "My record is six and we only stopped because she begged me to."

"That's..." he lightly runs a finger against my nipple, and I suppress a shiver, "a long time."

"And, unlike you, I know what I want." He teases my nipple again, just the barest of touches, and I don't stop the shiver that cascades down to my already pulsating core. "Right now, after enduring the hellish events of the past two days, I want..." another tease, another shiver, "no, I *need* to continue our conversation at the bistro, the one we were having before being so rudely interrupted." His hand leaves my face to unbutton my jeans as the other continues torturing me with waves of pleasure. "Do you recall the topic?"

He slips one finger into my wet center, instantly finding and teasing my g-spot. I bite my lower lip to stop the yelp. "Uh...remind me," I say, voice cracking.

Never taking his eyes from mine, he forces me to take a step back right against the table. "We sat at a table just like this..." Another feather light tickle with both fingers. Another sharp intake of breath and another quiver. "But all I wished to eat..." The other hand vacates my breast to aid in pulling down my pants and underwear only to press into me again. I almost come right then. "Climb on the table," Connor orders huskily as the bastard removes his finger from me. It doesn't occur to me to do anything but obey. My bare butt lifts and rests on the wooden table where we just discussed murdering people. And I absolutely don't give a damn. A small part of me knows I should but lust and anticipation silence that moron. That was then, this is now. All that matters is the now. Connor removes my shoes. "All I desired to do was lick..." My pants and panties fall to the ground. "Nibble..." I am totally naked from the waist down and I don't give a good goddamn. "To feast upon..." I should—*no*. No. The now. And in the now he falls to his knees before me like a disciple before a goddess. Perfect height, as if he and the table were made for just this moment. My legs part on their own in anticipation. He lightly kisses up from my knee to my thigh. "To *devour*..." He brings my right leg over his shoulder. "You..." he whispers a centimeter from my ready sex. The simple vibration of his words against my already frenzied sex sends it into overdrive. "This."

When his tongue flicks my clitoris that first time I think my eyes cross the sensation's so overwhelming. So delicious. He waits an agonizing second, an eternity, before he does it again. I run my hand through his soft auburn hair for an anchor. He flicks it again. Again. His own hand moves up my belly, my abdomen, under my shirt again to grip my breast. Another flick in time to him pinching my nipple. Again. Jesus Christ, that's good. I close my eyes to better savor all his expert work. The flicks and pinches gain momentum with a swirl and a kiss to that sweet spot thrown in to keep me off balance. The man truly has a silver tongue in all respects. My orgasm builds with every flick, swirl, and suckle. I don't know how much longer I can last...

Then he's gone.

He pulls away and my eyes fly open. I barely have time to blink before Connor's standing and quickly removing his own clothes. Oh, hell yes. His pants quickly fall to his ankles just as he grabs my waist as his mouth that still tastes of me mashes against mine. I take his rock hard erection in my hands to hasten the inevitable. He glides in gently, slowly filling me. Oh, that's even better. How the hell did I ever think I never wanted to do this again? We don't kiss, I hug his neck and moan into his hair with each perfect, thrilling collision. I wrap my legs around his waist to draw him in deeper. He can't be deep enough. He hugs me against him, our naked flesh fully connecting, so there's no space between us. We're one, locked in the delectable gluttony of it all. This man, this madness, how right and wrong everything we're experiencing is. Oh, I'm close. So close...

I open my eyes and notice the bar stool across the room levitating. Shit. Shit. Fuck it. I close my eyes again. He thrusts, hitting my g-spot for the first time, and I really lose it. I dig my fingernails into his scalp and cry out. "Come for me, Beatrice," Connor pants against my neck. "Let go. Come. Come."

When the orgasm shatters through me, I hold onto my lover for dear life as my body spasms around his still thrusting manhood. Oh, that's good. This is so good. But Connor's not done and apparently neither am I. He continues rutting me, a little harder this time, gliding right over my g-spot with pinpoint precision with each stroke and the fantastic tension begins building anew. Building...building...

Another wave of ecstasy ripples through me, if possible stronger this time. I'm so into savoring my own bliss I barely notice Connor crying out as he climaxes as well. Neither of us moves for several seconds as we regain our senses.

"That was fantastic," Connor pants, "bloody fantastic. Amazing." He strokes my cheek, and I finally open my eyes. He kisses me before smiling again. "I adore multi-orgasmic women. We can make a game of how many times I can make you come in an hour."

"Is that what that was?" I ask.

Connor chuckles. "Oh, my innocent Beatrice." He kisses me again. "We are going to have *so* much fun together."

Fun. Yeah. Fun. I can do fun. Can we have fun again now?

The man must be a mind reader because his erection grows inside me the moment I finish that thought. He did say he could go for hours.

"Care to try my game?"

I clench myself around his erection and grin. Fuck it. "Why the hell not?"

And he lowers me onto the table to begin the game. Let the good times roll.

CHAPTER SIX

THE SHALLOW END

Something I can now cross off my bucket list: joining the mile high club. We were barely in the air on our way to Las Vegas in Connor's private plane when I ticked that one off. Sex in public—a club bathroom to be specific—came the next day, pun intended. I can also cross off meeting a celebrity. I lost my shit when Connor waved over Brittany Spears and we all shared a drink together. April and I went to Vegas once, but hitting the town with a connected billionaire is a damn better way to do it. Dancing at the most exclusive clubs, shopping at every designer boutique, having a suite at The Venetian with the whole of the strip laid out outside the huge window, I could damn well get used to the high life.

With all quiet on the vampire front, Connor insisted on getting away while the getting was good. Four nights of debauchery, of dancing, drinking, fucking like rabbits, of having my every whim catered to was just what the doctor ordered. I didn't even bother to turn on my cell phone.

But the good times have to come to an end or at least get put on pause for a day or so. Fuck you, reality. I'm gently woken by a kiss to my bare neck. Ugh, three rum punches while sunbathing by the pool knocked me out. Or it could be the sleepless nights and more orgasms in four days than the entirety of my life catching up to me. I slept on the plane and must have dozed off in the car too.

"We have almost arrived," Connor whispers into my ear before kissing then licking my neck again. He says he can taste the sunshine on my skin like it's the rarest, sweetest vintage of wine. I'm positively brown with all the sunbathing I did. I woke around two in the afternoon and had a few hours to kill before he rose. Most of that time was spent at the pool enjoying rum punches, in the casino, or shopping. The nights were a hell of a lot more romping but the days did have their moments.

I open my eyes and even in the dark I recognize the one-story ranch houses with chain-link fences that comprise my, as I've heard assholes call it, ghetto. Just because it's filled with damn hard working immigrants and retirees does not a ghetto make. I sigh. I don't want to go home yet. I am not looking forward to the questions, the sighs, the disappointment about to greet me. That first night I returned home around three AM to pack and left a note explaining where I was going. Spur of the moment trip to Vegas with a friend and not to worry. I also left her a message I'd arrived safely and was having a blast. Probably should have phoned her again to tell her I'd be home tonight but that only occurred to me on the plane. Not sure of the welcome I'm about to receive. Probably not a party.

Her car's in the driveway along with a light colored Mercedes convertible I don't recognize and a Lexus convertible parked on the street. Maybe she is having a party. Oh hell, if that Mercedes is my brother Brian's new car I'm going straight to a hotel. I—

"Surprise," Connor says.

"What?"

The car stops and Connor's grin grows. "Do you like it?"

It takes me a second to put two and two together. "The car?"

"Yes! The Mercedes. Do you like it?"

"You-you bought me a car?"

"Well, technically it belongs to CM Holdings, but for all intents and purposes...yes. I bought you a car."

"Connor, thanks and all but...I-I can't accept it."

"Why on earth not? You mentioned you did not have an automobile. I have the means to provide you one."

"Connor, it's too much. It's too extravagant."

"The cost of it is about one tenth of what I just spent on our trip," he points out.

"I know but—"

He leans across and kisses my words away. "Use it until you purchase your own. There are no strings attached to this gift, I promise, fairest. You had a need, and I had the means to quell that need. Surely there is nothing wrong with that."

"I-I guess not." It still feels wrong somehow. See? This. *This* is why I didn't want to come back. I didn't say a word of protest when we spent thousands at Prada and La Perla. Maybe he's right, I do overthink things. He's letting me borrow a car, he's not buying *me*. This is what people do when they're in a relationship, try to fulfil the needs of their partner. Guess that's just a foreign concept to me. Steven was a closeted sociopath and Will never got the opportunity to show me he could. A horrible realization knocks me for a loop. If we count the first night at the club as the beginning of our romance, I've been with Connor longer than I was with Will. That is...so wrong.

"Beatrice, are you well?" Connor asks, bringing me out of my head. "You have grown...melancholy. You do not have to accept the car. It—"

"No, it's not that. I just..." I quickly kiss him to reassure him. "Thank you for the car. It was sweet of you to think of me."

"I have done precious little else since I met you, my fair Beatrice," he says, eyes crinkling as he smiles.

I kiss him again. "Call me tomorrow night, okay?"

"Must I wait that long? I have no clue how I shall restrain myself."

And one more kiss for the road. "Try. Bye."

I climb out of the car before he can work that devil penis magic on me again. I need a break from it, but only a small one. Give my poor, sore body a chance to recover. I am amazed I can walk. The driver helps me with my suitcase to the door. Damn am I sore but the good sore. After comparing Will and Steven I thought the only way to have good sex was with love. I didn't love Steven and sex became something I just put up with. My one night with Will was astonishing. Mind blowing. Perfect. And the sex with Connor wasn't as transcendent but it was still pretty damn great. Fun just as he promised. I can live with great fun.

But the good times cease rolling the moment I set foot in the house and see her expression. Nana sits on the couch watching TV, but when I step in her gaze immediately whips back to me. It's as if she cannot believe her eyes, like I'm a strange ghost, one she's not happy to see.

"Hi," I say as I shut the door.

"Bea," she says, rising from the couch.

"I'm home."

"Where the hell have you been?" Nana snaps.

"Vegas. You know that. I left you a note. Messages. I—"

The sight of the man stepping out of the hallway stops my words, my breath, my thoughts, the whole of my atoms, the whole of the world dead. Just *dead*. Normally he merely takes my breath away but that was then. In the before. Now my breath's gone for an entirely different reason. I think.

The last time I set eyes on him he lay in our med bay, most of him bandaged like the Invisible Man with only a closed eye exposed. I should have gone to his side, held his hand, sung to him and read him stories, as he had by my bedside when I was in a coma. But I couldn't stand the sight of him. So damaged. So weak. Both of us. And it was all my fault. I turned my back on him and never looked back. At least literally. I wish I had figuratively as well. Staring at him here, now, there isn't a trace of that night. Not a scar. No claw marks on his ivory skin, hell there isn't a golden brown hair out of place. He is still the most gorgeous, angelic creature ever to grace this earth. And he's here. In my living room. Staring at me with those gray eyes and a barely there sad smile on his full, reddish lips. "Hello, Trixie."

I don't know what to do. I don't know what I *want* to do. Run into his arms and not let go until the sun rises. No. Don't you *dare*, Bea. This is an ambush. He's here to bring you back. To make you confront everything. I can't. I can't. Not now. Not tonight. I'm too tired. I don't want him here. I don't even want to be here anymore. I'm literally shaking from shock and anger. They've been conspiring behind my back. Talking to each other, deciding my life for me. How dare they? How dare he just show up like this? I manage to unglue my eyes from the interloper to my grandmother. The traitor pleads with her eyes, her frown, for me to behave. To be grateful. No. hell no. "Did you ask him to come here?" I hiss.

"No," Oliver answers for her. My gaze whips back his way. "I came on my own."

"But I should have," Nana says. Her turn for MY glare of death. "I should have called him long ago, back when April suggested it."

"Oh, April's in on this too," I scoff. "Figures."

"She's terrified for you, Honey Bea. I am too. Especially after what I've heard about this man you're...dating."

I look at Oliver again. "Let me guess. That was *you*?"

"Yes. Absolutely."

"So you came here to poison my grandmother against my boyfriend?" I spit out.

"I came here because you are lost," he states as plain fact.

"And the fact I'm screwing a vampire other than you has nothing to do with it? Bullshit."

"Beatrice!" Nana says.

"Three months. Nothing. Not a call, not an email. I finally start enjoying myself and suddenly it's intervention time?"

"Yes, because this is not you," Oliver says.

"Yeah, well, it is now. Because being the other me...all I got was misery. Horror. Guilt. She was a chump. A moron. Good riddance to her. So go back to Kansas. Get the hell out of my house, Oliver. There is no one here who wants or needs your pitiful excuse of a rescue."

"This is my house, Beatrice," Nana says, voice steel, "and he is *my* guest. And don't you dare speak to him like that again. *Ever.*"

I ignore her. "I said get out. I rescind my invitation for you to be in this house."

"And I extend an invitation to *my* house," Nana counters.

"Just...get out!" I shout in frustration.

He stands his ground, all of him, even his face tensing in anticipation for my attack. "No," he says with finality. "You may scream, you may cry, you may beat me bloody, but I am not leaving you. Not like this. *Never*."

The determination in his gray eyes, in his voice, I haven't experienced either since we returned from Dallas, since the night we swore we'd always come for each other even if it were to the gates of hell. We'd climb that gate and drag the other out, taking on a hundred demons with our bare hands if necessary, no matter what. It is as if that promise were scrolled on our bones. Always there. A part of us. A covenant governed by God himself. It used to be wonderful. A security blanket that transcended distance and time. But right now it's a burden. My body's so heavy and the demons I've been keeping locked up deep, deep down know if I give into him, they'll be released. I don't want to fight them. I don't think I can. Not even with him by my side.

"Fine," I say, grabbing my suitcase again. "If you won't leave then I will."

"Bea—"

"Where are the keys to the Mercedes Connor gave me?" I ask Nana.

"I don't—"

"I am leaving this house even if I have to walk all the way downtown. Give me the God"—Oliver flinches—"damn keys, Nana."

"I did not know you could be bought so cheaply," Oliver says.

I'm not even going to dignify that with a response. "Keys!" Nana glances at Oliver who remains a stone cold statue. They both know me well enough to take my threat seriously. They should. I'm about ten seconds from walking out the door and calling an Uber. Nana hangs her head and moves toward the bar, picking up the key. When she's close enough, I snatch it from her hand. "Thank you."

"Honey Bea, don't do this," Nana calls as I turn toward the front door. "We love—"

I shut the door on her hollow sentiment. You don't ambush people you love and call them a whore. I hurry to the Mercedes in case they chase after me. They don't. I climb in, adjust the seat and mirror, and peel out without EVEN putting on my seatbelt. When I realize I should I can't get the damn thing on. I just yank and yank until I'm screaming in frustration. I have to pull over not three blocks from the house to regain my composure. I hit the steering wheel and scream again. I can't believe this. I can't believe I just stormed out of my own house. I can't believe I have nowhere to go. I'm kind of homeless. Guess I could go to a hotel. Of course I just came from a hotel. Ugh, just go to the club already. I don't want to be alone.

I ignore the seven texts and five voice mails from the past few days and just dial Connor. "Miss me already, fairest?" he purrs.

"Oliver just ambushed me at my house and I stormed out when he wouldn't leave."

He's quiet for a few seconds. "Are you alright?"

"I'm livid. I'm worried. I'm…exhausted. They've all been plotting behind my back, Connor. Nana, Oliver, April, probably even Javi. I-I-I feel like killing someone!"

"Well, do not do that. Of course if you do I will help you dispose of the body," he says jokingly. I would smile if I could. I don't have it in me right now. "Are you driving right now?"

"No, I pulled over."

"Good." He's quiet again. "Fairest, I *have* to work tonight. I have to get caught up. I shall be in and out until morning, but if you wish you may stay with me. You can take a bath and fall asleep in the spare room."

Oh, I was hoping he'd say that. "Are you sure? You're not sick of me?"

"Of course not. If I did not have a night full of meetings and paperwork I would have begged you to come home with me tonight. But now I insist. You should not be alone if you are this upset."

"Thank you."

"Are you alright to drive to the club?"

"Yeah."

"Then I shall see you soon, fairest. Bye."

After I slip this phone back into my purse, I pull back onto the street and take deep, calming breaths the whole ten minutes it takes to drive to the club. I call Connor again when I reach the private parking structure under the club. The gate lifts, and the man himself steps into the garage. It hasn't even been twenty minutes since we last saw one another. He strolls over to get my suitcase. "Long time no see," I quip.

Connor kisses my forehead. "I knew you could not live without me for too long." He wraps his free arm around my waist, and I rest my head on his shoulder as we meander to the door. "I see the Mercedes came in useful already."

We enter a narrow, dim concrete cinderblock stairwell upstairs. "Yes, a Mercedes is the perfect getaway car when confronted by well-meaning jerks."

He squeezes my waist as we enter the hallway to his apartment. This time he doesn't hide the code from me. Guess he trusts me now. We walk into his apartment. Oh, there's the table we had sex on. And the couch. Floor. All I'm interested in are the bath and bed. "If you compile a list I can send someone out to purchase you food and whatever else you require," Connor says.

"My own minions. Nice."

"My minions are your minions from here on, fairest. Use them well."

"Aren't you the most gracious of hosts." I flop down on the couch and sigh. "This is just for tonight."

"You are welcome to stay here as long as you desire," Connor says, sitting beside me. He takes my hand. "You had no idea he was coming to town?"

"No. None. I saw him and I just…my brain short-circuited."

"What did he say?"

"I didn't give him a chance to say much."

"Do you think this is related to Antonia?" Connor asks.

"Like she enlisted him to spy on you? I very much doubt it."

"But he is here because of me," Connor says.

"I think April called him. We had a huge fight a week ago. She was probably dialing his number before I even made it to my car."

"You fell out with your friend because of me?"

"Because of a lot of stuff." I lay my head on the back of the couch with a sigh. "I don't want to talk about it. I don't want to talk period."

"Do you believe Oliver will leave?"

I scoff. "Hell no. He made that crystal clear."

"What do you think he will do?" Connor asks, for some reason concerned, as if I were being stalked by a serial killer.

"I don't know. Nothing…bad. He'd never hurt me. *Never*. So there's no need to be the strong protective Papa bear, Connor. I had enough of that with Will, thank you very much."

"Yes, your wolf was most…overprotective. It must have been quite chaffing. And now Oliver is here to take over the role."

"It is coming from a good place," I point out to us both.

"Is it? Do you consider jealousy a good place?"

"What?"

"Fairest, three months of silence. No contact. None. Then the moment we begin seeing one another he must swoop in and save you from yourself out purely of the kindness of his heart? The timing is not suspect? He is not here for you, he is here for *him*. To drive a wedge between us. To poison you against me so you go rushing into his arms."

"That's not…" Okay, maybe. Probably. I sigh. "I'm tired. I don't want to think about this. I don't want to deal with it. Not tonight. All I want is a bath and sleep."

"In that case, fairest, my home is at your disposal. I should return to work anyway." He kisses me again before rising. "And make that list. Someone will purchase it immediately."

"Thank you. Really."

"Of course. I shall come check on you later. Call me if you need me."

I give him a smile, which he returns before walking toward the front door. He blows me a kiss before departing. Good. I lie down on the couch and stare up at the white ceiling, too tired to even decide what I want to do next. Every little decision is such hard work. A bath. Definitely.

I cart my suitcase up the stairs to the second level where his bedroom and bathroom are. I'm not quite sure I want to sleep in his bedroom, not because it isn't nice. It's *tres* chic with a thousand thread count Egyptian cotton sheets on the California King size bed with a chrome headboard, a large flat screen above the modernist dresser, a mini-fridge and microwave, and abstract art covering the walls. I think the painting over the bed is a genuine Pollack, but the lack of a single window and the fact the door's made of solid steel and locks like a prison door with only a keypad to open it gives the place a slight jail cell or at least panic room quality. I check out the guest bedroom but it's the same just sans TV. Jail cells for all. Maybe I should just go to a hotel. My yawn vetoes that idea. He's not going to lock me in like a prisoner, especially if I'm in the same room with him when he's literally dead to the world. If he trusts I won't kill him in his sleep, I can trust he won't trap me. Besides I'm dying to try out his Jacuzzi tub.

As the water fills, I retrieve my toiletry bag before stripping to nothing. Like the rest of the apartment the bathroom's all chrome and Venetian marble with one of those multi-spigoted showers with gray mosaic tiles. Our room at The Venetian had one of those state-of-the-art but we barely used it for cleansing purposes. The only things to get clean were my breasts. Connor's a boob man. Good thing I have plenty to offer in that department.

After adding the vanilla scented bath oil, I slip into the tub and flip on the jets. Oh, that's heavenly. I've so missed taking baths where I can spread out and let the water cover my whole body. Nana's tub is so small and shallow I barely bothered to use it. Some of the tension begins to dissolve out of my body as the jet at my back works an Oliver sized knot out. This is lovely. I'm definitely getting some of my vacation glow back. Maybe I can just pretend that horrible fight at the house never occurred. That it was a figment of my imagination. I sigh. Yeah, not even my denial skills are that masterful.

I always knew I'd see him again, I just always figured it'd be years down the road when I was on my death bed or when he needed someone to help extract out of a jam since I'm the only sucker who would actually show up to help. For such a "popular guy," as I've heard him called a million times, Oliver doesn't have that many true blue friends. I haven't met a one. People who want to kill him, sure. Women and men he's slept with, those are legion. Ride or die, pick you up from the airport, drop everything to save him friends, only me. And after tonight I may not even fit that category either.

Connor's probably right. Three months without a call or email to check on me, I'm with Connor a week, and Oliver *has* to come rescue me? He does have a jealous streak. When he discovered Will and I were together he lashed out, almost feeding me to my werewolf lover. It was the only time I've ever been truly afraid of him. If this trip is all about jealousy then God knows what he'll do to Connor. It's gotta be driving him nuts I'm with another vampire. I told him time and time again the fact he doesn't have a pulse and sees me as a Big

Mac creeped me out. Now here I am banging a guy with no pulse who keeps asking permission to feed on me. In all our nights of debauchery that's only one, okay *two* acts I've denied him. The other being still outlawed in several states.

So what is Oliver's plan? What does he want? What will he do next? I...am too exhausted to work on a battle plan. This whole mess will keep until tomorrow. After almost half an hour, I climb out of the tub, brush my teeth, and slip into the pink satin nightie I bought in Vegas. The black Egyptian cotton sheets feel equally luxurious against my skin when I climb into bed. I've missed having the finer things in life the past three months. My time at the F.R.E.A.K.S. mansion spoiled me with huge bath tubs, silken sheets, cloud bed, and every electronic gadget available at my fingertips. Once you've lived in Paris it's hard to go back to the farm and milk the cows. Guess it's the same with everything. What I've done and seen the past year, the high highs and the below rock bottom lows, all else in life seems so mundane. Boring. Trivial. Maybe that's why I'm so drawn to Connor. He's a safe danger, like a rollercoaster. Whatever the reason, at this moment, I'm glad to have him. He's been just what I've needed. I will get a hotel room tomorrow, though. I am truly exhausted and after a few minutes I drift off to sleep.

I'll die if I don't. Maybe that's better. My lungs, my legs, my throat, the cuts on my feet and arms all burn like glass shards covered in fire. If I give up, if I let him have me, it would stop. I just want it all to stop. Then why do I keep running? Habit? Fear of death? Could it be any worse than this? I'm just about to give up when I see *it* in the distance. Light.

A sign. I can make it. Maybe it'll be better if I make it into the light. Using what little reserve I have left inside, I fuel, I channel it to help me make that last long stretch. It will all be okay if I can make it to that light. Ignore the agony. Ignore the blood pouring out of me with each frantic step. *Just keep going.*

As the light grows closer, *he* does as well. Fifty feet. Forty. I can all but sense his snarling breath on my neck. *Don't look back.* Never look back. All that matters is the light. Thirty. Twenty. Ten.

The monster vanishes.

I step into the light, out of the woods into a clearing. It blinds me for a moment. I can barely make out the frame of a man stepping to the edge of the clearing across from me from his own half of the woods. But only for a moment. I'd know him even without eyes. I'd know his scent, his energy anywhere. Right where light meets dark, he stands. Smiling. Waiting for me with a huge, brilliant smile on his preternaturally beautiful face. But I can't take another step. I'm so exhausted even breathing proves near impossible. He knows it. He always knows. And he can't wait for me any longer. He takes one step into the light, and I haven't the breath to warn him. Oliver makes it three steps before the light singes him. That radiant smile twists into a silent scream of horror as his arm stretches out to me, as if I can pull him to safety, but there's nothing I can do. He burns to ash.

I awake with a gasp of shock, from both the nightmare and as the heavy door mechanically locking. It's so dark, even with my better than average night vision, I can barely make out his movements. I hear clothes rustling, his sighs as if the simple task of undressing takes all his fortitude, all before the bed shifts as he climbs in beside me. We never really slept together like this. Before dawn came, Connor would slink away to his coffin, leaving me alone. Guess he likes to sleep nude because that's how he comes to me. Clings to me. Connor spoons me, one hand sliding up to cup my breast through the nightgown as his manhood presses into my buttocks.

"Sorry I woke you," he whispers.

"I'm glad you did. I think I was having a nightmare," I whisper back.

"What about?"

"I don't remember," I answer truthfully.

"So we both endured nightmare evenings." He kisses my neck as he pulls my breast free over the top of my nightie. The tingles radiate from my nipple down between my thighs as he teases it with his fingers. "Is it alright if I make love to you?" he whispers.

Whatever happened in that nightmare wound me tighter than hell. Not to mention his deft fingers revved my motor the moment he began toying with me. "I'm still a little sore. Go slow."

He kisses my neck again. "With pleasure."

With my back still to him, his free hand traces up my leg, under my nightie to push it up, before removing my panties. I kick them off as his erection grows against my now bare back. As we both lie on our sides, I lift my leg enough for him to position his pelvis against my bottom and he gently, slowly enters me. The soreness rises as he continues inside but is overshadowed by that glorious sensation of fullness which prompts a quiet moan. "Is that alright?" Connor whispers.

"Yes. Keep going."

He glides inside me again with tender care, prompting another moan, especially as one hand returns to my breast. With the third thrust his free arm snakes over my bare hip until his hand reaches his destination, my engorged clitoris, toying with it in perfect sync to his other caresses. I close my eyes to savor the sensations. "You feel so good, fairest." Another thrust. "Like liquid silk." Another thrust. "Knowing you were here waiting for me was the only thing that helped me survive the night," he whispers before kissing my shoulder.

After another slow thrust, another tickle of my clitoris, another moan, I ask, "Why? What happened?"

Another gentle coupling, followed by his moan his time. "Oliver."

With that one word my pleasure quotient drops significantly. "O-Oliver was here?"

"He came to the club."

"Wh-what did he want?"

Connor stops moving, stops toying but remains inside me. "What do you think? He wanted you. Demanded I produce you immediately under threat of grievous bodily harm."

"He knew I was here?"

"He suspected and I confirmed, which precipitated a theatrical bandy of insults, aforementioned threats including castration and true death. There were even a few tense moments where I was certain he would physically assault me. It took two of us to eject him from the club. I did not think he could become so unhinged."

"You didn't...hurt him, did you?"

Connor's silent for a few nail-biting seconds before saying, "No, though I was well within my rights to do so. But I was merciful out of deference to you. Because of your...friendship."

"Thank you," I whisper before shifting my hips and squeezing my Kegels to spur him on.

Connor takes the hint and begins gliding and teasing me again. "But he only gets the one pardon, fairest. And I fear his envy has overwhelmed his common sense. He was almost feral tonight. Without a doubt he will say or do anything to achieve his ends. He has never been violent with you, has he? Perhaps I should assign guards to—"

I look back and press my lips to his to silence his words. "Stop worrying."

"I cannot. You did not see him tonight. Did not witness the bile and threats. Did not gaze into his black eyes. He has lost all reason, Beatrice." He pauses and stops moving again. "As long as he remains in the city, I want you to stay here. Where you will be safe." He rolls my nipple and clitoris in his fingers, and I can't suppress a moan. "Where I can take care of you." He begins thrusting again, a little harder this time. Another moan. "That is all I have desired since the moment we met." He thrusts faster now right over my G-spot. "Let me take care of you, Beatrice." He kisses my neck. "Let me take care of you." Oh, that's perfect rhythm. The perfect pressure in just the right places. "Let me take care of everything for you. You need not worry about a thing."

"Thank you," I gasp. "Oh, that'd be lovely."

"Anything for you, fairest." He thrusts again. "You are precious to me." He thrusts again and again as I moan, impaling me again. God, that's good. "So precious." He kisses my neck before another quick thrust. I'm getting close. "I will take care of you. Of everything."

Just give in. Just relax and give into him. And I do. I come gently this time, little light tremors that bring me peace and tranquility on a night I truly need both. I could use somebody taking care of me. He can't do a worse job than I have.

CHAPTER SEVEN

EASY STREET

What is so damn cold?

Over the past year I've woken in so many new beds in so many different hotels I should be used to this. It takes a second for me to gain my bearings. There's not light, not a speck which actually helps spark my memory. Connor's. That's what is so cold. My lover's all but dead body. A tiny chill snakes down my spine and not just from the cold. I've never woken beside a vampire the morning after. Normally I linger in bed but not today. Last night I wanted him inside my body and now I can't stand to be a foot from him. I sit up and turn on the light on the nightstand. He does like to sleep in the nude. Even pale as paper with a roadmap of tiny blue veins crisscrossing his back, bum, and arm, he's still handsome. Peaceful. I pull the covers up over his backside. His damn fine backside.

The clock reads 11:08. Oh, he's left a slip of paper with a seven digit door code and "XOXO" written on it. At least I can get out of the room. First, the bathroom. After the usual morning activities, I change into black jeans and my red and black star t-shirt before returning to the bedroom. He hasn't moved. He won't move until the sun sets or a little before.

I'm all alone. What the hell am I going to do with myself today? He wants me to stay indoors. Protect me from Oliver. I roll my eyes at that one. I can take Oliver without lifting a finger. And I'm safe from him during the day. Don't have to see or speak to him. Right now I don't have to do anything. No strings, no responsibilities, no…idea what to do with myself. Except eat. I'm starving.

Since there's no coming back into the bedroom once I leave, I drag my suitcases out of the bedroom.

"Do you need help?" I spin around and gaze down the stairs at the approaching woman, a gorgeous, tall, bi-racial woman with an awesome afro decked out in perfectly pressed chinos and white shirt. She smiles to reassure me. "Hi. My name's Krista Harris. His Lordship asked that I look after you while he slumbers. Here. Let me." She takes my suitcases.

"Are you leaving?"

"No, I uh, just in case I need something."

"Well, that's what I'm here for! Think of me as your fairy godmother. Your wish is my command," she says with a pretty smile. She sets the suitcases by the couch. "I've already made you coffee," she says, hustling to the kitchen. "Cream and lots of sugar, correct?" she asks, pulling those very things out.

"Yeah. How—"

"His Lordship left me a detailed list of your likes and dislikes, and I figure you can fill me in on the rest. There are also chocolate croissants, oranges I took the liberty of slicing already, and if you like I can squeeze more and fix you a fresh Mimosa," Krista says, smile never wavering. Okay, now it's getting a little creepy.

"Um, you don't need to do all that. I can make—"

She holds up the coffee mug and croissant for me to take. "But there's no need for you to. That's why I'm here. Why trouble yourself if you don't have to?"

This whole situation is so weird to me I can't think of a response. I just take the offerings from the Stepford wife. "Uh, thank you."

"My pleasure," Krista says as if she truly means it. She sits at the bar counter.

I sip my coffee. Damn near perfect. "This is delicious, thank you."

"I was a barista/actress before I became Jack's consort last year. You met him, I think. He has an eyepatch?"

"Uh, yeah. At the meeting."

"You impressed him," she says with a proud grin. "I heard you were the lone voice of reason and kept us from total war. *Everyone's* talking about you."

"Is that good or bad?"

"It's excellent. Apparently his Lordship hasn't taken a keen interest in someone for close to two decades. We've all noticed a change in him. He smiles more. He even took a *vacation*. You are so lucky. He is such a great man. A fantastic leader. And so handsome. I adore Jack, I love him, but if Connor crooked his little finger at me..." She sighs wistfully. O-kay. "Anyway, uh, I'm blathering on. Forgive me."

"It's okay."

With another Stepford smile, Krista turns her back, opens a drawer, and returns with a pad and pen. "So, I need to know what you wish for me to get you at the grocery store. I've taken the liberty of hiring a chef to come in tonight, a try-out of sorts. If you like what he prepares we can extend the job indefinitely, but you'll love him. I know it. He's willing to do all your meals. And do you have a preferred mover?"

"Mover?"

"For your belongings. I understand you've been living with your grandmother. Besides your boxes, will you also need your bed, dresser—"

"Wait. Wait," I say, holding up my hands. "Woah. Who said anything about movers?"

"I'm sorry. It was my understanding you would be staying here for the foreseeable future. For your own safety."

"I mean, I…I might stay a couple nights, but I'm not moving in. Does-does Connor think I'm moving in with him?"

Krista's smile wavers for a moment but it quickly returns. "No. Of course not! I must have misunderstood. All my instructions said was 'ask about her belongings.' I just filled in the wrong blanks. Still. I'm sure you'll be needing more than what you have with you. While I'm out I can swing by your grandmother's and get whatever you've left there that you need. His Lordship told me you and your family had a falling out. I know how that can be. My family and friends aren't that thrilled I'm with Jack either. Most people not in this lifestyle don't approve or understand why we choose to be with vampires. As if you can choose who you fall in love with," she says, rolling her green eyes. But I can say the friends I've made in the lifestyle are far deeper and richer than any I've known before. We're brothers and sisters. We're *family*. We take care of one another with no strings. No questions asked. And boy do we have fun." She chuckles. "And there I go again. Talking your ear off." She rolls her eyes. "Back to business. Groceries first, no?"

Okay, be it my year of investigative training or just my inherent bullshit instinct, whatever it is, my gut's telling me there's something off with this woman. It's as if she's coated me with slime. Like I'm on a used car lot with a saleswoman in front of me. Or a cult member. She did say she was an actress. They tend to be overdramatic. Or she could be overcompensating because I'm the boss' girlfriend. All I know is I'm massively uncomfortable. I want her gone.

I rattle off some of my favorite foods and she writes them down, smile never wavering like I'm Moses reading the Ten Commandments. "And from your grandmother's?"

No way in hell I want her at Nana's. "I can handle that."

"But if you don't have to—"

"I got it. Thank you."

For the first time, she frowns and even takes a step back. "I've come on too strong, haven't I? I can tell. I've made you uncomfortable."

"No, not at all," I lie.

"I have. I know it. I just…they've never asked me to do anything before. You're important to his Lordship, and he told me to make sure you wanted for nothing. Those were his exact words."

"I just, uh, I guess I'm not used to having—"

"Someone take care of you? No, I get it. I was the same. Little Miss Independent. I wouldn't take anything. Not money, not help, not from anyone because my dad told me it made you weak. But…since Jack…he insisted on pampering me. Taking the reins. Taking the weight off my shoulders. And he taught me that easy isn't bad. You shouldn't feel guilty about privilege. Life is hard, sometimes impossible, if easy is offered…why not enjoy it?"

I can't argue the logic. "Guess I could do with some easy. Worth a shot, right?"

"Right. So I'm going shopping and then coming right back," Krista says, smile finally returning. She scribbles something on the pad and rips it off. "This is my cell number if you think of anything else. Oh!" She turns around and picks an envelope off the counter. "This has a key to the door, the garage door clicker, and a corporate credit card. Just in case you want to go out. The card has no limit. Go nuts. Maybe go buy a whole new wardrobe. Leave everything behind! Might just be what you need. A fresh start. So few of us are given a chance. Take advantage."

Krista winks this time before retrieving her Coach bag and walking out. I've never had a servant before. Not even at the Kansas mansion. A maid service came in twice a month, but only did the communal areas. We took turns grocery shopping and cooking. I do hate grocery shopping. I grab a croissant and my coffee before flopping on the couch and switching on the TV. Yeah, that keeps my attention for all of a minute. What does a woman of leisure do all day? I really only have The Real Housewives to go by. So shopping, lunches, frenemies, and catfights. Suppose I could go out to lunch then get into a fight with my new best friend Krista.

That thought leaves a bitter taste in my mouth. A sycophant as my new best friend. Wonderful. Sycophants, vampires, groupies, killers, hello new social circle. A few months ago we all had guns pointed at one another now I'm their Prom Queen. Of course the moment I lose Connor's favor they'll be more than willing to slit my throat and treat me like a blood fountain. With friends like those…

I shut off the TV and let out a long sigh. What am I going to do with myself until Connor rises? Heck, what am I going to do *after* he rises? He seemed genuinely concerned about Oliver and my safety. He'll probably want me to stay here, or at least in the club. Clubbing's fun on rare occasions, but I am partied out after Vegas. Well if I am staying here I need something to occupy my time. And I don't want to play nice with Krista. I just know she'll insist on going with me. I need to stock up on books, DVDs, maybe a video game system if I'm stuck here or at a motel. So my choices are to go home and collect those or go shopping. What would a Real Housewife do?

I collect my car keys and contents of the envelope, throw them all into my purse, and hurry out of the apartment before anyone can stop me or ask questions. No such luck. At the garage stairwell, one of the bartenders is coming up as I go down. He does a double take when he sets eyes on me. "Oh. Hello."

"Hey," I say.

"Going out?" the twenty-something asks.

"Yeah."

"Is that...smart? The boss said that psycho from last night—"

"I'll be fine," I say shortly.

I take a step down and he takes one up, essentially blocking me in this tight space. "You know, if you're bored, we can always use a hand in the club—"

"Maybe later. Could you please..." I gesture him to move.

For a tense moment he doesn't move and stares at me, as if he's mulling over a complex problem, but then nervously smiles and backs against the wall. "Yeah. Sorry. Of course."

"Thank you." I hurry past him before…I don't know what.

"If you have any problems or whatever just call the club."

"Okay," I call back.

I finally relax when the building's out of sight. Of course that doesn't stop me from frequently glancing in the rearview mirror to make sure no one's tailing me. He wouldn't…no, he totally would. It seems he told his entire staff to keep an eye on me. What the heck did Oliver do last night? Dance the Macarena on a corpse or something? Okay, I know he means well—okay, I'm ninety-eight percent sure he means well—but I'm not sure I should stay at Connor's. There's a fine line between protective and smothering. Will had a tendency to cross it, and I hated it then as much as I do now. I'm not ready to eat crow with Nana, so hotel it is. I won't go back to Connor's until tonight, we'll talk, I'll get my suitcases and stay at a hotel until I find the nerve to talk to Nana. The last thought makes my stomach knot. Yeah, not even close to ready to face that mess. Any of my damn messes. But as Krista pointed out right now I don't need to. I don't need to do anything I don't *want* to. And right now all I want to do is…hell if I know.

I just drive awhile, testing out my new toy with the top down, until not even the radio can keep the thoughts at bay. Oliver and I used to do this all the time. Just driving, singing along to the radio, laughing our butts off and talking. I loved his stories about the past. How people used to live. About meeting kings. The art of courting. All the cities, the villages he'd visited. It was fascinating.

One night we lost track of time, somehow ended up in Oklahoma, and barely got back to the mansion half an hour before the sun rose. Will wouldn't look at me without a sneer a week after that. I'm positive he thought we'd spent the night in some motel going at it like porn stars. God if Will's spirit is still around what must he think of Connor and me? He'd be so disappointed, just like everyone else. He…ugh. Nope. Don't want to go down this road. He doesn't get a vote in my personal life. Not anymore.

With these thoughts coming fast and furious now, I pull into the mall parking structure. First stop is Hot Dog on a Stick for lunch. After working here in high school—I burned all the photos of me in those polyester shorts and hat—I couldn't stand to eat there but time wiped away my aversion. I missed the hell out of those corn dogs and lemonade when I was in Kansas. I sit in the food court, savoring the million calories I'm ingesting, and people watch for a while. Society women with dozens of shopping bags chatting on their cell phones. Teenagers skipping school with their friends. I catch sight of a blonde girl in a tie-dyed shirt with one of the groups but when I see her profile I realize it's not Mariah.

Mariah. I chuckle to myself. Who knew buying a girl a burger would result in my ex's death, uncovering a cult, and me falling into bed with a vampire? But that's life. If I'd chosen to leave my classroom thirty seconds later I never would have saved little Randy, my student, and been recruited by the F.R.E.A.K.S. If I'd kissed Will one of the trillion times I'd wanted to before, we'd probably be married with a baby on the way. If I'd trusted my instinct instead of my fear when Oliver begged me not to free Adrian Winsted, I wouldn't be sitting in a food court on the verge of tears again. Crap. I toss down my french fry. "Stop it. Stop it," I whisper to myself. Distraction. I need a distraction.

I hurry to the movie theater near April's salon and buy a ticket for the next movie playing. I've already seen it, but the ridiculous plot and constant explosions occupy my brain enough I don't think of anything else. Mindless entertainment, the new opium for the masses. I guess I needed my fix.

When the movie lets out I still have hours before Connor wakes. God, how do the socialites handle the boredom? I meander through the mall to the bookstore. My haven. When I was with the F.R.E.A.K.S. traveling around the country, I always made sure to locate a bookstore in town. When I needed something familiar, an anchor, I'd go and just browse or read magazines until I felt grounded in reality.

Today I browse the fiction sections, not finding anything since I was here last week. Time to lower my expectations, I guess. Suppose I could—

"Guess some things never change." I spin to my right and find April sauntering over. She's still dressed in her all black salon uniform but must have just gotten off work since her purse is slung over her shoulder. "Want to find Bea Alexander, go to the nearest bookstore." She stops a few feet away, folding her arms across her chest. "Yo said she saw you coming this way. Glad to see you're not dead."

I roll my eyes. "Always so dramatic."

"You disappeared off the face of the earth this past week," she points out.

"I went to Vegas."

"With *him*?"

"His name is Connor and yes, I went with him and had an amazing time. Came back super-relaxed. Happy even. Thanks for ruining that."

"*I* ruined that?"

"Yeah, you, Nana, and…him. All of you. Conspiring behind my back. Gossiping. No doubt betraying confidences. Scaring Nana with your conjecture. Bringing *him* to ambush me."

"Yeah, gee, what assholes we are, especially Oliver. Dropping everything to make sure you're okay. What a shit friend he is, no?"

"Probably because you told him God knows what. That Connor kidnapped me or something."

"Don't put this on me," she says. "He was coming here before I even said a word about Connor."

"Bull."

"Nope. We spoke once, *once*, right when you first got back three months ago then out of the blue, like one hour after you stormed out of my house, he called asking if something happened to you, that he just got a weird feeling, and he was going to make arrangements to come here. I figured *you* called him that night but he said no. But then yeah," she says, putting her hands on her hips, "When he called again I told him what was happening. I just damn well wish he'd gotten here sooner. What he told me about your new boyfriend…" She shakes her head. "Did you know before he became a, you know, he was already a Lord and led the charge in butchering a rival's village? He can't even blame being a killer on being a…you know, Bea. He was a murderous jackhole before he was even turned. And now you're living with him?"

"I'm not living with him. I stayed at his place last night—"

"And you were with him the night before and the night before…" She sighs. "At least tell me you're going home tonight and begging for your grandmother's forgiveness. Because you can yell at me, even at Oliver until your tongue bleeds, but don't you *dare* treat her like you've been treating us. Seriously, I don't recognize you right now. You're…mean. You're pushing away everyone when we just want to help like you've helped *us* a trillion times in the past. How can you not recognize we're doing this because we love you."

"Then love me enough to trust me."

"If you were acting like *you*, then I would. If you were sleeping with this guy because you like sex and he makes your feel great, hell yeah! Ride that pony. But you're doing this to fill some hole. You're doing it so you don't have to face what happened. At least with those stupid video games there wasn't a chance of finding you bled dry in a ditch."

"I won't end up dead in a ditch, April. I can handle myself. He touches me, I kill him."

"Okay, just the fact this is a topic we're rationally discussing in regards to your boyfriend should be a huge, major flashing red light, no? The fact everyone, *everyone* who cares and knows you is screaming they're worried about you should be too. And…you're not listening to a word I'm saying, are you? Guess I should just be happy you're not screaming at me this time."

"I'm listening. I am. And I am sorry I was so…dramatic the other night."

"I forgive you. You know we can have a trillion fights and I'll forgive you each time. It just hurts me, like physically hurts me, so much to see you like this. You have no sparkle. Even now with your rich boyfriend and fancy trips. And I don't know what to say or do anymore. What happened to you is so out of my wheelhouse. Just…know that no matter what, I love you."

The shame washes through me like acid rain. "I know. Thank you."

She squeezes my upper arm. "But if you don't apologize to your grandmother, and at least speak to Oliver once, this is the last time I'll talk to you until you do. They don't deserve that. And my best friend would know that. When she comes back to us, I'll be a phone call away." April kisses my forehead as I've seen her done to her kids a million times. "Hope to hear from her soon. I miss her like hell."

After a sad, apologetic smile, my best friend walks away without a glance back. I bow my head and will the pain in my gut away. She may as well have physically punched me. We've been as close as sisters for almost twenty years and it's as if she's given up on me. I can't even blame her. I've poisoned her with my misery and anger. I'd walk away from me too. God, that's *exactly* what *I* want to do. If I could get away from me, from this hell that is my life for even a moment, I'd sell my soul to do it. I truly would. I keep making these giant messes, and I just don't have the strength to pick up a mop.

I suddenly can't stand my usual sanctuary. Even the bookstore's been ruined. I don't know what to do. I don't know where else to go. I just have to leave before I start crying again. It's hard to even breathe, but I can run. So that's what I do. I run through the mall to my car, but when it comes time to make a turn out of the parking structure onto the street I don't know which way to turn. Instinct makes me want to move right to Nana's house. She'll be there now. Making dinner. Watching the news or chatting with my sister-in-law Renata about Marcus, my baby nephew. He's six months old and just learning to crawl. I've only seen him twice when Brian brought him over. My brother doesn't like me near the boy and after my return, his two times a month visits to San Diego came to an abrupt stop. Instead he or Renata come pick Nana up and bring her to their Beverly Hills home for the weekend. I didn't get an invite. Ever. Not that I've wanted one since I returned. Holding Marcus that last time three months ago resulted in me bursting into tears and scaring the boy. There's no way I could hold him now without thinking about what I lost. Because it's not just Will I grieve for. It's the life we almost had too. The house with a little garden we talked about. The children we both desperately wanted with his green eyes and my sense of humor. The seemingly endless nights of falling asleep all nestled together in bed. It was at my fingertips. I literally touched it. Now gone. Lost. Because of me.

I stare right. I *should* go home. Face the music. Apologize and promise to do everything Nana says until I'm forgiven. It's the right thing to do. But instead, when the person behind me honks for me to move without thinking, I

spin the wheel left toward Connor's. Guess I'm not ready yet.
One more day. Tomorrow. Tonight I'll test out my personal
chef, chat with my assistant, and try out a new page in the
Kama Sutra with my boyfriend. I've done right all my life. I
deserve a little easy.

I don't have the will for anything else.

CHAPTER EIGHT

THE HIGH COST OF LOW LIVING

"Are we having fun yet?" Connor asks as I walk over to him.

After all the dancing and hike up the stairs to the VIP area, I need to catch my breath and sip my rum and coke. My fourth tonight. Hangover hell in my future but that's tomorrow's problem. Those problems are stacking up though. Connor pulls me onto his lap. It is the only place to sit what with our massive entourage either talking, making out, or in one case with Jack and Krista, drinking her blood in the booth. A little impromptu get together with the inner circle courtesy of Krista. When I returned to Connor's, she was still there helping the chef unload Connor's new pots and pans. The vamp didn't own a single one. Dinner was delicious and Krista didn't say a word a word about me sneaking out, but I could see it in her eyes. She was hurt and a little scared, so I promised I'd stop by the club and meet the gang. Connor thought the party was a splendid idea. I got to wear my new off the shoulder black and pink Michael Koors dress that clings in all the right places. It was on the floor in seconds after Connor first saw me in it, but afterwards it's proved perfect for dancing.

Connor's been in and out of the VIP area, work permitting. I kiss him quickly and smile. "I am, thank you. How's everything?"

"The deal is going through tomorrow," Connor says. "Neil and Avril have it well in hand for now."

He slides his hand underneath my skirt between my thighs. Compared to what Raquel and Edgar are doing right beside us, this act is positively prudish, but I still move his hand a few inches down. Guess I haven't gone totally native yet. I finish off the rest of my drink before leaning against him and resting my head on his shoulder. "Do you have time to finish our conversation then?" I ask.

"Which one? The ridiculous one about you checking into a hotel for no rational reason? The one how it was not only rude but worrisome when you left without a word and would not turn on your phone?"

"No. You've talked those to death. I mean the one about me pulling my weight."

He kisses my exposed shoulder. "I enjoy your weight presently where it is."

I sit up to stare at him straight in those violet eyes. "Please, okay? I'm serious. Today with the cook, and the car, and Krista...it's too much. There has to be something I can do to help your company."

"Fairest, there is no need," he says.

"I want to. You can't lock me up and keep me like a doll. I need something to do or I'll go nuts."

"Well, what did you do between cases? You cannot have been fighting monsters all the time."

"I trained. Researched. Helped Nancy with her schoolwork. Played pool and video games. Hung out and shared stories with the others. Cleaned. Shopped."

"Then do that now," Connor suggests. "Is there anything you have wanted to learn? I can hire tutors—"

"Is there a reason you want me under lock and key? Is Antonia—"

"Beatrice, I merely want to take care of you as I promised I would. You have been through so much," he says, gently caressing the vampire bite scar on my neck, "*so* much, even in recent days. You need a safe space to focus on yourself and your recovery. Working a menial, soul crushing job will not achieve that end." He smiles seductively. "And yes, I do not wish your attention diverted away from me. If you worked during the day, you might be too tired to…play with me at night." He leans up and kisses me. "Merely give it a few more days to acclimate. And you can be honest with Krista if she proves too obtrusive for your liking. You are in charge. She works for you."

"She works for *you*," I point out.

He frowns. "I have no desire to spend another precious moment arguing about this. I am attempting to be kind to you, and you are throwing my kindness back in my face as if I have insulted or aggrieved you in some way. It feels as if I have presented you with a diamond and you chucked it into the rubbish for not being a ruby. You are, quite frankly, hurting my feelings, Beatrice."

"I don't mean to," I say. "It's not that I'm not grateful for everything. I just—"

"Well, it does not seem that way at present," he says, dropping his arm from around my waist.

God. Great. Now I've hurt someone else I care about. Who knew he could be so sensitive? He wore that same scowl/pout when I broached the subject of getting a hotel. I kissed and…well, put my mouth to other uses to wipe it away then.

"I'm sorry. I'm *sorry*," I say before kissing him. A probing, passionate, yummy kiss. I don't stop him from moving his hand under my skirt again. His fingers brush aside my panties, and I put up no resistance as his fingers enter me. I lean into him. I've seen far worse from vamps in social settings. Just go with it, Bea. No one's—

"I should arrest you both for indecent exposure."

Oh, God.

My eyes whip open, and I have to blink several times to make sure what I'm seeing is real. Please don't let it be. I pray this is just a nightmare. *Please be a nightmare.* But of course it isn't. Not even my nightmares are this horrific.

Oliver stands on the other side of the VIP rope, scowl affixed. It matches Connor's. At least his hand vacates my body to save me further embarrassment. Not that there's much more embarrassment to be had. I suppose Nana could be here too. I'd die on the spot then.

"How the hell did you get in here?" Connor asks, voice bordering on a growl.

"Ways and means," Oliver replies with a tiny smirk. Better than a scowl.

"You are not welcome here or even within my territory. I thought I made that quite clear last night. I *could* have you killed."

"Connor, that's—" I say.

"This does not concern you, Beatrice. He has violated vampiric law by ignoring a direct edict."

"And I am a Federal Agent and therefore not leashed by your murderous whims," Oliver counters.

"Are you here in an official capacity, Agent Montrose? Because if you are not, and if you are in league with Antonia as Beatrice informed me you are, then I am *well* within my rights to have you executed. Now I can add trespassing, espionage—"

"Okay, enough. Enough!" I say. "I have had enough male posturing bullshit to last twelve lifetimes. No one is killing anyone."

"Thank you, Trixie. I—"

"You shut up too," I snap. "You're not innocent in this, and we both know it." Great, now I have a headache and am seventy-five percent sober. I take a deep breath and quell my anger. "Just say what you came to say and leave."

"May we speak in private?" Oliver asks.

"After that display last night in my office, if you think I will let you be alone with—"

"*Let* her? I am sorry, does she need your permission to go to the toilet as well now?"

"Alright, now I have had more than enough of this disrespect and grandstanding," Connor says. "Jack, Edgar, please escort Agent Montrose to his vehicle," the two big men stand up, "and if he resists, meet force with force."

"No!" I say, leaping up on instinct. I step in front of the velvet rope and hold up my hands to stop the two glaring minions. "That won't be necessary. Oliver's leaving."

"Not until you speak with me," Oliver says, stonily.

"She does not want you here," Connor hisses.

"Right now *want* is not a luxury she can afford," Oliver says.

Jack and Edgar take a step forward. "No!" I state again, taking a step backwards toward Oliver. I glance at the glaring Connor. I've never seen him so livid. His jaw's tight, the veins in his neck bulge, and his nostrils flare. He's normally so calm, even when those men attacked him. This is bad. "I'll walk Oliver back to his car."

"Absolutely not!" Connor says. "I will not let you—"

"Yeah, the words 'let' and 'me' should never leave your mouth together again, Danny Boy," I warn. "I am walking my friend through public spaces to his car where he will drive away never to return." I spin around to face Oliver. "Because if he does, I won't stop what comes next." Back to Connor. "I'll be five minutes."

"This is—" Connor says.

"The end of this discussion. I will be back in five minutes," I say, voice hard before I unclip the rope, step beside Oliver, and we start down the stairs.

"You know, I do believe I just witnessed history. Someone finally stood up to his Lordship," Oliver says. "He—"

"Shut. Up. Or I will stake you myself." I hurry through the club without glancing back at Oliver until we're outside. "Where's your car?"

The bouncer, who probably won't have a job this time tomorrow, steps toward us. "What the hell is he—"

"I'm handling it," I snap.

"Ma'am, I am under strict orders from his Lordship to kick the shit out of this man if he—"

The bouncer grabs Oliver's arm and I step up to the huge man, jaw clenched and glare affixed. I almost want him to hit Oliver, and not just because I'm dying to beat someone to a pulp just to vent my fury. "Get your damn hand off him or I will pull your brain through your nose without lifting a finger. I said I'm handling it."

The bouncer matches my intense glare, no doubt debating his next course of action. Reason prevails. He releases Oliver's arm and takes a step back. "Whatever you say, *ma'am*."

"Thank you," I say, voice still steel. My glare whips back to Oliver. "You. Move."

"Yes. *Ma'am*," Oliver says with a slight smirk. I want to slap it off but somehow reign myself in. We start down the sidewalk, I hope to this car. "Just like old times, no? You saving me from thrashings."

"Not that you've never deserved them. Present situation included. What the hell were you thinking coming here tonight and picking another fight? I'm pretty sure he *does* have the right to kill you now."

"He will not dare for a multitude of reasons, the most salient being he would lose your affection."

"Yeah, don't bet on it."

"I already have. And won."

"I meant about him losing my affection. Especially after what you've pulled the last two nights." I stop walking and turn to really confront him. Face-to-face. "Showing up uninvited after months of no contact? Insulting me? Strong arming your way into Connor's office and acting like a psycho?"

"Is that what *he* told you?" Oliver asks before scoffing. "Did he fail to mention his part in the altercation? How he goaded me? Said the most vile, heinous, explicit things about you? And yes, I lost my sense for a regrettable moment, yet still managed not to throttle him. Because I realized what his game was. That is his MO., Trixie. Knowing the precise buttons to needle to get what he wants from others. He is a master, no *legendary* manipulator. The mere fact you share his bed proves it. He is taking advantage of your lost state, to what end I can only guess."

"Yeah, because he can't just like me for me," I hiss. "He can't think I'm sexy. He can't just want to *be* with me."

"I am sure he does. How could he not? But drawing pure, true affection from that man would be like drawing blood from a stone."

"Look, I'm not expecting him to fall head over heels in love with me. Hell, I don't even want him to. He's fun. He spoils me. It's nice. It's easy. That's it. Am I not allowed to have a little harmless fun for *once in my fucking life?*" I shout to the heavens.

"Not when you have chosen to run and hide and have your supposed fun with a python who is ever so slowly coiling himself around your neck. Well, I will be damned if I allow him to strangle and devour you merely because at present you are not strong enough to fend him off."

"I do not want you to save me from anything, Oliver."

"Yes, but you *need* someone to," he states as gospel. "And you have saved me so many times in so many different ways, it is more than time I take my turn."

"You don't owe me a fucking thing, Oliver," I say angrily.

"I owe you more than I can ever hope to repay even should I live another five hundred years," he states as plain fact.

His vehemence, his utter conviction in his words renders me momentarily speechless. He uses my befuddled state to his advantage, taking a step toward me. I can smell his cologne, his shampoo. I didn't realize how much I've missed that scent until this very moment. I'm suddenly transported back to that night in Colorado on my first case where I cried and cried in his arms as he sung me lullabies until I fell asleep. It was the first time in forever I felt safe. Cared for. Understood. But I'm not that girl anymore. That was back when I was innocent. Before I literally threw him to the wolves.

I take a step back before I lose myself to those memories. "You've repaid me, okay? We're even. You're absolved. And I appreciate you coming. I do. But you need to go back to Kansas and find someone else to point your newfound savior complex at. This is *my* life. *I* choose what happens in it. And right now I choose to finish this conversation and go back to the club and my boyfriend. And if he strangles and devours me…that's on me and me alone. Your five minutes are up. Don't come back or I'll let him do whatever he wants to you. Go home, Oliver. Just go," I plead.

"Not without you," he says.

"I am home."

"If you believe this is home, that *this* is where you truly belong, then you are far more lost than I knew." He stares down at the compass he gave me for Christmas with Will's wedding ring beside it on the chain. "But if I have to venture twenty thousand leagues into the abyss to pluck you out, I will." He looks up into my eyes. "Just as you did for me. Just as I know you will always do for me. Even if you do not think you wish to leave that void, or even deserve to, even if its allure has enchanted you as it did me for so long, I *will* help you find your way out. Because you are worth fighting for. Even if you do not believe it at present, I do. Because *you are*," he says with complete faith. "And until my last moment on this earth, I will do all in my power and beyond to make you believe it too."

I stare into his gray eyes and for a glorious moment I experience a sensation I didn't think I had inside me anymore. It starts in my stomach with the butterflies that then flutter through my whole body, their tiny wings fanning the embers almost extinguished by life into full blown flames. Of hope. And in this moment, I do believe. Oliver smiles, a pure radiant smile that somehow makes him into the most beautiful creature ever to grace this universe. "*There you are*," he whispers.

"Beatrice?"

Connor's brogue shatters the spell into a trillion tiny pieces. It jolts me out of our two person universe back into this less thrilling yet far more cold, frightening one. I can breathe in this realm at least. I quickly glance back at my boyfriend who stands half a block away with his arms folded across his chest, glowering as if he's just caught us screwing against the wall. Guilt overwhelms me all of a sudden, or maybe that's just a convenient excuse, I step back from my friend. Oliver doesn't hide his anger and disappointment as I do. God, that expression, those piercing eyes and frowning mouth, are worse than a shiv to my heart. I actually cringe and have to return my gaze to Connor. "Everything's fine," I call to him. "I'm coming."

"Do not go," Oliver says.

I turn back to Oliver but stare at his chest. "Don't make this any worse. Please. Just go. Please. It's not worth it. *Go.*"

Head bowed, I turn my back on Oliver like a coward and begin toward Connor. He lowers his arms from his chest and smiles as I approach. A slightly smug smile I kind of want to rip off his face. I pass him with a word. I don't want to speak or be spoken to ever again. Talking just seems to cause more turmoil and troubles. More confusion. Connor at least keeps his distance as I make my way in a daze to the club because I don't know where else to go.

The glaring bouncer opens the door, all but growling at me as I pass. I suppress the urge to hiss at him like a cat. I zoom straight to the bar. "Vodka shot." Mathilda, the bartender, glances back, I presume at Connor, then fills my shot glass. I chug the nasty crap and shudder. Still, I ask for another. Connor must grant her permission because Mathilda fills the glass again. Another shot and another shudder. I've never gotten black out drunk but tonight seems like a good time to try it out. Probably should have done it from the moment I touched down in San Diego. "Another."

"No, we are returning to my apartment," Connor says, taking my arm, "before you pass out."

"No! I want to dance again!"

"Beatrice—"

"Leave me alone!" I pause. "Just…not now."

He studies my pained face with a straight scowl but does release my arm. "Fine."

Motion. Must stay in constant motion. No quiet. No rest. Thoughts come when I don't.

I stumble toward the dance floor and begin gyrating with the equally fucked up horde. All of us here trying to drink, to dance, to screw the shittyness of life away if just for the night. What the hell is so fantastic about reality? Who needs it? Here's better. Dancing until I die. At least you die having fun instead of...tears suddenly fill my eyes, but I blink them away. Just dance, bitch.

I dance to two more songs until my arms and legs begin to ache and the vodka begins its job. The whole world, the whole of me blurs and dulls just like before *he* ruined everything. Home. Hope. Two made up concepts that only exist in the human mind. I don't have either? Here is home, this dance floor, because it makes me happy. Kansas and the F.R.E.A.K.S. aren't home. I don't belong there. Probably never did. And hope? I have hope. Hope is the hangover isn't too terrible tomorrow. See? Nothing to fight for or against, Oliver. If this is the abyss, the dark side, it's a hell of a lot better than where I was before.

Except I have to pee now. See? Stupid reality sucking away all my fun. I must be drunker than I realized because I can barely walk straight toward the toilets. Damn it, the line is all the way down the hall. I'll go back to Connor's and—

Wait, I know that guy. I stop dead at one of the tables along the wall where a chatting foursome, one of whom I vaguely recognize. I have to blink to buy my brain time to make sure I'm right. Thin frame, long stringy hair, white peasant top, busy beard, yeah it is so him. The asshole vamp who abused his teenage consort then ratted me out to Connor for trying to help her escape him. Pathetic little prick, couldn't even face me man-to-woman. Had to hide behind Connor. My eyes jut to the girl he now has his arm around dressed in a matching peasant top. Her I've never seen. She sure as hell isn't Mariah, though they appear the same age and with the familiar hollow cheeks, frail frame, and bruises not quite concealed by make-up. Looking at this new lost girl my whole body tingles with fury. Out of nowhere the table they sit at suddenly flips, doing a full one eighty, spilling the drinks all over the couples. The startled and confused group all leap away from the table.

"What the hell?" Moon Lipmann gasps. "What—"

Peering around for the source of this unexplained occurrence, Moon finally lays eyes on me. "Boo, asshole."

It takes him a second to place me too, but the moment he does fear quickly morphs into anger. "I-I remember you. The F.R.E.A.K. who assaulted me."

"And you're the pathetic shithead who likes to starve and beat little girls." I stare at the doe-eyed teen shrinking against her boyfriend. "This your latest victim? What happened to the last one?"

"None of your business," Moon snaps.

"The hell it isn't. Where is she? Where's Mariah?"

"I don't have to answer to you, bitch," he spews back.

That's it. I lose my mind with that last word. Be it the booze or rage or both, the bastard flies against the back wall, pinned by my invisible grasp. His friends gasp again. Guess they've never met a psychokinetic before. I step toward Moon and his three companions give me wide berth. Nice friends. "I'll ask you again, asshole. Where is Mariah?"

"Let me go! You're cra—"

My grip on his heart as I squeeze stops his words. "Where is Mariah?" I squeeze harder. "Answer me or I *swear* I will fucking kill you. I—"

"What the hell is going on here?" Connor asks behind me. "Release him. Now."

I glance back at the infuriated Connor and concerned Krista, whose probably been watching me for him this whole time. Narc. "Not until he tells me where Mariah is."

"Sir…" Moon whispers.

"Agent Alexander, cease this assault now!" Connor booms.

Those first two words knock some sense into my addled brain. I release his heart after those two words and the rest of him by the end of his sentence. Moon falls to his knees, clutching his pained chest. The very least he deserves. If we were alone I'd do what I'm dying to and kick him a few times in the ribs. I take a step back in case my resolve breaks.

"I-I wa-want that woman arrested. Th-this is the second time—"

Connor merely raises his hand, and the vamp shuts his mouth. My boyfriend peers at me with the same disdain he has for his underling. "What happened?"

"He won't tell me where Mariah is." My head whips Moon's direction again. "He beat her and scarred her and did who knows what else to her before, and now he won't tell me what happened to her."

"And I told her it's none of her damn—"

Connor holds up his hand again, silencing the worm. "This is easily remedied. Tell Agent Alexander where the woman is, and we can go our separate ways."

For a flickering movement something close to terror flashes across Moon's ferrety face. I've seen it a dozen times as I questioned perps, and in that moment I know she's dead. He killed her. The bastard…it's like a literal punch to the stomach. Bile rises into my throat. "She left me months ago," Moon says. "She packed up her shit and left, I think home to her parents, alright?"

"Liar!" I roar as I lunge toward him again.

A tight grip latches onto my arm, stopping me.

"Krista, please escort Beatrice to my apartment. I will be there shortly."

"Connor—"

"Beatrice, I shall handle this. Leave. *Now*."

Even in my drunken, crazed state, I'm cognizant enough to be afraid and not push my luck. Plus I'm pretty sure I'm about to throw up and really need a toilet. "Fine. Kick his ass for me, Danny Boy." With my narc shadow in tow, I stumble a few steps before Krista grabs my arm to steady me. Why is walking so damn hard? The world spins so much the nausea becomes almost unbearable. I barely made it to Connor's downstairs bathroom before puking.

"Gross," Krista says. "I'll, uh, go get you some water."

Oh crap, I think I puked in my hair. I pull it aside when I throw up again.

Krista returns with a glass of water but the cold tile floor feels so amazing against my cheek, I don't move. I don't think I could move if I wanted to. I concentrate on stopping the world from spinning. Oh alcohol, I love and hate you so, though the dial is more toward hate right now.

I hear muffed voices in the living room, no doubt with me as the topic, but I don't care. The alcohol's still doing its job there at least. A few seconds later the voices stop and a few more after that someone steps into the bathroom. "Are you alright?" Connor asks sternly.

"I think I drank too much," I mutter against the lovely floor.

"How astute of you," he says.

"Did you arrest that child killing bastard?"

He's silent for a moment. "No."

Though the word twists and turns and the nausea returns, I force myself to sit up and face the stony Connor looming in the doorway. "Why the hell not? He killed his consort! He killed a teenage girl, Connor."

"And he swore under oath that she left him months ago."

"Of course he said that! Oath or no oath, he's not going to admit killing a helpless, love-struck teenager. I-I told you what he was doing to her at Christmas, Connor. Or don't you care?"

"She is also one of my subjects. Of course I care. The matter was investigated then and if I can recall correctly, the girl refused to take it further."

"And that was it? You talked to her once and decided that was enough? You let her...stay with that evil asshole and never thought about her again, didn't you? *Didn't you?*"

He tilts his head to the side. "Now are we talking about my alleged indifference or yours right now?" I can't handle his scrutiny right now. I look away. "Is that why you assaulted him? Why you embarrassed me, placed me in an untenable situation, made me appear weak to my subjects for the second time in one night? Because Oliver stirred up some misplaced sense of remorse inside you? The man is a master manipulator, Beatrice. I have personally seen him seduce a nun with a few minutes of conversation. He will say or do anything to get what he wants from you, and in your current frame of mind, you are all but powerless to resist." I chuckle wryly. "What?"

"Nothing. He just said the exact same thing about you. That you're taking advantage of me. Using me."

Those violet eyes narrow as his mouth and shoulders drop, I think in disappointment with a hint of sadness too. He shakes his head before sneering at the ceiling. "I do not…" His pained gaze returns to me. "What have I done, Beatrice? What have I asked you to do for me that would give even the slightest credence to those suspicions? Have I asked you to use your gift against my enemies? Turn your back on your morals and ethics to better *my* life? What have I done but attempt to make *your* life easier? Enjoyable. And what strings have I put on those attempts? Or are you so far gone it is impossible for you to believe someone can genuinely care for you and expect naught in return? Because I do. I genuinely like you. I could even…" He stops that train of thought. Thank God. "It has been…decades since I have met a woman I can engage with both intellectually and physically. Who is both gay and responsible when it is called for. So perhaps I am using you. I am using you to bring a bit of fun and joy into my frantic, maddening, dangerous existence. But if I am guilty of that crime then so are you, fairest. So is every human currently coupled on this earth. And I will remind you, you are not a prisoner here. The front door is wide open. You can leave whenever you fancy. But do not expect it to remain unlocked should you chose to use it. On the other side is a one way road back to where you were before with no return. The choice is yours, Agent Alexander, and quite frankly after tonight…after this conversation…I almost wish you were halfway through that bloody door already."

He steps out of the bathroom, I think before his veneer breaks down further. I sit stunned for a moment. Another far too familiar wave of guilt crashes through me. I hurt him. I genuinely hurt his feelings. Blood from a stone my butt. I manage to stand up and though the world somersaults a few times, I walk into the living room where Connor just stands with his back to me and his head hung a little. "I'm sorry," I say as I approach.

"No, I am sorry," he says, not turning around. "I did not mean what I said. I lost my composure. That is not...like me."

I reach him and wrap my arms around his torso, resting my head on his shoulder blade. He hugs my forearms with his own. "At least I now know you're not the emotionless automaton everyone says you are. I just wish I didn't have to piss you off for you to show it."

"If I appear cold or indifferent...it is how one plays the game. The mask, the façade has saved me and mine countless times."

"Well, you don't need it around me, okay?" I kiss his back. "And I'm sorry I made you look bad in public. It didn't even occur to me that was possible."

"No, I...should have not ordered you about as I do others. Oliver is your...*friend*. You have every right to converse with him whenever you choose. I merely knew that if you did, *this* would happen. He would use every trick to cast suspicion upon me, upon my motives, and we would quarrel. Worse, you would believe him and..." He ceases speaking and just kisses my hand. "I merely want you to be happy, Beatrice, and he upsets you. I want to spare you as much pain as I can."

I kiss his shoulder again. "And I appreciate that. I do. You are the only thing that's made me happy in months." I squeeze him tighter. "And I like you too."

He chuckles and kisses my knuckles again. "Then you are the member of a truly exclusive club." He releases my arms and slowly turns around to face me, that crinkle-eyed grin of his greeting me. "One I hope I never give you cause to leave." He kisses my forehead. "Now let me get you cleaned up and into bed." He kisses my forehead again. "Oh, I do not envy being you tomorrow."

I look up into his gorgeous eyes. "And Mariah…"

"The situation is now delicate, fairest. You assaulted him without provocation and used your gift to do so in clear sight of humans. The law dictates I punish you and inform your former colleagues. With the truce with Antonia sitting on a razor's edge, and us still under intense scrutiny, the incident could draw you and I into peril as well. So for now we must let it go. Let Mr. Lipmann calm down and forget." He brushes a stray strand of hair from my cheek. "But I promise I will investigate the matter."

"But—"

He shushes me and places a finger over my lips. "This is for *your* own good, fairest. To protect you as I promised I would. Trust me, Beatrice. Please." I don't have any fight left inside me tonight, so I simply smile and nod. That brings a smile to his face. "My word, you are a handful woman. A beautiful…" He kisses my forehead. "Enchanting…" Another kiss. "Infuriating…" He scoops me up like a bride and I chuckle. "Handful. But well worth the trouble."

As he carries me upstairs, I almost believe those words.

Almost.

CHAPTER NINE

TRUE DETECTIVE

Hangover. From. Hell.

What the hell was I thinking? What the—? I can't even finish that thought as I throw up again, making my aching head and beat up body flare with pain again. This is so bad. Never again. So not worth this. Maybe if I blacked out it would be but not only is there the physical torture but the mental torture accompanies it at the same intensity. Mariah and Moon. The fights with Connor. The scene with Oliver. At least one of those troubles ended on a nice note. Connor drew me a bubble bath, massaged my shoulders, and even washed my hair for me before tucking me into bed without attempting sex. He even left the light on in the bathroom so I could move around the dark bedroom with minimal stumbling. If only he were awake now to turn me into a vampire so this pain would go away.

The shower helps with the physical torment a little. The rest not so much. Horrid flashes come into my head fast and furious. Oliver's face when I went to Connor. Mariah's face when I last saw her in that house. When I left her. That fleeting look of terror when I confronted Moon and knew she was dead. I don't care what Connor said last night. I failed that girl. I should have followed up. Kept going to that house and befriended the teen. Or at least put another scare into her abuser. But I didn't give her a second thought until now. What if he'd killed her in a fit of rage right after I left? That is when an abused woman is most likely to get killed by her partner, when he finds out she plans to leave him. Life got insane at Christmas, but as a sworn officer of the law it is literally my job to protect the innocent. Another failure. More blood on my hands. Well if I can't save her, I damn well can find her body. Give her a proper burial. Let her family know what happened. Show her someone cared. Let her soul rest in peace.

What I did last night was stupid. I never should have gotten physical and spouted off my suspicions. I tipped my hand. Of course now he has Connor keeping me in check, he probably thinks he's golden. He's gotten away with it. And though Connor promised to investigate he's got so much else on his plate, and God knows what will happen in the future. This isn't a priority. What's one dead teenage girl involved in a domestic? Well she damn well matters to me, and I have nothing but time on my hands. I pull my aching carcass out of the shower, drink two glasses of water, down another Alleve, and dress in jeans, sneakers, and pink t-shirt. I know Connor said I shouldn't be doing what I intend to, but if all goes right he won't find out until I have proof against Moon. He'll still be pissed, I'm sure, but the damage will be minimal to him. I just have to not get caught.

Krista's watching television downstairs in the living room when I come down with my suitcases again. My gauntlet to pass through. She tattled on me more than once...

"Afternoon," I call cheerfully.

Krista leaps off the couch to help me. "Hi! How are you feeling?"

"Mortified. I don't know what got into me last night. I'm so sorry you had to see me like that."

"If I had a dollar for every time I saw someone in our circle barf, Jack and I could buy our own island." She set the suitcase down beside the couch and I do the same. "Matt, the chef, was here earlier. He left you a smoothie that works miracles on hangovers. It cured mine."

"Where is this magical elixir? Gimmie."

With a smile that matches mine but is actually genuine, Krista hurries to the kitchen as I sit at the bar. The smoothie is a rusted color and reeks of raw meat even from here. I take one sip of what can only be described as old blood covered Brussel sprouts left out in the sun for a week. I literally gag and push it away. "I am not that desperate. I'll just get Starbucks on my way to the hospital."

"Hospital?"

"It's just a check-up." I lift my bangs to show her my ragged scar. She cringes. "I had a car accident a few months ago. The doctor scheduled one last CT scan to make sure everything healed right." All of this is true, it just happened a few weeks before. "It's nothing."

"I could come with you," Benedict Arnold offers.

"There's no need. I just wait in the lobby for an hour or two, then lie in a machine for a few minutes. I'll bring my Kindle. And actually…I am going to be late!" I leap off the stool and rush to get my purse.

"I really think I should come with you," Krista calls.

"Why?"

"Because…moral support?"

"Or because you got in trouble with Connor for leaving me alone yesterday?" I ask.

Her mouth falls open. "I-I-of course not!"

"Look, I don't need or want a babysitter, and I'm thinking you have things you'd rather do than be glued to my side all day in a hospital waiting room. As long as we're both here when Connor rises who is to say we didn't spend the day together? I won't tell if you won't. Regardless, you're not coming with me. Enjoy your day."

I turn my back on her and walk out. She doesn't utter a word of protest. I even make it to the garage without encountering another soul to question me. The fates are with me for once. When I pull onto the street I breathe a literal sigh of relief. Now if everything else goes as smoothly, Moon will be in handcuffs by night's end.

Quite a few of the F.R.E.A.K.S. cases I worked on began as a missing person's investigation. Unfortunately since Mariah was an official consort her case falls under vampire jurisdiction. A consort is like an honorary vampire and bound by the same laws and rights as a real vampire. The only times the F.R.E.A.K.S. are allowed to intervene is if a vampire begins killing anyone outside their own species or their acts draw press attention. This case doesn't meet the criteria. That however does not mean the F.R.E.A.K.S. can't be unofficially helpful. At least I hope so.

"Hello?" Carl asks over the phone.

Carl Petrovsky, F.R.E.A.K. for close to a decade. George recruited him from a psychiatric hospital after poor Carl attempted to cut his own hands off. That may seem crazy to most but not when the offending hands—all his skin really—can tell him your emotions, thoughts, secrets, the limb removal's understandable. The poor guy can't be touched, not even hugged, let alone…anything else. I thought psychokinesis was a burden.

Despite his own curse, and generally introverted personality, we did manage to become close with our love of books, old movies, and him just being a trustworthy, good, good guy. He even saved me from killing an innocent woman once and never told a living soul or brought it up to me again. Hope I can count on his discression and aid this time too.

"Hi, Carl. It's Bea."

There are several seconds of silence on his end. "Uh, hi," he chuckles. "This is a surprise. How-how are you?"

"I'm okay. I'm okay. What about you? I heard you guys just finished a case. Are the new recruits pulling their weight?"

"So far so good. Devin's a tech wiz, something we've been sorely lacking, and Claire, his wife, held her own when we took down the rogue cabal."

"It's always vampires, isn't it?" I ask with a scoff.

"Seems that way, no? And on the topic of bloodsuckers…did Oliver make it to San Diego alright?" Carl asks. "We haven't heard from him since he left."

"Yeah, he's here. He's fine or was last night when he almost started a fight in the middle of the club."

"That sounds like him. You should have seen him about a week ago. He was convinced, dead convinced, something had happened to you. He had George agreeing to let him borrow the jet to get to you when the cabal case came in. George had to all but blackmail Oliver to come with us. And he was a nightmare the whole case. Snapping at everyone. Couldn't concentrate. I preferred him before."

"Before?"

"When he was just quiet, gone most of the time when he wasn't in his room playing video games, I think with you." Shit. I thought it was Nancy most of the time. Weird. "I think there was a whole week where nobody saw him. George had to force him back for a case. He did the work, whatever Chandler assigned him, but barely said a non-work related word to anyone. Not even Nancy. I've known him for years and never saw him so…Bea, he didn't even flirt with Claire. Not once." Dear God. If his mouth's moving he's flirting. I don't know what to say. Carl fills the silence first. "We all miss you, you know. Wolfe's fighting with Chandler after every other order. He's even thought of transferring out. Nancy's been acting out. Not doing her schoolwork. Talking back. She actually ran away to see that boy Logan in Oklahoma. I think they…I think the Doc put her on the pill. And the job. Jesus, Bea. We all have new scars. Literal scars. I was on light duty for a month after a golem case. Rushmore is gone. They could barely re-attach his arm after that golem literally ripped it off."

"Jesus! Is he all right?"

"He'll never have full use of it again. His career with the bureau is over. His first replacement Allerdyce lasted one case before transferring out. We're supposed to be getting two newbies but who knows if they'll last. I know George has been trying to call you. He talked it over with a couple of us to see if we'd be okay with you coming back. Pretty sure you still have your job. If you want it."

My stomach seizes. "I don't…you guys would trust me? After what I did?"

"You'd be on double secret probation with everyone, but we know you were in an insane situation, Bea. None of us knows what we'd do if we were in your shoes. It was a dumb decision, but we all know how much it cost you. You won't make the same mistake or anything close to it again. Plus the newbies are hopeless investigators. And Chandler's all but become a dictator even during interviews, all bull in a china shop. You were good. Great. A true detective just like Will." Carl pauses. "He thought so too. Will. When you left at Christmas he told me so after apologizing for acting like an asshole all those months. You impressed him, Bea. No easy feat. Almost impossible if you ask me."

I blink back a few tears and wipe the lose ones away. "I miss him."

"Then honor him. Keep the good fight alive. Come back. Come home."

I sniffle. "You sound like Oliver. He says he's not leaving until I go with him."

"That sounds like him. No doubt he means it too. He took indefinite leave."

"Wonderful," I scoff.

"Are you in trouble like he thought?"

"No, I'm…I'm just dating Connor and yet everyone's acting like I'm sitting on an atomic bomb."

"Connor? The vampire who helped us stop your ex?"

"Yeah. And everyone seems to forget that fact. That, though he had no reason to, he put himself and his people in harm's way to stop a group of serial killers."

"Yeah, fairly sure *you* were the reason, Bea. Didn't he also try to convince you into being his mistress by threatening to kill you and your family?"

Why does everyone insist on bringing that up? "Yeah, but I called his bluff." I don't want to go down this conversation path again. "And now I'm helping keep his vamps in line. I'm investigating a possible murder now. I know this vamp killed his consort, an eighteen-year-old girl, and I just need to find the evidence."

"Ah. And let me guess, you want my help."

"All I need is for you to do is check the missing person's database for this girl. Her first name's Mariah, I assume spelled like the singer's. Blonde hair, eighty to a hundred pounds, about eighteen, blue eyes. Check the age range from fifteen to nineteen in case she was lying. And if you could also check the coroner's offices for San Diego city, county, and every other county within a hundred mile radius for girls, probably Jane Does, matching that description from mid-December to present."

"That it?" Carl asks.

"For now."

"You owe me, Bea. I will collect when you come home."

I don't say anything for several seconds. "I'm probably not coming back, Carl. I can't...I don't think I have it in me to play hero anymore. I don't think I want to."

"Says the woman spending her free time trying to find a teenage girl she barely knew," he points out. "Bea, there are certain things about ourselves that no matter how hard we try, how much we may want to change them, they're just...us. And fighting against yourself is just wasted energy and time when you of all people knows how precious that time is. So stop fighting a pointless battle. You are...a true detective. You are a good person. And a lot of people need you. Not just us. Think of the countless people out there who are alive because you saved them. And think of those out there who *will* live because of you. It's a burden, believe me, I know. But it's also a privilege. Your life means something important, Bea. Just don't forget that, okay?"

I turn down Nana's street and take a deep breath. "I won't. Thanks."

"I'll call when I've finished the searches."

"Thank you. Really. I will make this up to you somehow. I gotta go. Bye." I hang up before I become a blubbering idiot again.

They want me back. They *need* me back. It truly never occurred to me they could have problems like that. Rushmore almost lost his arm? Nancy's running away and having sex? In my year we lost two people, Agent Konrad and Irie. Nancy was a mess after Irie, Agent Wolfe too, but Oliver and I banded together to make them both smile at least once a day. I can't believe he didn't do that again. The new recruits should help with firepower at least. They'll be fine now. Will wanted us to quit anyway. We were halfway out the door. This turmoil was inevitable. Right?

My body grows heavy with this new emotional baggage. Oh, stop it, Bea. I park my car in the empty driveway and sigh. I can't think about them now. I have more than reached my limit on guilt. Let me unload the ton marked "Mariah" before I even glance at the newest brick.

Nana is volunteering at the library as I'd expected so I slip into the empty house unmolested. There are a few goodies I need before I begin the investigation in earnest. I collect my silver nitrate MACE, silver plated handcuffs, lock picking kit, three silver daggers, my Glock, 9mm with holster, my one box of silver bullets, and Bette. Doing this feels wrong without her. I also pilfer Nana's binoculars, a few bottles of water, and some granola bars. I consider leaving a note but haven't a clue what to say. Sorry? I'm fine? Don't worry about me? It'll have to do. For now. I scribble those paltry words on the whiteboard on the fridge. I just hope this gesture doesn't make her worry more.

With my purse of destruction safely stored in the car, I drive off toward the Premiere Lanes Bowling Alley. I haven't set eyes on that place since Steven dropped me off all those months ago on our last "date." Mariah called me, scared out of her mind, begging me to pick her up. I know San Diego well enough to recall approximately where the house was, but it was dark and I was mostly concerned with keeping her calm to recall exactly where I drove that night. I also tried Google but came up empty for an address or any trace of Mr. Lipmann. Hard way it is. Always.

I waste almost an hour driving up and down suburban streets hoping a house will pop out of me. It had a stucco roof, there was a chain-link fence, and I think it was brown. Of course that describes eighty percent of the houses around here. Okay, this could have been a dumb idea. Connor would have the address but then he'd forbid me from investigating, we'd fight, and yeah. Just keep driving, Bea. Trust yourself. Remember. Half an hour later and still no joy. It's around here somewhere. I know it. I—

Oh, hell yes.

Light brown. Chain link fence. Blacked out windows. A brown '69 Volkswagen Bug in the driveway. If that hippie douchebag doesn't live here I'll eat Bette. I circle the block then park down the hill in front of the house with a "For Sale" sign on it. No nosy homeowners to call the cops or bug me. My car will stick out, but hopefully they'll just think I'm another realtor or buyer. Hopefully I won't be here too long. I collect my arsenal, save for Bette, and ready myself. If I do this right I won't need a thing. I hide the gun under my coat and the rest in my purse. I keep my head down as I move toward the house. No one's around, no one stops me, not even when I walk through the gate. With the windows blacked out or boarded up, I can't see inside the house. I circle the house and don't find a single one to peer inside. I do hear a TV on and plates rattling inside when I reach the backyard. I can't see through the blackout curtain along the sliding glass door, but I assume the girl from last night must be in there. Fudge. I scurry back to my car and climb inside. Oh heck, I hate stakeouts.

I definitely did not miss this part of the job. Sitting in a sweltering car, waiting for hours on end. The TV shows make police work seem so interesting. Thrilling. In reality that accounts for about five percent of the time. The rest is this. Long, long spates of boring nothing. Sitting as I am now, staring and willing for that five percent to come. I settle in and switch on an audiobook I brought for this very contingency. This very dull contingency.

On one case, a succubus in Virginia, Oliver and I went twelve hours, sundown to sun up with nothing to show for it. He was always the best stakeout buddy. We'd talk about the book or podcast we were listening to. He'd tell stories of his colorful past. We'd sing along to the radio and see who could sound the worst. He even gave me his coat to cover myself when I had to pee into a Starbucks cup. He laughed his butt off with that one.

Half an hour and nothing happens except I eat the granola bar. Moon's new girlfriend may not leave the house at all today. I don't even know her name. I—

My phone rings mid-chew. Carl. "Hi," I say.

"Hey. So I did the searches. Negative on bodies matching your description, but a possible on the Missing Child Database. Your phone have photo viewing capabilities?"

"Yeah."

"Sending you the picture now." A picture comes through a few seconds later. She's a few pounds heavier and far tanner, but that's her. That's Mariah. "Bea?"

"It's her," I say.

"Mariah Celine Wilson, disappeared a year and a half ago from Salton Sea at age fifteen. I pulled her record in Salton. In and out of foster care, arrested for shoplifting, and ran away twice. The latest foster mother reported her missing. No leads, barely any follow up."

"At least she has a full name now," I say.

"I can contact the police to let them know we had a sighting. They can help."

"Not yet. We don't have enough to bring to anyone yet. Plus this is vampire business. She's a consort."

"A sixteen-year-old?" Carl asks.

"Remember vampiric laws haven't caught up with the modern world. If she's thirteen, she's fair game. Give me until tomorrow night before contacting them, okay?"

"Need anything else?"

"Actually yeah. Run searches on 4562 Vida Ave, Chula Vista. Names, utilities, a phone number would be a lifesaver if you can find it."

"Wouldn't your boyfriend have that?"

"Um…he didn't."

"I'll see what I can find. Call you back soon." He hangs up.

Mariah Wilson. Sounds like you had a hard time of it even before you fell in love with an abusive psycho bloodsucker. Maybe that's all you ever thought you deserved. Maybe you thought people showed love with their fists. Poor girl died being bullied. Unloved. Thinking no one cared. Because they didn't. Well, someone does now honey. I'll find you. I'll see you get a proper burial if I can. And I *will* punish the bastard responsible.

Another half an hour of nothing, Carl calls me again. "Got your info," he says. "The house has been owned by Moon Lipmann since 1968, utilities all in his name. There is a listed phone number at that address. Got a pen?" I get one and he gives me the number. "Need anything else?"

"Not that I can think of right now. I cannot tell you how much I appreciate this. I owe you one."

"Buy me Starbucks for a month when you get back," Carl says.

"You got it," I say without thinking. I shake my head. "Thanks, Carl. Bye." I hang up.

Okay. How to play this? I need her gone for at least an hour in a way that's not gonna cast suspicion on me now or later. Tacoma. Yeah, that ploy worked once, it should again. I do a little more research, and gather all the info I need before dialing the Lipmann number. She picks up on the fourth ring.

"H-Hello?" I assume the girl from last night asks.

"Yes, hello, is Mr. Lipmann home?"

"No, he's, uh, gone until tonight."

"Well, this is Olivia Smythe from California Electric Company. I am calling to inform him that due to months of delinquent payments, we will be shutting off his electricity in one hour."

"Wait, what? No, he, like, paid the bill."

"That is not what our system shows. However, if you have proof he paid the bills as you said such as cancelled checks, you can come down to your local representative branch. If you don't you can go there and pay with a credit card, cash, check or cashier's check."

"Uh, I have, like cash."

"That's fine. The amount due is five hundred thirteen dollars. Do you have a pen and paper? Here is the address of the office." I give her an address near the real office building. She'll think she wrote it down wrong. "Please come in as soon as possible. You can speak to any of our representatives in the office there."

"Okay. Thanks."

"Have a nice day." I hang up.

Now to see if she fell for it. Will taught me that ruse on our third case. Tacoma, Washington. A witch selling love spells and potions. Lucky me, I got to spend hours alone with my crush. We started to get to know one another on that stakeout. Started to become friends. It was so difficult to draw him out at first. Lots of "Can we talk about something else" or "It's not that interesting," but eventually he opened up. Even flirted back as his face blushed. Why didn't I kiss him there and then? I wanted to. *So* badly. I'd like to think he'd have kissed me back. So much could have been avoided if I'd been brave then. It's so bizarre how such a tiny decision could impact so much of one's life and you never know until it's too late.

Ten minutes later the new girlfriend hurries out of the house. In the sunshine she's even paler than last night. And I'd bet a grand the huge sunglasses she's wearing have less to do with the sun and more to do with the bruise peeking out their side. Asshole. The girl climbs into the ancient Bug and speeds away, leaving clouds of exhaust in her wake. I don't waste a second. Re-assembling my arsenal, I climb out of my car and hustle up to the house again. The teenager was in such a hurry she forgot to lock the front door. How considerate of her. I just stroll in.

The house is exactly as I remember it. He even replaced the Grateful Dead poster frame that broke when I threw him against it. Should have ripped out his heart then. More hindsight to keep me awake at night. No time for self-flagellation now. I have a murderer to catch.

A quick sweep of the kitchen proves fruitless, just tons of tofu sprouts, granola, and a bag of blood. Nothing in the living room either except a lone photo of Moon and his new lunch box at the beach with the stars behind them. Hall closet, guest bedroom, and another spare bedroom full of vinyl records and a tiny bed are also free of traces of Mariah. Crud, maybe he's not the moron I thought. Maybe he burnt or gave away all her stuff. I sigh. Just keep going, Bea.

The master bedroom's next, and it's here I run into trouble. The door has a padlock on it. Ugh. Okay, I can do this. I remove the lock pick kit Will gave me on my birthday. I received the one lesson and it shows as I struggle with the lock. Ten minutes of swearing, pacing around to quell my frustration, and even a pee break I still can't get the damn thing unlocked. I could just kick the door in but they'd know I was here. Okay, I'm giving up. For now.

The garage is next, and I run into another road block. Mr. Lipmann appears to be a hoarder. Great. I stare at boxes and boxes of God knows what stacked to the ceiling with rusted bicycles, magazines, and more than a few rats scurrying around in the few places there's room to move. God, he could hide Mariah's body in here, and it'd never be found. I don't smell decay. No, the neighbors would complain about the stench. I don't know where to begin. I close my eyes. God I wish Andrew were here I'll have to do my best. "Mariah, if you're still here, if your spirit is still here...help me. *Help me.* Help—"

Something clangs nearby, and I open my eyes. A shovel continues falling down suitcases a few feet away. Worth a shot. I have to literally climb over boxes to reach the suitcases. As I get closer, I see it. A streak of blood across the canvas fabric of a duffel bag. Is this it? I close my eyes again and try to access the memory of the night I came to rescue Mariah. She was packing a duffel bag. This is it. I think so. I snap a picture of the blood splatter with my iPhone before opening the bag.

Hello.

Inside I find nothing but clothes and a few photos of Moon and Mariah kissing at the beach like the photo of the new girl in the living room, and way too many of Mariah naked or engaging in sexual acts. I snap photos of these. Disgusting but not incriminating. Nothing else but more clothes. I put everything back in but when I shift the bag I notice another vaguely familiar sight. A purse saturated in dried blood. I snap a picture before carefully opening it. There's not a lot in there either except for breath mints, gum, a card redder than white, and a pink plastic wallet. I open the wallet. A few dollars in cash, a picture of Mariah hugging a little girl, and a driver's license with a photo of Mariah but with the name Mariah Lipmann and this address listed. Fake. Claims she's twenty-one. I snap photos of everything, including the card. *My* card. Even with all the blood I can make out my name and the FBI seal. Motherlode. I think this'll be enough to convince Connor. I put everything back in its place and do a quick look through of the garage. Nothing stands out. I climb my way back to the door.

I'm running out of time. The question becomes do I keep at the bedroom lock or—

The decision's made for me. I'm close enough to the driveway in here I can hear the Bug choking out exhaust as it pulls up. Crap. When I get back to Connor's I am so practicing my lock picking until he rises. I hustle to the living room as I hear a car door shut. Back door it is. I brush aside the heavy blackout curtains and open the sliding glass door. I'll have to leave it unlocked, hopefully the only sign I've been here. Girlfriend will chalk it up to her own fleabrainess. I quietly shut the door and let out the breath I held. This better be—

It's in the mid-eighties today but a chill runs down my spine, as if someone traced a melting ice cube from neck to tailbone. I've experienced it enough on the job to know the cause. A ghost. I don't have Andrew's mediumship gift, but we've been through enough haunted houses and cemeteries with the man to know a real ghost when I sense one. When it wants me to sense it. I turn around but of course don't see anything. Just the small backyard that's more dirt than grass. Another chill. What are you trying to tell me, Mariah? I walk the length of the lawn and when I put one foot on a long dirt patch there goes the chill again. I stop dead. This patch is about five and a half feet long. Another chill comes when I move to the next same sized dirt patch. Crap. I count three more patches. Jesus.

Before I can move to the next one, there's a noise inside the house that catches my breath. I have to get out of here. I take a quick picture of the backyard as a whole before running to the side of the house and sneaking back to my car. I start the car and drive off. Maybe not all of them are bodies. Maybe none of them are.

Yeah. Right.

The purse should be enough. It has to be. And if Connor won't help, I know a Federal organization that will. A small smile crosses my face. I did miss this. Investigating. Beating the bad guy at his own rotten game. Maybe I am what Carl claims. A true detective.

Will would be proud.

CHAPTER TEN

SWEET AND VICIOUS VENGEANCE

"You did *what*?"

Okay, not the reaction I hoped for. My boyfriend glares at me, even baring his fangs. I stand my ground, even squeezing my shoulders and straightening my back. A large part of me knew this would happen, the fury, hell that he'd dump me on the spot for going against his wishes, but this is more darn important than us.

"You heard me. I have proof Moon Lipmann more than likely killed his consort Mariah, among others."

"And how precisely did you gather this evidence?" he asks, jaw now clenched.

"I searched his house."

"You broke in."

"No, the door was unlocked. No breaking involved. And I made sure to leave no trace I was ever there. I *am* a professional, Connor. I've done this before."

"You cannot…" He grunts, lightly punches the dining room table, and takes a step back. "I told you I would handle the situation. I forbid you from—"

"Yeah, as I told you before, no one forbids me from a thing," I say, voice hard. "And you said you'd handle it someday. *Maybe*. But right now there's another teenage girl living with a child killer who cannot afford someday. And look at it this way. Not only have I taken an item off your endless

To Do list, but outside of us two who is to know you didn't task me with this job? That you asked me to instead of telling me not to. There's no face to save."

He lets this logic sink in, the sides of his mouth slowly untensing. "Who else knows about this?"

"Carl from the F.R.E.A.K.S."

"Oh, for fuck's sake!" he says, literally throwing up his hands.

"He just did some research for me. There's nothing on record, nothing official." I pause. "At least not yet."

"Beatrice!"

"He promised to give us two days to handle it in house. But police are already looking for Mariah. She's in the law enforcement database. And if my hunch is correct, and there are more bodies in that backyard, not all of them will be his consorts, which does give the F.R.E.A.K.S. jurisdiction."

"So you have boxed me in. Given me no alternative but to—"

"Do your job? I shouldn't have to take a play from your book to get you to do the right thing, Connor." I fold my arms across my chest. "Hell, if you weren't on the receiving end of this, I'd bet you'd be damn proud of me. You've been a good teacher."

My boyfriend stares across the table at me, face suddenly a stone mask, as he works the angles in his mind. "Fine. Show me your evidence."

I lay out the photos, my notes about Mariah, my theory. That mask of his never wavers. "I'm no expert on vampiric law, or how much evidence is required to convict him, but this should be enough to at least check out his backyard, right? And if you have a medium on staff they could talk to one of the ghosts there too."

"I do not believe that will be necessary," Connor says. "This is…good work. I will send my people to bring Mr. Lipmann here and investigate the backyard."

"Is there enough even if I'm wrong about those patches being bodies?"

"If that is the case then I will *get* the evidence when I interrogate him."

"Thank you," I say with a smile.

"There is no need to thank me. It was me, after all, who asked you to investigate this matter," he says, all business.

He nods and begins walking toward the door.

"Connor…" He turns around, face unreadable. "I wouldn't have done this behind your back if it wasn't literally life and death."

"I am just…disappointed that you did not trust me. That you lied to my face when you promised to do just that. How can *I* trust *you* now?"

I don't have an answer for him. Because at the end of the day I didn't trust him. "This was a special circumstance. This was *me* cleaning up *my* mess. I can't mop them all up, but this one I could. And for the first time in months, I felt like me. I felt good. I *needed* to do this, Connor. Can you understand that?"

Connor gazes down, the tension waning. After several seconds, he says, "I will try."

That's the best I can hope for right now. "Thank you."

"Please wait here. I shall return in an hour or so and we will put this mess to bed."

"Okay."

After a curt nod, he walks out. I all but flop into the dining room chair. The gourmet Ahi salad and soufflé my personal chef whipped up sits half eaten and will probably stay that way. I've lost my appetite. I couldn't have waited until after my dinner to spring this on Connor. Really, I want to run. I want out of this apartment, away from him could I? I can handle someone being angry at me, disappointed not so much. And his disappointment kind of makes *me* mad. There is no downside for him to what I did. He doesn't have to waste resources or time investigating. A potential threat to his reign is being eliminated. It would be worse if Moon killed again *after* Connor became aware of the issue. He should be thanking me, proud, not scolding me like a stern father.

This whole "obey me or else" attitude of his is getting to me. I'm not an underling, I'm his girlfriend. And if he wants some blind follower who just fetches his slippers and awaits his every command, he should get a damn dog. Maybe he's not used to dating a modern woman with drive and a mind of her own. For a centuries old vamp the feminist movement has relatively been around for like a year. Well, he better learn to accept it or…what, Bea? This was meant to be a fling. A rebound. Fun. Instead it's been fights with everyone I love and now him. The sex has been great but all else weighs on me. I should be happy, right? Living the dream with my rich, sexy boyfriend catering to my every desire. Then why do I have to keep telling myself I'm lucky? Why don't I *feel* it like I did when I was investigating today?

I clear my plates, do the dishes, and return to my lock picking training and the *Doctor Who* marathon. It's not nearly as much fun watching the show without Oliver's snarky commentary but my other task helps keep my interest. Five hours of practice before Connor woke and I can now open a padlock, handcuffs, and Connor's front door deadbolt within minutes. Once I master the kit I'll move onto bobby pins, regular pins, and my bra's underwire. Will once opened a jail cell with that last one. It was damn impressive. Of course not fifteen minutes later I lost all respect for the man when he wanted to leave Oliver to his torturers. Guess I shouldn't be too surprised by Connor's reaction to my rebel ways. Will was all "my way or the highway" too. It pissed me off then too. Guess that's my type: unyielding control freaks. Will's came from a place of insecurity, I don't know where Connor's comes from. That makes me nervous.

Yet here I am in his apartment, waiting around for him to beckon me. Shit, I'm practically living with him. A man I don't really trust. I put the lock down and sigh. I think I need a night away from here. From him. From everything and everyone. A place where I can breathe. Yeah, I'm doing it. After this Moon business gets settled, I'm going to a hotel. Just not before. I'm not moving until that bastard's faced justice.

I don't have to wait too long. Almost an hour on the dot, there's a knock on Connor's front door and Avril steps in. "His Lordship requests your presence downstairs. Please come with me."

About damn time.

Avril leads me down the stairs and into the underground garage where Edgar and another vampire stand sentinel by a concrete wall. As we weave through the cars toward them, Edgar presses on the wall, which slides a door sized slab to the right. Hidden door. I can hear the sobs and screams through the hole. My stomach clenches with each wail of agony. You never, *ever* get used to the sounds of pain and misery coming from another living being. I guess the day you do is the day you become a true monster.

If the sounds weren't bad enough, the sight of what's occurring inside this 14X14 concrete tomb now adds chills to the mix. An impassive Connor and Jack stand on either side of the bound Moon, who has been forced to his knees. Literally. Blood already drips onto the plastic tarp below him from his broken nose, slashes to both his cheeks, and the tears flowing from his eyes. "Please, please, please…" he sobs.

My whole body becomes a pillar of stone. I know this man is a murderer and God knows what else, but still. His utter terror and torment bring revulsion and guilt all through me.

"Sir, Neil phoned," Avril says, all business. "He sensed six bodies in Mr. Lipmann's backyard."

"Then with his confession, the burden of proof has been more than met," Connor says. Moon just sobs harder. "Call Neil back and tell him to wipe the girl's memory of the past six months, give her some money, and drop her at a shelter."

"And the bodies?" Avril asks.

"Contact Det. Harvey Berry. He will know how to handle the situation for us."

"Very good, sir," Avril says with a little bow before leaving the cramped room. Lucky her.

The concrete slab slides shut behind her. The reek of metallic blood grows heavier the moment it does. The adrenaline. Even his sobs grow louder, each one ratcheting up the tension inside me to another level. "He-he confessed?"

"To your Mariah's demise, yes," Connor says. "However, a decade past, he registered another consort with me, a Jennifer Carson. She will no doubt account for one of the other bodies. Tell Miss Alexander what you told us, Mr. Lipmann."

Moon simply continues sobbing. After a few seconds, Jack kicks the pathetic man in the stomach. The vamp shouts and doubles over in pain. "Lord Connor gave you an order!"

"Is that necessary?" I ask.

Jack glares at me and Connor purses his lips in disapproval. "Yes. It is," Connor says. "Talk, Mr. Lipmann."

Moon lets out a few more sobs before croaking out, "I-I didn't mean to kill her. I didn't."

"Tell Miss Alexander precisely what you told us," Connor instructs again, "or I will remove your tongue and make you write it out in your own blood."

"I...I..." he sobs. "She was going to leave me! She was leaving me! The police questioned her, and she lied, she stayed, but...but we fought again. She was going to call you again. And she was leaving me!"

"The night you and I met, he beat her to death," Connor finishes.

"You son of a bitch," I growl.

"I didn't mean to!" he wails. He looks up at me, pleading with his eyes. "I swear! It was an accident!"

"Six times?" Connor asks.

"Those were...yes. They wouldn't stop bleeding. I-I lost my temper. I was stupid. They...I'm sorry. I'm so sorry."

"Who were they?" I ask.

"I don't know! Just some girls!" Right. Just some girls.

"And Jennifer?" Connor asks.

"I...yes. Jen. Oh, Jen, I'm so sorry," he sobs as he peers away from me again.

"We need names for the other girls," I say. "The others you butchered."

"I didn't know their names! I don't remember—"

"You don't remember the women you murdered?" I spew out.

"I didn't mean to—"

"You didn't mean to," I shout, before grabbing his jaw and forcing his eyes up to mine, "but you did! You killed the sixteen-year-old girl who loved you! Who trusted you! Who wanted nothing more than to spend her life with you! You betrayed her! Then you threw her out like fucking trash! You're a pathetic, weak, selfish, bastard who never, *ever* deserved her!"

"I'm sorry! I'm sorry! I'm sorry!" he sobs and sobs and sobs.

I release his face. I'm so disgusted, so infuriated, I can barely breathe. I can barely do anything but tremble. I take a step back before I give into my deep, deep desire to beat this bastard to death. "No, you're not. You're just sorry you got caught."

"I'm sorry. I'm sorry. I'm sorry," he continues to wail.

"Do you have any other questions for the prisoner?" Connor asks me.

"No. Let's get this over with."

"Very well. Gary 'Moon' Lipmann, I hereby sentence you to death for the murders of your legal consorts Jennifer Carson and Mariah Wilson. Sentence to be carried out immediately."

"No! Please no! Please don't! Please…"

Connor ignores his pleas as Jack reaches over to the nearby table covered with knives, pliers, and other torture instruments, instead picking up the sword. It's huge, easily five feet long, with a gilded hilt. Strangely, Jack holds it out to me. "What?" I ask.

"We assumed you would like the honors," Connor says.

"Y-you want me to…"

"*You* caught him. You wanted justice. Here it is," Connor says. He grabs the sword himself before thrusting it at me. "Take it."

Connor holds out the sword for several seconds, just staring at me. I reach up and take the sword. Jesus, it's heavy. Thirty pounds maybe. It will do the job, no question. A quick smile crosses my face as I twist around and position the sword over Moon's neck. His sobs become full wails. "Please, don't! Please, please, please…" over and over again. I raise the sword, and the bastard gazes up at me, blood dripping from his eyes and cheeks. Pathetic. But suddenly it's as if someone's punched me in the gut. I'm nauseous, pained, and a little frightened. What the…?

He deserves to die. He *needs* to pay for what he did to those women. The world needs to be protected from the likes of him. Then why can't I bring the sword down? I know I'd take almost orgasmic satisfaction as the sword slices through his spine knowing I stopped him. I caught him. *Me.* So just do it, Bea. Kill the bastard.

But something stops me. *I* stop me. I lower the sword and take a step back. "What are you doing?" Connor asks curtly.

"I…can't kill him."

"Why on earth not? I thought this is what you wanted."

"It is. But…I think that's the issue. I want to kill him."

"Then do it! What is the problem? You have killed before," Connor says.

"But not because I *wanted* someone dead. It was always in self-defense, never in cold blood."

"And this is justice," he states plainly.

"No, it's vengeance, Connor. If I do this, it's not for Mariah, it's not for the other girls. I'd be doing it because I *want* to hurt him, to kill him, because it would make me feel good, and taking a life should *never* do that. It's what separates us from…him."

"You put this in motion, Beatrice," Connor says, voice hard. "This was the inevitable outcome. You were correct about him. There is nothing wrong with taking satisfaction in that. In taking pleasure in winning."

I stare at my lover, who believes every word he's said, and get a chill. I have to suppress a shiver. "Is that what it is to you? A game?" I spew out.

"Of course not," he says, but I don't believe him. Another chill. He shakes his head. "Very well. Give me the bloody sword." He snatches it from my hand, and without a moment's hesitation, my enraged boyfriend raises the sword and brings it down on Moon's neck. One slice is all that's required. The head falls onto the tarp as blood spews from his neck until the rest of him flops to the ground too. They claim the brain's still conscious seven seconds after beheading, and as Moon's eyes stare up at me in terror, I believe it. Shuddering, I turn my back on the scene.

"Are you alright, Beatrice?" Connor asks.

I can't look at him either. "I don't…I think I need to sit down."

"Jack, please escort her back to my apartment then return to help Edgar with this mess."

I'm in the downstairs bathroom with the door shut. Not even splashing cold water on my face cleanses me even one percent. I can't look at myself in the mirror. I flop onto the toilet lid and rest my head in my hands, taking deep breaths to try to calm myself.

I barely get out three breaths when there's a knock on the bathroom door. "Beatrice?" Oh, God. Leave me alone. Give me one damn...Connor comes in without an invitation. "Are you alright?" he asks with genuine concern. He kneels in front of me and cups my hands in his. I look up, met with sympathy and concern. I still want to snatch my hands away. "I thought this was what you desired. He deserved his fate, Beatrice. This world is a better place without the likes of Moon Lipmann. You should not feel an ounce of guilt for your part in what occurred tonight. And I am sorry if I caused you distress by asking you to execute him. That was not my intention. Quite the opposite in fact. I thought it would make you happy, and that is all I want to bring you. Happiness. Please forgive me for my behavior tonight and for misjudging you. I am simply not used to being around...the pure hearted. You did my territory a great service catching that fiend. I will find a way to repay you. I promise."

I stare into those violet pools of his, and just feel...tired. Weary. I don't have the strength to push him away as he embraces me. "I think I'm going to get a hotel room tonight."

His cold body stiffens before he releases me. "What?"

"Just for tonight," I assure him. "We've been together every night for over a week. And we keep fighting. I think we're wearing on each other's nerves. I'm sure you've been neglecting your work, and I...I need to be alone." I caress his cheek. "Just for tonight. I really think it'll do us both good."

He opens his mouth, probably to protest, but I give him a quick kiss and rise. I sidestep him out of the bathroom into the living room. My suitcases are right where I left them this afternoon in the corner.

"Or we could fly to London," Connor says behind me. "We could leave tonight. I could even introduce you to Lord Byron. Then onto Paris. Both are beautiful this time of year."

That sounds damn tempting, but I still collect my suitcases. "I thought you said you were too busy for a long vacation."

"I make time for what is important," he says, "and right now there is nothing more important to me than you."

Stay strong, Bea. For once don't give in. Don't. Stick to your damn guns and get the heck out of here. "It's just for tonight, Connor. London and Paris will be there tomorrow night. Here." I set down one of my suitcases. "I'm leaving this here so now I have to come back, okay? And I am coming back." I think. I walk over to my pouting boyfriend and kiss his frowning lips. "I'll call you tomorrow night. I promise. This isn't me walking out. Leave the door unlocked. Will you?"

"Of course," he whispers.

I smile up at him. "Thank you." I give him another quick peck. "Talk to you tomorrow."

I keep my smile plastered on until I'm safely in my car and let out a jagged breath. There was a part of me that wasn't sure he'd let me go. Because we both knew the moment I walked out that door, hell the moment he took that sword from me, things would never be the same between us. Because this isn't fun anymore. It isn't easy. My fault probably. I just had to play detective, bring life and death into our little oasis. But I just couldn't help myself. And I'm actually damn proud of myself that I couldn't. Maybe Carl's right. A true detective can never retire even when she has every reason to.

Why are all my blessings curses?

CHAPTER ELEVEN

UMBRELLA

I've always wanted stay at the Hotel Del Coronado. They filmed one of my favorite movies, *Some Like it Hot*, here. Marilyn, Tony, Jack all graced these halls. I come to the beach nearby all the time, but only set foot inside the hotel to use the bathroom or to buy something to drink. Well, I can cross staying the night off the old bucket list. The only problem is I can't stand being here. Not the hotel's fault—my room's beautiful and room service is wonderful—my fault of course. I managed an hour of alone time before I literally began pacing the room. Every time I stop a flurry of images and thoughts flood in. Mariah's blood covered purse. Connor's sneer. The weight of that damn sword in my eager hands. Moon's decapitated head staring up at me. More than twice I considered returning to Connor's and screwing our brains out until I haven't any energy left to think. Maybe then I could stay still. Why the hell don't I? Something inside stops me from getting in my car. I need to be alone. I need to sort my head out.

I always get like this after we close a case. You go, go, go and then when there's nowhere left to go, it's hard to shift out of overdrive. Normally Oliver and I would drive around and talk about what we'd been through or hit the mall or go to Dave and Busters to get goofy. Twice we convinced almost the whole squad to come along for that last one, save for Chandler, Will, and Rushmore. Even George joined us for some skeeball and karaoke. Those were good nights. God, I miss them. I—

My phone buzzes on the charger. Probably Connor. I'm shocked he hasn't called sooner. I should at least tell him I reached the hotel safely. But the number's isn't Connor. It's a Kansas area code. Shoot, I forgot to call Carl with an update. I pick up. "Hello?"

"Hello, Agent Alexander," Oliver says on the other end.

My stomach clenches at the sound of his melodic voice. I need time to mentally prepare for moments like this. I close my eyes to focus on calming down. "Uh, hi."

"I just got off the phone with Carl. He wanted me to check on you. See if you required further assistance in your murder investigation."

Of course Carl had to call Oliver. Who *isn't* talking about me behind my back? "Actually, no. The matter has been dealt with. I was going to call Carl tomorrow with that update."

"It has not been twenty-four hours since I saw you last, and you have solved a murder? That is impressive even for you, Trixie."

I can't help but smile. "Actually, I solved six but who's counting?"

"Six?"

"A vamp named Moon Lipmann was going full Bluebeard on his teenage lovers."

"My my. And how precisely did you get involved?"

I sit in the lounge chair by the window and sigh before laying out the whole tale, starting at Christmas all the way to the beheading. It just pours out, every embarrassing and gruesome detail. The weight of the ordeal lifts as I get it all off my chest. Oliver doesn't utter a word, even after I stop talking. Several tense, pregnant seconds pass before I ask, "Oliver? Did I lose you?"

"No, I am here," he says solemnly. "I am simply in…awe."

"What? Why? I screwed up, Oliver. I turned my back on that girl and never gave her a second thought. I was just cleaning up my own mess."

"Trixie, you are not the world's designated sin-eater."

"A what?"

"In some societies, when a loved one died, there would be a ritualistic meal where all the sins of the departed would be infused in the food. A family member would then eat the meal, taking on all the transgressions of the person so the deceased could rest in peace. You did all you could for that girl, more than most ever would. *She* chose to stay. *She* chose to ignore the lifeline you threw her. And even still you went above and beyond to bring her justice, to stop other innocents from meeting her fate. How can you feel anything but pride in yourself, is beyond me. So stop flagellating yourself, woman, and take the bloody victory lap you deserve."

God there he goes again. Saying the exact right thing at the exact right time. Forget the super-speed, strength, and near immortality, *that* is his true power. "A victory lap, huh?"

"It is far better than what I know you are doing now, blaming yourself for all the mistakes others made. Do you recall the pusher case in Mississippi? On the flight home all I bloody heard was how you should have suspected the grandson sooner, even though none of us did either. Even though, in the end, it was *you* who proved it was him. Even when we landed you paced around the mansion, beating yourself up—"

"Until you dragged me to the roller rink. We stayed until I could barely breathe, then you sat me down and told me if I didn't stop torturing myself and finally listen to reason you'd steal all my Hitchcock DVDs and change all my internet passwords."

"And you listened and accepted my deserved praise. As you should now. Remember, I still know your Amazon, Netflix, and e-mail passwords, my dear. The threat remains," he says overdramatically. For the first time in a while I actually laugh. "So, take your victory lap, Trixie. Or else."

My smile grows wider. "Okay."

There are several seconds of silence before he says, "Would you care for company on our jaunt?" My smile wanes a little. "That is if Connor trusts you enough to loosen his stranglehold on you for an hour or so."

"Actually I'm on my own tonight. We decided it was time for a night apart."

"*We* decided or you did?"

I roll my eyes. "Really? And you were doing so well."

"Fine. I will not say word one about your paramour unless prompted. I give my word." He pauses. "We always venture out together after a case. This may not have been an official F.R.E.A.K.S. investigation but keeping tradition alive is most important."

"I'm just the only one who'll do karaoke with you."

"And I have been deprived of my guilty pleasure for three months now. Do not make me suffer a moment longer!"

This draws another laugh. I never laugh more than I do when I'm around him. I'd forgotten that. "Okay, fine. You win. I'm at the Hotel Del Coronado, room 205. Come pick me up."

"I am on my way, Trixie. See you soon." He hangs up.

I throw on my black jeans and new silk flowery purple and yellow tunic before slapping on some make-up. Oh I wish there was time to do my hair. A side ponytail will have to do. Cute. Some clunky black jewelry and my black leather motorcycle jacket, and I'm ready. I relax on the bed with the television and wait. Yeah, alone time can be overrated. Guess I just needed away from Connor. Okay, I knew that was the case but how do you tell your boyfriend that? I just hope he doesn't find out. Although we never said we were exclusive. Not that this is a date. It's just...tradition. Yet the television can't fight back the creeping guilt. How would I like it if he were shagging Avril on his desk right now? Okay, not comparable, Bea. There will be no sex tonight. You're not cheating. You're hanging out with a friend. Stop the damn guilt. Try to enjoy yourself. Oliver's right, you've damn well earned it.

About ten minutes after I sit down, there's a knock on my door. My heart leaps into my throat. *He's here!* I shut off the TV and do a quick mirror check. I'm no Heidi Klum but I clean up nicely. Once again, not that it matters. Oliver's seen me with stitches, covered in blood and gore and once— shudder—in a bathing suit. And this is *not* a date. I nod to my reflection and walk to the door. Of course compared to my friend here in the looks department I'm a mucous covered troll. Tonight Oliver's gone casual in black jeans, the buttoned up black and white checkered shirt I bought him, and a cerulean undershirt poking above the collar. Drool. "Hello, my dear," he says, all smiles. "Are we ready?"

"As we'll ever be." I step into the hotel hallway right beside him. Double drool. He always smells so damn good. Fresh cologne with a hint of lavender.

"You have a destination in mind?" he asks.

We start down the hallway side-by-side, our arms grazing one another. "I could go for some air hockey and karaoke."

"You read my mind, dearest."

When we reach his car, a convertible—the only kind of car you should rent in Southern California—he opens my door like a gentleman, even performing a bow. I chuckle at his ridiculous act and roll my eyes. That bit got old months ago but it gained new life when I pointed that fact out. He does love to annoy me. My friend climbs into the car, locates our destination in his GPS, and off we go for a harmless night of fun. It's quite hard to get into a fist fight or grind against a guy at Dave & Buster's even with a few drinks in you. Not that I plan to imbibe tonight. That last hangover is too damn fresh in my memory.

"I'm not allowed to drink tonight," I tell Oliver. "No matter how much I beg, you have to stop me."

"Hard drugs are fine, though?" he asks, mock serious.

I scoff. "Of course. I'm not a saint, Oliver," I say in the same tone. We smile at one another, and I sit back to enjoy the breeze and eighties music he put on especially for me. "Bette Davis Eyes." The day I get sick of this song is the day I was replaced by a pod person. I lip sync to it as Oliver grins. When the song ends, he even applauds. "Thank you, thank you. I'm here all week." We ride a little longer just listening to the music. He keeps stealing glances at me. "What?"

"Just that you look quite fetching tonight, if I am allowed to say so."

"The top's Ralph Lauren. I got it in Vegas," I say.

"You went designer shopping without me? I am wounded. I have not been shopping in months."

"The student has surpassed the teacher," I say with flourish. We smile again. "Why haven't you been shopping? Nancy loved going with us."

"She…has not been herself," he says, the sides of his mouth twitching.

"Yeah, Carl told me about her running away and…you know. Logan. Did you talk to her about it?"

"No."

"Why not? Did *anyone* talk to her? It's kind of a huge deal, Oliver, losing your virginity."

"She is a smart girl. I am sure she knows about contraception," he says.

"It's not just about that. There are emotions involved. A storm of emotion. Fears and guilt and happiness and a billion other thoughts and feelings come up your first time stirs up. And if not you, then who? Out of everyone left, you're the one she's closest to except George and he's like her Dad."

"You sound disappointed in me," he fires back.

"Damn straight I am! She lost Will. Me. Irie. Apparently Rushmore too. She's been acting out like a teenager in pain does, and you did nothing? You're better than that," I say, folding my arms across my chest.

"As always you give me far too much credit."

I roll my eyes. "Oh, don't even. You *know* you are. We both know you're a good, intelligent, empathetic person no matter how hard you pretend you're not, so stop putting yourself down. You know it pisses me off."

Oliver glances at me, the corners of his mouth forming a momentary smile before looking away again. "I will try to refrain. But you should know your absence has caused…much turmoil. Strife. Emotionally and physically. No one is themselves."

"Carl already took me on a guilt trip, okay. I'm sorry you've had to do all the violent heavy lifting in the field. But you have two new werewolf team mates to back you up now."

"They are not you. They do not possess your instincts. Your keen mind. Creativity. *They* could not have accomplished what you did today in less than twenty-four hours. I doubt even our new dictator could either."

"Has Chandler really gotten that bad?"

"A by the book, rigid, control freak with no sense of humor or creative bone in his body leading a traumatized, grieving, understaffed squad of monster hunters? No, it has been a dream. At least Wi—" He stops himself. I know what he was about to say. I'm just glad he didn't.

"Well, if he's so terrible then take over. You have seniority."

"I am no leader, Trixie. I have neither the tools nor the drive to be one either. Unlike Agent Chandler, I recognize that and am man enough to admit it."

"Then Wolfe? One of the rookies?"

"You?" he posits.

My stomach clenches hard enough I grimace. We are not going here tonight. "Okay, topic two off the conversation menu tonight. *That.* No Connor, no more me returning to Kansas. Got it?"

"Assertive. An excellent trait in a leader," he says with grin #2, tips of his fangs showing.

I don't smile back. "I mean it."

"Why? What else do friends converse about besides work and love? The weather?"

"Yes, and isn't it lovely tonight? We're expecting fog tomorrow morning though." This time he doesn't smile. I sigh. "I just don't want a lecture tonight about everything I'm doing wrong in my life. Let's make a deal: I won't lecture you, you won't lecture me."

"Fine. No lectures for either one of us. I can agree to that." He pauses. "So. It is lovely tonight. Too bad I will miss the fog though."

"Ha ha." We ride in silence for a minute. "We're out of practice, aren't we?"

"I do not know. We have already had a chiding, a small argument, and made up all within five minutes. We are right on schedule," he says with grin #1.

"Really? Then what comes next?"

"Rampant flirting, more chiding, followed by flirting, flirting, and more flirting."

"Best get on with it then," I say with a smirk. He returns the gesture. With mine still affixed, I look out the window at the valleys going by. "How did this tradition start? I don't remember."

"You wound me, Trixie," he says mock seriously. "It was on the case right after the Dallas fiasco, with the teenage witch accidentally casting love spells. You were stomping about because of Will's...ill attitude towards you."

"Oh, right. One of our easier cases. A few threats and the girl was scared straight. Would that they were all that simple."

"Was Mr. Lipmann's?"

"A couple hours work, no violence against me. Yeah. Thank goodness," I say.

"I am surprised Connor blessed the endeavor. Six humans murdered by one of his subjects under his nose, perhaps over decades. That will be hard to spin politically, especially in light of his recent Cuban Missile Crisis with Antonia."

"Yeah, he...wasn't exactly thrilled with me when he found out. He more or less ordered I wasn't allowed to take the matter further until he gave me the go ahead."

"So of course you began your investigation the moment he used the word, 'ordered,'" Oliver says with grin #1, full fang.

"It had to be done. Lipmann already had a new girl living with him. Some things can't wait for politics." I pause. "It shouldn't be too bad for him, right? I didn't just hand Antonia cause to break the cease fire, did I?"

"No. Cuba and America can continue plotting behind each other's backs as always. Although it was foolish of Connor to assault her men as he did."

"They attacked us first."

"Only after he uttered every gay slur before going into graphic detail how he intended to violate them," Oliver informs me.

I stare at Oliver. "He did?"

"According to Antonia, yes. And he used the same tactic with me the other night. Five minutes of conversation, pushing my every button, describing your...sex life in pornographic detail, and even I lost my composure. He knew precisely what he was doing. It would not surprise me if he planned both attacks. Antonia is right to worry, even without you in the equation."

"She's worried?"

"Of course. To Antonia, having you firmly on Connor's side is the equivalent of Castro possessing the Death Star."

"Why? I don't have anything against her. I want no part of their little squabble. I'm just his...friend."

"A friend who helped remove the Lord of Dallas from power. Who slew over a dozen vampires in the course of a day. Who can kill any lifeform on this planet with a mere thought, vampires included. And you are sharing the bed and physically defending her sworn enemy. Anyone in her position would be concerned. *I* am concerned."

"Why? Do you think she'd hurt me?"

"It is not Antonia I am weary of, Trixie," he chuckles wryly. "Forget me and Antonia. The man almost goaded you into committing cold blooded murder tonight."

"Someone had to carry out the sentence. Connor thought I should be the one to see the job through," I say.

"Yes, it was for *your* benefit. It had nothing to do with the fact you would literally have blood on your hands, under his authority. That you would have literally killed for him. With him claiming to have authorized the investigation, for all intents and purposes you would be part of his organization. Officially."

"It wasn't like that."

"*This* is why I am concerned, Trixie. You are playing chess with Bobby bloody Fischer and Spasky at the same time thinking the whole time you are playing Checkers. Worse, Fischer had asked you to bet your body, your soul, your friends' lives on the game all the while toying with you, letting you believe you are winning."

I don't want to hear this. "I thought I made it clear Connor was off limits."

He glances at me, takes in the slight scowl and tilted head, and knows me well enough to discontinue this conversation. He turns back to the road. "Fine."

"Thank you." Great, now the warm fuzzies have blown away leaving a slight, uncomfortable chill between us. It's as if a thousand tiny icicles prickle my skin. Judging from his set mouth and slightly hung head, he senses it too. I've hurt him. I know him as well as he knows me. We ride in uncomfortable silence for a few seconds before I can't take it anymore. "What? Say it. Just say it already!" I snap.

"You...used to trust me. That is all."

Shit. That's not all, that's...everything. I want to tell him I do, because I think I still do, but go with the truth instead. "Don't take it personally. It's not...you. I don't think I can trust anything or anyone anymore. Myself included."

More silence, then, "Truly? Because in five centuries I do not believe I have ever trusted or respected anyone more," he states as plain fact. "I suppose I will simply have to show you what I see."

"Which is?"

"Though much is taken, much abides; and though
We are not now that strength which in the old days
Moved earth and heaven; that which we are, we are,
One equal-temper of heroic hearts,
Made weak by time and fate, but strong in will
To strive, to seek, to find, and not to yield.
-Tennyson."

"You think that's me?" I ask.

"Oh, yes," he says without a shred of doubt. "And I shall make you believe it as well." He looks me square in the eye, gorgeous pure smile just for me on his perfect face. "Until my dying day and beyond."

For the second time in less than a day the butterflies, the flames spread through me in a moment of exquisite, pure, radiant joy. "I've missed you," I whisper, voice cracking a little. "I've missed you so freaking much."

"I am positive it is nowhere near as much as I have missed you, my darling," he whispers back. Oliver takes my hand and presses it to his lips. "Nowhere near."

Impossible.

*

"Still got it."

I slip the plastic gun back in its holster and step away from the arcade game. I so prefer killing zombies this way, just for the lack of the stench alone.

"You cheated," Oliver says.

"The heck I did. And you're one to talk Mr. 'No I'm not using my supernatural vampire reflexes' during air hockey."

"I am wounded you think so little of me. Cheating? Me? Never," he says dramatically.

I chuckle. "Knew it, you dirty, dirty cheater man."

"Well, you are more than welcome to take me somewhere private, pull down my trousers, and spank me for my transgressions," he says with grin #1. "Repeatedly. For hours. And *hours*."

I keep chuckling but know my cheeks turn red and warm. "*Or* we can get me something to drink. Killing zombies always makes me parched."

"I like my suggestion better."

Me too. "Come on." My stomach gurgles. "Actually, can you order me a Sprite? I have to use the bathroom," I say to Oliver.

"Of course."

"Be right back."

I hustle to the toilet. That room service food I had earlier has not been kind. As I'm washing my hands, my phone buzzes. Again. I check it and of course it's Connor. One voice mail and two texts in an hour. I haven't listened or read them. Fudge it. I shut the phone off completely. Hopefully he'll just think I went to bed.

I return to the bar where Oliver sits on a stool oblivious to the fact ninety percent of the patrons surrounding him steal covert glances or downright stare to get the hunk's attention. Par for the course when I'm out with him. I sit on the stool beside him as couples enjoy their dinners and a teenage girl butchers "Material Girl" with her friends clapping for her in a nearby booth. The food may not be gourmet, but I have never left Dave & Buster's without a smile. Just lots of people having fun being silly. Better than Prozac.

"Is all well?" Oliver asks, sliding the Sprite my way.

"Fine. I know better than to mix fries and caffeine. I should be okay now." I sip my soda. "So. What now? More skeeball? We might have enough tickets to claim a mustache comb with one more game."

The bartender walks over to Oliver with a mug of beer. "Compliments of the lovely ladies down the bar."

I glance over at the pretty blondes giggling to one another as they wait for Oliver's reaction, which is none. If the man actually drank he would have died of cirrhosis years ago from all the drinks people in bars send his way.

"Please thank them for me," Oliver says.

I glare at the women, raise an eyebrow, and throw my arm over Oliver's shoulders, claiming him. The women share a familiar look—what the hell is he doing with her—then begin whispering about me. To his considerable credit when we're out alone together he keeps the flirting with other women to a minimum. I guess he saves that for when he's out alone.

Oliver chuckles and I lower my arm. "What?" I ask.

"Nothing. Simply…I do adore it when your jealously comes out to play."

"I've told you before. It's not jealousy. It's…the rude don't get to win. And at least I didn't put the vampire whammy on them like you did that guy in Oklahoma who flirted with me."

"*He* was insufferable. Even you thought so." Grin #2, some fang, forms on his lips. "And if you need to tell yourself jealousy plays no part in your proprietary actions, by all means do. Just do not cease such actions. It will lead me to believe you do not care." The grin falters a little. "I have experienced those doubts enough for several lifetimes, thank you very much."

I don't know what to say. My stomach clenches as I stare at his slightly crumbling face. He's trying to keep the evening light, but I can read his face like a book. "Oliver, I never—"

"Oliver M, come on up!" someone says over the loudspeaker.

We both peer around for the source, both landing on the man by the karaoke machine waving my friend over. I glance back to Oliver. His happy mask is back. "Oh, I forgot to mention. I signed us both up for a song each." He slides off his stool. "And I hereby invoke my right to throw down the gauntlet."

My eyes narrow. "No."

"Yes," he says with grin #1, full fang, before backing toward the stage.

"Not here! I live here!"

"The gauntlet is down. We must abide by the edict!"

"Oliver..." I hiss before groaning.

He climbs onto the small stage and takes the microphone. "This tune is for the only person in this world I would make a total fool of myself for simply to put a smile on her beautiful face. Enjoy the show my dearest darling. Do not forget to smile. Maestro, if you please?"

It hasn't even begun, and I already have a darn smile.

Oh, God. This is my own fault. On one of my drunker nights out I dared Oliver to get onstage and not only sing Katy Perry's "California Girls" but perform the dance moves from the *Just Dance* video game too. He agreed, only if I did the same to "Hey Ya." I was practically rolling on the floor watching him act as if he were on *Celebrity Lip Sync Battle* but as I did the same with my song, shaking everything like a polaroid picture. It became a thing when Carl, Wolfe, and Nancy came out with us and Oliver "threw down the gauntlet" to us all. I got a stich in my side laughing as Carl discoed out to "Dancing Queen."

"Never Gonne Give You Up" by Rick Astley begins playing and there he goes. Oliver has many, many talents but singing is not one of them. He's a better dancer, but this song doesn't give him much to work with. In the game there's just lots of pointing, spinning, blowing kisses, and posing like a superhero, all of which he performs with a serious expression and gusto. Yet there isn't a person in the room without a grin or laugh escaping them, me included even when I'm shaking my head and hiding my face in embarrassment. He is such a dork, at least around me. I've infected him with my silliness.

As the song ends, he blows me one last kiss and leaps off the stage like Superman, all to uproarious applause and hooting. He bows to his adoring fans and swans toward me, smug smile affixed.

"O-kay, well, that's a tough one to top," the MC says. "Up next we have Trixie. Come on up and show us what you got."

Oliver's smug smile grows. "Your turn."

"I hate you," I whisper as I get off my stool.

"I think circumstances have proved that is an impossibility."

I sneer at him before walking to the stage. If he chose some song like "Afternoon Delight" or "Like A Virgin" I may actually commit cold blooded murder tonight. I take the microphone and breathe a sigh of relief when Rhianna's "Umbrella" cues up. This is the one song I get a higher score on when we're playing the video game. I've never sung it outside of my car before, and I've never danced sober, but here goes.

I zero in on my challenger. He is the only person in this room. My beautiful, beaming best friend. I remember every dance move from our nights in front of the Wii. Within seconds I completely forget I should be embarrassed. I just give into the words and the ridiculous amount of fun I'm having making an ass out of myself for him. Rhianna couldn't do it better. The reason he chose this song dawns on me during the first chorus. I put as much heart into the words as I can. When the song ends and I perform my last shimmy, Oliver's the first one off his stool, giving me a standing ovation with such pride I've never seen in anyone's eyes before. It makes me feel lighter than air.

Everyone else liked the show too because even the rude blondes applaud. I take a bow before returning to my friend, who just scoops me up in his arms for a huge hug. "You are such a jerk," I say, hugging him back. "I adore you as well." He kisses the top of my head. "My ungrateful umbrella girl."

*

After three more rounds of Skeeball—and me winning him a My Little Pony sticker set—the busy day finally catches up with me, and I begin to yawn. It's well past midnight and has been a hell of a day. I worry I'll fall asleep as Oliver drives me back to my hotel. God, the last thing I want is for the night to end though. I know the feeling's mutual. We sit in the car in the hotel parking lot for several seconds. "Do you want to take a walk on the beach?" I ask.

"You read my mind," Oliver says with grin #1.

We follow the path past the hotel to the beach and stroll in the moonlight side-by-side with only those lapping waves making a sound. Huh. Like a week ago I was in this very spot asking for him to help me. And here he is. By my side. Guess you can sometimes get what you need.

I didn't realize there's a full moon tonight. I barely used to notice the moon, and after Will I hated the damn thing. I don't think it'll ever be just the moon to me ever again. Especially a full moon. Right now there are hundreds of werewolves around the world running with their packs or locked up in cells to protect the people they love from themselves. I watched Will in a cell once. It was torture for him, and downright disgusting at times for me. That would have been my life once a month until the day I died, but I would have done it. I loved him enough to clean up his piss and shit and ectoplasm covered fur while he tried to maul me all night. *That's* what I see when I stare at the moon.

"Beautiful night," Oliver says.

For a moment I had forgotten he was here. I suddenly remember the last full moon we experienced together. He was furious Will and I were together. He lost his temper, forced me to kiss him, then tried to force me toward my enraged werewolf boyfriend. I never knew Oliver was capable of purposely hurting me. Of course not a week later I assaulted him and locked him in a freezer just for attempting to talk sense into me. And that same night he risked his life to save the man I loved...for me. Yet here we are, goofing off, talking, hugging as if nothing happened. We only get a few friendships like that in a lifetime, and that's if we're lucky. I have two and despite my best efforts, they're still intact. I could call April up right now and with a simple "I'm sorry," it'd be like old times. Everyone screws up but only the best of us can forgive and forget. Not just for our own sakes either. Forgiveness can be almost as powerful as love. Sometimes it *is* love.

"Penny for your thoughts," Oliver says, nudging me with his shoulder.

"I was just thinking about forgiveness. I want to..." I stop walking and face him, "I'm sorry for how I treated you the night you arrived and for last night. I shouldn't have...it wasn't you. None of it was *you*. Ever. Since the beginning, since we first met, you have been..." Damn it. I gaze down, hoping maybe the right words are there. They aren't. There aren't enough words in all the languages combined to express what this man means to me. I shake my head. "I'm sorry. I'm truly sorry. The last thing in this damn world I want is to cause someone I lo—care about a moment of pain. And it's like that is all I'm capable of doing right now. I'm not fit for human consumption. I'm just so...*furious* and sad and frustrated and frightened and I want to cry and punch and scream and crawl into a ball and never move again every second of every day since I..." My mouth snaps shut. I'm not—

"Say it." I look up at Oliver, whose face is as serious as cancer. His eyes bore into mine. "*Say it.*"

"Since I...almost got you killed. Since I...murdered Will," I say, voice cracking.

His expression doesn't change. "Is that what you truly believe transpired that night? That you threw me to the wolves and murdered your fiancée? That every crime that occurred that night was due to you?" he asks, voice hard.

"Oliver..." I look away.

"My actions, all our actions that night, were our own. *I* chose to chase after William. Patricia Winsted chose to rape and murder men—"

"And *I* chose to pull that trigger. I chose to—"

"Save my life. You chose to save my life from the mad, wild animal literally ripping the flesh from my bones. Tearing out my throat. Letting me bleed out like a stuck pig. If it were anyone else but William would you have felt a kernel of guilt?"

"But it was," I say. "It was."

"*That* was not William, Trixie. That was Patricia Winsted's monster. A soulless beast wearing William's skin. He was gone the moment she enchanted him."

"But she never should have had the opportunity, Oliver. She was there, in front of me, the whole time. I was just so distracted, I wasn't paying attention. She was *right there*, and I—"

"You were not the only one working the case, Trixie. You are not the only one to bear the responsibility. Even William—"

"*No*," I growl, even pointing my finger in his face. "Don't you dare—"

"Say he should have remained at mobile command or recused himself from the case the moment he realized he was susceptible to her influence? Or perhaps I should point out he should have been able to withstand her magic or come to his senses when faced with the power of true love?"

"Stop."

"Or fought through his madness, his bloodlust, his animal nature the moment he laid eyes on you whilst he feasted on my liver?"

"Stop," I hiss as I move away from him.

"Perhaps you simply did not love him enough," Oliver continues. "Perhaps you failed to make him believe you truly loved him. Perhaps, deep down, he knew how weak, how damaged, how ugly you are and wanted simply to get away from you by any means necessary."

I spin around to face this hateful man. "Stop it! Why are you saying these things?"

"Because you are thinking them," he says, voice steady as he takes a step toward me. "Because they are possessing your mind. Your soul. Because you are drowning in them. These-these bloody ridiculous thoughts that have no basis in reality. And William would agree with me. I loathed the man at times. He was boorish, uncreative, ornery, and treated you like manure for months because he was too weak, too frightened to reveal his true feelings to you. But I do not doubt his love for you. The moment you arrived, he sparked to life. He smiled. He laughed. He softened. He dreamed. He hoped. *He adored you.* Fleeting though they were, you provided him with some of the happiest days of his life. And he would destroy himself if he knew how you have been behaving because of him. Torturing yourself. Burying your justified anger and choking on your misplaced guilt. Let it out, Trixie. You have every right, *every right* to be angry, even at him."

"You think I'm angry at *Will?*" I spew.

"No, I think you are *furious* at him, and that is the root of all this madness. You are enraged and you are guilty for feeling that way, which in turn spurns more fury. You are the ourobourus eating its own tail."

"That's nuts. *He* was victim in all this. Th-that bitch turned him into her slave. He didn't know what he was doing. He couldn't help himself. Literally."

"And I literally almost died at his hands. You still literally had to put him down like the mad dog she made him." Oliver steps toward me, so close I doubt there's an inch between us. "Darling, it is not rational, but when have emotions ever been rational? When has life? When has naught to do with love?" He gazes down into my eyes. "I am asking you, I am *begging* you my darling, you have to forgive him. And you have to begin forgiving yourself. You have to embrace your anger. Let it out. Let it go. Unshackle yourself from his corpse, crawl out of his suffocating grave, and scream to the heavens. Let whoever is listening hear your primal rage and let that fury spark you back to life. If not for me, if not for your family, for April, then do it for yourself. Do it for William. Let the man rest in peace knowing he did not kill you that night because if you do not do this, he will have in all but body."

I already have tears in my eyes, all my muscles have knotted, and I can barely breathe. The weight's too much. I can't move. I can't think. I just want to crawl into a ball and hide. "I don't think I can—"

"You can do this," Oliver says with absolute certainty. "You know you can do this." He caresses my wet cheek and smiles. "You *have* to do this. Just let it go, my darling. Let him go and come back to us. *Please*."

Staring into those loving, determined eyes, experience the soft touch of his thumb caressing my cheek, that same spark from last night rekindles, burning inside me. I can do this. I can do this for him. Twice he walked into certain death, once to save my life and once to save my spirit. I can goddamn well do this for him. My dark angel. My best friend.

I close my eyes and step away, turning my back on him. I open them and stare up at that moon. "Will, I…" I croak. "I-I don't know if you can hear me. I don't know if you're listening. Of course listening to me was never one of your strong suits," I chuckle as I wipe a tear away. "I-I hope you are now. I hope whoever else is out there, God, the universe, whoever, is listening too because…I have a lot to say, and I only want to say it once. But to Will, I…I loved you. I loved you the only way I could, with my all. We would have had a good life. You would have been a good husband. An even better father. You would. And I am so-sorry for the part I played in taking those experiences away from you," I say, voice as brittle as the rest of me right now. "I am so sorry, Will. You didn't deserve what happened to you, what she did to you. What she made you do. You were a good man. A great man. And a part of me will...love you until the day I die. You were my first love. And you helped me believe I was worthy of love in return. Thank you for that gift, Will Price. Thank you."

I swallow my tears, gaze down, and take a few breaths to buy me time to find the courage to say this. "But...*fuck you.*"

I stare up at the moon again, my scowling mouth trembling. "It may not be fair but fuck you. Fuck you for every time you pulled away from me. Fuck you for making me question if I was a good agent. Because I am. I was even better than you and that fucking killed you. Fuck you for every time you left the room when I walked in. Fuck you for treating me like shit for fucking months because you were too proud to admit you were jealous. Fuck you for not kissing me the thousand times you wanted to. Fuck you for always pushing me away because you couldn't admit you loved me. Fuck you for making me fall in love with you. Fuck you for not being strong enough to fight that psycho bitch. I was there, right fucking there, begging, pleading. Did you even try? Did you even try to fight for us, because that's all *I* did. And fuck you for that. Fuck you for the million opportunities you never took that would have never put us in her path. We could have been married right now. Had a baby on the way. But you took that from me too, you son of a fucking bitch!

"I would have done, I *did* everything I could for us! Me! And it wasn't enough for you! You couldn't do one goddamn thing for me! I *begged*. I was right there in front of you, begging for you to stop, to leave her, and you wouldn't! You wouldn't listen. You *never* listened. You were killing my best friend and you wouldn't fucking listen! And fuck you for hurting a hair on my best friend's head! *He* didn't deserve that either! So fuck you! Fuck you William Price for making me pull that trigger! Fuck you for dying and taking our children and our life with you! Fuck you for leaving me alone in this fucking fucked up world with nothing but guilt and shame and anger left! Fuck you, fuck you, FUCK YOU!" I shriek at the top of my lungs until there's no air left in them. Until my shaking legs cannot support myself, and I fall to my knees in the sand still shouting.

The sobs begin a second later, huge wracking sobs I can't control. Oliver's arms scoop me up from behind, and I fall against his body as I just sob and sob as he pets my hair and hugs me a sweet lullaby until I'm all cried out. Until I'm empty of sorrow. Of guilt. Of anger. Until I'm no longer suffocating and can breathe in the crisp, clean ocean air once more. Until there's nothing left but peace and gratitude for the man holding me. I never want him to let me go. And he won't. Not when I've just found my way back to him, the one who believes in me even when I don't believe in myself. Only *he* could make me a believer.

CHAPTER TWELVE

THE MOTH AND THE FLAME

I don't know which is worse: an alcohol hangover or emotional hangover. With either one it's almost impossible to drum up the energy to get out of my luxury hotel bed in the morning. I only have the drive to order room service and pad to the bathroom when needs be. The question becomes around noon do I extend my stay another night or check out. Since I don't think I can leave in time for check out, I choose to buy another night whether I use the room or not. It's only money.

It's only after my second order of room service at lunch that I even begin to feel human again. It's like after a massage. When you begin there are all these stress knots but after the massage the knots are gone but working them out released lactic acid, leaving you sore for days. Get through those days and you're home free. Suppose it's the same with emotional knots. My body has emotional poison pumping through, working its way out, but it's a good pain. A necessary pain. I don't know, I feel almost…free. Cleansed. As if my soul doesn't weigh several tons and I'm carrying it around like a quarry full of boulders anymore. How did he know? How does he always know the exact right thing to say or do? How does he know what I need even when I don't? Centuries around humans no doubt. For once I'm glad I'm so damn predictable. Maybe he can tell me what I'll do next because I have no freaking clue.

I'm still exhausted mid-afternoon but bored to tears. It's been awhile since I've been this exhausted. Oliver had to practically carry me back to my room. He put me in bed, removed my shoes, tucked me in, and I think I was asleep before he even left. Such a gentleman. I need to think of a way to thank him. I already have to name every one of my eighteen children after him at this point. Right now all I can do is apologize until my gums bleed. To Nana and April too. The Beatrice Alexander Apology Tour should begin today. Before I lose my nerve.

After forcing myself out of bed and into some clothes, white capris and royal blue blouse, I trudge to my car and leave the Coronado. I want to pick up a few things from home. Of course my resolve wanes when I see Nana's car in the driveway. Crap. I shut off my Mercedes and just sit for a few seconds. I can do this. I need to do this. She's gotten the worst of it from me in the past months. I have to begin making amends. For both our sakes. With a sigh, I climb out of the car.

Nana's sitting at the dining room table working on a puzzle with a courtroom show playing on the TV when I let myself in. She peers over at me, and once I see the smile on her round face, my nerves wane. "Hi…Nana," I say.

"Honey Bea," Nana says as she rises. "Are you okay?"

"Yeah. I'm good. I'm fine. I'm sorry I…worried you." I pause to gather my strength. "That's, uh, actually why I stopped by. I came to…I had a sort of epiphany last night. A come to Jesus moment, Mrs. Rodriguez would call it. I've been horrid. A total cow these past few months. Worse, I knew I was doing it. I knew I was treating you like crap, but I couldn't stop myself. I didn't even want to. No one has the right to hurt people no matter how angry they are, especially the people they love."

"I didn't take it personally, Bea. I knew it wasn't about me."

"It still wasn't right. Especially how I behaved the other night. Both other nights," I chuckle wryly. "I was horrible to you at April's then again when I got back from Vegas."

"You were surprised," Nana offers.

"No excuse. I even knew you'd done it to help me, and I still yelled at you. I still walked away without a word. I didn't let you know where I was going. I didn't call after that. I've been selfish. And I'm sorry. I love you. I am...*so* sorry."

"Honey Bea, what you've been through, what you had to do..." she moves toward me. "You talked about it a little, but I had no idea just how horrific what happened was. How Will was brainwashed, kidnapped, how you beat then freed a suspect trying to find him. How you saved Oliver's life doing what you did. How you begged and pleaded and how Will still didn't listen. Oliver told me *everything*, even what you endured before Will. Your first case. What happened to the squad, and how you were caught in the middle. What happened to Steven the night he died. What you've been through, honey, I'm surprised you're not barking mad."

"He told you...everything?"

"Yeah. And I'm so glad he did. It helped me understand you more. He's a good man. He cares about you a great deal."

"I know. I think you were right to...welcome him here. So I apologized to him, and now I'm apologizing to you. I was caught off guard and didn't handle the situation well. I'm sorry. Again."

"I forgive you. Of course I forgive you. Come here."
She hugs me. Tight. I swear sometimes hugs are better than
sex. I embrace her back. "I love you. *So* much. You are so
loved, Beatrice. Please don't ever forget that. All we say, all
we do, comes from a place of love."

"I know, Nana."

She releases me and cups my face in her hands before
kissing my nose. "You're a good girl, Bea. You deserve to be
happy. And now you just have to decide where you'll find that
happy."

"I thought it'd be with Will," I say. "I wanted it to be
with Will. I have no idea what will make me happy now. I
don't even know if I have any happiness left in me."

"Of course you do. It just needs a spark to come back
to life and a little help stoking the embers. If that means going
back to Kansas with Oliver or staying here and teaching again,
I support you either way."

"That's the problem. I don't know what will make me
happy. But I guess, at least, I kind of want to find out now."

Nana smooths my hair, cups my cheeks, and kisses my
forehead again. "I'll start dinner, okay? Spaghetti? You'll
stay?"

"Yeah. Sounds great. Or I can make it. My culinary
skills are getting rusty."

"You don't—"

"I want to. You sit. Finish your puzzle. Let *me* take
care of *you* tonight."

I kiss her forehead and move to the kitchen. I haven't cooked beyond microwaving in months. We tried to take turns making dinner for the whole squad in Kansas but with all our erratic schedules and cases I only cooked two to three times a month. Usually it was spaghetti or hamburgers with french fries, nothing special. I didn't have the energy since getting back to San Diego to even try, but the skill quickly comes back. I actually feels good, accomplishing something concrete and having the proof of my work. It even tastes good.

I'm cleaning up the dishes when my phone buzzes in my pocket. Oh, fudge. Connor. I was hoping…well, maybe later. I let it go to voice mail and finish the dishes. Of course all the joy from dinner wanes after that call. I've managed to put him out of my mind all day, now here he is. Waiting on my phone. Sometimes technology really sucks.

I excuse myself to my bedroom and shut the door. I could be a coward. Never call him back. Send an e-mail asking he bring my suitcase back here when I'm out. But the truth is I don't know if I want to end things. The relationship always had an expiration date, we both knew that. Or at least I hope *he* does. But I like him. If we slow things down considerably then that expiration date could be months in the future unless I return to Kansas and…okay, did that thought just enter my brain? *Go back?* No. Hell no.

But—

Stop! I don't care that most of the time I freaking loved the job. That I miss the squad something fierce. That I was damn exceptional at it. That it sounds like they're falling apart. That it gave me a sense of purpose as if God himself were speaking to me. That not going back might mean I'll only see my best friend once or twice a year, if that. All or nothing. That's what we are, and we can't be nothing. But it's not worth it. The broken bones, the watching people I care about die, the terror, remember that, Bea? You joined to gain control of your gift. You've done that. You can go back to teaching. You can go on Match.com and find a husband. Have children. It could still happen. Of course the idea of returning to teaching makes me physically grimace and the last time I tried dating someone normal he turned out to be a sociopath. Maybe April's right. I am attracted to darkness. Will had it. Connor sure as heck does. Oliver—

Okay, stop. Jesus. *Connor*. Focus on Connor.

I will not be a coward anymore. He's been good to me. If we are over then he deserves a face-to-face talk. Plus I really don't want to peeve off the ruler of San Diego if I can help it.

I listen to his message. "Hello, Beatrice. I was merely calling to check in on you. I hope all is well. I am thinking of you. Especially certain parts of you," he purrs. "Please phone me back. There is actually something I wish to discuss with you, something mutually beneficial to us both. I hope you will find my proposition amenable. So…please…phone me back. I wait with baited breath. Good-bye."

God, he sounds so sincere. I press re-dial and he picks up on the second ring.

"Connor McInnis."

"Hi, it's Bea," I say.

"Hello," he says almost cheerfully. "It is wonderful to hear your dulcet voice. How are you? Where are you?"

"I'm visiting my grandmother. We just ate dinner."

"Lovely. You sound well. A night away seems to have done you wonders."

"It did."

"Well, perhaps I can improve your mood further. I want to show you something."

"Is this the mutually beneficial proposal you mentioned in your voice message? Is it business or personal?" I ask.

"Which option will grant me an audience?" he asks.

I shake my head and smile. "Just so you know I'm staying at my hotel again tonight. Or my grandmother's."

"Perhaps I can change your mind. But will you meet me?" Connor asks.

Maybe when we meet face-to-face I'll know what to do. "Okay. Where?"

"I can send a car—"

"No, just give me an address. I can drive myself."

"Very well. Do you have a pen?" He gives me an address in downtown San Diego. "I shall meet you there in an hour."

"Okay. See you then. Bye." I hang up.

Why is my whole body tense? Probably because this is a bad idea. He won't hurt me, at least not physically. I just don't want any drama. I've confronted enough unpleasantness lately, I'm not sure I can handle a drop more. But I'm doing this. No more hiding.

Getting past Nana proves easier than I thought. We chat a little while watching *Jeopardy*—I know exactly one answer—but I keep my eye on the clock and hand on my cell phone. I'm surprised Oliver hasn't called to check on me. Maybe he's waiting for me at the hotel. Crud, should I call *him*? After the meeting with Connor. I'm sure we'll have lots to discuss after. Or if he calls before. Okay, *if* he calls before I leave the house, I'm not going. He can come watch *Jeopardy* with us. Nana probably likes him more than she likes me right now anyway.

But he doesn't. I don't get off that easy. I tell Nana I'm going back to the hotel. Not a lie exactly, I'm just taking a detour on the way. A strange detour at that. The GPS leads me downtown to the Gaslamp District, just a few blocks from the club. After parking in a structure, I have to check the address because I find myself at a vacant storefront between a clothing boutique and upper-end furniture store. Both of those have people inside so I don't think he called me here to murder me. My destination is all white walls and wooden floor.

There's a light on inside the empty shop, so I try the door. It's open. "Hello?" I call.

A second later Connor steps out from the back room, holding a folder, as always looking dapper in designer black jeans, white V-neck t-shirt, black vest, and necklaces just like the night I met him and most of our nights in Vegas. Rock star casual. Dumping him loses a few points. He smiles that crinkly eyed smile of his and there goes another point. My libido only gets a third of the vote though. "You came," he purrs in that accent. Another point.

"Of course," I say.

He strides toward me, smile never wavering. The kiss, a mere peck on the lips, adds another point. Oh, crap. Let reason prevail. I do kiss him back. He steps away first. "I missed you last night," he says. "I did have the opportunity to catch up on work, though. You have been bad for business, fairest."

"*Me* corrupting *you*. Bet you didn't see that coming," I quip with a smile.

"Now there is that beautiful smile of yours," he says with his own growing. "I was concerned after last night's…unpleasantness, I would never see it again."

"The wonders of a good night's sleep and room service in bed," I say, my smile wavering. Not a total lie.

"Wonders indeed. And I am honored you were willing to leave your little paradise to meet with me. Especially after my abysmal behavior last night and the night before. You were following your moral code. I am simply not used to being with someone with such a code. I am also not used to people disobeying me. My yes men and women have dulled my conflict resolution and empathy skills."

"So there's been no blowback like you feared?" I ask.

"No. Not yet anyway. I have managed to keep the situation relatively quiet. Not even a mention in the newspaper. The police have ID'd half the bodies, including your Mariah. Once the selfish anger passed, I realized...how impressive what you accomplished was."

"Thank you. And you have to know I didn't pursue it or leave last night to punish you. I—"

He raises his hand to stop me. "Of course I do. And you were correct once more. We did require a night apart. To breathe so to speak," he says with a quick smile. "To think. And it occurred to me I am not as adept at modern courting as I believed I was. I have not seriously wooed a woman in decades. Before women's liberation even. My past paramours were more than content with the parties, the gossip, the trips. You require more. I even respect that," he says with a smile. "Which leads me to my proposal." I raise an eyebrow. "It is not that sort of proposal, I assure you. This is strictly business." He glances around the store. "What do you think of this space?"

I peer around too. It's medium sized, good lighting, good location. "It has potential, but I'm no expert. Why?"

"Because I have an eye to turn this space into an independent book shop, and I want *you* to build it from the ground up. To run it. With all the big shops closing, independents are on the rise fiscally speaking. The big bookshops that remain used to be community oriented but now they barely sell books. I envision this store as filling that gap. We would sell coffee, books, but also host author events. Live music. Poetry readings. Book clubs. We would turn it into an intellectual salon worthy of Gertrude Stein herself."

"And you want me to play Gertie?" I chuckle. "Connor, I don't know the first thing about running a store let alone building one from the ground up."

"I would put you in contact with consultants already on my payroll. I have almost two dozen small businesses— clothing, restaurants, art galleries—that the team have built. They know codes, permits, vendors, and you would work closely with them."

"If you have them then why do you need me?"

"Because I doubt a one of them has ever cracked open a novel, let alone attended an author reading. Do you know why so many businesses fail? The one thing they lack?"

"Luck?" I posit.

"*Passion.* Love of what one does. It sustains you during the dark times. It drives you even whilst naught but fumes remain. This would be your shop. I would remain a silent partner, purely a financial backer and sounding board should you require one."

"You'd be my boss?"

"Partner," he insists, "one you can buy out or walk away from at any time. I will put that in the contract."

I stare at my boyfriend for a few seconds. He does paint a pretty picture no doubt. It's practically a Monet. It's a wonderful offer. Almost a dream come true. But deep down it feels a little like the snake offering Eve an apple. "And you just came up with this idea last night?"

"No. I had my consultants begin their research whilst we were in Las Vegas after you mentioned you could not find a bookstore anywhere. Their reports, which I have right here, are yours to peruse." He hands me the file he holds, his finger lightly brushing my own. "Of course it may be better if you return to my apartment so we can review them together."

Oh, God. I came here for clarity but now my mind's cloudier than ever. I want to go with him, listen as he sells me on this amazing opportunity between rounds of cunnalingus, but I find myself saying, "Not tonight, okay? I still...need time. Especially now," I say, holding up the file.

"I understand. I am disappointed, but I understand. I can be most distracting," he says with that damn eye crinkly grin.

"You certainly are," I say with a matching grin.

"I would be even more distracting in Paris," he says. "*That* offer always remains."

There goes another point. I do want to see Paris. Okay, *why* was I ever considering breaking up with this man? Luxury trips, great sex, now my very own bookstore? He's whipped up another Monet. I just... "One offer at a time, Danny Boy, and business should always be gotten out of the way first."

He fake pouts. "An excellent mind frame for a business partner, terrible one for a lover. I am both impressed and annoyed."

"I live to keep things interesting."

"And you succeed." He smiles again. "Well, at the very least, allow me to walk you to your car. In this instance I will not take no for an answer."

"How almost very gentlemanly of you. Okay."

"Give me one moment." He turns and walks to the back room. Just to the car, Bea. That's as far as he's getting tonight. The lights shut off and a moment later Connor returns wearing a leather jacket. Just to the car, Bea. "Ready, fairest?"

I do allow him to slide his arm around my waist after he locks the door. He glances over his shoulder before smiling at me and holding on as I start us toward the car. Dang, he even smells lovely, like expensive cologne. Just to the car, Bea. Just to the car.

We round the corner and he glances back over his shoulder again. This time his body tenses beside mine, and he squeezes my waist tighter. "Beatrice, do you have a weapon on you?" Connor whispers, barely audible even with his lips pressed to my ear.

"What?" I whisper back.

"I fear we are being followed," he whispers. "A vampire. I noticed him milling around the store before you arrived. Now laugh."

I let out a little giggle, but inside I'm battle ready. F.R.E.A.K.S. training proves handy again. Every muscle tenses, my senses heighten, and my mind begins on strategies. I don't have a weapon except my power, which is all I really need. There are people on the streets so he won't attack, I don't think. "Are you sure, darling?" I ask gaily.

"Not completely," he says, "but we shall see, no?"

We act the happy carefree couple strolling down the sidewalk as I keep an eye on our shadow in the glass of the storefronts. He's about ten steps behind. Tall, bald, Latino, talking on his phone or pretending to as he glances up at us. I rest my head on Connor's shoulder. "What should we do?" I whisper.

"Get to your car," he whispers back.

"I'm not leaving you alone to deal with this."

"This is not your fight," he whispers.

"I am not leaving you alone," I hiss.

Connor squeezes my waist again and kisses my cheek. The vampire's still behind us half a block later. What's his game? Wait until we're isolated then pounce? We can use that to our advantage. The two-story parking structure is in sight. A good a place as any. But when we turn right toward the structure, Baldie turns left. I breathe a literal sigh of relief. When we walk into the structure, I say, "He's gone."

Connor looks back before smiling at me. "Thank you."

"What for?"

"For refusing to leave my side. I am sorry for my paranoia."

"Is something going on?" I ask.

"Always, fairest."

"Well, in that case, I'd better drive you back to the club. F.R.E.A.K.S. escort service at your disposal."

"I would prefer if you escorted me back to your hotel room."

"Sorry. *That* is not part of the service. I—"

Something hits me from behind, and I'm falling to the ground sideways before I put cause and effect together. I don't recognize what's happened until the pain in my wrist starts. It's not as terrible as when I broke my arm, but it's still a shock. I turn over just as Baldie literally stabs Connor in the back as another man slashes him across the chest. There's no time to piece it all together. The bald vamp flies right and the one behind Connor glides left. I leap to my feet as Connor attempts to yank the knife still lodged in his back. "Connor!"

I barely take a step toward him when Baldie vampire appears right in front of me, knife already slashing toward me. On reflex I hold up my hand to stop him. White hot pain rips across my hand. "No!" someone yells. "Not her!" We both glance at the second assailant. "We're not supposed to hurt her."

I lose a second to take that information in, but Connor tackles Baldie. Both collapse to the pavement, fighting for the knife. My lost second ends. I kick Baldie in the face and in his haze Connor whacks the knife out of his hand. The other man vanishes, I hope for good. Baldie knees Connor in the groin, causing Connor to roll off the vamp. Before I can do a thing, Baldie vanishes as well. He's just gone. Connor holds onto the family jewels, bleeding everywhere. I have a split second to choose my course of action. Help him or chase them. I hate that my first instinct is pursuit. To catch them and find out why they attacked. I loathe unanswered questions.

But I quash the urge and move toward Connor. "Get up," I say as I bend down to help him do just that. "We have to go." I pick up the knife before wrapping my arm around Connor's waist to aid the hobbling vampire quickly to my car. I guess our assailants decided to cut their losses. I hope so. I lean Connor against the car to retrieve my keys from my purse. He makes it to the passenger side alone. I unlock the doors and let out a ragged breath as I turn on the engine. The trembling starts as I maneuver us out of the structure. We're safe. I think.

"The club," Connor groans as he shifts uncomfortably in his seat.

"Are you okay?" I ask.

He holds up his bleeding hand with a grimace. "I think they used silver blades. Bloody hell, that hurts." He shifts with a groan. "Are *you* alright?"

"Just my hand. I'm okay." Club. Get to the club. I'm making such a bad habit of not keeping the promises I made to myself. "Who were they?"

"No bloody idea. Morons. That is who they were. *Dead* morons if I ever locate them." He presses his good hand to the slash on his chest and groans. "Thank you."

"For what?"

"You saved my life. He was about to slit my throat."

"Do you think—"

"I do not know! I do not know," he says through gritted teeth before removing his cell phone from his jeans. "Neil? Meet me at home with a med kit. I was attacked. We are a minute away."

One minute later I pull into the club's garage right beside the secret torture room. Though Neil rushes over to us from the stairwell door, Connor manages to climb out of the car unassisted. His super-healing must have worked its magic on his groin but with a silver knife his hand and back still drip blood. Heck his shirt is more red than white now. He may need actual stitches. Keeping one hand on the purloined knife, I scan the garage in case the vamps followed us here. We make it to the stairwell and his apartment unmolested. Safe.

The first thing I do is locate a dish towel for my own dripping hand as Connor sits at the dining room table, shrugging off his coat with a wince as Neil hovers around him. "No, check her first," Connor orders.

"No," I say, "really, it's not that bad. It's not deep. I just need a bandage. Check him, especially his back."

Neil opens the first-aid kit before cutting off Connor's shirt. The gash across his pectoral is about as shallow as my gash and the stab wound on his shoulder is small enough a few stitches should do him, which is exactly what Neil begins to do. I look away. "We already have people canvassing the area," Neil says. "We will find them, sir."

"Bring them back alive if you can," Connor says with a wince. Stitches suck.

"Is there anything else to go on, sir?" Neil asks.

"They said I wasn't to be touched," I add. Both men look my way. "To be hurt."

"Antonia," Neil whispers to himself.

"We do not know that," Connor says.

"Who else? Who else would care what happened to *her*?" Neil asks with derision. Still not my biggest fan I see.

"Why would Antonia care?" I ask.

"She would not. *Oliver* would," Connor says with another wince. Stitches *really* suck.

"But why would she do this now? You have a truce. And what would she gain if you were just randomly killed?" I ask.

"Because you—" Neil begins.

"Neil, no," Connor cuts in.

The men exchange an angry glare but Neil's lip curls up before gazing my way. "Because *you* made us appear weak. Because you proved Connor could not maintain control of his subjects. Because the whole of San Diego and beyond have noticed how distracted he has become. Because of you we *are* weak for the first time in decades. Of course people will take advantage."

"I said shut your mouth," Connor snaps and even leaps up. "Do not speak to her in that manner. *Ever.* Leave. Go do your bloody job and find the bastards who did this to us!"

The men continue glowering at one another, Connor's lip curling into a snarl for several tense seconds until Neil finally gazes down at the floor. "Yes. *Sir*," he says with disdain. The vamp glowers at me as he walks past and out of the apartment.

"Is what he said true?" I ask.

Connor turns to me and frowns. "Will you please finish dressing my wounds?"

My boyfriend sits back at the table, shoulders slumped. With a sigh, I grab the suture kit. Giving stitches is almost as horrible as getting them. Neil finished most of his back but not his chest. After I finish the stab wound, I move in front of him to assess his chest. The six inch gash still bleeds but experience tells me it isn't deep. It shouldn't need sutures. I find another dish towel, wet it, and begin wiping off the blood on his chest. Facing him, staring at his pained face and strained eyes, I can't help but ask, "It's my fault, isn't it? Was this because of Lipmann and last night? What I did? The truth."

"Your actions did not…help matters, no," he says.

"And how long have things been so…worrisome?" I ask.

"Since we returned from Las Vegas," he says, eyes down. "Despite the truce, there have been rumors Antonia was up to her old tricks whilst we were gone. We have been investigating, of course but uncovered no concrete evidence."

"Why didn't you tell me?"

"There was nothing you could do," he says before reaching up to caress my cheek with a sad smile, "beyond what you were doing. Providing me a ballast. Comfort. The only pleasure and joy I currently have in my life. An oasis I so desperately needed where I do not have to be strong. Stern. Quixotic. Where I can be..." He runs his thumb across my lips. I'm still so pumped full of adrenaline I can't stop the shiver of lust. "Myself. I had no idea how much I needed that. *Need* that. You. You are worth a thousand verbal lashings and a little bloodshed, fairest."

Oh, please don't. Please—

He leans in and kisses me. Oh heck, he did it. Okay, don't kiss him back. Don't...crud.

My traitorous lips move against his and within seconds I'm wrapped in his bare arms, pressed against his chest as our hands rove each other's bodies. I can't seem to stop myself. He tastes like mint and a tang of blood. Like him. My hand hurts but the pain is soon forgotten. Connor pulls off my shirt and bra. God I love the sensation of his cold hands on my tender breasts. His fingers rolling my erect nipple. Never ceasing his caress, he rises from the chair to lift me up so I have no recourse but to wrap my legs around his waist.

We don't stop devouring one another the whole trek upstairs to his bedroom. We fall onto his bed with him on top, grinding his pelvis against mine. With the first thrust of his erection against my own engorged sex, what little resistance inside me gets snuffed out. I've wanted him inside me since the parking garage. Guess I've found my kink. Dangerous situations. Thrill. This man needs to get inside me, to screw me senseless *right now.*

We're tearing what's left of each other's clothes off and are naked within seconds. His mouth finds my nipple, suckling and flicking in time to his fingers playing inside me. He is so damn good at that. His other hand begins kneading my other breast, rolling and tugging my nipple in perfect coordination until he finally kisses me. Deeply. Almost as deeply as he thrusts inside me, until he reaches my end. That implosion is so shocking, so pleasurable it takes me another thrust before I notice the foul copper taste suddenly in my mouth. Blood. Enough I want to pull away from his kiss, but when I try he grabs the back of my head to stop me. I have to swallow down the blood. After a second he breaks the kiss to trail his lips down my neck as he rolls me into the sitting position. I prefer this position. I like being in control. We face one another as I straddle him. This time I choose the rhythm. I lower myself onto him and ride him up and down, up and down as he suckles and flicks my nipple again in time to my own movements. Oh, Jesus, that's good. That's—

A sharp pain crosses my breast. My eyes fly open at the same time his mouth leaves me. A small, shallow cut on the swell of my breast bleeds a little. "Sorry," Connor says before kissing me again. The taste of blood remains strong. "Sorry."

That's the problem sleeping with a man with fangs. At least he's never attempted to bite me. I'm not about to let this accident stop my fun. I close my eyes and continue riding him as he takes my cut hand, kissing and licking the wound. Blood.

It must be driving him mad smelling it. But I don't care. I've found that sweet, glorious spot his head rubs against in perfect rhythm. He kisses me again and that taste assails my mouth again. Ignore it. Just keep going. I'm close. Up down, up down. God, that's good. I—

He decides to take control again, flipping me onto my back once more. The moment I'm beneath him, he drives into me harder, faster like a piston on high as I wrap my legs around his furiously pumping waist to drive him in deeper. I cling to his back and kiss his shoulder for some ballast against the overwhelming carnality. He traces something on my forehead, over my heart while whispering words I don't understand. I don't care. He's found that magical spot inside me again, and I'm nothing but that ecstasy he bestows upon me. Connor kisses and licks my hand again before another coppery kiss. He thrusts faster, faster, good. So good. Faster…the strange words, I think in Latin, continue even as he kisses me, as he licks the blood from my still weeping hand. I'm coming…I'm coming…with one final thrust he drives me over the precipice while at the same time pressing my bleeding hand against his chest as he does the same with his own sticky hand to my cut chest.

When I return to my senses, when the orgasm finishes rollicking through me, I open my eyes. My wounded hand covers his cut chest and vice versa. After I take that odd fact in, how gross and bizarre that fact is, I then realize he has a strange, circular symbol scrawled on his forehead in blood. What the…?

I suddenly want him as far from my person as possible. I yank my hand from his bloody chest and nudge him off me, out of me, before backing as far away as I can on the bed. Connor doesn't seem to notice or care. He's...angry. He scowls deep that enough there are creases in his forehead, and he refuses to look at me. He mutters, "Shit," before shaking his head and climbing off the bed. Without a second glance my way, as if I no longer exist, he strides out of the bedroom to the bathroom. If I wasn't so freaked out for myself I'd probably be worrying about what I did to displease him. In truth I'm *so* glad he's gone. I touch my own forehead and my fingers come away with blood. My chest too. The scrape is only about an inch long and shallow but there are still smudges of the blood from his own hand along with the vestiges of another sigil. A chill courses through me. I cover myself but the blankets can't help with this kind of chill.

I hear the bath running and a few seconds later Connor steps out of the bathroom wearing a robe and blank expression, the blood now gone. His sins conveniently wiped away. "I have run you a bath," he says emotionless. "And there is a first-aid kit under the sink to dress your wounds. My saliva should have helped though."

"Uh, okay..." I say, clutching the sheet.

He nods. "You should remain here tonight," he says as he moves toward the closet. "It may not be safe for you out there. After her failed attempt tonight, Antonia may become more desperate, Oliver be damned."

"Uh, okay..." I say.

"I shall be at my office most of the night should you require me. Someone shall keep guard outside."

"Uh, okay."

He quickly pulls on black slacks and sweater before striding out of the room without another word or glance my way. Fine by me. I wrap the sheet around myself and scurry to the bathroom, shutting the door behind myself and even locking it. Safe. I finally feel safe now. It...something isn't right. Something's shifted. Wrong. I don't know what. Everything was fine, pleasant even, until I opened my eyes. The moment I did it was as if he'd just violated me on some level. Not sexually per se but...I stare at myself in the mirror. He *did* draw the same symbol on my forehead. Another chill cascades down my spine. I wipe whatever that *thing* is off my body as soon as I can and gargle the taste of blood out of my mouth with toothpaste. Maybe the blood made him crazy. Our second night together he asked if he could bite me and I said no. He's never tried to, not even tonight. But it's as if he did. I don't know. Something is off, and I hate that I can't put my finger on what. I sigh. Right now I just want to get clean.

The bath isn't filling fast enough. I jump in the shower. My hand and chest sting under the hot water. At least they're healing already. Vampire saliva should be bottled and sold for billions. I scrub and scrub until my skin stings as much as my cuts. It takes a couple minutes but I finally get clean enough. I wrap myself in a towel and listen at the door before returning to the bedroom. He isn't there. He's off putting out the fires I helped ignite. A vampire I've never met probably wants to hurt me or worse now I've thwarted another of her nefarious schemes. How is it I'm not officially a F.R.E.A.K. and this crud keeps happening to me? I am just a trouble magnet.

But in this moment…I don't care about any of that. I wouldn't care if there were a legion of bloodsucking undead out there to battle through. I want to get out of this apartment. I want to go back to my hotel, take a bath, and eat cake as I figure out what the heck's bothering me, but I've learned the hard way if someone's gunning for you, being alone isn't the smartest move. Which is the lesser of two evils? I'm uncomfortable here but possibly in mortal danger out there.

I grab one of Connor's robes and peek out of the bedroom door downstairs. No one. I'm uneasy as I leave the bedroom to retrieve my purse and clothes and don't relax even a little until I'm back in the bedroom. Getting dressed helps too. After changing into black leggings and blue tunic, I sit on the bed with a long sigh.

I want to leave. I want out of here so freaking bad it's as if the walls are closing in like in the Temple of Doom or something. I've actually been imprisoned before and though the digs are nicer here that sensation is the same. Antonia won't hurt me, at least not intentionally. Of course I did just assault another of her minions, self-defense or not. But I'm only a target because of Connor. If I tell her we're done maybe she'll leave me alone. Because we are done, aren't we? Yes. *Heck yes.* Great sex, traveling, and my own bookstore are not worth this. But it still doesn't change the fact I assaulted her men, so what the heck do I do? I'm dialing Oliver before I even finish that thought.

"I was wondering if you were going to phone," he says, no doubt with a grin. "I—"

"Antonia tried to kill Connor tonight," I cut in.

"*What?*"

"Connor was walking me to my car, and these two vampires came at us with knives."

"Are you alright? Trixie, are you—" he asks urgently.

"They cut my hand, but they stabbed Connor. We fought them off."

"And why do you suspect Antonia was involved?"

"Because one of the men ordered the other one to leave me alone. That *she* told them I wasn't to be hurt."

Oliver's quiet for a few seconds. "This makes absolutely no sense. They have a truce. She knows how powerful you are, *and* that you have an affinity for Connor. She would be mad to attack now, especially with you literally by his side."

He's right. I don't know the woman, but I know enough. She's not about to send just two thugs after an incredibly powerful vampire like Connor, especially when the Federal Agent who decimated a dozen vamps in one minute might be with him that night. And why not attack him when we was alone in the store? "Okay, then if not Antonia, then who? All his other enemies wouldn't give a second thought to hurting me."

Oliver's silent for a few seconds. "What occurred after the altercation? How did Connor behave? What did he say or do? Was *he* acting oddly?"

"Not…" I don't want to share intimate information with Oliver, especially with what just happened so raw. Maybe I was reading too much into it. Maybe it was some vampire thing. They can be into some freaky, kinky stuff. "He, uh, there was this weird thing that happened when we were, uh…you know."

After a heavily pregnant pause, "What precisely?"

"He…kept licking my wounded hand and pressing it against the cut on his chest. He also…I think he'd bitten his tongue or something because when he kissed me, I tasted blood, like a lot, and—"

"Did you swallow his blood?"

"I had to. Yeah. Why?"

"Did he draw symbols on you with blood? Sigils?"

"How did you—"

"Did he say anything?" Oliver cuts in urgently. "In Latin or even English? Did he force you to say anything in return?"

"He didn't force me to do anything," I insist, "but the Latin thing, yeah. He was whispering, and I think it was in Latin. Why? What's going on?"

"Do you feel different? Revitalized?"

"No, just freaked out, a sensation that's growing by the second. What is going on Oliver?"

"Beatrice, you need to leave. *Right now*. Is Connor still there?"

"Uh, not really. He's next door at the club. What—"

"Are you under guard?" he asks.

"I-I don't know. Oliver, what—"

"They will attempt to stop you. You must not let them know you have fled. Get somewhere safe, somewhere public, and then call me. I will come get you. Do not take that car he gave you. I have no doubt there is a tracker on it."

"Oliver, what the heck is going on?" I snap.

"He…attempted to make you his familiar."

I draw a blank. "His what?"

"It does not matter now. All that does matter is you get as far away from that sociopath as possible."

"Oliver, he's not a—"

"Trixie, *he* organized the attack tonight. He-he attempted to force his *soul* on you. You need to leave and you need to leave *now*," he says desperately.

That desperation and terror in his voice make me nauseous and my stomach was wobbly to begin with. "Okay. Okay," I say, leaping up from the bed.

"I am leaving my hotel now. Get out of there and call me on my mobile. I shall be downtown in ten minutes. People and lights. Get to people and lights."

I grab the suitcase I left here last night. "What about Nana and April? He'll—"

"I will call and take care of them," he says firmly. "Your *only* concern is getting out of that apartment undetected. Which you should be doing. Now."

"I am." I open the bedroom door and peek out. Still alone. "I'm leaving now. Just get my family to safety, okay? Nothing else matters."

"Be careful. I am on my way."

"Thank you. See you soon."

I hang up, slip my phone into my purse which I wrap around my torso, and hurry down the stairs with my suitcase in tow. I do a quick look around for anything else I've left and realize I don't care. I'll buy whatever I've left again. I listen for noise at the front door. Okay. I don't hear a thing beyond my own pounding heart. With a deep breath, I open the door. No one left or right down the hall. I can't take the car, so I go toward the club. There's bound to be cabs or Ubers outside. I pray there's a crowd already. I—

Just as I shut the front door, I hear footsteps to my left toward the garage. By the time my head whips that way, Jack steps into view. I freeze. I don't know how to play this. "I'm just...I'm leaving. I'm going home."

"That is not advisable, Ms. Alexander," Jack says, slowly approaching me.

"I don't care. I'm doing it anyway." I take a step to the right toward the club but before I get to take another, he's right in front of me, blocking my path. I gasp but his expression remains neutral.

"You should go back inside. For your own safety," he says in monotone.

I thought I was ready for this. The confrontation. The fight. I've been mentally psyching myself for this moment since I got off the phone with Oliver. I've faced this situation over a dozen times on the job, heck I've faced it this week, but once it's here no prep, no experience helps quell the terror. There will be pain. There will be blood. Here it comes.

I stare straight into his one brown eye. "Move or I move you," I growl.

That eye narrows. He appears menacing enough with the eye patch alone. "Get back inside or I will contact Connor—"

I break right, but Jack steps in front of me again. That's it. I'm in no mood for the dance. I fling him backwards down the hall hard enough he leaves a dent in the wall. Reaching in my purse, I take off running before he even reaches his destination. I make it through the club hallway door before he grabs me by the hair, yanking me backwards. The moment I stop moving I hold up the silver MACE, spraying it in his good eye. That eye, the skin on his face, boils and burns. Jack releases me now he's far too busy screaming and holding his face. Screw my suitcase. I sprint through the door into the hallway to the club. Shoot, it's still too early. The club is only a quarter full, if that. Empty space everywhere. As the music pounds around us, nobody pays me any attention as I maneuver quickly from group to group, using them as cover. Just get to the door. Just get to the door—

A hand wraps around my right forearm holding it so tightly I whimper, but worse I drop the MACE just as another hand takes my other arm. Edgar keeps squeezing until I fear my bone will shatter but Avril's the one with the scowl. "One false move, and I rip your jugular out," she hisses right into my ear. "Come on." She yanks me toward her.

"Help me! Someone—"

Avril suddenly smashes her lips against mine to shut me up. She releases my arm to hold the back of my head so I cannot get away, but Edgar practically forces my arm behind my back. He pushes and Avril pulls me back the way I came. The psycho finally breaks our "kiss" when we reach the first hallway. I literally spit in her face the moment I can. Bad idea. The cow punches me in the stomach so hard I lose my breath and double over. Heck, I see stars. Before I can recover, Edgar picks me up like a bride and within two blinks I'm back in Connor's apartment.

I'm tossed onto the couch, literally gasping for air and curl into a ball. At least I'm not sobbing like Jack at the sink. "Let me see! Let me see!" Avril says behind me, I guess to Jack.

Edgar whips out his cell phone but never removes his gaze from me. "Yes, sir. The apartment. Quickly." He hangs up.

Oliver was right. I didn't completely believe it, that Connor was capable of what Oliver claimed, but I haven't a doubt now. And he's coming.

I can't walk. Even if I hold all three against the wall as I leave, they'll catch me in seconds. I'm screwed. I have to sit tight, see how this plays out. Wait for an opening then escape by any means necessary. *Any* means.

Not one minute later, the front door opens. I can still barely sit up to watch as Neil and Connor swan into the apartment. If I weren't already nauseous from the punch the sight of him would do it. I lay down again.

"Is she alright?" Connor asks someone.

"She sprayed him with silver. I washed his face, but—
" Avril says.

"Get him home and get him blood. He should be fine."
Connor rounds the couch to face me. His face contorts in
anger. "Did someone strike her?"

"It was the only way to immobilize her, sir," Edgar
says. "I had no choice."

"Wait in the hallway. I shall deal with you later,"
Connor snapped.

"Sir, she has been proven violent. She—"

"Go. Now." Like a good henchman, Edgar nods and
walks away without another word of protest. When I hear the
door shut, Connor kneels in front of me, trying to catch my
gaze. "Are you alright? Should I fetch a doctor?"

"I'm fine," I pant through the pain. At least I can
breathe now. "Why are you doing this? I was just coming to
see you in the club. I was just trying to—"

Connor frowns. "I believe we are past pretending,
no?" He rises. "I knew I lost you the moment you left last
night. Before perhaps. The moment Oliver arrived."

"I don't know what you're—"

He holds up his hand to cut short my words. "Please.
Stop. At least give me the courtesy of not insulting my
intelligence." He frowns again. "What was it? Our lovemaking
tonight?"

What's the point? I drop the confused expression for
my true, pure rage. "Is that what you call it?" I spew.
"You...psychopath. You tried to make me your...familiar
against my will. You tried to force your soul on me."

He frowns. "I knew there was little chance of the gambit succeeding, but desperate times call for desperate measures. And it was not an easy decision to make. I never enjoy forcing anything upon a person, you simply left me with little choice. I *am* sorry. Truly."

"Little ch..." My mouth flops open, and I sit up despite the pain. We're not alone. Neil's by the door, blocking it. "*Why?*"

"You were leaving me, and I need you," he states emotionless.

"Need me?"

"Against Antonia. I told you before, you are one of the most powerful psychics in the world. Who would not wish to acquire a nuclear bomb when engaged in war?"

"So this...us...was all about *Antonia*? You-you slept with me, you made me care about you, you tried to make me...*love* you just so I'd kill your enemy?"

Connor sits on the couch beside me, his frown growing sympathetic. "Not just," he says sincerely. He tries to touch my hand, but I yank it away. His frown deepens. "I meant everything I told you. I do like you. I *could* love you. I truly...wanted to take care of you. I still do. And fairest, please recall, you came to me first. *You* continued to come back."

"Because you manipulated me from the start. We-we didn't just end up in that bistro in LA, did we? You knew those men would be there. You wanted them to attack you so I'd come to your rescue. So I'd be pulled into this crap between the two of you. So I'd...sleep with you."

"I never manipulated you into my bed," he says defensively. "You chose to come every time. Even tonight."

"Really? Those men who attacked us weren't Antonia's. They were yours. You know I'm...turned on by danger. They attacked us, they cut me so you could do your insane ritual. How is that not manipulating me, Connor? Just because you didn't hold me down and rape me doesn't make what you've been doing to me in any way, shape, or form, okay."

"I was using you as you were using me, merely for different ends, fairest. For you I was solely a means to hide. To forget. To make your Oliver jealous. That is what people do. We use one another. We *give* and we take. And I was willing to give you your every heart's desire. Travel. Money. Power. Love. A life free of strife and worry, not just for yourself. Your grandmother could move out of that hovel. Your friend April's children could attend the finest schools and colleges. If you wished to have children, I would move stars to make it possible. And it is still possible, fairest. Simply forget tonight. If you accept I will never, ever harm you. You can have your bookstore. You can become one of my advisors. Create charities. Save people like Mariah. No more lies, no more tricks. You will become my true partner. My familiar. You will become one of the most powerful people in the supernatural community. Is all that not worth the life of one vampire already set on your destruction?"

For a moment, a fleeting moment, I actually consider the offer. Nana wouldn't have to count every penny. My godchildren would be set for life. And it's not as if I would have to necessarily stay with him. He could buy me a house in London or Paris. I'd have my own life, just one bankrolled by him. It sounds...nice. But when the moment passes I instantly hate myself for even contemplating this. For considering selling my soul to this devil for cash. When did I become so shallow?

I lean in so our noses practically touch and stare him in the eye. "My power is not for sale. My conscience is not for sale. My body is not for sale, and my soul sure as heck isn't. Not for anything."

Connor leans back. "Very well." He frowns. "You do, of course, realize if you are not on my side in this…I know where your grandmother lives, Beatrice. Your friend April and children Manuel, Carlos, and Flora. Where they attend school. That Oliver Smythe Montrose is staying at The Hampton Inn, room 304 within my territory. One phone call and I will round them all up. I will lock them up until I take them to the garage one by one, starting with the children, torturing them, right in front of you until you agree to become my familiar. And you must know I cannot let you leave here."

I tilt my head to the side. "Yeah…what did I say about you using the phrase 'let me?'" I growl.

With all my mental strength, I fling him upstairs through his open bedroom door. The moment he takes off like a rocket I direct my focus to Neil behind me. I visualize and squeeze his vertebrae hard enough I hear them crack. As Neil howls in pain and collapses to the ground, I leap off the couch. Sadly he'll be fine by tomorrow, but he can't run after me now. Which I do. I *run*. I literally run for my life. Again.

I make it out the front door and immediately notice Edgar coming in from the garage exit. The way I need to go. Before I realize I'm doing it, he's flying toward me then past me at the rate of a bullet. He hits the wall at the same speed. The wall crumbles around his body as blood splatters around the back of his head and out his nose and eyes. I take off toward the garage and when I reach the stairwell door, I glance back. Edgar's slumped on the ground, unconscious. Perfect.

Just as I'm about the open the door, there's movement out of the corner of my eye. My gaze whips that direction again. Connor stands at the apartment door, snarling at me. Then he's shrieking in agony as his legs crack and twist unnatural angles as I hobble him at the knees. He collapses to the floor like his flunkies as I open the door.

My head throbs like a mother as I sprint down the dark stairwell to the garage. Empty. I continue sprinting toward the closed gate. Shoot, I don't have a card to open it. How...? Luckily my subconscious is already on the job. The gates flies up, gears grinding in protest. A sharp pain, like an ice pick being stabbed into my prefrontal cortex, makes me cry out. But I keep running.

People and lights. People and lights.

I make it down the small alley to the sidewalks of the Gaslamp district. People and lights, but not good enough. Those people keep staring at me as I hustle down the sidewalk with no destination in mind. Hide. I need to hide. Most of the boutiques are closed but the restaurants are open. Two blocks from the club, when the pain in my head almost blinds me, I have no choice but to seek refuge in a restaurant. The teenage hostess actually gasps when she sees me. "Ma'am are you—"

"There's a man. He's stalking me. Can I please hide in your bathroom until the police arrive?" I huff through the agony.

"Uh, yeah, of course," the teen says. "Let me take you to my manager."

The teenager leads me through the dim restaurant toward the back. I keep my head down because I guess I must look a fright judging from my escort's grimace. I finally wipe the wet stuff off my nose and upper lip and see its smeared blood. I must have pulled a telekinetic muscle. I haven't used the full strength of my power for months. I'm shocked I didn't pass out.

The hostess knocks on a door marked "Manager," and a few seconds later it opens. A middle-aged man with a goatee, I assume the manager, takes one look at me and gasps. "Sir, this woman says she's being stalked."

"Uh, come in. Come in," the man says, gesturing me into the small office with only a desk and filing cabinet. "Madison have you called the police or—"

"No, don't call the police. I need to call my contact in the FBI," I cut in, falling in the spare chair. "He-he was on his way already. No one else can know I'm here. He's probably already sent people out looking for me. If anyone does come, just lie. But you're not in any danger. I swear."

"Okay, Madison you stay back here with her. I'll stay up front," the wonderful manager says before pulling out a first-aid kit from under his desk. "Here. Should we call an ambulance or—"

"No. It's just a nosebleed. The agent coming is, uh, about six feet, light brown hair, thirtyish, named Agent Montrose."

"Okay," the manager says.

"Thank you for this."

"Of course." The manager nods to us both before leaving.

I pull out my cell phone from my purse still slung around my torso. Thank Christ for small mercies. Oliver picks up on the second ring. "Trixie?"

"He made his move. I got out. I'm in a restaurant, Il Trattitore on 3rd. The manager's up front waiting for you, Agent Montrose."

"Are you alright?"

"I'm fine," I lie. "Grandma and April?"

"I spoke to them. They are both on their way to a hotel. I purchased them rooms at the Sheraton in Chula Vista under false names. I—"

"No, you need to physically go get them. April first. Escort them all the way to their rooms."

"Trixie, I—"

"He threatened the children," I cut in. My new best friend Madison gasps. "I'm safe here. And *I* can defend myself. *Make sure they are safe.*"

"Very well."

"Thank you. See you when you get here. Bye." I hang up and notice my hands are trembling so bad I can barely open the first-aid kit.

As I dry swallow the aspirin, I call my grandmother's cell phone. She picks up on the third ring. "Bea?"

"Have you left the house?"

"I'm walking to the car right now. What—"

"Just get to the hotel. Don't let anyone know where you're going, not Mrs. Ramirez, not Brian, nobody."

"Did that man hurt you?"

"Don't worry about me. I'm safe. Just get to the hotel, okay? And don't leave."

"Well, how long will I have to be there?"

A good question I have no answer to. "I…three days, okay," I lie. "Just three days." I sniffle some of the blood away. "I-I'm sorry for this. I'm so sorry. If I hadn't…I…" I can feel the tears coming. No. Nope. I can't fall apart right now. "Just call me when you reach the hotel room. Oliver's going to check on you. Don't let anyone else in until tomorrow morning. I love you."

"I love you too. Bea—"

I hang up before the tears begin.

"Wh-what happened?" Madison finally finds the courage to ask.

I turn to the teen, smiling sadly. "I learned there's no such thing as self-destruction. There's always collateral damage." And after another sad smile, I lay my arms then head on the desk. I pray this detonation doesn't completely destroy everyone I love.

CHAPTER THIRTEEN

ENEMY OF MY ENEMY

The staff at Il Trattitore are lovely in my hour of need. Madison escorts me to the bathroom to clean up. A waiter brings me water and garlic bread sticks. My adrenaline rush comes to a standstill five minutes after I arrive so the shaking begins in earnest and I grow drowsy. I can't sleep no matter how much I want to because every second I have to be prepared to defend the good Samaritans if Connor's people come after them. He's certainly coming after me. The manager calls back twenty minutes after I arrive to tell us someone just stopped by asking after me, but he told him he hadn't seen me. It doesn't mean someone else won't pop by or that the minion believed him. The searcher could have gone to get a posse and planned to slay the whole restaurant for all I knew. That call prompts another adrenaline spike then withdrawal. Where the heck is Oliver?

Poor Madison actually shakes after the call even more than I do. To distract her I begin asking questions about her life. She's attending classes at my old Alma Mater, the University of San Diego studying psychology. I pray she makes better choices than I did after college. The talk calms us both down enough our trembles stop. She's telling me about her girlfriend Asha when there's another knock on the door.

"Trixie?"

I leap up and unlock the door. The moment I lay eyes on Oliver, my strong front blows away. I practically collapse into his open arms. He embraces me back, squeezing so tight it hurts. I don't care. He could break all my bones and I'd still never want this hug to end. "Are you alright?" he whispers desperately.

"I'm fine. I'm okay." We continue hugging for apparently too long because the manager clears his throat. I let Oliver go and look at the manager and Madison. "Thank you for everything. Really. You may have saved my life tonight."

"What should we do if they come back?" the manager asks.

"Tell the truth. I came and got her," Oliver says. "But they will not trouble you further, I am positive of it."

"Okay," the manager says.

"Thank you. Really. Thank you," I say again before Oliver wraps his arm around my waist and leads me down the tiny hallway back to the restaurant.

People always stare at him, women especially, but when we pass through the restaurant and eyes jut our way, I instantly tense up. I felt relatively safe in the small office but in this semi-open space I'm too exposed. Any one of the dozen or so patrons could be Connor's agent. They could leap up at any moment and just slit our throats before we even know it's happening. My body tenses with each step and Oliver squeezes me tighter around the waist to comfort me. It's worse when we step outside. They could be in any car, they can zoom in from even the tops of buildings. My gaze juts everywhere. Every movement, every person gets my attention. Oliver's convertible is down the block, and no one attacks us. I can actually breathe once both car doors shut. He had the top up as if he'd anticipated my need for an enclosed space. My savior starts the car and pulls out into traffic.

"Are you truly—" Oliver asks.

"April? The kids?" I cut in, my jaw still trembling from the adrenaline.

"Enjoying their two room Presidential suite as best they can. I checked in on your grandmother as well. She is fine. And hotel security is aware of the situation and will keep an eye on them."

"Are they…angry?"

"They are frightened and put out, but they will be fine."

"How? Connor practically owns the city. He's immortal. He's pissed. He's patient. They can't live in a hotel forever."

"We can send them somewhere. Florida and Disney World for a week or two," Oliver offers. "We shall find a way to make the best of it."

"Then what? I should have…I should have killed him. Tonight. I should have ripped his heart out of his ribcage. Neil may have killed me, but at least it'd be over. They'd be safe."

"Do not talk like that. If you had killed him, if you had survived, perhaps even if you had not, there would be no guarantee his followers would not punish your family or me in retaliation. His inner circle are a loyal sort. No, the only way to truly keep them safe is to dismantle his entire organization."

"Oh, is that all?" I chuckle wryly before the words sink in. All we have to do is topple a centuries old empire when I can barely think or control my own body. My hands, my legs, all of me trembles.

Oliver reaches into the backseat and retrieves a coat, handing it to me. "Here." I wrap myself in the jacket. It doesn't help the chills much. I'm not cold, I'm in shock. "Perhaps you should try to sleep. We will not reach our destination for several hours."

"Where are we going?" I ask.

"To the one place, the one person, who is a true match for Connor."

"Antonia," I say. Brilliant. The woman whose men I assaulted. Who I convinced that Connor wasn't an immediate threat. "She'll help me? Why?"

"The enemy of my enemy is my friend," he says. "And in this instance, lucky for us, she is actually a friend."

"Yeah. *Friend.* And how long exactly have you two been *friends?*"

He glances over at me. "If by friends you mean lovers, we were together a few years. We came to America together. Braved the ocean, the prairie, and superstitious settlers together."

"A few years? For you that's like fifty years of marriage." I pause. "Did you love her?"

"Depended on the day," he says with a smirk. I don't smile back. His drops. "I did. I do. She is one of the few people I ever encountered who has gone out of her way to help me while expecting precious little in return. Sadly I took advantage of that fact one too many times, and she had no choice but to cast me aside."

My eyes narrow. "What did you do?"

"She placed me in charge of one of her budding businesses, a large shipping company, that would have cornered the market, and I neglected it. I wished to travel, to attend parties, explore, enjoy myself, and drumming up clients and submitting permits simply did not seem that important."

"She wanted you to grow up, and you wanted to stay in Neverland," I say.

He nods. "It was almost a century later we finally reconnected, and she told me she had been grooming me to become the number two in her empire, but at the time I believed it was solely her way to keep me on a leash."

"She wanted you to reach your potential, to discover your worth," I say.

"Yes. And I failed her at almost every turn. I let near on a century pass before I could face her again. It took her years to rebuild what my negligence destroyed in mere months. But she forgave me. She even admitted my suspicions were correct, that it was in part an attempt to keep me close. She is one of the few people I have ever considered a true friend. Someone I wholly trust. I trust her with my life. And yours. She will protect you. She will know how to proceed."

"And if you're wrong? Forgive me but I've never had much luck when I've met your exes."

"She is different. Truly. We came to Los Angeles a few years before the railroad and after the Civil War. Then it was a mere village. A lawless, wild village, but had such potential. She purchased parcels of land on the waterfront, then where we discovered the railroad stations would be constructed. She built that shipping company despite my fumblings, invested in multiple factories, she even helped expand the harbor at San Pedro to make it a major trade hub. She is a billionaire possibly hundreds of times over and is the first and only ruler of Los Angeles. Connor arrived in San Diego a decade later, easily dispatching Lord Alonzo who held that territory for twenty-five years, and immediately began expanding into Antonia's. It did not help relations between our warring factions that Lord Alonzo was Antonia's occasional lover. She immediately challenged Connor to a duel, but he declined as he always does. The woman always knew what she wanted, and what trials and tribulations would be met along the way. She is a master swordswoman. World renowned among my people. Which is why *he* attempted to make you his familiar. To finally have an edge over Antonia in a duel."

"What? How? I wouldn't defend him after what happened."

"Entering the familiar bond…there is no greater connection in this universe. None. It is the literal joining of life energies, of souls, between human and vampire."

"What?" I ask.

"It creates a metaphysical bond. You each give part of your energy, your life-force, your magic to the other. The human becomes stronger and healthier, and the vampire can withstand the sun and silver better. Not to mention the sharing of dreams, emotions, the thoughts of one another as the bond grows deeper."

"So the human gets a taste of invincibility and the vampire humanity. Sounds like a win-win to me," I say. "Why don't more vamps do it?"

"Because the vampire gives away a portion of their immortality as well. The familiars age slowly but do age. And when the familiar dies, or vice versa, so does the vampire. The average life span is a hundred fifty years."

"Oh. Why would a vamp agree to do that?"

"It is a rare bond, but if the human does not desire to become a vampire and the pair wishes to be as close as possible, then the ritual can be performed. However the most frequent time the ritual is conducted is when the vampire is near death and it is the only way the human can save them."

"Well, Connor didn't do it for any of those reasons."

"No, he attempted it to gain your telekinesis. It is part of your life-force after all. He would personally gain the talent—"

"And use it during the duel. Bastard. But he'd only enjoy the win for like a hundred fifty years which is like a decade to you vamps."

"Perhaps he is aware of a counter ritual to sever the link once you had served your purpose. Perhaps he believed if he dispatched you before the bond strengthened he could survive the severing. Perhaps after over a century of losing to Antonia he is blind to everything but victory. I do not know, and I do not care. It did not work. That is all that matters."

"And you trust this woman not to have the same notion? Connor likened me to a nuclear bomb. What if she just wants to detonate me too?"

"Then...I will protect you."

"Even after all I've put you through the past few days? Even though you're in danger, again, because of me and my stupid choices?"

He looks over at me. "Until my dying day. And beyond."

I believe him. I reach across and take his hand, squeezing it. He squeezes it back. "Thank you," I whisper. "You..." I wipe a tear off my cheek with my free hand. "I don't deserve you. I don't."

"Trixie...I would not be here if that were true. Where do you think I learned this chivalrous rescuing nonsense from?" he asks with grin #3, no fang.

"All my fault, huh?"

"Yes. You have turned a perfectly despicable vampire into some self-sacrificing, respectful, compassionate...nice guy," he says with fake disdain. "Shame on you."

I actually smile. "Sorry to disappoint you but I'm pretty sure deep down that's who you've always been."

"Well, *you* encouraged him to come out and play. Now it seems I can barely get rid of the bugger."

"Sorry. I guess Antonia and I were right. You just have to live with it now. You're a good man, Oliver Smythe Montrose. Maybe the best I've ever met. And I guess I'll just have to keep saying it and expecting it until you believe it too."

He studies my face for subterfuge but of course can't find any. I meant every word. His beautiful face softens, and he gives me a genuine smile. "Then I had best keep you safe until my dying day as promised because I only believe it when it comes from your beautiful lips."

"Is that the only reason you keep saving me? For my ego stroking?" I ask.

"No. I do it for the same reasons you always come to my rescue. Because I made a promise. Because you are my best friend, and I would miss you more than words can describe if I lost you. Because...you would do the same for me without hesitation. Without question. And besides, it is my turn to rescue *you*."

"So we're just going to go round and round taking turns saving one another like a maddening Mobius strip until one of us drags the other into the grave with them?"

"Or until we find a way to cut the strip and live happily ever after," he counters with a genuine smile.

I gently remove my hand from his and my mouth slowly contorts into a frown. "I don't think I believe in happily ever after." I look out my window and press my head against the glass. "Not anymore."

After a second, Oliver takes my hand again. "Then I suppose I will just have to keep proving it and expecting it until you believe in it again too."

Somehow he brings another small smile to my face. I squeeze his hand before pulling mine away again to wipe the tears away. If anyone can do it, it would be him.

*

I must have fallen asleep within seconds of ending our conversation because I shut my eyes to San Diego while Eric Clapton played on the radio and the next thing I knew Phil Collins croons about the air tonight and the neon signs of Los Angeles shops whiz by. Despite my nap, I don't wake refreshed or even a little less exhausted.

"...there. Where should I park?" Oliver asks beside me.

I peer left and he has his phone pressed to his ear. He glances over at me and quickly smiles. "No, I shall find it. I see the lounge now. See you in a few minutes." He hangs up. "You are awake. Just in time."

We pass the red and purple sign for The Crimson Lounge, a medium sized bar where hipsters vape outside on the sidewalk. Unlike the surrounding buildings with boutiques and restaurants, the bar is a story taller with the brick painted black. Classy. We turn the corner toward the beach then down an alley into a small fenced parking lot right at the edge of the sand where a familiar Latino man waits. The side of my mouth twitches as we park and he moves toward us. He seems perfectly recovered from the beat down we gave him last week. *The enemy of my enemy. The enemy of my enemy.*

Oliver doesn't seem worried about the man so I unbuckle my seatbelt and climb out. If he kills me at least I can do it with the smell of the ocean and the sound of the crescendoing waves behind me. But I don't need to worry. The Latino eyes me up and down even though Oliver reaches him first. I tug the jacket tighter around myself. His icy gaze doesn't help my chills. Nor does the open surroundings.

Connor had to know I could come here and could have men ready to kidnap me. My adrenaline begins pumping again. "Alejandro?" Oliver asks the man.

"Yes. Come on. We have kept watch, but he still may have agents out here," Alejandro says, reading my mind.

Oliver waits for me to walk over then wraps his arm around me, pulling me against him. "You are safe now. I promise," he whispers as we trail behind Alejandro.

He scans the area, we all do, as we cross the alley to a door with three literal bolts across it which Alejandro open. I feel safer already. Or possibly more trapped. Definitely closer to trapped when we enter the dark hallway and he bolts the three locks on this side too. A woman dressed in red and purple uniform like a cigarette girl from the twenties strolls down the hall with a nod to Alejandro and flirty smile for Oliver, who doesn't even look at her. We're led around a corner then up a staircase two floors to yet another door. Alejandro knocks. "Ma'am?"

"Enter," a woman says.

The moment of truth. We obey.

My first impression of Antonia is she's not nearly as pretty as I'd envisioned. Not that she isn't attractive just striking is more accurate. She resembles a late thirty-something Anjelica Huston with the same tall, dancer's body tonight dressed in black leather pants and purple silk kimono top. Her nose is too large, Roman, her lips too small, but her prominent cheekbones, large almost black eyes, Mediterranean skin, and thick dark brown hair keep her from being homely. Who the heck knows what she thinks of me with my damp, unbrushed hair, bloodshot eyes, and fifteen pounds of extra weight. The familiar Chinese standing man beside her is far easier to read. He practically glares at me. Better than our last meeting where I beat up him and his partner, the same partner who moves to his side. The trio appear imposing standing on the other side of her huge desk with the whole of the art deco bar and lounge behind them seen through the glass. People talk and drink in a place out of *The Great Gatsby* one story below us. I doubt they can see us. If things go south I can blow out the two-way glass, toss the vamps through it into the bar, and run. Oliver probably has no such thoughts, he simply smiles at the trio. Still better safe than sorry.

Antonia moves her gaze to Oliver. "No trouble getting here, I assume?" she asks with only a hint of an Italian accent.

"No. None," Oliver says.

"My spies say he is still combing San Diego for you two and her family. Are you sure they are hidden well enough?" she asks him.

"Yes. My FBI colleagues are aware of the situation and will be moving them to a safe house tomorrow where they will be under guard until the situation resolves itself."

"I didn't know that," I say.

"I contacted George after you fell asleep."

"Well, if needed, I have homes in Rome, London, and Rio. They are welcome to stay in any of them," Antonia says with a pleasant smile.

"I don't...thank you. We'll see," I reply as I smile back. "That's very kind of you. Especially after..." I look at the men. "I am so sorry about the other night. I had no idea he planned the whole confrontation. I just saw you hit Connor and...I'm sorry. Truly."

"Fault lies on both sides," Antonia says pleasantly.

"No, he planned the whole event. He knew they'd be there. He manipulated them into attacking him to bring us closer or whatever," I say, rolling my eyes.

"And *they* should have seen through his artifice and walked away," she says. "But that is all in the past. You are a welcome guest here. More than welcome, an honored guest. As is our mutual friend here."

"Thank you, Toni," Oliver says with a nod.

"Yes. Thank you. Thank you so much," I say, voice breaking.

Antonia's smile wanes. "Oh, dear Agent. I am forgetting my manners. You look as if you can use a drink. Or six. You as well, Ollie. Alejandro, Jin, please take dear Ollie here to get some of our reserve and have Robin bring Agent Alexander a Brandy. It will help quell your nerves, dear."

She wants to divide us. She's up to something. She—

Oliver squeezes my waist. Antonia's eyebrow pops up slightly. "I am a tad parched," Oliver says before removing his arm. I begin trembling slightly as if his arm were the only thing holding me together. A distinct possibility. "Gentlemen, let's let the ladies alone to their gossip about me."

"Nice to see the FBI did not beat the ego out of you, Ollie," Antonia says with a smirk.

"An impossibility, darling Toni," he says, ever the charmer. He gives me a quick, reassuring smile, before looking at the men. "Shall we leave them to it?"

"Your ladyship, I—" Jin says.

"Go. Now," Antonia says without taking her eyes off me. The men continue to glare at me as they pass me out of the office, Oliver at their side.

"Do you have AB negative? It has been weeks—" Oliver says pleasantly before they shut the office door.

And then there were two.

"Jin was concerned that tonight's drama was all a ploy to get you inside my home to assassinate me," Antonia says nonchalantly. "It is understandable. Your reputation precedes you, and he has experienced your...talent firsthand. And let's not forget you have already aided in the dethroning of one Lord this year, another ex-lover of our Oliver I might add."

"You're not worried?" I ask, still shaking a little. Even though my skin tells me it's warm my internal thermostat is turned down to twenty.

"You are not worried I may try the same tricks Connor allegedly did? Or that I may have just decided that killing you would ensure he can never get his grubby little hands on your power again?"

"The thoughts...crossed my mind. Your reputation precedes you as well, your Ladyship."

"And yet here you are. Alone. With me," Antonia says.

"And you with me," I point out.

She smiles again. She's almost pretty when she smiles. "Then we must both trust dear Ollie with our lives."

"I certainly do," I say without hesitation.

Her smile grows. "As do I. Good. That is settled. No duels to the death tonight. Now sit down, darling. You truly do look as if you are about to collapse."

I'm not a hundred percent convinced she won't hurt me, but I am a hundred percent convinced my legs will give out if I don't sit. I take the chair across the desk from her, and she sits in her throne as well. Anyone watching would think we were about to start a business deal. Guess we kind of are.

"Do you require a doctor, darling? I do smell blood on you. My Robin was an army medic. She can—"

"No. I'm fine. The cuts were shallow, and I already dressed them."

"And those wounds came from my alleged attack on you tonight?"

"Yeah. But then Connor admitted he set the whole farce up. Right before I broke his legs," I say with a hard edge.

Antonia smiles again but the knock on the door wipes it away. "Enter."

A tall, blonde woman with a lantern jaw and the shoulders of a linebacker dressed in khakis and pink halter top steps in carrying a tray with two glasses. Growing up in San Diego I've seen my share of trans men and women to realize she's almost fully transitioned or is far down that path. Antonia studies my reaction as the woman walks past. I must pass her test because the vamp smiles at me again. "Agent Alexander, meet my consort and our resident medic Robin Abbot."

Robin hands me the glass of Brandy. "I think this is for you," she says with a smile too.

"Thank you."

"Robin will be taking care of you during the day," Antonia explains.

Great, and I just shook Krista. "Okay."

Robin hands Antonia her glass of blood with a kiss. "The spare rooms are ready for them," Robin says.

"When we are done here I am going to need you to check Agent Alexander's wounds. And do you mind entertaining our other guest while we speak?"

"Your stupid gorgeous ex? You do spoil me," Robin says before kissing Antonia again. "Love you."

"Love you too," Antonia replies.

After another smile and kiss, Robin leaves the room. I take a sip of my Brandy. "Your consort seems nice," I say politely.

"Yes. She is. We have been together for the past seven years. I intend to turn her when she decides if she wishes to fully transition or not," Antonia says, sipping her blood with her pinky up. "Connor never mentioned I had a consort? I suppose if he had he would have also had to mention giving Robin's name, e-mail address, and prior home address to multiple hate groups in an attempt to bypass the law and have her killed."

My heart literally hurts with this information. "He did that?"

"I have no proof, of course, but who else? In our little war of attrition any destabilization is a victory. A Cold War is death by a thousand tiny pinpricks to see who takes the longest to bleed out. Over half a century of this, having to be on one's toes twenty-four seven, friends and family caught in the crossfire, it is exhausting. Connor must feel the same to attempt such a drastic measure." She sips her blood. "I wonder how long he had been planning this. Perhaps from the moment he heard of you. Your exploits in Dallas created ripples through our community you know. Almost a dozen dead or maimed, including a Lord, in less than twenty-four hours is quite impressive. He must have recalled that article about you saving the boy and put two and two together. He probably did ample research and just had to lie in wait until you returned home."

"*You* seem to know a lot about me too," I point out.

"I compiled a dossier when Oliver phoned me back in December when you returned to the state and I even helped a bit to locate you when you were abducted. When Oliver told me you returned to San Diego three months ago I kept an eye and ear on you. Three months of nothing then I blinked and you were in my enemy's bed. I was shocked how quickly you moved in with him. Shed blood for him. Betrayed Oliver again for him. I—"

"I never betrayed Oliver," I cut in.

"Really? It was my understanding you and Oliver were as thick as thieves before then you threw him over for some werewolf and that even though you slayed your fiancée to save our Oliver, you quickly abandoned him without a word."

"That's not...I didn't throw him over. We were never a couple. And I didn't abandon him either. I came home to recover. And not just my body. As you may have noticed I haven't exactly been the picture of mental health and good decision making even before I came back. I almost got Oliver killed. I couldn't...face him. Or that. I figured he'd either hate me or force me to deal with what I did to them both, and I wasn't strong enough for either, okay?"

"So you were a coward and instead of speaking to him, you betrayed him with Connor."

"I didn't betray him! We're not a couple."

"Darling, one need not be physical lovers to betray a person who loves you," she points out.

I close my eyes so I don't have to look at this chick. "It was never my intention to hurt or betray anyone. Especially not him, okay? Oliver didn't factor into my decision to date Connor at all. I just wanted to...not be me for a while. To have fun. That's it. That's all. How the hell could I have seen all this coming?" I open my eyes. "Go on. Tell me."

Antonia frowns. "You knew what he was, Agent Alexander. Who he was. What he was capable of. Oliver warned you. From what I hear your family did as well. It does not sound as if you were deluded enough to think you could change him. No, any armchair psychologist would tell you perhaps you chose him because a part of you hoped he would kill you. That his darkness would swallow you whole."

My mouth flops open. "You don't...you don't know me, lady," I snap.

"I am over six centuries old, darling. I have known many yous. Mind you, you have more reason than most to act and feel the way you do, and I have always been a huge proponent of personal freedom, so if you desired Connor to turn you into a husk then dispose of you as he saw fit, it is your life, Agent Alexander. Have at it, darling." Her face contorts to form a menacing glare. My stomach seizes. "However, not only has your little brush with self-destruction impacted my livelihood, but it has also put one of my dearest friends in mortal peril. I would have killed you the moment I heard you were entangled with Connor, but Oliver pled for your life. He even threated me with the true death should I ever move against you. I never knew he had such backbone. I feel I should point out, *darling*, he even came to San Diego knowing full well Connor would flay him alive at the first opportunity. You mean *everything* to him, little girl. And the fact you refuse to even acknowledge that fact makes me want to rip your ungrateful throat out, forget helping you clean up your mess. Make no mistake, Agent Alexander, the only reason I am providing you sanctuary instead of a shallow grave is my friend requires protection and would not accept it unless I extended the same courtesy to you. Are we clear?"

The shakes the brandy had helped reduce returned during her speech. "I understand," I whisper, looking down at my trembling hands. "You must really love him."

"To know him is to love him, darling. Even *you* have to admit that," she says smugly. "He and I traveled in the same circles in Paris for years. He was simply one of many I played with, at least until my consort Jean suddenly died. Hit by a carriage, trampled by horses, just a freak accident. I was devastated. Inconsolable. He was one of the great loves of my life. I withdrew from society, locked myself in our house and could not find the drive even to eat. And the only one of my so-called friends, vampires I had known for centuries, who came to check to see if I were truly dead was our Oliver. Of course he played the visit off, saying he solely wished for the name of Jean's tailor. But he brought me blood as well. As he did the next night, and the next, and so on until I could actually face leaving my crypt and re-enter the world. He remained by my side every step on my path back to life. I suppose I fell in love with him for that. I certainly saw another side no one else seemed to, himself included. His compassion. His strength. Yet he always denied these traits when I exhaulted them to his face."

"Yeah, he still does that," I say.

"It took me years to realize he acted that way was because it was far easier to be the lover and fool than live up to his full potential. Not to mention it is fine if he fails wearing that mask but if he fails or is rejected being his true self then he may crumble. I pushed him to remove that mask, and there were moments here and there where I succeeded, but perhaps I pushed too hard or too often. I demanded when patience was the correct avenue. I just *knew* he was capable of more. Or perhaps…he did not trust me enough to be his true self around me. We were together over five years. We crossed an ocean and continent together. Braved storms, Indians, settlers, the elements together. He kept me sane as I built the foundation of my empire. Built the foundation on Los Angeles itself.

"Yet, for whatever reason, he felt the need to revert to old habits. I gave him an opportunity I knew he could thrive at, and he squandered it in favor of adventuring and whoring. We were barely a couple by then, I was far too busy I suppose, and perhaps drawing him into my empire was an attempt to keep him in the fold. Instead it drove him away. I did not see or hear from him for close to seventy-five years. He admitted he had been avoiding me. I told him there had been no need. I had forgiven us both decades before."

"You don't seem the forgiving type," I say.

She smiles. "I forgive fumblings, especially those I helped incite. We are all imperfect beings. Mistakes occur. As long as we learn from those mistakes, help clean up the aftermath, and they never occur again, forgiveness should always be the goal. Even of ourselves. And I missed my friend. He apologized, as did I, and we moved on. Lucky for you, no?" she asks with a raised eyebrow. "Twice over actually. You know it was *I* who convinced Oliver and Lord Peter of Washington D.C. to suggest our Oliver join the F.R.E.A.K.S.?"

"What?"

"Have you heard this tale? You know how Oliver came to be a F.R.E.A.K? What does Mona McGregor call it, 'The Goodnight Massacre?' Witches do tend to be overdramatic."

"I read the case file. I even met Anna West, but I never asked Oliver too many questions. He seemed uncomfortable talking about it."

"The man grows a conscious at the strangest times," Antonia says, rolling her eyes.

"Faced with the dilemma of killing a child is not a strange time to grow a conscience," I snap. "What he did was incredibly brave, especially when he knew it could mean his own death."

"He phoned me from a gas station right after he dropped the girl off with the police. I had never heard him so frightened. He did not know how to proceed. He knew Peter, would be legally bound to execute him and the other idiots, but he just kept going on and on about those dead humans and the child. I told him to return to Washington, that I would speak to Peter on his behalf. Of course Peter was cleaning up another mess with the werewolves and could not be reached until almost dawn. We were all up well past dawn trying to untangle the new crisis. Oliver seemed resigned to prison or worse, but when Peter mentioned the F.R.E.A.K.S. were understaffed, I knew it was a perfect solution. I even called in my favors with George to get him to agree. There were so many backdoor dealings, werewolves with vampires, vampires with witches that day, I lost count," she chuckles.

"Wait, you know George?"

"Oh, I know George," she says with a sly grin. I don't want to know how she knows my boss, but I can guess. "I am a member of his little co-op even. Oliver's position was one of its first success stories. And I hear he has been an adequate addition for the past thirty years. Not to mention had I not intervened, you two never would have met. You are welcome."

Vampires, always with the grandstanding. "Then thank you. Twice over."

"Then let's begin showing our appreciation, shall we? I need to hear *everything* that transpired between you and Connor since your introduction at Christmas. Any business deals, any acts as Lord you witnessed or overheard, especially as they relate to me." She punches something into her computer before moving the webcam on top. "And I am recording this. Speaking is Lady Antonia Sabatini of the Los Angeles territory interviewing Special Agent Beatrice Alexander in regards to Lord Connor McInnis of the San Diego territory. Let us begin with your first contact with Lord Connor. When did it occur and what were the circumstances?"

I spend the next hour plus sharing every, *every* intimate detail of my relationship with that monster. Antonia grills me as if I were a hostile witness on the stand at the trial of the century. The more I hear myself speak the more I realize just how much that psycho played me. How insidious his machinations were. How he could explain away everything, how he emotionally manipulated me, and I just refused to listen to my instincts. How surface he kept it all because he knew that was what I wanted. I *wanted* him to have the control, how I think deep down I wanted to be manipulated. I walked into his trap with my eyes almost wide open. I knew what he was. I knew he was a scorpion just as I knew I was the frog. I let the bastard ride on my back anyway and yet I'm still shocked he stung me. Not just stung me but stung my entire frog family. The bastard's even trying to sting the tadpoles.

Antonia remains neutral, her expression not giving away even a hint of an emotion. She no doubt thinks I'm just pathetic and weak. The more I hear myself talk, I sure as hell think it. And in one final act of humiliation, I pull down my shirt to show the knife wound on my chest.

"And you never gave your consent to become his familiar at any stage of your relationship?" Antonia asks as I cover myself.

"I didn't even know what a familiar was until Oliver explained it to me after the…assault occurred."

"So you never consented to become his consort, familiar, or have any position in his court or business?"

"No. I was just…his girlfriend. Except for attending a meeting regarding the orchestrated altercation between your men and him, and the Moon Lipmann investigation and execution, I had no dealings in his professional life. Or wanted to."

"But he did admit to coming into my territory to incite my men with the sole purpose of instigating a fight and attempting to force you into a familiar bond to gain control of your psychokinetic power to use in a duel against me."

"Yes," I say.

"Thank you, Agent Alexander. Interview ending at 2:23 AM." She shuts off the webcam with a smile my way. "Excellent job, darling. I shall be sending this recording to the King. We may, *may* have enough now to begin banishment proceedings."

"How long will that take?"

"I do not know," Antonia says. "A week perhaps. I—"

"A week? I have to stay here a week? My family—"

"Will be taken care of," she assures me. "If they do not wish to remain where they are or go to my homes in London or Paris then I can arrange for a suite or two in Orlando. Your brother and his family can meet your grandmother and friends there as well. Disney World, SeaWorld, Universal Studios, those should occupy them whilst we sort this out."

"Maybe," I say, staring down at my empty glass. The brandy barely lasted five minutes after I began my story. It did help with the nerves. I'd forgotten I was holding the glass. I put it on her desk. "Honestly. Would he go after my family?"

"Possibly," she says. "Yes. By now he has to have sussed out you are here. He has spies in my network, and it is the most logical course of action for you to have undertaken. Which means he will have deduced you have turned informant and that I will send your testimony to the King, which begins the clock on his possible removal from power."

"Possible?"

"Technically he has not broken the treaty. There have been no invasions, no outright skirmishes. He has not drawn undue attention to us. There has not even been cause to call in the F.R.E.A.K.S. By the letter of the law you were a willing participant. There was no physical duress. *He* did not lay a hand on you you did not desire him to, even tonight."

"But the men who attacked us. He admitted—"

"You are in law enforcement. It is not what you know, it is what you can prove. Beyond his word you have no proof, and he will just turn around and claim you were a lying woman scorned. You have made up this entire story because you were upset he ended your liaison. *He* will have many witnesses to testify to his version of events."

"And the King would believe him over a F.R.E.A.K.S. agent?"

"Once again, technically, you are *not* a F.R.E.A.K.S. agent at present. Suspended for dereliction of duty and emotional instability. Even in the 21st Century how many domestic violence and rape cases have been thrown out or not even brought to court by the DA's office because the majority of the world believes the victim had it coming or is just a crazy woman?" she says with a sneer. "You believe it is better in our literally antiquated vampire society?"

My lip begins trembling. "So that's it? My family has to hide forever, I have to stay here forever, and Connor gets away with it?"

"Not necessarily. We do have a few marks in our favor. Your affiliation with the F.R.E.A.K.S. for one, tenuous though it may be. I will phone George about your predicament and he can advocate for us to the King. The F.R.E.A.K.S. are meant to remain neutral in vampire disputes unless human life has been taken, but there is a credible threat to one of his agents, our Oliver, so George can at least toss his weight around. Your affiliation with them may also deter Connor from harming your family and friends. They are humans after all, and if he harms them, the F.R.E.A.K.S. can officially step in. He may take that chance though, simply because it is the only way to lure you out and have you agree to anything and everything he desires. With your talent, even his diminished use of it and you forced to fight by his side, he could potentially topple the King and F.R.E.A.K.S. himself."

"So the longer he can't reach me, the more desperate he becomes, and the more danger my family is in."

"So we do our damndest to keep them and you out of his reach."

"In the off chance the King decides to intervene. Possibly. Maybe. Somewhere in the distant future," I say harshly as I fight back tears.

"That is the best I can give you, darling," Antonia says.

Fudge it. I don't have the strength to hold back the tears anymore. They drip down my face and I swipe them away. "And if he does capture my family or Oliver…what will you do? Will you let me go?"

She doesn't answer. She doesn't have to. I knew the answer even before I asked it. I'm a prisoner here now. Still a pawn in this wretched game that began before even my mother was born. And it's all my fault.

She smiles again. "You are no doubt exhausted," she says as she presses a button on her desk. "Robin has prepared you a room, and tomorrow I will have someone purchase you anything you require. Make a list before you fall asleep. Anything and everything you desire will be provided. You are an honored guest after all. My home is yours for the duration."

There goes that politician's smile of hers again. God, she and Connor could be the same person. No wonder they loathe one another. "Please do know," she continues, "please do accept we are on the same side, darling. Accept it, if not for your sake than for Oliver's. We have cast our lots together for the duration, and I will do all in my power to keep you and your loved ones safe from harm. I only ask you show me the same courtesy. You rest. You have earned it. I shall take the reins from here."

There's a knock on the door, and Robin steps in. "Yes?" Robin asks.

"My love, Agent Alexander is ready for bed. Please check on her wounds as well," Antonia says, picking up her phone.

"Of course," Robin says.

Guess I'm dismissed. Finally. I rise from the chair and the ground sways a little under my feet. Maybe the brandy wasn't the best idea. I can add it to the Mt. Everest size list of terrible decisions I've made lately. Robin strides beside me, taking my arm and waist to steady me. "Come on. Let me help you."

"Thank you," I whisper.

Robin leads me out of the office into the hallway. "Are you okay?" she asks me. "Are you still bleeding?"

"No. I-I'm really fine. They weren't deep. His saliva mostly healed them. I really just want to go to bed."

"I think we can manage that," Robin says with a smile.

We walk the way I initially came to the small stairwell, going down only one floor to another hallway but stop at a door. We enter a supply closet and after Robin closes the door she moves aside a shelf to reveal a metal door with a keypad. When that door opens there's another short stairwell and another door and keypad. Strangely we walk through a large, long hallway that has to be the length of the building next door. Smart. Antonia doesn't live next door but the building after that. They take security seriously around here.

After another two doors, we finally reach her home. Alejandro sits on a black leather couch channel surfing as Oliver paces around the mostly black and white living room with damask wallpaper the same colors. I especially like the entire wall of a high definition television set up with curtains around it showing a night scene of a balcony overlooking London. There are no windows so it must help with the claustrophobia. I'll bet there isn't a single window anywhere. That bothered me at Connor's too. It truly is a prison. Oliver's tightly wound body relaxes the moment we see one another. The feeling's mutual. I want to run straight into his arms, but Robin doesn't give me the chance. "Toni needs to see you both," Robin says as we continue walking.

"Are you alright?" Oliver asks me.

"Fine," I say quietly. "Tired."

"I'll get her settled in the guest room," Robin says. "You two better get in there. Now." Alejandro shuts off his television and rises. Oliver glances from Robin to me to Alejandro then back to Robin. "You know better than to make her wait, gorgeous. Your girl here's in good hands. I promise."

"Go. It's okay," I say.

Oliver walks over and squeezes my shoulder. "I will be back," he whispers.

I nod, and Robin starts us moving again. Our destination is a large bedroom with the same color scheme and level of luxury as the rest of the apartment. There's even a TV screen in place of a window showing a starry night and full moon behind the gauzy curtains. Oliver's bedroom in Kansas has the same display. Robin has performed her hostess duties to perfection. Lying on the bed are a thick robe, a coral maxi dress and white pashmina along with a UCLA t-shirt and gray sweat pants I think will fit.

"I guessed you were a ten by twelve. They should fit even if I was wrong. I'll be in the guest living room if you need anything else. There's a fully stocked kitchen too. I'm a health nut but make a list and I'll go shopping tomorrow. The shower's through that door," she says as she nods to the bathroom door. "The toiletries are already in there."

"Thank you."

"You'll be okay. It'll all be okay, hon," Robin says, rubbing my arm. "We'll keep you safe."

"Thank you."

"You get some rest." Robin smiles again before departing. Finally.

The last hour's been one long déjà vu trip. I've replaced one vampire lair, one minion watching over me for another. At least Connor let me leave. He no doubt had people following me, but I could leave his apartment. Antonia won't be that loose. Ugh, I can't think about that. Not right now. I don't even have the strength to take a shower or change into the pajamas Robin gave me. I just shove all the crap on the bed onto the floor, kick off my shoes, climb under the covers in the fetal position, and let the floodgates of heck wash through me.

How did this happen? *How did this happen?* How have I screwed everything up so badly? Everything I do is wrong. I ruin everything I touch. I'm poison. A plague. I should be locked up forever. Quarantined. Everyone would be better off without me. Everyone. They're already in misery, in pain, terrified because of me. I need to be eradicated before I spread my death to those I love. But I don't know how. I don't know what to do. I'm back in North Carolina as I stared at the fiancée I just murdered holding my best friend as he bled almost to death. My world has shattered again this time truly because of me, everyone around me is bleeding to death. It's me. It's all me. It's always me. *I'm* the monster. The abomination. The villain. How did this happen? How did I allow this to happen? I suppose it doesn't matter now. Because one thing hasn't changed.

I know what should happen to villains.

CHAPTER FOURTEEN

COME WHAT MAY

Even my own body believes I should be tortured for my crimes. I'm exhausted in body and soul, but every time I'm at the precipice of sleep, I either jerk awake or begin the adrenaline trembles. I give up after an hour and take yet another shower tonight just to stop the shakes. It does help my body so I only have mild Tourette's symptoms now. I dress in the sweats and get back in bed with only two tries on putting on the pants. Yet sleep still won't come. I just want to sleep. I just want to sleep. Let me sleep. I shut my eyes tight. Just let me sleep. Let it all go away. Why won't it just go away? The tears begin spilling out of the corners of my eyes and suddenly I'm sobbing. I just want to go to sleep. I want—

There's a tiny knock on the door I barely hear. A second later my door opens but I don't have the strength to open my eyes or stop sobbing. "Trixie? Trixie…" Oliver says as he shuts the door. With only the fake nightscapes' glow and my haze of tears I can barely make out his outline. I feel the King sized bed shifts as he climbs on beside me. "Darling? Darling…" he pulls me into his arms and for the millionth time in my life I literally cry on his shoulder. "It is alright. It will all be alright. I swear to you. I swear it will, my darling," he whispers as he kisses my hair.

"I'm sorry," I sob. "I'm so sorry."

"Hush. Hush," he whispers, kissing and petting my hair.

"Why does this keep happening? Why? Why? I'm so tired. I'm so tired of *everything*. I thought I was a good person. I always try to be a good person. Why does this keep happening to me? Why can't anything ever be good? Why does everything I touch, everything I do, fracture and mold? Why can't it stay good and easy? What have I done to deserve this? What?"

"Nothing. You have done nothing, my darling. Nothing," he whispers.

I cling to him tighter. "It never gets better. Never. Why won't it ever get better? I do everything, everything I can and it never gets better. I'm so tired. I'm so tired of messing everything up. *I'm* horrible. I *am* horrible. It's me. It's always me. I am an aberration. A blight. I never should have been born. I hate this. I hate it. I hate letting everyone down. I hate hurting everything and everyone. They'd be better off without me. They'd be better off," I sob so the words are barely intelligible. They would. Him especially. I believe it with every fiber of my soul. I pull away from him and sit up, my water logged eyes bugging out of my head. "You need to go. You need to leave *right now*. Go. Go back to Kansas. You-you-you shouldn't be here. You need to go. He-he won't hurt you if you're *there*. Go. Just go."

"I am not going anywhere," Oliver says calmly.

"No, you have to go. *You have to*. He'll hurt you. He'll kill you. You have to go. Go. Just go! Go!" Near hysterics now, I begin shoving him, but Oliver grabs my wrists and I begin flailing. "No, let me go! Let me go and go!" I yank my arms from his grip and stare straight into his eyes. "Go. *Now*. There is *nothing* for you here. There never was. I am not going to sleep with you. Never. Ever. *You* did this. You did. You ruined everything. It was all fine until you got here," I hiss. "I don't want you here. I was happy. I was happy with him. But you ruined it, just like you ruined it with Will. You made him hate me for months. You bit me. You scarred me. You attacked me just because I chose him over you. I would rather have him, have Connor, in my body than you. And you know why? You know why I will never, *ever* sleep with you? Because I see you for what you truly are. Vain. Shallow. Manipulative. Immature. *Selfish*. And that is all you will ever be. Will was a trillion times the man you are. And Connor...at least he knew he was nothing but a quick lay and a good time. So leave because I don't want you here. I never have and never will want you. So go. *Now*."

I wish I could see his eyes, but in the dark I can barely tell he's there. The only sound comes from my shallow breaths. Neither of us moves or speaks for several seconds. "Are you done?" he finally asks calmly as I think his eyebrow rises. My own mouth twitches. "*I* have seen *Lassie* as well, my dear. It never worked on the dog either."

I crumple in on myself and the tears begin anew. "Just go...please...please..." Even after all the horrible, untrue things I just spewed at him, Oliver still pulls me into his arms again. "I'm sorry. I'm sorry."

"I have heard far worse, and from those who actually meant the words," he says.

"You need to go. You *have* to go. He'll kill you. Please go. Please..." I hold onto him tighter. Oh God, I want to melt into his body. "I'm not worth this, Oliver. I'm not. You've done enough. You've enough for me, angel. I can't...watch you throw your life away for me again. You are worth ten of me. Don't you know that? How can you not know that? I'm no good, Oliver. I try to be, but there's just something toxic about me. I destroy lives. Steven. Will. My mother. My brother. I ruin everything and everyone I come into contact with." I sniffle. "My grandmother, my best friend, her *babies* are in fear for their lives because of me." I pull away to grab his head, even digging my fingers into his cheeks. He can see me in the dark better than I can and I bore my eyes into his, my whole body trembling. "*Run*. Run far and fast. *Please*. Run for your life while you still can and never look back. Please. Please. *Please*. I'm not…worth it. I'm not."

I swear his eyes stare straight into mine. "You have no idea, do you? None."

"What?"

He takes my hands from his face to hold them before staring down at them. His shoulders slump. "Darling, I am five hundred fifty-seven years old. Five hundred fifty-seven years I have existed on this planet. I have set foot on almost every continent. I have met beggars, kings, demons, spirits, housewives, movie stars. I have watched humanity evolve from believing the moon was supernatural to walking on it. From having a common cold kill to the transplantation of organs. I have seen and done all. I have lived a life most would only dream of. Beauty. Wealth. No limits. No guilt. No consequences. If I wanted it, I took it. I have slaughtered without mercy. I have lied, I have used, I have been cruel when I had no cause to be. That was the world I inhabited for over five centuries. Monstrosity was allowed, expected even. Just as I knew what *I* was expected to be. Even before I became a vampire," he chuckles wryly.

"My course was set from before I was even conceived. I was born to be a farmer like my father and his before him. It did not matter that I loathed it. That I was wretched at it. That I woke most mornings wishing I had not. But it was my fate. As it was my fate to be...people always told me I was handsome, and naught else. *Never* anything else. The girls in the village blushed and giggled, tempted me even, but the church said to wait for a wife. So I did...until one mistake, one drunken night when I barely knew my own name. Sarah knew what she was doing. She wished to be the one to finally seduce the village beauty. To this day I do not believe she ever liked me let alone loved me. But she paid for her transgression. We both did. She fell pregnant, and there we were. There *I* was. Performing a job I hated, a husband to a woman I near despised, and making a mess of both. The only bright spot in my life were my children. I loved them. I *adored* them, Trixie. To this moment I miss them as I would a limb. And they were enough. Yet I lost them the moment Alain fed me his blood and turned me into...this monster. A monster forsaken by...the deity. I had been good, pious all my life, and how did He repay me? I lost my soul. I lost my children. So why not enjoy my new life of leisure? Of the flesh?

"But even as a vampire I was solely my body. My face. What I could do for them. And what did I know? Vampire, human it had always been that way. Perhaps it was survival. Perhaps I was not strong or intelligent enough to break out of that role. Even when it became dull. When I derived no more pleasure out of sex or luxury or touring the world. So when the opportunity to break out, try something new came about with the F.R.E.A.K.S., I was actually looking forward to my new role. The hero. The investigator outsmarting the baddies with my keen intellect. But they all knew what I had done. How I stood by as my so called friends slaughtered an innocent family. How I allowed Asher to kidnap Anna. Her being on the team did not help matters. She could barely look at me. They all could not. They wanted nothing to do with the killer foisted upon them. So I kept to myself and on cases I played my part. The muscle. Nothing but a body once again. I should know after five hundred plus years the more things change the more they stay the same. Thirty years of towing the line. Going through the motions as I always had. Because...that was all anyone ever expected of me. Wanted from me.

"Even when you arrived I viewed you as barley more than another conquest, especially after I saw how infatuated William had become with you. I had to win. But then...you trusted me. *Me*. A vampire you barely knew. Who I gave no reason to. Yet you let me in on your darkest impulses and fears. You listened to my advice and took it. You stood up to the man you were infatuated with to save my life. Even after I maimed you," he says no doubt looking at the scar on my neck, "marked you, you did not hesitate. You forgave me. It was as if it never occurred. And if those were not miraculous acts to me, you...risked your life to save mine. *Nobody* has ever gone out of their way for me just *because*. You do not want me simply for my body or what I can do for *you*. You truly believe I am clever. Kind. Intelligent. Worthwhile. And you have not stopped pressing me, helping me, proving to *me* that I am. You made me think, you made me *know* I can be more. You showed me how to care about myself. About others. Because you demanded it of me. And you. *You*, this compassionate, bright, funny, loving, beautiful creature, if you think I am worthwhile, then I must be. no? You...make me a better man. You help me *like* myself. What is that against death?"

Before I can stop myself I lean forward and hug him. I practically cling to him for life. He embraces me back and for a moment all is right in the world. "You always give yourself such little credit. How can you not see what I do? You *are* a good man. And I'm sorry for what I said before. I didn't mean it."

"I know. I forgive you," he says immediately.

"I'm just so tired. And scared. If anything happened to you again because of me..."

"Here. Lie down, darling." He pulls away and gently presses me into the pillow. "Lie down."

I rest my head on the pillow, and he lies down beside me, both on our sides so we're facing one another. "I am so sorry for what I said," I say.

"It is not as if none of it were untrue," he says. "I can be vain, immature, shallow, and vindictive. I did maim you. I did...lash out because I was jealous of William. There is no excuse for what I did that night in the cages. *None.*"

"You scared me," I admit. "That wasn't like you."

"It is no excuse, none, but when I discovered you and William were together, I knew he would take you away. He would do his damndest to end our friendship."

"I wouldn't have let him," I say.

"Darling, you were planning to leave the F.R.E.A.K.S. already. It was the natural course of the situation. Where would I fit in between PTA meetings and cooking meatloaf? It would not be your fault. Or mine. Not even William's truly. It would just be...life. But you would still be gone. I was furious. At William. At the fates. At you. I lost the course of myself. I was immature and cruel. I am a work in progress. But I regretted my actions the moment they occurred, and I swear on all I hold dear, it shall *never* happen again."

I nod. "I believe you. And I forgive you. Just as I hope you forgive me. I locked you in the freezer. I let you run off to almost certain death."

"Darling, I would have done the same had the roles been reversed. In truth I would have done more. I would do anything to save the person I loved. I knew what you were doing. The cause. And I knew what *I* was doing when I chased after William. Those I forgave long ago." He pauses and looks down. Away from me. "But...you left. You left without a single word. You did not visit me in the infirmary. You packed up your life in Kansas and just ran away. You refused to return any calls. You abandoned me without a thought or glance back. As if I were disposable."

For the first time through the whole of this horrid night, all the confessions and emotional turmoil of the past few hours, this is the first time he's been visibly pained. Now we're up close I can see his forehead's creased and eyes weary. This makes my heart physically ache. "That wasn't...I..." I let out a ragged sigh. "That wasn't about *you*. I didn't do it to hurt you. I...I saw you. In the infirmary. Right after the Doc stabilized you. You were still in a coma from the blood loss. All your wounds. Because of my *brilliant* decisions," I chuckle sadly. "My own body was broken but nowhere near as mangled as my mind and soul. One unkind word, one look of anything but pure unadulterated happiness, and I would have shattered. I would have picked up a scalpel and slit my own throat. There was every chance you would hate me, and then I would fully and completely lose you too. It would have all been for nothing."

"That was not the case," Oliver says. "That would never be the case, Trixie."

"I know. I knew that. Eventually."

"Then why would you still not speak to me?"

"Because...I didn't want to move forward. Process it all. Admit I was angry at Will and the universe. To face it all like you forced me to do on the beach. It was me. It was all me. *All me.* It was wrong, I even knew it at the time, but I didn't care. So I'm sorry. From the bottom of my soul, I am sorry. It had nothing to do with how I...feel about you. I missed you every hour of every day. I was just lost, and I wanted to stay that way. I wanted to stay still. Catch my breath. Let something, anything, be uncomplicated. And *we* are...not uncomplicated. Or shallow. That's one of the reasons why I began seeing Connor. There was no chance of falling in love with him. We'd sleep together, we'd travel around the world, and we'd just have fun. No risk, all reward. And if something happened to him...like it has to everyone else around me...okay. Not the end of the world. Or at least that's what I keep telling myself."

"What do you mean?"

"Look at what's happened. *Again.* Out of all the men in San Diego I could have had a fling with I chose one who a few months ago tried to blackmail me into becoming his mistress? I could have picked up some accountant in a bar or signed up for Tindr. I purposely sought out a dangerous sociopath. Worse, I kept going back."

"He was manipulating you," Oliver says.

"I knew he was a killer. A manipulator. Ruthless. I *knew* he was selling me a bill of goods with trips and parties. But at least with him I knew he was no good. I mean, I've slept with four men in my life and three have tried to kill me."

"Darling, what they did is not your fault," Oliver says.

"Isn't it? I *chose* those men. A known sociopath who drinks blood and uses people like tissues. Steven had the ability to kill strangers inside him the whole time. And I knew

Will had rage inside him. He literally turned into an almost uncontrollable monster monthly. And you're—" I stop myself from traveling down that road. I close my eyes.

"And I am..." Oliver says quietly. He touches under my chin and my eyes open. His own eyes are sympathetic. "A soulless corpse. A philanderer. A murderer forever embraced by the darkness the whole of humanity fears."

"You're not soulless," I whisper.

"Most would disagree with you," he says. "But the others? I am. I am literally a creature of the darkness. But my darling...so are you."

I cringe and close my eyes again. "*No.*"

"Look at me, Trixie," he says gently. I obey. "Do you know what would have happened had you galloped off into the sunset with William? What truly would have occurred? Because my darling I see it as clear as a cloudless night. He would have stifled you at every turn. The man was inflexible. It was his way or no way. He lacked creativity, had no imagination, and could not understand those who did. And this was *before* he was forced into our dark world. He was a creature of the light before his attack, someone who loathed the darkness he now found himself enveloped by. Forced inside him. He was too inflexible to adapt, to embrace its countless beauties. He could not accept he was part of that darkness now and was in constant battle with that part of himself. And if he could not love himself wholly, if he loathed that essence inside himself, how could he ever love you the way you deserved? And how could you love him when you were in the same quagmire of denial and self-loathing?"

"Stop," I whisper and close my eyes.

He cups my cheek with his cold hand. "Do you remember what I said to you after your first case? When you feared you were a monster?"

"You called me a goddess," I say with a small smile. "And in the past year that opinion has not changed. That belief has *never* wavered." He pauses. "You asked me how I could not see what you do in me. Yet how can you not embrace all that I see in you? Your strength. Your determination. Your moral compass. Your compassion. Your—"

"Darkness?" I whisper.

"Yes," he states plainly. "But my darling, what is wrong with darkness? It is beautiful in its own way. Without darkness we would never know the moon and stars exist. That there are fireflies. Never see the majesty of the aurora borealis. And without darkness how could we appreciate its contrast? Darkness is not in and of itself wrong. It is not dangerous or evil. Corrupt. It is the only those if you choose to perceive it that way. To wield it as a weapon or use it to harm others. Or you can choose to embrace its complexity. Its depths. Its freedom. Those in the sun view it as different, unfathomable and therefore evil, but it is simply other. And there is nothing wrong with *other*. There is nothing wrong with *you*. Your darkness is a part of you, and it does not solely come from your talent. Your gift will always set you apart, yes, but it is not what defines you. It is a tool just as your empathy, your intelligence, and creativity are. And to those in the sun...those are not assets. Most do not possess them and therefore cannot understand them. And my darling, even if you were not born with your gift...you would never belong in their sun. You were not made for an ordinary life, no matter how much you desire to be. *Beatrice Alexander, you were meant for an extraordinary life*," he says with a smile.

He wipes away my tears as tender as a kiss with his thumb. "I know this is not what you wish to hear. I know you have always envisioned your life comprised of the PTA and meatloaf you charged toward with William. It is what you have strived for. The light at the end of your tunnel. That you believed you would reach it and all would be right in the world. But it would be a small world. A stifling world that would slowly crush your spirit. Your essence. There would not be a day or even an hour where you would not think 'There is more out there than this.'" Because you were meant for *more*. You were meant to influence the lives of others. To protect them. To make an indelible mark."

"I don't want that, Oliver," I say.

"Want and need are two entirely different animals, darling," Oliver says. "*Want* threw you into bed with a viper. Need led you to the F.R.E.A.K.S. Where you truly belong. Where you unlocked your strength. Your courage. Your purpose. Who you truly are. A goddess."

I chuckle wryly. "*Right*. A goddess of bad decisions and misery. Oliver, I tortured a man. I led you and the squad into a trap. I let Patsy Winsted die. I shot—"

"William. Yes," he cuts in. "But why did you pull the trigger? You had a moment to decide. In spite of it all, in spite of the fact he was literally tearing me apart, he was the man you loved. The avatar of your bright, brilliant future. You had every reason to shoot him, yes, but every reason not to as well. My ego is not so huge that it was simply you choosing me over him. So why did you?"

"Because…it was the right thing to do. He was killing you for no reason beyond rage. *Anyone* would have made the same choice."

"No, they would not," he states as plain fact. "*I* would not. If you were murdering someone, even a person I cared about, I could not do what you did. I could not kill you for anything or anyone. Not if there was even half a chance you would return to me. I faced that very dilemma when I found you freeing Adrian Winsted. I could not lay a hand on you, let alone kill you. Your instinct is always to do the right thing, the just thing. I am in awe of that. Just as I am in awe of your way with people. How you make them comfortable with a few sparse words. Your creative mind that makes connections with a few moments of thought. Your natural leadership abilities. Being able to take control during chaos and deftly moving us toward order. I have had over thirty years to hone my investigative skills and on your first case you surpassed even me. Eventually you surpassed our leader William. You solved cases in days that would normally take us weeks and saved dozens of lives in the process. And you came alive with us. You blossomed. You became...a goddess."

"I don't want to be a goddess," I whisper.

"I do not want to have to drink blood every night to survive, but if I did not I would have died over five hundred years ago a poor, desperate, melancholy farmer who loathed himself. It has been torture at times. Hell. There have been moments I wished I had died that farmer. But there have been far, *far* more moments where I thanked fate or the universe or...Him for that night five centuries ago. And without it...I never would have met *you*.

"All of life is give and take, my darling. All we can hope for, any of us, is that the good outweighs the evil. You were given a gift from birth that you could wield to help or destroy. But you have that gift and nothing will change that. It is a part of you just as your eyes are. I know what you want, but my darling, it is not what you *need*." He takes my hands in his. "And you *know it*."

All I have ever wanted, *all*, is a normal life. A house. Children. A man who adores me. Why can't I have that? Everyone else does. But not me. Because he's right. Of course he's right. I will always be me. No matter where I go in the world, no matter how hard I've ever tried, I can never stop being me. I couldn't stand by and let those vampires attack Connor. I couldn't stop myself from running full steam ahead in the Lipmann case. In the three months since I left Kansas investigating that murderer was the only time I felt like my old self. People do change, they can at least, but they can't change everything. Not what's at their very core. The blind don't just suddenly see. Gay people cannot change their sexuality. A true sociopath doesn't wake up able to feel empathy. I will always be different. I will always be a creature of the darkness. I've adapted to the light well enough for pure survival, but I will never truly belong there. Not the way I want to. I will always be me. Different. Kind. Damaged. Funny. A killer. A savior. A freak.

I move against Oliver, who instantly wraps his arms around me as I do him. I rest my head on his shoulder. "I'm so sorry I left without telling you. I'm sorry I made you think I didn't care about you, for causing you a moment of pain or doubt, because...*nothing* could be farther from the truth. I think you're just about my favorite person in this whole wide world, Oliver Smythe Montrose. I've never laughed as much as I do with you. I've missed you like a drowning woman misses air. Talking to you. Just being in the same room as you. You're my best friend." I hug him tighter. "But you're wrong about one thing. *I*...don't deserve *you*. I don't. Because you are clever. You are intelligent. And above all, you are kind. You are the most beautiful person I've ever known, inside and out. And I am so, *so* lucky to have you in my life, Oliver. I will never, ever take you or us for granted again. *Ever.* To the gates of hell, to the valley of death, I will always protect you. I will always adore you. I will always find my way back to you. I will *always* come for you. Until…my dying day and beyond."

I pull away to look up at him through the darkness, and I swear his eyes are rimmed red with his own tears. He caresses my hair and smiles. "Trixie…I…"

I know what he wants to say. What every girl wants the man she adores to say. But a part of me doesn't want him to. I'm too fragile. Too broken for anything but *this* right now. Will's love, Connor's poison are still inside me. It's not the time. This is too important. Because it can't be taken back. But a larger part silently prays that he says it. That he kisses my lips until they crack and bleed. That he makes love to me until dawn rises. That we lay in each other's arms until the world ends. I sense that same hunger in him from his tense body. His fingers digging into my scalp. I know it because I know *him*. He's waiting for me to choose. So I have to be the person he thinks I am. The person he deserves. And he deserves what he's offering, all of me.

I close my eyes and rest my head on his shoulder again. I can't be another person who uses him for my own selfish needs. "Oliver, I—"

He hugs me tighter. "It is alright," he whispers, kissing my head. "I know. I understand. We have all the time in the world."

Of course he knows. Of course he understands.

And once again I fall into sweet sleep safe in the arms of my best friend. My dark angel.

Where I belong.

*

"Oliver...?"

I awake from a dreamless slumber alone. The moment I realize he's gone all my muscles lock as a surge of adrenaline courses through me. It's unnatural not being in his arms, not pressed against him in this moment. I don't recognize my surroundings or why my chest and hand hurt. I'm so terrified I gasp and sit up. A second later my brain reboots enough for it all to come back. Even when it does I still have a hard time breathing regularly. I still *need* him here. It's as if I'm skinless, just exposed nerve endings that even the air hurts. Worse, what if Antonia's done something to him? What if her plan all along was to entrap then force me to fight for her by any means necessary? She'd need Oliver out of the way. Or he could be locked up as leverage to keep me in line. Friends or not I wouldn't put it past her. I have to find him. Even if there's a battalion of her minions in the hallway, I'll go through them all. I have to find him. I climb out of bed.

There's no army of minions in the dim hallway. In fact there's nobody. Thank God. The hallway has half a dozen closed doors, most with keypad locks on them. I'm afraid to knock. I don't want to disturb anyone and get yelled at. Or worse. "H-hello?" I call down the hallway. I hear movement, footsteps, in a room to my right. I stand up straight and tighten my fists, ready to fight if needs be.

The door opens and Antonia's number two Jin steps out of the room in gray sweats, black hair in need of brushing. He takes one look at me and scowls. "What?"

Yeah, he's not a fan. As long as he doesn't attack me, I don't care. "I-I'm looking for Oliver."

"I believe he is with Antonia," Jin says. "Anything else?"

Yeah, I don't like his attitude. I fold my arms across my chest. "Yeah, you can take me to him."

"I don't—"

"I want to see him. *Now.*"

The side of his mouth curls into a cruel smirk for a moment before he really smiles. "You are the guest, Agent Alexander." Jin looks back into the room. "Just be a minute, *mi amour,*" he says, I assume to Alejandro, before closing the door. "Right this way."

I follow Jin down the hall through the living room then down another small hallway that dead ends to a door with another keypad. I wonder if there's a security expert who handles all vampire homes. Or they just kill whomever they hire. Jin punches in the code, blocking my line of sight as he does, and we enter a small apartment. The posh living room is far homier than the guest wing's with a robin's egg blue accent wall that matches the pillows on the fluffy white couch, arm chair, and circular art deco chandelier above. The only antique is the oil painting of Antonia, I assume from the Renaissance era judging from the square neck blue velvet dress and circular jeweled cap she dons. I wonder if she knew the Borgias and Medici's. For all I know she's really Lucrecia Borgia and simply changed her name. It would explain a lot.

This thought barely forms when I hear a grunt. Then another. A woman's moan. A man's. My gut clenches. *No.*

The noises call to me. I don't want to go, I try not to, but I cannot help myself. I cross the living room to the hallway with photos of Antonia and Robin, Antonia, Alejandro and Jin, Antonia and movie stars, even one of Antonia and Oliver in disco garb on the walls as the noises grow louder. The door at the end of the hallway is slightly ajar. Don't look, Bea. Go back to bed. Don't. *Don't*...

The naked trio lie tangled in bliss, Oliver in the middle with Antonia pinned on the bed underneath him and Robin behind him, setting the rhythm of the event. For all three. Oliver throws his head back in ecstasy, even kissing Robin, before returning his attention to Antonia, kissing her too. Bile literally rises into my throat. I've turned around from this horror show before I realize I've done it. Thank you, body. I rush past the smirking Jin, and he's suddenly falling to the floor. That's what he gets for being a bastard to a telekinetic. He's lucky I didn't break his legs like I did Connor's. I might have except I just want to be *away*.

When I reach my bedroom I slam the door shut once, twice, but it doesn't help. After the third time I slide down to the floor against it. At least Jin didn't see me cry. I managed to hold back the tears until I was in here. The moment my butt hits the floor, I burst into sobs again. I can't even shut my eyes because all I see is him. *Them.*

He said he understood. That he'd be patient with me. I'm shocked he waited until I fell asleep. I know I have no reason, no right to feel betrayed, but I want to scream and cry and claw all their faces bloody. How could he do this? To me? To us? I thought we'd...I curl into a ball and hug my knees. Maybe it wasn't his idea. Maybe he felt he had no choice. Maybe it was the price for my residence here. I don't know which scenario is worse. God help me I know which one I prefer.

I'm drawn to the darkness, he says because I am a part of that darkness. Perhaps he's right. And perhaps I should begin embracing that part of myself. To let the abyss inside me spill out and have it devour them all. It's only fair.

There's barely any of *me* left in *their* wake.

CHAPTER FIFTEEN

CHECKMATE

He never returned. I stayed awake as long as I could but only managed an hour before I couldn't help myself. When I wake, my body stiff from hours of inactivity, there's no sign he came back. He usually left me water or a note. He's probably in there with *her,* their naked limbs wrapped together, and the moment the sun sets they'll be ready for another round. Or five. As I get dressed and brush my teeth and hair, I can't stop thinking about it. Them. After all Connor did to me, after having to literally run for my life, after our gut wrenching talk and all the revelations, walking in on their *ménage-a-trois* tortures me the most.

Once again I'm trapped with nothing but time on my hands. Nothing but my thoughts. I try to watch TV but of course all the crap that is my life practically suffocates me. I can't even follow the darn Kardashians. I pace around the small space like the caged animal I am. The door isn't locked but I'm hesitant to leave the relative safety of this room. I don't know what the rules are. I wish I could go for a walk on the beach—it's *right there*—but I know I can't leave the building. Connor has to know I'm here by now. He's smart enough not to storm this place, even in the daylight, but God knows what he's set in motion regardless. For all I know he has my grandmother, April and the kids locked away. I try their cell phones but they're off. Smart. It's easy to track a cell phone when it's on. I wish I had the number for the hotel, what names they're registered under, but maybe Antonia moved them. Maybe she'll use them to keep me in line. I shouldn't have trusted her with them. I shouldn't have trusted Oliver about *her*. She could have bamboozled him just as Connor did me. "Goddamn it!"

I can't stand it a moment longer. Around ten AM I put on the clothes she gave me, a coral maxi dress and white pashmina with flip flops, and brave the world. The dim lights in the hallway allow me to see a few feet in front of me, but I don't hear a thing. All the doors are closed too. So much for hospitality. What if I needed medicine? Or what if I were hungry? Okay, I am hungry. I thought Robin was supposed to take care of me. She's no doubt still asleep after last night's sexual gymnastics. She gets screwed the fun way and in turn screws me the annoying way. Story of my damn life. I could always knock on their door, heck knock it down with my mind, and demand she make me breakfast but then I'd have to see *them* together so that's not really an option. The bar might have food. It'll definitely have booze.

The doors to the bar have freaking keypad locks too. Most open with little telekinetic effort but the last one to the bar is heavy enough I get a twinge when I slam the door aside, cracking the wall around. They can bill me.

I find myself in the back of the dark, empty lounge, its gold and silver décor no longer glittering like last night and find the lights before I locate my destination—the bar. With the sunlight streaming through the skylight above the VIP lounge, I see it's nice outside, all blue sky and sunshine. And I'm stuck in here with the beach mere yards away. Yeah. Booze. I find the Belvedere vodka, Kahlua, and cream in the mini-fridge. White Russians, Starbucks that will fudge you up. I think I'll drink all day. Puke all over the guest room. Make—

"Freeze!"

My gaze juts toward the voice. Robin, dressed only in a peach kimono robe, holds a gun on me from the hallway to the back of the club. She sighs in relief as her body visibly relaxes. Even without make-up and unbrushed hair she's prettier than me. Beotch.

"Oh, shit, Agent Alexander, you scared the crap out of me," she chuckles as she lowers the gun. "I thought Connor..." She begins walking toward me. "Did you do that to all the doors?"

"I didn't have the codes," I say brattily, adding ice to my drink.

"I overslept. I'm sorry," she says before reaching the gilded bar. I suck down my strong drink and suppress a shudder. Too much vodka. "You really did that to that last door? It's solid steel."

"I once lifted a Hummer over my head, so..." I take another sip.

Robin sits on one of the stools. "Wow. No wonder Connor wants you so badly."

"Yes. For my *mind*," I say bitchily, channeling my inner Bette Davis.

Robin's jade eyes narrow at me. "Are you...okay? It's kind of early to be drinking."

I roll my eyes while taking another sip. "Aren't we the considerate one?" Another sip. "I want to talk to my grandmother and best friend. I want to make sure they're okay."

"Okay. Of course. Oliver gave me all the details. He—"

"Oh, I know he gave you all the *details*." Another sip. "*Repeatedly* I'm sure."

Robin slow blinks at me. "Oh. That's what this is about." She starts playing with a strand of her bleached blonde hair. "I-I thought you two weren't...you're not a couple. And it was just a bit of fun. I don't—"

"We may not be a couple, but he is my...friend. And he wouldn't have left me and done...*that* if your girlfriend didn't pressure him or take advantage of his emotional state. He—"

"Uh, you need to stop right there, honey bunch," Robin says, holding up a finger. "First off, Toni didn't pressure him to do jack shit. He came to us upset and confused about your little conversation in bed last night. He told us all the shit you've put him through the past few months too." My face falls. "Yeah. He told us *everything*. And from my perspective it sounds like the only one taking advantage of him is *you*. You almost got him killed more than once. You pushed him away. You abandoned him. You humiliated him. Dragged him into this current bullshit we *all* have to clean up now. So honey, *you*—who have been fucking another guy for weeks now—don't get to judge or be pissed off that a single man found a little comfort when he needed it and you wouldn't provide it for whatever reason, you ungrateful bitch. We're all here, bending over backwards, to solve the giant clusterfuck you've brought to our doorstep."

"*I* brought?" I huff. "Your girlfriend and Connor have been at each other's throats for over a century. If anything *I* was the one dragged into this. I didn't want *any* of this! I didn't ask for any of this!"

"Well, you're in it now," Robin says. "Your family's in it now. It is what it is, Agent Alexander. It's not going to magically resolve itself. Life doesn't work like that. You have to put in the work. And right now that work is for you to decide what you are willing to do to clean your mess, and it is your mess. You need to decide how far you're willing to go to do what's right. For yourself, for your family. Your friends. Everything else should just be white noise. And you getting drunk and picking fights with people trying to help isn't going to drown out that noise. Will it? Get your head in the game, honey bunch. Put your big girl pants on, grab a gun, and start fighting. If not for your sake then for the people you love's."

My righteous anger from just a minute ago evaporated with her words, instead replaced with something worse. Shame. Nope. Not that. Stop it, Bea. I have nothing to be ashamed of. *I* didn't start this war. *I* didn't feel the need to comfort a vulnerable man with my penis. Anger. Anger's good. Better. I can handle anger. I—

There's a pounding on the front door of the bar not fifty feet away. We both gasp and spin in that direction before glancing at one another again. We don't know what to do so we just remain still and quiet. Probably a delivery or something. They pound again.

"LAPD! Open this door or we will break it down!"

We exchange another confused look. I shrug. Robin slowly climbs off the stool while picking up her gun again. I move around the bar to join her as a united front. Ready for—

The door literally falls off the hinges inside the club just as three men with automatic rifles storm in. Thank Christ I immediately notice the word "Police" written on their Kevlar and their badges hanging around their necks or I'd snap their necks with my mind.

Robin immediately drops her gun and we both raise our hands as they shout at us to, "Put your hands on the back of your heads and get down on the ground. On the ground!" the one in the lead says as SWAT and a man in a windbreaker advance toward us. We obey. The three men in tactical gear swarm around us, rifles pointed just as they're trained to do. Like the FBI taught me. The man in the windbreaker with a suit underneath his Kevlar approaches behind them.

"Beatrice Suzanne Alexander?" he asks.

"Y-yes?" I gasp.

He removes his handcuffs and bends beside me. "Beatrice Alexander you are under arrest for the assault and battery of Connor McInnis and Neil Kilkelly."

"What?" I ask as he slaps the cuffs around my wrists.

He continues the Miranda warning as my head swims. This is a freaking farce. *I* assaulted *them*? He's using the police to do his dirty work now? Gotta give him credit, it's a clever ploy. If he sends his own people not only does it violate the treaty but he knew I'd fight back against them. I can't do anything to these men. Neither of us can. The officer yanks me off the ground and one of the tactical team points his gun at me. The other two remain on Robin. "Do you understand these rights as they've been said to you?"

"Y-yes."

"I'll get you out," Robin says.

"She'll be extradited to San Diego County after processing and arraigned probably later this afternoon," the officer pushing me toward the door says.

"I will get you out! I will stay on top of this! She has powerful friends in the FBI! If anything happens to her…" Robin shouts.

The officer manhandles me out into the almost overwhelming sunlight I longed for just minutes ago. I wish I could shield my eyes. The cuffs cut into my wrists. I *could* easily escape but if this is in the real system, I'd be a fugitive. I'd have to hurt these men. The F.R.E.A.K.S. may be able to smooth things over, but I don't know. I half expect some of Connor's minions to drive by and grab me or for the officer to just hand me over to some goons, but he actually does take me to the back of a police cruiser. The tactical team returns to their own car with only one getting in with us.

"Is-is this for real?" I ask the men.

"What?" the tactical officer asks.

"Do-do you work for Connor? Are you taking me to him?"

"Ma'am we work for the county of Los Angeles, and we are taking you to county lock-up where there's a van coming to take you back down to San Diego for arraignment," the plainclothes officer says.

"So this is legit? He really filed charges?"

"Yes, ma'am. Last night right after you assaulted them. SDPD told us where you'd be early this morning." The driver pauses. "I saw the photos. You really did a number on them."

Yeah, nice try jerk. Getting me to talk about my crime. I learned that tactic too. "And let me guess, it was a Det. Harvey Berry who facilitated all this?"

The driver glances back at me. "How did you—"

I scoff then chuckle wryly. "Yeah. Welcome to the farce, gentlemen. You've played your roles to perfection. Delivering me into the arms of the devil." I rest my head on the back of the seat and close my eyes. "Maybe it's where I deserve to be."

*

Have you ever been so tired that the mere act of blinking proves as difficult as running a marathon? Not physically difficult just that it's one more pointless activity that needs doing and you just don't see the point of. Where you're exhausted in your every pore, every atom? Twice before in my life I've experienced this. The first time was sitting in the reception area of a Phoenix police station after talking to the case officer from Child Protective Services when I was eight. My mother had just killed herself and I had no idea what would happen to me next. The officer mentioned some grandmother I'd never met was on her way for us, but I didn't know the woman. All I knew was that the mommy who loved brushing my hair while humming show tunes, who read me stories at night, who made the best pancakes ever, was gone. Dead. And according to my brother it was my fault. It was a lot for a child to handle, so I more or less shut down. The second time was on the flight back to San Diego three months ago. We'd buried Will hours before, I was all but fired from my job, and guilt over both suffocated me. I do now what I did those other two times: curl up, close my eyes, and stay as still as possible as abject misery and guilt drown me.

I've been fingerprinted. Strip searched. Photographed. Cavity searched. Forced to bend over naked and examined to ensure I don't have contraband stuffed in my vagina or anus. Manhandled onto a van for an hours long trip back to San Diego sitting beside a jittery meth addict also enduring alcohol withdrawal. Shoved into another holding cell that reeks of urine, feces, and body odor with more drunks, gang members, and meth addicts picking their faces to a bloody pulp. I sit on my bench in the corner of the courthouse holding cell, hugging my knees while resting my head on them with my eyes shut as I'm called a white bitch and *puta* and cunt by some of the others. I barely hear the insults. I travel so deep into my own head, into the inky abyss, the other prisoners may as well be in another dimension.

Just me and my thoughts. My plans. It becomes so clear what I need to do. The only solution. I saw it last night even before Oliver came into my bedroom. After he did what he did with Antonia too. I just don't know if I can pull this off. If I can even bring myself to do it. If he'll—

"Alexander, Beatrice?" a woman says over the intercom at hour three in the bowels of hell. I slowly gaze up to find a guard on the other side of the door. "Come to the door, put your hands behind your back, then turn around."

Like a zombie, I obey. The guard cuffs me through the metal slot before opening the door. Once again I'm marched through beige halls past other guards and criminals, some struggling against one another. An exercise in futility. Pointless. A waste of energy. I've learned my lesson, so should they.

Our destination is a small interrogation room where a familiar woman waits. Krista has the nerve to smile at me as I'm cuffed to the table by the guard, yet I don't feel a thing. Not annoyance, not anger, just a void. The guard promptly leaves and a moment after the door shuts, Krista's smile grows. "They think I'm a paralegal for your lawyer."

"I don't have a lawyer," I say in monotone.

"Of course you do. One of the best in town. Connor would never leave you in the lurch," she says pleasantly. "You'll be arraigned, I'll post your bail, and eventually all charges will be dropped. It'll be like it never happened."

"Is that why he sent you? To deliver the good news?"

"I'm here to talk some sense into you, girlie girl," she says. "I mean, look where you are, Bea. You're in jail when you could be in Paris with Connor, shopping at Chanel and—"

"*Connor* put me in here," I point out.

"You didn't give him a choice. He's been so worried about you he's barely gotten any sleep today. That Antonia could have been torturing you. Holding you hostage. She—"

"Is that what he told you? He's doing it all for my benefit? Jesus, I knew you were dumb but—"

"I'm not dumb," she cuts in. "If anyone's the dummy here, it's y-o-u," she spells out. "He wants to give you *everything*, girl. Power. Money. A life traveling the world with no worries or responsibilities. And not just for you. For your family too. He'd take care of you all. He'll give you anything. What's that Antonia offering, huh? Nothing, right? Come on, Bea. You know life's mostly horrible. For every one good thing that happens there are ten bad. The deck's stacked against most of us. The rich and powerful war and it's us peasants that suffer. Playing by the rules, being good, whatever the hell that really means, where has it got you? And it's not like Antonia is an angel here. She's just as evil and immoral as Connor. She just wants to use you like he does, but at least *he* knows your worth."

"*She* never threated my family," I point out.

"*Yet.*" Krista leans forward. "You're stuck between a rock and a hard place. That's just a fact. It isn't going to change. And all you can do…is do *you*. What loyalty do you owe that bitch?"

A flash of Oliver screwing her enters my mind.

"None."

"Then get yours' girl. They did this to you. All you can do is make the best out of it. Besides, it's not as if you have much choice." She leans back and pulls out her cell phone. "He wanted me to stress he'd rather this be done civilly, but…" She holds up her phone to reveal a photo of my sister-in-law Renata walking to her car holding my baby nephew Marcus. My stomach clenches. "Forgot about them, didn't you? We didn't." She puts her phone back. "Antonia didn't either. Our guys noticed her guys parked out front. Connor told me to tell you he can protect them. To remind you that the moment Antonia hears you're back with us she *will* take measures, no matter whose friend you are. Connor *wants* to protect them. He really does care about you, Bea. Truly." Krista rises from the table with a sympathetic smile. "There's only one thing to do, and it is the *right* thing to do. Just give in already. Stop fighting this, Bea. Stop fighting him. You'll be a lot happier if you do. And he just wants you to be happy."

Krista half smiles before spinning around and banging on the door. It opens and Krista departs. I just stare at that door, still numb before laying my head on my arm and shutting my eyes again.

Okay. *Okay.*

The guard escorts me back to the holding cell where I resume my impression of a rock on the beach, thinking thinking thinking away and not feeling a damn thing. When planning a massacre a person should feel *something* right? I don't. An hour, maybe less, passes before the guards round us up for the arraignment. Connor's lawyer meets me for all of two minutes and is exactly like I envisioned him: hurried, bored, and the kind of man who owns a pen that could pay my rent for a month. At least he lets me borrow it. And I do hope he charges Connor for the scrap of paper and ink.

When it's my turn at the dock, even without the handcuffs on, I keep my hands balled into fists. And aren't I the popular gal. In the first row of the gallery I find Krista and one hulking goon I recognize from my nights at the club. In the back, by the door, Robin with three giants of her own flanking her. I knew she'd be here. Brave of her. She smiles at me but I don't return the gesture. I couldn't even if I wanted to. I just stare at the bored judge as the clerk reads off the bogus charges. Two counts assault and battery with a hundred thousand bond ready to be paid within the hour. Not two minutes later I'm sent back to the holding area to wait again. Back into my shell to refine my plans. One hour later, I'm filling out paperwork and being escorted out of the holding areas a relatively free woman. Bully for me.

I don't even get thirty seconds out the door before both factions pounce. Krista and her goon rush from the left of the courthouse and Robin and her three from the right. They must not have spotted each other until now. Once they do, both rush to be the first. Krista beats them by three steps. "All set?" she asks me as if the opposing team aren't there.

"Agent Alexander?" Robin asks.

Krista turns to Robin. "Who are you?"

"Who are *you*?" Robin asks.

I don't have the energy to prolong this nightmare. I'm ready.

"Robin…" I say, stepping her direction. I smile and take her hand.

She glances down at our hands then up at me, confused. "What—"

"Robin…take your pathetic little minions here and fuck off back to your bitch girlfriend. While you still can."

Her eyes narrow. "What? I don't…you don't have to go with them. We can—"

"Protect me? Take care of me? Excellent fucking job you've done so far, *honey bunch*. All you and your girlfriend have managed to do is piss Connor off further and literally screw the man I lo—" I stop myself again and grimace. "You can't do shit for me. Only *I can*. And I am." I step toward Krista, but then stop and turn back around. "Oh, and Robin, don't forget I know where you all sleep. Where you live. If *anything* happens to my family, I will bring that building down. I will crush and burn you all alive. That is a promise. Now run back to your master...slut."

I give Robin one last shit-eating grin before moving to Krista. "Let's go." The goon takes my upper arm, but I yank it away. I look the man square in the eye. "Touch me again and I'll rip out your spine vertebrae by vertebrae, smiling as you scream."

I bump past him as I saunter away. They follow at a close distance down the hallway and out of the courthouse. The sun still hangs in the sky with about two hours remaining. I close my eyes and enjoy the sensation of that natural warmth on my upturned face. I savor the slight breeze on my skin and the faint scent of the ocean that's always on the San Diego wind. Life makes it so hard for us to remember to take a moment to enjoy these simple pleasures of the world. These simple delights threaten to bring tears to my eyes.

"Bea?" Krista says behind me, ruining the mood.

That's all I get. A few seconds of bliss and peace. I open my eyes and spin back to face her. "Let's get this over with, shall we? Mustn't keep our master waiting."

CHAPTER SIXTEEN

THE VILLAIN IN MY OWN STORY

At least I've made the bastard's life harder today. Per Krista, Connor's barely slept all day and spent all last night healing and organizing the arrest to "get me out of enemy hands" as Krista calls it. I just sit in her car with the window down and head resting on the door lavishing in that sunshine. But like all things in this life, it's over too fast. We reach downtown and the skyscrapers blot out the sun, and its completely taken away from me when we turn into his underground garage. Even without knowing there's a secret torture room here this place would feel like a tomb. They fixed the gate, and the moment it shuts, my heart leaps into my throat. I'm really doing this. *Am I really doing this?* Yes. Darn straight I am. Get out of the car and be the bad bitch they need you to be. Ruthless. Cold. Hard. You've learned from the greats.

A goon gets the car door for me, and I climb out with my shoulders back and chin up. I don't wait for them to follow. I know where I'm going. What I'm doing. This minnow has evolved into a shark and its time to swim.

Neil stands at the entrance of the apartment hallway staring down with a scowl that I assume he wishes could kill me as I come up the stairs. Seems he's fully recovered from last night. Not a dent or scratch. Jerk. I smirk anyway. I'm positive he'd preferred the goon had taken me out to the desert and shot me in the back of the head, but when do we ever get our heart's desire? I continue smirking at the silently seething vampire. "Hello, minion. See you're not ready to kiss and make up yet. Not surprising I guess. I can't recall ever seeing your lips do anything but kiss Connor's ass."

"You—"

"Bitch. Cunt. Yeah. *Whatever*," I say, rolling my eyes as I pass him at the top of the steps. Down the hallway two guards flank the apartment door and both reach into their jackets as I approach. I stop at the door and smile at them both. "Gentlemen."

Neil finally reaches the apartment door and pounds on it twice. "Come in," Connor calls from the other side.

And away we go.

Connor sits on the sofa with a laptop beside him and cell phone pressed to his ear. Looking at him in a pair of khakis and royal blue button down no one would ever suspect he's a cold blooded killer. Considering what I did to him last night I expect a greeting like Neil's but instead get passivity. He simply nods at me before returning his attention back to his call. "Avril the moment the sun sets I expect everyone here. I have not been able to reach Edgar's consort all day. He needs to rise now. Send someone there." Connor listens for a moment. "We shall see. Get it done." He hangs up the phone before finally looking at me with a frown. "You look dreadful, fairest."

"Fleeing one's psychotic boyfriend then spending the day in jail does that to a gal," I say with a cruel grin.

"Yes. I must apologize for my…tactics. It was—"

"Your tactics? Like trying to force your soul on me? Accusing me of a felony? Those tactics?"

"Yes," he states as plain fact. "But desperate times call for desperate measures. I—"

I roll my eyes. "Oh, for God's"—the vampires wince—"sake, just shut up. Just shut the fuck up. After *everything* just please do me the courtesy of stopping the bullshit. Desperate times…fuck you, asshole. This was you, Connor. This was all you and your boredom and dumbass ambition and pathological need to win so you can feel good about yourself. End of. It's fucking pathetic. You're as insecure as a teenage girl, and I see right through you. So save the spin and let's just get down to brass tax." I pause. "Ten million dollars."

Belittling him didn't get him to drop the poker face but those last three words do. His eyes narrow. "Ten million dollars?"

"With a million every year after as long as I live. Plus you pay for my godchildren's college all the way through their doctorates if they choose to go that route."

"I do not…"

"That's it. That's the price for half my soul."

Connor, Neil, heck the guards all stare at me in disbelief and confusion. I stand here under their scrutiny, back straight. Connor catches my eyes, peering in deeply to find the subterfuge. He won't find any. I mean every word.

"You suddenly wish to become my familiar? Just like that?" Connor asks. "You know what it entails."

"Yeah. You get to use my power in your dumbass duel, and I get to live the picture of health for an extra hundred twenty-five years as a millionaire."

"And this is acceptable to you?" Connor asks.

"No. *None* of this is acceptable to me, asshole," I snap. "I would kill you dead here and now, but I'm sure you have a contingency plan for that. Probably something to do with my baby nephew, you evil fucktard." His mouth twitches into a momentary smile. My blood chills a few degrees. I don't let it show. "There are obvious trust issues here on both parts. I get that. You don't trust me not to kill you here and now and I sure as hell don't trust you won't slit my throat the moment you have your precious LA territory. Which only leaves us…mutually assured destruction. As I understand it as your familiar, I can't kill you without killing myself and vice versa. That fact will give us both insurance. You hurt my family, reneg on your end of the deal, cue destruction. On your end not only do you get my power, I will damn well fight by your side tonight just to keep my own ass alive. When the bitch is dead, we go our separate ways and I never see your smug face again. After tonight the only contact we'll ever have is the yearly payoff. I will have no further part of your business, and you do not call me unless your life is in mortal fucking danger. You will cease to exist for me. We kill the bitch, we're done."

He's been scrutinizing me during my whole proposal with one side of his mouth curled up. "You would truly do this? Sell your soul and murder a woman who took you in last night?"

"Well, let's face it, what choice have you left me? Either of you? You're both going to keep swatting me around like cats who've caught a mouse for how long? Years? And forget about me, fuck me, what about my family? At least this way the bullshit ends tonight, I come out with enough cash to keep my family comfortable, and I get to start a new life away from all this violence. Away from you. Win-win."

"Not for Antonia," he points out.

"Her problem, not ours," I say with a sneer.

"I glean you two did not get along as well as she had hoped," Connor says.

I grimace. "No. We got along just fine…until I walked in on her and her girlfriend fucking Oliver. So…"

Connor chuckles. "Of course. Hell hath no fury like a woman scorned." He shifts on the couch. "And what of your gallant, lantern jawed hero?"

"What about him? You don't touch him," I say forcefully. "He's covered under the family clause of our little Faustian deal here."

Connor chuckles wryly again. "Do you honestly believe he will stand idly by whilst you assist in murdering his friend and lover?"

My mouth twitches. "He said he would. She-she pressured him last night. Took advantage. He'll see the light. Eventually. But you don't touch him regardless."

"And if he attempts to touch *us*?" Connor posits.

I stand up straighter. "Then he would have made *his* choice, wouldn't he?" I swallow. "But it won't come to that. Not if we stick to my plan."

"*Your* plan?" Neil asks with derision.

My gaze whips his direction. "Yeah, asshole. My plan. The plan of a woman whose led close to two dozen missions as a Federal Agent. Who spent all fucking day in jail with nothing but time on her hands to work out every angle that gets her family out of danger and ten million dollars in her bank account. Now shut up and listen." I return my attention to Connor. "We move tonight. *Now*. We have precisely two tactical advantages over her right now: she thinks I'm a weak moron and the element of surprise. As last night's attempted metaphysical rape proved, you can't trick someone into becoming your familiar. I have to be willing. As long as she has my family, logic dictates I won't do anything to jeopardize their lives. So I wouldn't readily agree to be your familiar. But you do have me. You would just possibly torture me until I agree, but that would take time. Not to mention the longer we wait the bigger the chance one of her spies discovers I'm your familiar and all bets are off. Still with me?"

"Oh, yes," Connor says with pride.

"She'll be scrambling tonight to get me back and fortify, to gather intel, so the majority of her underlings will be out. But I know where she works. Sleeps. I know the layout. I suggest you gather a small tactical team, hire us a plane, and we arrive at the bar in force before it opens. An ambush. Then…you finally accept her duel in front of whoever's there. One of three things will happen: one, you fight with your bright and shiny new talent and win, two, she'll reneg and you'll win by default."

"And the third possibility?" Neil asks.

"Well, the most likely occurrence is she'll say no, you'll win by default, and with nothing left to lose, she'll start a big ass fight in an act of desperation, hence the need for your best and brightest but once again, a lot of you and few of her. You win anyway."

"We cannot simply all-out attack her. The King—" Neil says.

I look at Neil. "Has already seen my testimony from last night and knows what a bad boy Connor here's been. However, unless *he* has a familiar with telekinesis you don't know about, after tonight's takeover, not only will Connor be richer and probably more powerful than this King, but in a one-on-one fight, he can take him too." Back to Connor. "So. Clock's ticking, asshole. You in or not? Best accept before I change my mind."

My cautious ex-boyfriend stares at me but asks Neil, "Did our people notice her having contact with any of Antonia's? Any phone calls?"

"No," Neil says. "She made no phone calls and the only visitors were Krista and our attorney. Antonia's he-she was at the courthouse but as you heard what both Krista and Charlie said they spoke only in their presence. And, if she is willing to be your familiar..."

"Mutually assured destruction," Connor says with a smile my way. "You know, I have never wanted to throw you on this couch and fuck you so badly as I do now."

"After the familiar ritual if you ever lay a finger on me again, I will rip your dick off and feed it to you, death be damned."

Connor rises from the sofa. "Well, a hundred twenty-five years is several lifetimes. I may win you over again yet."

"Please. Like you haven't already begun looking for a way to sever the tie without killing us both. A hundred twenty-five years wouldn't be enough for a greedy son-of-a-bitch like you."

Connor slowly moves over to me, stopping less than a foot away and his eyes never waver from mine. "You know me so well, fairest. And here I thought I knew you."

"Yeah, well, as someone pointed out to me today, what good has being me gotten me? Time to try being like everyone else. Greedy. Selfish. *Cold*."

"Finally wiseing up, I see."

"Ten million with another million every year. Protection for my family. No contact unless life and death. Accept my terms and you become the most powerful vampire in America, if not the world. So just say yes already and let's get this the fuck over with."

Connor smiles again, those violet eyes crinkling. "To mutually assured destruction, fairest." He turns to Neil. "Charter the plane and cars. Get *everyone* here."

"But not too many," I order. "Only people you trust implicitly otherwise one of her spies could catch wind and fortify. Strong but surgical."

"You heard our General. Hop to," Connor orders. Neil rolls his eyes but obeys, whipping out his cell phone and moving to the other side of the room. Connor returns his attention to me. "So...shall we begin?"

I glance at the guards and Neil. "Can we have some privacy please?"

"And be alone with you and a knife? I think not."

"Still don't trust me?" I ask.

"I shall in a few minutes."

"Fair enough. I'll get the knife, you get my money, Danny Boy."

"Non-silver please, fairest."

"Aww. You're taking all the fun out of this for me," I say.

"I shall make sure you have plenty of fun tonight. *Partner.*"

With an eye roll, I turn away from the vampire. As Connor returns to his computer to make me a millionaire, I find a butcher knife in the kitchenette. My hands tremble as I pick it up. I can't back out now, no matter how terrified I am. I don't know what to expect. Will this hurt? Will it destroy what's left of my soul? In the end, it doesn't matter. It's going to happen regardless. I just don't want to prolong any of this. I want this night to be over. I just want it all to be over.

Connor types away at his computer and I set the knife down between us. I help him complete the transaction. In less than a minute I become a bonafide millionaire. I used to live in trailer parks, out of a car at times even. Dirt poor. And now I have more money than I know what to do with, and I don't feel a damn bit different. Nana can finally live in a house without bars on the windows. April won't have to worry about choosing between doctor visits and groceries for the week. It's a life changing amount of money and I don't feel a thing. Not happy, not guilty, just nothing. Connor looks over and smiles. "Congratulations. You are now a wealthy woman. How does it feel?"

"Like I sold my soul," I say. "Imagine that."

"When you are sunbathing in Turks and Caicos with a martini in your hand next week I am sure that feeling will be different," he assures me, patting my hand. After that first part, with a glower, I yank it away. He frowns at the rebuff. "I have kept my end of the bargain. Your turn."

My stomach seizes. Okay. *Okay.*

Before I lose my nerve, I pick up the butcher knife and slash my still healing hand where his minion cut me last night. "God—" he winces right along with me, "damn it that hurts! Ugh!" I clench my jaw. "Over the heart too I assume?"

"Yes. I can—"

"I got it," I snap. After another deep breath, I slice where he "accidently" hurt me last night. He begins removing his own shirt. "We don't have to have sex during this, do we?"

I hand him the knife. "It would aid the process, yes, but can be avoided as long as enough blood is exchanged and both participants are…open, spiritually, with one another. Kissing, touching and exchanging blood are required though." He cuts his palm and across his heart with winces. "We can always attempt the ritual once without copulation but if it does not work then we may have no choice."

I'm so dead inside and out I probably wouldn't feel a thing regardless. Just close my eyes and think of England, right? Become a literal whore, but at least I'd be a high priced one. "Fine."

"I have to paint the sigils on your head and heart in our mixed blood," he explains. He dabs his own bleeding hand then mine with the same finger before drawing on my forehead and over the wound on the swell of my breast before doing the same to himself. Sigils. I've seen witches use these to seal spells and ward away bad energy. Just looks like squiggles in a circle to me. "Now…we begin. We must share a great deal of blood. Ingest it. Beginning with me. I have to bite you."

My nose crinkles up. "Goddamn it. Fine."

I push my hair to the side and bare my neck. He isn't gentle. Those fangs sinking in, piercing my skin, hurt a lot more than the cuts. Even worse than the pain of his fangs in my neck is the sensation of him touching me. His hand in my hair, his tongue licking and lips suckling my open wounds. Pure hell.

It seems like an eternity but can only be about thirty seconds before I begin growing woozy. He finally pulls away from the blood feast only to kiss me. The blood filling my mouth at least distracts me from the kiss. I can actually tell there are holes in his tongue just like last night. My own has no option but to mingle with his when I'm not swallowing enough blood to almost trigger my gag reflex. Another thirty seconds of this disgusting act and he moves back to my neck. Then we're kissing again. My neck. I'm almost grateful for the blood loss. I'm so relaxed and don't even care he's really kissing me now. Running his good hand through my hair as he did dozens of times before. He pulls away this time to stare in my eyes and clasp our cut hands together. "That is my girl," he whispers. "Give in fairest. Let go."

He kisses me again for several seconds before returning to suckling my neck. The wound's healing so he has to bite again. My own blood pours out. I must have lost three pints by now. Connor stops his feast again to pull me on his lap. Of course he has an erection. I don't care. I'm so woozy I barely notice as he bites his own wrist again and the blood spews out. As he moves the wrist to my mouth and I continue to gulp down the disgusting liquid. He begins whispering in Latin again, "*Sanguinem sanguine meo.*" He pulls away his wrist. "When I drink you say it." He returns to my neck and grinds his pelvis against mine as I repeat the phrase. This time he only suckles for a few seconds before making me feast from his wrist as he says, "*Caro de carne mea,*" then back to my neck as I repeat the phrase. Back to drinking from him as he repeats the first phrase. Then I do my part as he switches to my neck. Again with the second phrase. As he grinds against me. Repeat. Repeat. He finally looks me in the eyes and says, "Blood of my blood, flesh of my flesh, we are of one soul, one body. Always mine, always thine."

He begins saying it again, chanting it, and I know I'm supposed to say it with him. We repeat it like a mantra ten times, twenty, his pelvis massaging against mine and mine his, eyes never leaving one another. Twenty times. I sense it, I *feel* it grow with every word. Building, building like an orgasm in every cell. The world falls away and all that remains are his eyes, that erection, those words. It grows and grows until…he releases my hand and instinctively with those final words we press our hands to each other's chests.

Boom.

The moment we say the word "thine" as we touch, its as if I spontaneously combust with energy. I'm ripped apart into stardust and instantly rebuilt again. And I'm on the floor. With all the furniture flying around the room from the blast zone. It takes me a moment to re-enter my body but it's different. I recognize it instantly. *I'm* different. I should be exhausted but I'm still buzzing like a battery and panting as if I swam the English Channel. Thinking comes next. I glance around the room to find his the goons picking themselves off the ground too as they toss off the debris from the coffee table and chairs I exploded. I seem to be intact too. My wounds hurt but I touch my neck and only come away with minimal blood.

"Beatrice?"

Connor's scared. Terrified. Excited. Confused. I *know* he's these things before I turn to find him also on the floor a few feet away. I know it as if he had just said those very words to me. And his skin. Peaches and cream instead of just cream. It's almost…human. He stares at me. No, at something at my feet. A piece of what was once his coffee table. He stares, his eyes crinkling this time with concentration. The piece of wood flies across the room. Connor smiles which quickly becomes a laugh. Guttural, pure joy laughing, the kind where my new soul mate rolls around on the floor cackling away like a lunatic.

"We did it!" he laughs to the heavens. "I did it! I won!"

I fall on my back and stare up at the ceiling too. Yeah. I won.

*

"No asshole, you have to focus. *Focus*."

"I am!"

"You want to get us both killed? Fine. If not then fucking focus!"

We've been staring at a row of books on the bar for one full hour and none have lifted. Fun with telekinesis training while the vampire version of Seal Team Six, consisting of the full inner circle of Jack, Neil, Edgar, Avril, Thomas, the bartender Mathilda, and others I haven't met have all en massed at the apartment or are out assembling the arsenal and travel arrangements, but we both agreed the wagon trail won't depart until Connor moves all these books. First we needed blood transfusions, then separate showers followed by a steak dinner for me. I can't remember ever being so hungry in my life. Guess that's part of my new normal. Along with sensing what Connor's feeling, heightened hearing, clearer vision, and my hair looks like its commercial ready, and my skin's glowing as if I were pregnant. I think my breasts and butt are perkier too in my black turtleneck and jeans. I've lost ten pounds and ten years. So far I can see the appeal of being a familiar.

Connor continues staring at the book then groans in frustration, lowering his finger. "This is impossible."

"You did it before, right? With the wood? And once you've got it, you've got it. It's like riding a bike. Just block out everything else. Nothing exists but the book and your will to lift it. So lift it! Lift!"

As I instructed earlier, he raises his finger to focus where he wants the power to go. No joy yet. I expect this to take another hour at least. I'm enjoying watching him fail time and time again. Life's small pleasure—

The telephone beside us rings, breaking his concentration. He groans again. "Bloody hell!"

Neil picks up the phone. "Yes?" The minion listens and whatever is said on the other end brings a smirk to his face. "No. Please send him up." Neil hangs up, still smirking. "Special Agent Montrose demands an audience. He is on his way here."

My face, my stomach, my composure all fall. No. No, no, no, no, no...

Connor chuckles. "Oh, my night grows even better. This should be interesting."

There's no place to sit after I destroyed most of his living room and kitchenette, including the chairs, so I just stand here willing my legs not to give out. What the heck is he doing here? Him being here is not part of the plan. Why...? Stop, Calm down, Bea. It's done. It was done the moment I arrived here. Before. Nothing's stopping this now.

"No one hurts him," I order. "Not one fucking finger is laid on him."

"We will be civil if he extends us the same courtesy," Connor assures me. There's a knock on the door. "Enter."

Oliver, flanked by two other vampires with guns, rushes into the apartment. For the first time ever I am genuinely sickened by the sight of him. Heck, I can't even look at him. I gaze down at the floor, but I know he's staring at me, at first elated I'm in one piece, but the longer he doesn't say anything I know he's growing horrified. That last guess comes from the glee Connor's experiencing this moment. I hope *he's* choking on my despair. "Oh, Trixie. Wh-what have you done?"

"What I had to."

The room remains pin drop silent. "You...made her do this. You—"

"No, I did not," Connor says happily. "*She* had to convince *me*."

"What? No. I…Trixie?" I don't reply. "Why? Why would you do this?" I think he takes a step toward me. "Why—"

I finally peer up at him. "Because I had no choice. Because your *girlfriend* didn't keep her end of the bargain. Because my family deserves better."

"Not to mention the ten million dollars I paid you," Connor adds.

Bastard. Oliver glances from him to me, and I gaze down again. I hope Connor chokes on my shame too. "Trixie?"

"What? *What?*" I look back up at him. "Don't you dare fucking judge me, Oliver. You…" I take a step toward him. "*You* have absolutely no right to come here and judge me. Not you. Not after what you did to me last night."

"What? I…I do not…"

"'You're a goddess. You make me a better man. I know. I understand. We have all the time in the world, '" I hiss. "How long exactly was all the time in the world? Ten minutes? Twenty? How long between when you left *my* bed and when you stuck your dick into *her*?"

His face contorts into shock and horror. "Trixie, I—"

"I saw you. With them. With *her*. I woke up alone. Terrified. I couldn't find you. So one of her asshole minions took great glee in bringing me to her bedroom. And you…never came back. You left me alone. Did she pressure you into sleeping with her? Made it part of the deal to keep me safe?"

He has to look away from my gaze this time. "No. She would never—"

"So it just…happened? Like *this* just happened?" Another step. "Your girlfriend failed me. I was manhandled out of her fortress, forced to the ground, had a guns on me, strip and cavity searched, and delivered straight here while the woman you said would protect me slept naked beside you. Guess what? *He* won. There was nothing left to do. Nothing else I could do except stop fighting. End this bullshit. I choose to get mine. For my family. To protect them. And you."

"You…sold your life to him to protect me? By agreeing to butcher my oldest friend?" Oliver asks, voice trembling. "Do you honestly think I would just stand by and let you harm her?"

"*You* said you would. Last night. Or was that just an empty sentiment too?"

"What?"

"What I did to Will. You said you'd always come for me. Do anything for me. You'd walk into hell with me. *No matter what*. Prove it. Me or her."

"Trixie…"

"Me. Or her. We're taking the bitch down. Tonight. You can be on the winning side, *my* side like you promised and fight with us. With me."

"Or you are against me," Connor finishes for me.

Oliver stares at me as if he doesn't recognize me. "This is wrong."

"It is what it is," I say. "Me or her."

"This is not you. It—"

"It's me now," I cut in. "Me…or her."

"I-I…cannot. I cannot support you in this. This is madness."

My whole body slumps. "Yeah. That's what I thought." I literally turn my back to him to face Connor. "Lock him up somewhere. Get him the hell out of my sight."

"Trixie—"

"But don't hurt him. We may be able to use him tonight," I say, returning to the books.

"Get your hands off me! Trixie!" Oliver calls behind me.

"Down to the garage. Watch him closely," Connor orders. "Only hurt him if necessary."

"Trixie! Beatrice! Get your hands off—"

I hear fist connect to body before Oliver groans in pain. I wince myself but don't turn around. If I look at him I'll crumble. A few seconds later the groans cease and the door shuts. I rest my head on my arms on the bar. This wasn't supposed to happen. What was she doing, letting him come here? She should be protecting him. She doesn't give a crap about him. And still he sides with her. She—

"Well, that settles that," Connor says.

"What?" I ask.

"We now have concrete proof that you love him more than he loves you," Connor says no doubt with a smirk. "Interesting."

It takes every ounce of restraint not to punch him until he has no face left. "Shut the fuck up and get back over here. Unless you want to die tonight, you need to learn this. *Now*."

Connor moves over to me. "Yes, General," he says with a salute. God I so prefer him sneaky and Machiavellian to chipper.

"Point to focus. Concentrate," I whisper into his ear. "The book wants to lift. You are its master. Every atom is yours to command. Feel them. Focus on them. They belong to you. They are yours. Now force them to do what you want them to. *Lift. Lift.*" The book shakes but doesn't lift. "Lift!"

The book finally moves an inch off the bar. It falls a millisecond later. Connor chuckles. "I did it. I—"

"Again," I order.

Connor stares at the book and after three seconds, it levitates again. "Hold it…lift it higher…set it down." The book does all three.

"Holy shit," Neil mutters.

Connor laughs again. "I did it. I—"

"You can celebrate when you've moved them all. Lift!" The next book levitates, then the next, the next, one by one until all six have had a turn. "Good job. You're a quick study."

"Thank you," he says with pride.

"Now sweep Neil's legs from underneath him."

"What?" Neil asks.

Connor waves his hand, and Neil's legs go sideways. The man collapses to the floor as all the other minions laugh.

"By Jove I think he has got it," Connor laughs.

Connor points at what's left of the sofa and it moves a few inches off the ground too. "Take it easy there," I say, stepping in front of him. "You're a newbie. Don't blow your wad. We'll practice more on the plane. I think we're ready." A huge grin stretches across my face.

"Let's kill the bitch."

CHAPTER SEVENTEEN

SEE THE LIGHT

Sixteen. Sixteen times I've sat on a private plane soaring through the air, off to fight monsters. To put my life on the line to save innocents. Werewolves, trolls, witches, zombies, ghosts, a basilisk, even creatures I'd never heard of. I'd faced them all down and emerged victorious. For the most part. But those victories were due in large part to the people around me. Will and his tactical experience. Carl risking his sanity every time he had to take on the emotions of a victim. Andrew interviewing witnesses only he could. Nancy's enthusiasm cheering us on. Wolfe, Chandler, and Rushmore taking on the busy work and having our backs even though they're just ordinary humans against literal monsters. And Oliver. Always by my side, always backing me up or pulling me back from the bad plays. All of us F.R.E.A.K.S. A messed up family who rarely saw eye-to-eye on a thing, but when it counted, we came together and saved the day. Killers, monsters, abominations on the side of the angels.

Glancing around this plane, all I see are devils. Twelve sadistic, ruthless sociopaths all filled with glee at the prospect of tonight's massacre. None more so than my soul mate. Even without our new psychic link I'd be able to sense his excitement and joy. The vamp's barely stopped smiling since we left his apartment. To think I used to adore that smile and those crinkles around his eyes. Right now I want to slice his face and lips off. Me, I still don't feel a damn thing save for the nerves below the surface occasionally threatening to boil over. Those moments Connor stares over at me with a grimace himself. I'm harshing his buzz. We just return to training. Avril's had her gun flung out of her hand, Neil's been knocked to the ground, and two parries with the silver sword wielded by Edgar were swiped away with a flick of Connor's finger. Yeah, I'm with twelve devils who would gladly see me dead. And I chose this. I chose to do this. And what happens when we land will be on me too.

The situation might be bearable if not for the bound and gagged vampire with a gun trained on him staring at me through the half hour flight. I do my best to ignore him, I need to concentrate on Connor's training, but I can always sense his eyes on me. I thought about convincing Connor to leave him in the secret garage room to spare him tonight's horrors, but he could be forgotten in the aftermath and starve down there. There was some talk from Neil about slitting his throat in front of Antonia to further demoralize her, but I threated to rip his heart out if he tried. Even after he chose *her*.

Just as Edgar thrusts his sword at Connor, Connor flicks his finger and Edgar's wrist twists. Connor frowns, but the pilot announces we have to fasten our seatbelts. I sit beside Connor on the couch. "I was focusing on the sword, not his arm," Connor says. "It should have flown out of his hand."

"I told you, you're a neophyte and a lot of the power is instinct or emotion based in the beginning. The important part is you can use it at command. All you need is one swipe of her legs or loss of the sword and she's dead. That is *if* she accepts the duel. If it's war then your instincts will do the rest in the battle."

"What if she does accept the duel, sir?" Neil asks. "You kill her and then what? Her people will not just embrace their new ruler with open arms."

"We know who her top people are. We call them in or track them down and kill them, of course," Connor says. "Even if they swear fealty. We must put down the rebellion before it even begins."

"Yeah, great start to your reign, psycho," I say. "Killing without provocation. Gonna put their heads on spikes too?"

"I do this for you as well, fairest. Those in her regime will retaliate against you and your family to wound me."

"Whatever. I'd still forgo the spikes," I say snidely.

From this vantage I can't help but view Oliver out of the corner of my eye. He stares at me with such derision and scorn it turns my stomach. It physically hurts. Connor senses it and glances from me to Oliver. "Jack, please strike Agent Montrose."

Before I can protest Jack socks Oliver square in the jaw. I gasp as Oliver slumps against the wall. "Do *not* look at her in that manner. She is the only reason you still have your precious face. *I* wanted to cut it off and present you to Antonia, but *she* talked me out of it. If you live to see another night, it will solely be because of Beatrice. Show some bloody gratitude." Connor places his hand over mine to comfort me, but I quickly snatch it away. Connor scoffs. "Another one who can use a lesson in that virtue."

"Silence is a virtue too," I say smugly.

And that's how we land, in silence. Neil arranged two vans to meet us at the private air strip. What the drivers must think as we equip our knives to our belts, our guns with silver bullets, and a Kevlar vest for me. Soon they think nothing. They're quickly hypnotized to forget us after we reach the club. I watch as Jack shoves Oliver into the other van, my friend pleading with his eyes for me to come to my senses.

My stomach clenches again. Staring back into his sad, terrified eyes, I suddenly want to take it all back. I don't want to climb into this van. I don't want to go into that bar. I want it to be four hours ago when my soul was my own. Where I wasn't walking towards death beside a man I loathe. I don't want to fight and kill.

I close my eyes before the tears begin. What have I done? *What have I done?* I thought I wanted this. It seemed so clear, the solution, and that rightness, the clarity, clouded all emotion. This *was* the only solution. It truly was. I made my decision. It's too late to back out now. Now I just have to see this through. To the bitter end.

"Beatrice?" I open my eyes and Connor stands in front of me, studying my face. "Why are you sad?"

"He hates me." My jaw tightens. "Maybe he's right to."

I brush past him toward the van, climbing into the front seat away from the rest of them. The twenty-something driver, now nothing more than a zombie, stares straight ahead. I suddenly hate this man. He gets to forget tonight. He gets to return to his pretty girlfriend, his small apartment he loathes, and his dreams of selling his screenplay or whatever. In this moment I envy him down to my marrow. I envy his normalcy. Oliver was right. I was never going to be normal. Those weren't the cards I was dealt. My hand was aces and eights. The dead man's hand. Time to play.

The nerves finally hit the vamps on the fifteen minute ride to the bar. If Connor's any indication they'd be literally pooping their pants if their digestive system worked like that. He's more excited than nervous though. I listen as they talk through our assault plan again. Connor actually had a blueprint of the lounge and building next door. The bar's website said it was closed tonight for repairs so crowds shouldn't be an issue. After disabling the security system, a program Connor already had like the blueprints, three will enter from the back and the rest of us in from the front. We take anyone inside hostage and if Antonia isn't there, we have someone text her. Torture them if they don't comply. She comes, end game. We talked through every contingency like if she comes with multiple vamp guards or if she's in her fortress next door to the club. "I've destroyed her doors, I can do it again," I told them.

Connor takes a call from one of his spies ten minutes out. No activity at the bar save for Robin and her hired goons returning a few hours before, and Alejandro going out and returning alone. We circle the street twice. No one out but couples strolling on the beach behind the bar. Police may be an issue but a few mental whammies should take care of them. Guns are a last resort to avoid the police. We pass the lounge a third time and Connor's nerves reach uncomfortable proportions. Of course with my own who can tell? I'm a hairsbreadth from throwing up.

"Sir?" Neil asks behind me. "I think we are clear."

"Right," Connor says quietly. "Very well. Stop the car."

The driver pulls up to the bar, and the moment the van stops, we pile out. I'm shocked my legs don't buckle when my feet hit the pavement. The rest, minus the three for the back assault, climb out of their van, Oliver included. The air is thick with the ocean, and I can hear the waves lapping. I close my eyes and take a moment to enjoy that sound. That breeze. Maybe after I'll—

"Beatrice," Connor says as usual ruining everything.

I force my eyes open. The team's advancing toward the bar, with Jack shoving Oliver that way. Later. I rush over to Connor's side, my hand on my gun. I wish I had Bette. The rest of the team clutch their swords to their chests until we hear the security system's been disabled.

I will not wince.

I will not cry.

This is the way it has to be.

God, give me strength. And forgive me.

Connor opens the unlocked newly installed front door.

Antonia, Robin, Alejandro, and Jin all sit or stand around the bar when we enter. Connor's grin stretches across his face as he strolls in as if he already owns the joint. Alejandro and Jin jump off their stools, and Antonia's head cocks slightly to the side but we get no further reaction.

"Hello old chum. I love what you have done with the place," Connor says, gesturing around. "It *has* been forever."

"Connor," Antonia says emotionless, "and friends. Yes, it has been awhile. Fifty years since you last came uninvited to demolish the place."

"Well, this time I have been invited Lady Sabatini."

"Oh, really? By whom?" Antonia asks.

"Why *you* of course. I have come to finally grant your request for a duel."

Antonia smirks, calm as can be. No one on either side seems to notice or care. "Have you now? Then let us follow protocol please."

"Very well. I, Lord Connor McInnis of the San Diego territory hereby accept your challenge of a duel to the death for all lands and titles in each other's names, Lady Antonia Sabatini. Unless, of course, you refuse the challenge you instigated and hereby forfeit said lands and titles."

"No, I accept," she says cheerfully without hesitation, smirk growing.

She reaches under the bar and returns with a silver sword with a jewel encrusted hilt. At the same moment, on cue, vampires carrying all manner of weapons from M-16s to baseball bats with chains and nails begin filtering out from the back rooms. Robin pulls out an Uzi from behind her back. "However, I would be remiss not to remind you that the forfeiture clause now goes both ways, *darling*."

More and more of her vampires filter out behind their leader, so many our group begins slowly inching back toward the front door. No escape there. I hear the beeping of a backing truck, no doubt blocking that exit. Connor's entourage begin glancing at one another with fear and confusion as even more of her army fill the now claustropbic bar. Antonia's smile never wavers.

"You knew we were coming," Connor says, voice cracking a little. I count nineteen to Connor's twelve, and they all have Kevlar. No wonder I'm all but drowning in Connor's fear.

"Of course we did, silly goose," Antonia chuckles. "*She* told us you would be."

All eyes turn to the smirking woman she just gestured at.

Me.

As Connor takes a moment to wrap his mind around this news, as they all do, I lift Oliver into the air and toss him toward Team Antonia while slowly backing that way too. "Surprise, Danny Boy."

"'*Will trick him into accepting duel. Will come tonight with a small team. Have ambush ready. Know he has spies. Must be secret. Protect my family and Oliver*,' " Robin reads from the slip of paper I passed her when we shook hands at the courthouse. The lawyer who lent me his pen and a scrap of paper is going to regret that act when there's no one left to pay his bill. "'*Kill them all.*'"

"Yeah, you dropped the ball on that Oliver bit there, partner," I say as I glance at Antonia.

"No, I knew you would protect him. It was an acceptable risk to help sell your cover."

"You...planned this?" Connor asks.

"Like I told you, I had nothing but time to think after you had me tossed in jail. I knew I couldn't prolong the enviable any longer. I had to pick a side. And if you thought for a *millisecond* I'd choose the side of the psychopath who manipulated, lied, threatened, and even tried to metaphysically *rape* me, Danny Boy, you never knew me at all."

Connor nervously glances around the room. "It-it matters not. You are still my familiar. I still—"

"Try moving something, Danny Boy," I cut in. "Try the leg sweep. Heck, try picking up an empty glass."

He meets my smug eyes and horror fills his violet orbs. He moves his finger in my direction. Nothing. He tries again as Antonia chuckles. "I—"

"Yeah, I had you pointing so I knew what you were trying to move, moron," I school him. "It took *me* twenty-six years and intensive training to get the darn thing to work properly. Did you really think you could master telekinesis in a few hours? One thing you can always rely on: vampire hubris."

This new variable sinks in, not only to him, but to all his followers. Yeah, that's right. Checkmate jerks. Inside he's petrified, I literally feel it, but outwardly he retains his composure. "If I die, you die," he points out.

I nod and the corner of my mouth twitches. "Oh, I know," I say, voice cracking. "I know." I shrug. "But I did it anyway. I couldn't have my family suffer anymore because of me. I'm the common denominator in this psycho psychodrama. My choices brought me here. I should be the only one to suffer the consequences. Not them. If I have to die to save them, so be it. And if you knew the first thing about true love, real love...you would have seen this coming a mile away. *Fairest.*"

His lip twitches. Then he chuckles. And chuckles. Then begins to guffaw. "Oh. Oh, Beatrice! I—"

Suddenly his laughter stops as he stabs the vampire closest to him with the sword through the side of the man's Kevlar.

Chaos erupts.

One side begins firing, I don't know whose, but the gunshots overshadow the stabbed vamp's wail of agony. The first of many. I don't have time to pull my own gun, to even process one percent of the madness, before someone grabs me and yanks me backwards up and over the bar. I land on the other side of it just as the mirror above shatters from the bullets that should have hit me. Connor yells, "Be careful! She dies, I die you idiots!" on my tumble over the bar but only realize he's spoken when I land on my bad arm. A jolt of pain cascades up to my shoulder. My savior crouches beside me, shielding her head with her arm from the shards of glass. Groans, screams, wails, roars, above all gunfire on the other side of the bar physically hurt me as much as my arm does. Robin glances over at me. "You okay?"

"Yeah," I pant. "Thank you."

"No," she shouts, even touching my hand. "Thank *you*." She smiles. "We'll watch out for you family until the end, okay? We will. I'll make sure of it." She squeezes my hand again. "At least you got to choose your death, huh? Make it mean something. Get to go out fighting."

Sitting here as the agony, the blood, and torment I helped cause reigns on all around me, I realize…no. Not like this. I don't want my last moments to be this. Chaos. Madness. This isn't my fight. My war. It never was. I think I've earned…peace.

I squeeze Robin's hand back. "Take care of Oliver for me."

I don't have much time. I crouch with my head down, out of the line of fire, and rush toward the bar's edge and the back area. Men and women from both factions remain locked in battle even down the hallway. Blood spatters the walls as they slash and hack at one another. I glance around for Oliver but with the war raging, I can't see his face. No, he…*there*. He's toward the back rooms wielding a sword, locked in battle with Edgar, one of the three who took the back door. Oliver swats Edgar's gun away with the sword just as Edgar fires into the wall. Before he can try again I pick Edgar up, flinging him toward the thick of the fighting to die with his friends. Oliver's gaze whips that direction, and the moment he sees me, his purloined sword drops either in shock or relief. "Trixie," he gasps, every letter dripping with emotion. "Trixie, what—"

Every person in my path joins Edgar in the main room without me even having to consciously think of tossing them. The moment I reach Oliver, I throw my arms around his shoulders in a hug. "Get me out of here. The beach. Now."

Without hesitation he scoops me up. It's my stomach and ears that clue me into the fact we're moving faster than normal as he super-speeds through the back of the club. In a blink we're at the back door where one of Antonia's vamps stands sentinel. No escape. No survivors. "Let us through," Oliver orders.

"Sir, I—"

"Let us through or I shall kill you myself," Oliver roars. "*Now.*"

No time. The metal door with the bolts on both sides flies outward as if it were nothing but a piece of aluminum foil. My brain aches but the job's done. The guards on both sides barely have time to react before we're speeding away again. In two blinks we're at the edge of the ocean, the waves gently rippling on the shore. Oliver sets me down, and we face one another. Even in the dim moonlight I can see how pained his face is. He's in agony because of me. He cups my cheeks and I place my hands over his. We both begin talking at the same time.

"I'm sorry. I'm so sorry for what I said back there. I didn't mean it. Not a word. You weren't supposed to be there," I say talking over him. "I can't believe she let you go there. I—"

"What have you done? What the hell were you thinking?" he asks desperately at the same time. "Trixie what have you done? Why did you do this? How could you do this? I—"

We stop speaking at the same time too. My breath trembles along with the rest of me, along with the rest of him. "Why?" he pleads, blood filling his eyes. "*Why?*"

"To protect my family." I squeeze his hands on my face. "To protect *you*. They'd just keep using you all. It was my fault. I dragged you into this. It had to end before they hurt you."

"So you...sacrificed yourself? Your life?" he asks, voice cracking with the rest of his face. "You commit suicide?"

"It was the only way," I whisper as our tears fall. "I-I...I don't want to die. I don't. I thought I did for months, but..." I stare down and let out a real cry. "It had to end. It had to end before you got hurt."

"And *this* will not hurt me? Trixie, this will *destroy* me. I—"

"Listen," I hiss through the sobs. "*Listen*. I-I...don't know how much time we have, okay? I don't want to spend it fighting. So please just listen. I need...I need you to tell my grandmother she was the best thing that ever happened to me. That every-everything I learned about being a good person, I learned from her." My chin begins trembling. "T-tell April I couldn't have asked for a better sister. That I co-couldn't love her more if she were my flesh and blood."

"Trixie..." Oliver whispers, pressing his hand harder against my face.

"And Brian. Tell him I forgive him. And George. *Nancy*," I say, barely getting her name out, "the rest, pl-please tell them they helped me be brave. I-I-I don't think I was before. Tell them."

"I...I will."

I nod rapidly. "Thank you. Thank you," I say breathlessly. The fear's overwhelming as if I've already been thrown into my grave. "I...I...can you just hold me, until..."

He stares into my eyes before pulling me into a hug. We cling to one another as we have so many times before. I lower us to the sand and take a moment to savor the scent of the sea, the twinkle of the stars and moon on the calm water, and especially the sensation of this man against me. His scent. His strong arms cradling me. I run my fingers through his silky hair as his embrace tightens. Yeah. This. This is a good death. Surrounded by beauty. By love.

"I told you so," I whisper to him.

"What?"

"When it mattered, despite the pain it would cause you losing me, you did the right thing just like I knew you would." I move to gaze at his face. Even with his cheeks covered in blood he's still the most beautiful creature ever to grace this earth. "I am…*so* proud of you, Oliver Smythe." I cup his face this time and he kisses the side of my palm. "You are the best man I have ever met. You *are* good. Kind. Intelligent. Caring. Never doubt it for a moment. Nev—"

A sharp pain rips through my side. A phantom pain I know is Connor's. I wince and Oliver's mouth opens in terror as his whole body tenses. But I'm still here. Still alive. But my own horror doesn't wane.

I don't want to die.

I don't want to leave him. I'm not done. I still have so much more to do. People to protect. Monsters to slay. Laughs to have. Friends to joke with. Love to make. The world to see. I don't want to die. What have I done? What have I done?

"Trixie? *Trixie?*" Oliver gasps.

I gaze back at the agonized Oliver. "Oliver…I'm scared. I'm scared. I don't want to die." I don't want to die." Another metaphysical stab assails my shoulder blade. I cling to Oliver as the pain ricochets through me. "It's happening. It's happening…" I gasp.

"Look at me. Look at me!" Oliver roars. I meet his eyes. "You are the strongest person I know. You will fight, and you will come back to us." He has to literally swallow his emotions to get the words out. *"To me.* You *will* come back to me. Do you hear me, my love? You...come back to me. Like you promised. You promised. So you will literally fight death itself if you have to, my love. Do...do not take the only light I have left in this ugly world. Please. Please," he gasps before quickly kissing my trembling lips.

I rest my forehead on his and cup his jaw. "I lov—"
What?

That last word remains on my lips when I instantly find myself standing on the top of a small hill staring at two willow trees and a short wrought iron fence with a man waiting amongst the gravestones almost a hundred yards away. I know where I am by that sight alone. Kansas. Home. The sun rests above my head yet this world is dim, almost as if a mist hangs over everything though I don't see a single cloud anywhere. The air's off too, still but not stifling as if the world's stopped spinning. Huh. Okay. I glance back and find the mansion, all three stories of it, sitting amidst the empty American plain and gentle hills. I remember the first time I drove up the road toward it, so nervous and excited to begin my new life. Those sensations grew when I saw my new home, like something out of Jane Austen. Now through the giant bay windows of that library I instantly fell in love with, I catch Andrew sitting in his favorite lounge chair reading a book with his fingers as Carl and Nancy play chess. The manor of misfit monsters where we're safe to be ourselves. To be brave. I miss them so much. My friends.

But I mustn't keep *him* waiting. I spin back around and begin the long walk to the cemetery.

"I like what you put on my headstone," Will says with his back to me as I pass through the cemetery's gate. I move beside him and stare down at the gray stone. "'Beloved son of Albert and Susan and husband to Mary. A hero 'til the very end.' Not precisely true, but—"

"The heck it isn't. Will Price died transporting a murderous werewolf into custody. Everything after that was not Will Price. Will Price *was* a hero...until the end." I gaze over at him. God, he's exactly as I remember him. Tall, thick, that Roman nose settled between those exquisite emerald green eyes staring back at me with such kindness. "Have you been *here* all this time?"

"No," he says with a smile. "I just came to see you while I had the chance. While you needed me."

"I'm...I'm dead, aren't I?" I whisper breathlessly.

"For the moment." He pauses. "Or longer if you wish to be."

"What?"

Will returns his attention back to his grave. "You're wrong, you know. Will Price truly died seven years before you ever met him. I died the moment my Mary did. The man you met was just a walking corpse. Hell, the zombies we fought had more life in them than I did, Bea. You of all people know what I'm talking about. What you've put yourself through these last three months? It was eight years for me. At least until I realized I was falling in love with you." Will looks at me again with that smile still affixed. "Until you told me you loved me. You sparked me back to life, Bea. And even when that woman...that love was still inside me. It's inside me now. It's a part of me until the end of time itself. Just as my love for you is in your every atom too. *We* were special. But *he's* right too. You were meant for an extraordinary life, Beatrice

Alexander. And no matter how many houses or children we would have had, each day would have been a fraction dimmer than it should have been. True happiness would be just beyond reach.

"And you'd know it. You'd sense it. And you'd resent me. Baby, you…are destined for a greatness you cannot even fathom. For struggle, for strife for damn sure, but for such wonders and pure happiness as well. Oh, the places you'll go, baby," he whispers with pride before his smile slowly fades. "But it has to be your choice. You *could* come with me. You could be with your mom. Find peace. Just give in." I just shake my head. "But we both know you made your choice before you even got here. There are so many battles left for you to fight. Lives to defend. A world to make your permanent mark on. To improve. And…you did make a promise after all. He needs you. And you need him."

It would be so easy to go with him. To remain at peace forever. Placid. Tranquil. Dreamlike. But even now, with the man I loved beside me, I sense its wrongness. I don't belong here. Not yet. Since the moment I arrived I've felt a tether being tugged on. Their need. *Him.* His desolation. His destruction. Because of me. My true soul mate's in agony. I'll take him with me if I stay. We'll never find one another again. He'll go where I can't reach him. I'll damn him. But it's not only him I sense. It's lives I'm meant to save. The children I'm meant to have. Friends still to cherish. Love to embrace.

I look at Will with his serene smile. "That's my girl."

"I loved you."

"I know. I loved you too. And thank you...for having the strength, the courage, to save me twice over." He grabs me, kissing me with all his soul. I kiss him back with all of mine. "Now go and give those evil bastards the hell you were born to, baby. And I'll be here. Cheering you on. Make me proud, baby. I love you."

And he's gone. Vanished. I'm holding nothing. "I will. I love you too."

Okay. *Okay.*

I smile to myself and smooth my hair before staring up at the sky. The haze has burned away leaving nothing but a bright orange sun with blues, purples, pinks, and oranges above. There is such pure beauty in the world if you take the time to appreciate it. "Okay," I whisper to whoever's listening as I hold onto the compass on my necklace *he* gave me. To always find my way back to him. "I'm coming for you. Just light my way home."

And as always he doesn't let me down.

My eyes fly open to darkness. To stars. To him.

I come back to him.

And always will.

CHAPTER EIGHTEEN

WHERE WE BELONG

"No, flank him, Devin. Flank him! Now cast firestorm, Oliver. Now. Now! Yes...yes! We did it! The Gorgon's dead! We are the kings and queens of Azeroth. Oh, yeah!"

Nancy pushes her chair away from the table, arms up in victory. "Go F.R.E.A.K.S. Guild! Yeah!"

Devin smiles at me over our laptops. "That was awesome. It usually takes me at least four times to pass that boss. We did it in two."

I look over at Oliver. "Well, we would have done it in one if *someone* was quicker with his spells."

Oliver places his hand over his heart. "Please forgive me, fearless leader, but considering I am a mere level eight amongst you level thirties, I believe I did an admirable job."

"Okay, for a newb, you didn't suck," I concede. "We may not kick you out of the guild."

"*May*," Nancy adds.

The newly minted *World of Warcraft* F.R.E.A.K.S. Guild sits around the barely used dining room table vanquishing virtual orcs, ogres, and necromancers from the safety of the mansion. My new teammate Devin and I have spent the past few days bonding over our mutual geekiness. Seems there weren't many gamers or sci-fi/fantasy enthusiasts in the Eastern Werewolf Pack. I've met their leader Jason Dahl so I wasn't that surprised. I've yet to see Devin in the field against real dangers, but he took direction well in the game so

~ - 334 - ~I have hope. Surprisingly even Chandler seemed if not happy then relieved at my return. I foresee many pissing contests between us for tactical control of the team, but I'm prepared for the battles. Of course no one has been giddier at my return than Nancy. She's barely left my side, even spent the night in my room catching up and crying my first night back. And then she even begged me to come with her and George on her college tour at the University of Oklahoma tomorrow, but George shot it down. He said it was in case I was needed in the field, but I think he just wanted to spend time alone with her before we lose her to adulthood.

And thinking of tomorrow…I check the clock on my laptop.

"Shoot, guys, it's past one. Nancy, you've got to be up in six hours," I say, logging out.

"Crap, it's that late? Claire's gonna kill me," Devin says of his wife upstairs in the bedroom next to mine. I've barely spent much time with her beyond our gym session today, but she seems nice. "I'm not supposed to play for more than four hours in a row."

"You are home all of four days and already seem to be a corrupting influence, Trixie," Oliver quips with grin #2.

"Shut up." I rise from the table. "Go on, Nancy. You do want to look your best for Logan tomorrow, don't you?"

She blushes behind her thick hipster glasses as she packs up her laptop too. "Shut up."

"Yes, please make sure to send our regards to your lover for us," Oliver says with that grin.

"Oliver!" I snap as Nancy's blush deepens. I turn to her and lean in to whisper, "Just remember the pill takes a month to work. Make sure you pack the condoms I gave you, but if you don't feel like sleeping with him, you don't—"

"Oh, my God!" Nancy says loudly as Oliver winces. "Stop! Stop talking! I swear coming back from the dead turned you into such a nag!"

"Sorry. Just enjoy yourself, okay?" I say.

"I will. Jeez. Night," she says as she walks out of the room with Devin close behind.

If becoming a nag is the only side effect of my resurrection, I am lucky indeed. I don't remember dying, I just remember Oliver's face as he begged me to come back then some Good Samaritan performing CPR on me as Oliver held my hand, sobbing beside me. I was dead for a whole minute. If I went to heaven or hell or anything in between I don't remember. Probably a good thing. Apparently I'm one of only a handful of familiars through the centuries to survive when my vampire didn't. The theory is that the link was so new and tentative it was weak. Or it was the CPR. Hurrah for modern medicine. Either way I'm alive and kicking while Lord Connor McInnis and all his inner circle died in the same misery they spread to the world. Sadly so did almost half of Antonia's army, but I'm sure the fact she's now the most powerful vampire in North America behind the King consoles her. I actually had to meet with a representative of the King to explain the whole mess before I left San Diego. If I helped or hindered her new regime I don't know or care. My family's safe. I wish they could have been rich and safe, but since the ten million was technically for a hit, Oliver convinced me to donate it to charity. I made the donations to battered women's shelters and youth centers in Mariah's name. If it stops one girl or woman from meeting her fate, I was glad to do it.

No one seemed that surprised when I announced I was returning to the F.R.E.A.K.S. I had to wait for the felony charges to clear, thank you George, which took a couple of days but there wasn't a moment I've doubted my decision then or now. Nana cried at the airport, April teared up a little too, but I could literally sense their relief as I departed. It was as if the moment I came back to life it was all I could think of. All doubts, all fears, were wiped away. *This* is my path. This is my home. Right here. With them.

"Night guys," Devin says as he walks out.

"Night!" I say as I collect my laptop. Oliver remains across the table staring at me with grin #2. "What?" I ask. He's barely left my side either. Nancy's taken the day shift and Oliver the night.

"Nothing," he says, grin #2 becoming #1, full fang.

I know what he's thinking. No. Nope. I *will* resist. It *cannot* become a habit. "Right. Well, good game. See you tomorrow night. Sleep well."

"See you soon, my dear," he calls as I walk away. Willpower, Bea. Willpower.

As always, when I pass Will's old bedroom, my heart literally aches a little. It gets better each time I do it but for now I can handle that ache. I even went inside his room my first night back. All traces of him had vanished, even the mattress and curtains. A blank slate for its next occupant in the manor of misfit monsters. I couldn't help myself. I carved B.A.+W.P. in a heart in the doorframe. He deserves to be remembered, to be honored in this house. I will be the keeper of his flame.

I do my bathroom routine and change into my pink cotton pajamas before climbing into my bed. Soft as a cloud, just as I remembered it. I had a busy day today helping Nancy prepare for her trip, spending time at the gun range with Wolfe, getting my butt handed to me in the dojo by black belt Claire, then the game marathon. I feel every activity in my muscles. Yet like so many nights since my death, okay since Will's death, the anxiety grips me. It has gotten worse since my resurrection though. I can't relax. With no distractions, memories and feelings of Connor, of what he did to me, of what I did to Adrian Winsted and a thousand other terrible memories and regrets, can't be kept at bay. In San Diego I'd fire up the PlayStation or mix Ativan and vodka but look where that landed me. George did insist on me seeing a therapist, a former F.R.E.A.K. I've Facetimed with once, to help with the PTSD, but until a breakthrough I'm doomed to sleepless nights and days. The only natural remedy has been…no. In the two weeks since my resurrection, I've averaged every other night. It is a hairsbreadth from becoming a habit. I…for God's sake, there are worse habits to have. I need sleep.

Fudge it. Heck, I'm shocked I held out this long.

I knock on his bedroom door and before I even lower my arm, it opens. Oliver stands on the other side already in his own silk pajamas with a soft smile on his face. All for me. "Do you mind?" I ask apologetically.

"Never," he says.

As he shuts the door, turns off the lights save for the moonscape in the "window," I walk over to the bed and climb under the covers. He joins me in bed, above the covers, before wrapping his arm around me, cradling me. I nestle back against him, instantly beginning to relax. My oasis. In his arms. It hasn't gone beyond this. I hug his arms tighter against me. He's never remotely pressured me for more. But this is more than enough for us both. I close my eyes and begin drifting to sleep. After all we have all the time in the world.

And beyond.

ACKNOWLEDGMENTS

First, to all of you who write, Tweet, review, even send me presents. I have the best fans ever. Thank you.

Thanks to my Betas: Susan Dowis, Ginny Dowis, and Jill Kardell for their corrections. Any mistakes are mine and mine alone. I especially thank you for letting me know this book made you all cry. I love hearing that.

Thanks to the Peachtree City library for being a wonderful place to write and edit. All the staff there are so lovely.

And finally, thanks to my brothers Liam and Ryan for being wonderful roommates. Your support and just general not smacking me in my more emo moments did not go unnoticed. I adore you both.

ABOUT THE AUTHOR

Jennifer Harlow spent her restless childhood fighting with her three brothers and scaring the heck out of herself with horror movies and books. She grew up to earn a degree at the University of Virginia which she put to use as a radio DJ, crisis hotline volunteer, bookseller, lab assistant, wedding coordinator, and government investigator. Currently she calls Atlanta home but that restless itch is ever present. In her free time, she continues to scare the beejepers out of herself watching scary movies and opening her credit card bills. She is the author of the Amazon best-selling F.R.E.A.K.S. Squad, Midnight Magic Mystery series and The Galilee Falls Trilogy. For the soundtrack to her books and other goodies, visit her at www.jenniferharlowbooks.com .

BCPL
Baltimore County
Public Library

CPSIA information can be obtained
at www.ICGtesting.com
Printed in the USA
LVOW13s1911150817
545103LV00012B/572/P